P9-DEG-907

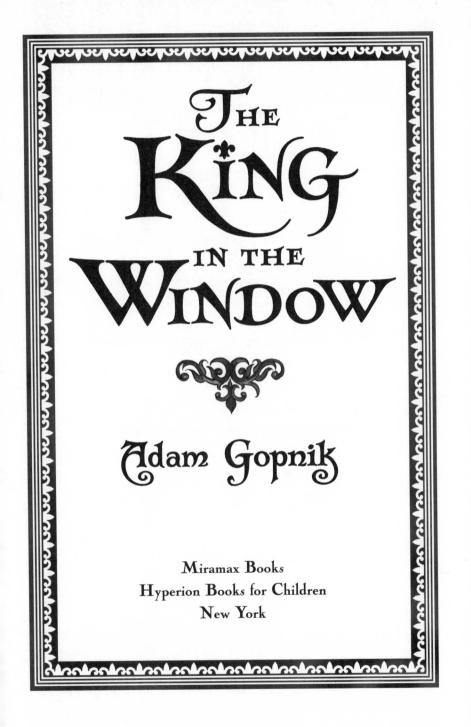

THE KING IN THE WINDOW

Adam Gopnik

Miramax Books
Hyperion Books for Children
New York

Text copyright © 2005 by Adam Gopnik

Illustrations copyright © 2005 by Omar Rayyan

All rights reserved. No part of this book may be reproduced or
transmitted in any form or by any means, electronic or mechani-
cal, including photocopying, recording, or by any information
storage and retrieval system, without written
permission from the publisher.

For information address Hyperion Books for Children,
114 Fifth Avenue, New York, New York 10011-5690.

First Edition

1 3 5 7 9 10 8 6 4 2

Printed in the United States of America

This book is set in 13-point Cg Cloister

Designed by Christine Kettner

Handlettering by Leah Palmer Priess

Library of Congress Cataloging-in-Publication Data on file.

ISBN 0-7868-1862-X (hardcover)

Reinforced binding

Visit www.hyperionbooksforchildren.com

For my wise, witty, and watchful son
Luke Auden, who gave this book its
title, gave its villain both his names,
listened to its many pages many times,
and offered its author the finest piece of
editorial advice he has ever been given:
"Just bring the cool bits closer together."
If there are any cool bits in this book,
he inspired them; if they are still too far
apart, it is not his fault.

And in memory of his godfathers,
Kirk Varnedoe and Richard Avedon,
who loved Paris, thought for
themselves, and showed me the way.

PART ONE

Chapter One

A Stone in the Street, a Boy in the Window

IF OLIVER HAD simply smiled and joked with his parents while he was wearing the gold paper crown, or if he had just remembered to take it off after dinner, as he had always done before, the window wraiths might never have mistaken him for royalty.

Instead, because he was a born worrier, and because he had homework to finish for the next morning, and because he was exasperated with his parents for being so childish, and just because (as he explained much later to Mrs.

Pearson) he pretty much forgot that he had it on, he wore the crown all through dessert and washing up. He had even kept it on his head at the end of the evening while he sat at the kitchen table and practiced making shadowpuppets.

And so that night, because Oliver wore the crown, the boy in the blue doublet appeared in the window for the first time.

It was the night of Epiphany, during a bitter and freezing winter in the city of Paris, where Oliver lived with his mother and father. It is often said that Paris is a happy and beautiful city, where people in love like to walk hand in hand and stare at each other, and, although this description is mildly goopy, it is also mostly true, at least beginning with April and ending in October.

But in the winter Paris is another place. It is dark and cold and sad and mysterious. If you begin the school day, as Oliver did, at eight in the morning and ended it, as Oliver did, at four thirty in the afternoon, then six months go by in which you never once see sunlight. The sun has set by four thirty, and the streets are often empty by eight o'clock, with people crowded inside the golden-lit apartments and cafés and restaurants. In the evenings, the gray-violet skies always look as if they are about to snow, and never do.

Just that afternoon, for instance, right after school, Oliver had kicked a pebble home alone from his school on the Right Bank to the Left Bank, where he lived with his parents, and at every corner he had turned, he saw only streetlights and long shadows—trees with black limbs silhouetted against the twilight—and crowds of people with their scarves pulled tight around their throats, looking down as their heels went *clack!* as they wove in and out against the narrow stone pavement, and looking up at the charcoal sky above, which was still not snowing.

It had been a very cold and lonely walk home for Oliver that day. Oliver had been born in America, in New York City. His parents had moved to Paris with him when he was only three, and when he visited New York now, he found it exciting but a little frightening. Paris was his home, although he didn't always feel quite at home there. Oliver was often very lonely, but he had never been as lonely as he was this winter.

For years his father had met him every day after school on his way home from his office on the rue Fleurus. They would almost always find a perfectly smooth stone on the street in front of the school, and then kick it all the way home together—all the way across Paris, across the Jardin des Tuileries and the rue de Rivoli and the bridge to the Left Bank. But last year his father's office had closed, and now he worked at home, and he didn't come to meet Oliver after school. "You're a big guy now," he had said. "You can find your own way home."

It was true that he could find his own way home. But he didn't *want* to find his own way home. He wanted company, and conversation, and he almost never had any of either, from his Parisian schoolmates, who had their own lives to lead, and led them without Oliver. Ideally, he thought to himself, ideally he would have walked home every day arm in arm with a chain of very fashionable people, exchanging jokes and confidential secrets. And even if his father wasn't fashionable or witty, at least he had always answered his questions. *What's the most expensive thing there is? Why are there so many languages in the world, and where did they come from? Why is there an infinity of numbers and not an infinity of letters? Why does it never snow in Paris?* . . . How had Oliver's father answered that one? Oh, yes, it never gets quite cold enough in Paris to turn the rain to snow. . . . Sometimes Oliver would ask so many questions that his father would just laugh and say "Ollie! Trust me."

Tonight, Oliver had tried to lift his spirits by kicking a pebble home himself. This stone wasn't even perfect—it was beautifully smooth, but it had a kind of weird white blemish on it—and he hadn't felt his heart lift one bit as he kicked his stone across the city. Up and down the narrow streets, and across the great gray violet boulevards—kicking a pebble home alone felt, well, empty, and Oliver had been so unhappy that he had at last kicked it right off the Pont Royal, one of the many bridges that runs across the river Seine and connects the Right Bank of Paris to the Left Bank.

Or rather he had *tried* to kick it off the bridge. He had struck it with all his might—but then the pebble must have hit a part of the bridge railing that Oliver couldn't see. Somehow it had bounced right back at him and lay there on the pavement before him, like an eager puppy. Oliver was so annoyed by this that he had kicked it again, toward the water, from the other side of the bridge. But this time, too, it must have struck someone's ankle—"Hey, that's enough from you!" a man had barked reprovingly, looking at him in anger as he stood among a crowd of Parisians, staring up at the new lights that were being strung up and down the Eiffel Tower and there the pebble was again.

And the odd thing was that he thought that he had heard the man bark at him even before his toe had struck the stone.

This third time he had really kicked it hard and watched it fly off the bridge and land with a barely audible *plop!* in the water. It was twilight, and dark—but he was sure that he saw the pebble skim right across the water and come back up on the other side of the bank, along the quai, the paved walkway that ran by the river on the Left Bank.

Oliver was astonished. He must be getting *much* better at kicking than he had thought . . . probably all that soccer practice, even though he wasn't big enough to make the school soccer team. It was so peculiar that, after he crossed the bridge, Oliver took a detour down the stairs to the quai to pick up the pebble, and had then kicked it home, as hard as he could, pretending to be Thierry Henry, the great French soccer star.

But no matter how hard he struck the pebble, *this* time it just flew lightly along the pavement, a few feet at a time, and then almost seemed to be waiting patiently for Oliver to kick it again, as though it wanted to go home with him, until at last he and the pebble both arrived at the courtyard of the building where he lived with his parents.

Leaving the pebble in the courtyard, he had taken a deep breath to drink in the Parisian winter air: in Paris in the winter, there is a special kind of keen, smoky smell that penetrates everywhere. It seems to be made up of strong cigarettes, black coffee, scalded milk, and burning wood. Then he walked up the narrow stairs to their third-floor apartment, to be embarrassed one more year by celebrating Epiphany with his parents.

One of the ways that people try to cheer up through the dark months of a Paris winter is at the feast called Epiphany. "Christmas isn't such a big deal in France," Oliver had once explained to his best, unfortunately faraway, friend, Charlie Gronek, of Allendale, New Jersey. "I mean, it's a big deal, but it's not the whole world, the way it is in America. Epiphany is just as big, really." Epiphany comes on January 6, and it celebrates the night when the Wise Men reached the stable at Bethlehem. ("If they were so wise, how come they got there so late?" Oliver had asked his parents when he was four, and they had laughed and repeated it to everybody for weeks, even though it had been a perfectly sincere question. What was worse was that they were still telling it *now*, eight years later, as though he had said it yesterday.)

So on this Epiphany night, Oliver was sitting with his parents in the kitchen of their apartment on a little street called the rue du Pré-aux-Clercs. Although they had a dining room on the other side of the apartment, they almost always ate dinner at a little round blue table in the kitchen next to the window.

"They make wonderful almond filling at Saffray," Oliver's mother was saying as she looked admiringly inside the cake that they were about to have for dessert. At Epiphany in Paris, everyone shares a cake called a *galette des rois*—the cake of the kings. A *galette des rois* has puff pastry outside, with a little design of leaves or wreaths on the top, and inside it is filled with almond cream. There is always a prize hidden inside the cake—a bean, or sometimes a tiny toy, or a golden angel. Whoever finds the prize in his slice of cake becomes the king, and gets to wear the gold-paper crown that the ladies in the bakery hand out when you buy the *galette des rois*.

"What beautiful almond filling . . ." his mother said, intent on the cake.

From years of experience, and because he really was not a complete idiot, Oliver knew perfectly well that she was really searching to see where the prize was, so that she could make sure that it was in his slice. Oliver would have to pretend to be startled when he found the prize in his piece.

"It's funny," his mother said as she peered at the almond filling. "I had ordered a *galette* for six people, so that Oliver could have extra, but they only had this small one left. They said that someone else had come in and taken ours, by mistake. And you know who it was—it was Madame Farrad! Neige came up here to look for you—"

Madame Farrad was their *gardienne*. A *gardienne* in

Paris is someone who looks after the building, and usually lives in a small ground-floor apartment. He or she collects the mail and watches the doors and takes out the trash. Madame Farrad was their *gardienne*—and she was a gloomy and suspicious woman, with a beautiful daughter.

Neige was her daughter's name. (*Neige* is the French word for "snow.") She was just one year older than Oliver, who had been playing with her since he was little. She was extremely beautiful, Oliver thought privately, but a bit, well, extremely difficult.

"Neige came up here?" Oliver asked. Missing Neige was one more thing that made today utterly lonely and rotten. They had had a stupid quarrel about six months ago, and she had hardly spoken to him since.

"Yes, darling. But I told her that you hadn't come home yet. You two don't seem to talk together as much as you used to. Is something wrong?"

Oliver was thinking about whether to tell his mother about the quarrel—it had been *really* stupid—when his father looked up from the paper. "Did you offer to exchange them back?" he asked Oliver's mother sharply.

"Are you joking? That would have been a real *crise*. I was glad to let her have our big one," his mother said. Madame Farrad was a very argumentative and sullen lady, and Oliver knew that his mother hated to get into long discussions with her, much less have an argument about the size of an Epiphany cake.

"Ty," she said. Oliver's father was staring off into the

window, as he often did these days. "Ty," she repeated. "What is it?"

"I better go check my e-mail. Something may be coming in. Be right back," he said, and dashed out of the room. His mother sighed. She hated it when people interrupted family occasions. She lived for family occasions, and more and more often his father seemed distracted when they took place.

Oliver's father was a writer for a newspaper in America, and every day he disappeared into his "office"—really, it was just a little room near the dining room—and Oliver would hear the keys of his computer clacking away. Faxes would come in from America in the middle of the night, and often Oliver's father would get up to read them, and then reply on his computer. When Oliver was little, he had loved the *brrring* of the faxes as they arrived, and the sound of his father clacking the keys, because both sounds seemed exciting. But now that he was older he thought that they made his father sad, and tired, and when he heard them in the middle of the night, he went back to sleep.

"It's that story about Gil," his mother said quietly to Oliver, shaking her head. "He's sort of obsessed with it."

"You know how he is about his work, Mom," Oliver said, trying to reassure her. "Especially now that he's trying to write about Gil."

Oliver knew that his father had been working for several months on a story about the great computer tycoon Gil Hornshaw. Gil was his father's oldest friend. Back in college, many years ago, he and Oliver's father had been roommates. "He was like Thomas Edison in a tie-dyed T-shirt back then," his father had told Oliver once. Then Gil had been hurt in a skateboarding accident, his father had explained to Oliver, and it had left the right side of his mouth paralyzed; ever afterward his face was set in a sarcastic-seeming half smile.

Gil Hornshaw (Oliver knew the story by heart, he had heard it so often) had offered to make his father a partner in the little computer company he had started. But Oliver's father had refused, because he wanted to go to France and write, and Gil's company had become a computer giant. Now Oliver's father and mother often joked about how much money Gil made every day compared to how many years it would take for his father to earn the same amount.

Only a few months before, Gil had announced that he was coming to Paris to demonstrate a "breakthrough," a strange and special project that would be based in the Eiffel Tower and somehow "be a quantum leap in engineering," and he had called to ask Oliver's father to write about it. "It would be an exclusive, Ty," Oliver had heard Gil say kindly to his father over the online connection.

Gil often would send streaming video of himself, answering questions, over Oliver's father's computer. Peering through his father's half-open door late at night, Oliver could see Gil Hornshaw's famous crooked half smile and open shirt, sending itself, in that herky-jerky way of computer videos, all the way from Seattle to Paris. Oliver even kept a little snapshot of himself with Gil, his arm around Oliver, in his wallet. It had been taken during the one visit he had made with his father to Seattle.

"Yes. Your father *is* obsessed with Gil and his project," Oliver's mother said now. Then she just looked away. "But it's not just the project, whatever that is. It's his whole way of looking at—" She caught herself, and then turned away and went over to the counter where the cake waited.

Oliver knew that she hated for him to think that his parents were unhappy.

Oliver quietly walked over to the window and looked out into the courtyard. There was nothing there, just Madame Farrad, staring up at the window, and disappearing into her tiny house in the courtyard. Oliver heard her speaking sharply to Neige from inside.

When his father came back from his office, Oliver's mother placed the cake on the table with great formality and lifted the slices onto their plates. Then they all bit in. Oliver poked around in his slice with his fork, and soon found something hard and bright inside it. The prize, of course. He withdrew it with his fork.

It was a shiny, small gold key—the kind of old-fashioned key with two stubby prongs that you see jailers holding in cartoons about medieval dungeons. As his mother exclaimed, pretending to be surprised, Oliver held the key up for a moment and examined it. He had to admit, they had done a very good job at Saffray. The key was much heavier than you expected it to be, more solid and actually keylike.

The two prongs of the key were even grooved and worn, as if they were ready for a lock. Well, Oliver guessed, *galette* prize-making must be a very competitive business these days. . . .

Then his parents did what they always did. They both stood up and his mother very ceremoniously placed the crown on Oliver's head while his father saluted him. To anyone looking in from the window, it would have looked like a very solemn coronation, even though Oliver was twelve years old. "*God*, Dad," Oliver muttered—but he didn't say it very loudly.

"Oliver, darling, do you remember how the first time you ever got the crown, you wouldn't take the crown off for three whole days—" his mother began to say. She seemed much happier now. He was glad for that but he had been *three years old*, for God's sake—and then they were talking as though this were something that had happened centuries ago to somebody else, and not to a living, breathing person who happened to be sitting at the table that very minute, and was being embarrassed. His parents, Oliver thought, had sort of, well, fallen out of time a little since they had moved to Paris. They still acted as though he was three, which was what he had been when they came here. They went on chatting, while Oliver sat with the crown on and looked out the window.

But, in a weird, exact-opposite-of-what-he-intended way that Oliver didn't have a word for, it was just because his parents had so exasperated him with this tedious behavior that he forgot to take the crown off this time, too. And so the crown was still on his head when Oliver sat down with his French history homework—in French, homework is called *devoirs*—at the kitchen table, while his father disappeared into the living room to read another newspaper and wait for the ten o'clock news to come on.

This sixth of January would have been, for Oliver, One of Those Days, if all of his days recently hadn't been One of Those Days. Oliver went to the Ecole Fontenelle, a *very* hard, serious French school, which is saying a lot, because all French schools are hard and serious. All the students had to memorize long lists of things: the number of continents, and the races of man, and the departments of France—those are sort of like the states of America—and their chief products. Once, when he was visiting Charlie Gronek in Allendale, New Jersey, Oliver had gone to Charlie's school, and he could hardly believe how different is was. The kids all wore whatever they wanted to wear—mostly sneakers and big T-shirts that fell outside their pants—and they called the teacher Joni and they gave reports on Madonna videos. By three o'clock, it was all over. The teachers at the Ecole Fontenelle were perfectly nice, Oliver explained to Charlie, but they wouldn't even look at you until you had recited the principle products of the department of the Gironde, and you certainly couldn't call them Joni.

Tonight, Oliver had *devoirs* to do on many subjects, but most important of all, he had a paper due for his rhetoric class. That was the class he hated most. Rhetoric is the study of ways of saying things: if you say something as

15

though you're talking to a crowd, that's one kind of rhetoric; if you say it as though you're talking to a friend, that's another. It's an important subject in France, but all it did was confuse Oliver even more completely than he was normally confused by school.

In order to settle his nerves before he sat down at the kitchen table to actually write that paper, he decided he would drink a bottle of Orangina and practice making shadow puppets in the pleasant warmth of the kitchen.

The kitchen was a comfortable place to be in the evenings. The dishwasher and the dryer would usually both be running, and they made a nice sound. When Oliver visited Charlie Gronek in Allendale, New Jersey, he was shocked to find that Charlie's parents had a whole room, like a garage, for the washing machine and dryer, which made a racket like the Paris metro coming into a station. The French dishwasher at Oliver's house just made a nice, throaty gurgle, and the dryer hummed and expelled sweet warm air into the kitchen. Often, he would sit and hum, or even sing to himself, while he heard the homey sounds and read a good book.

The windows of the kitchen looked out onto the courtyard of their building. They were the kind of old-fashioned windows—the kind that open like doors—that American people call French windows and French people just call windows. The glass in the windows was slightly rippled, and thick, and antique.

After dinner, his mother usually let down the blue-and-white-striped blinds that she had bought for the kitchen windows. Tonight, Oliver kept them down and turned on one of the kitchen lamps straight up so that it was like a spotlight. He had learned to make shadow puppets with his hands when he had been in bed for two weeks after he had his appendix out, a few years before, and he had become quite expert at it. He could make a bird that flew, a dog that opened and shut its mouth, and even a dolphin that rose from the sea and dived back down.

Oliver was still struggling to master the hardest shadow puppet in his instruction book, which was of a bird that rose up with two immense fluttering wings, like an eagle's. In his book it was called the King's Sign, and the diagram showed that you were supposed to weave your fingers together until your wrists practically broke from the strain. It didn't explain why it was called the King's Sign, though Oliver assumed that if a king wanted to play with shadow puppets, he would naturally want an impressive-looking one, like an eagle rising. Tonight, he worked on it for about five minutes, but it didn't look anything like an eagle rising—more like two porcupines arguing—and so he stopped and pulled the curtains up again.

Oliver often liked to pull the blinds up and look into the courtyard while he was reading. You couldn't really see much—just your own reflection, in the black night, coming back at you from the window. Sometimes, when Oliver was little, and the three of them were having dinner in the kitchen, he liked to wave to the family in the window—his mother and father and him. They seemed so close and near, but somehow still like another family, right there.

He looked down in the courtyard now, past his reflection in the window for a second, and was surprised to see Neige wearing her winter coat, and staring up at his window. He looked down again, and thought about opening the window, but before he could she was gone and he was staring only at his own stupid reflection. Stupid, he thought—he still had the crown on. He must look foolish.

And then he whispered, with a slightly bitter smile on his lips, because he was really so grown up now and his parents didn't know it, "Here I am. The King in the Window. . . ."

For a moment, he thought he heard a gentle knock on the window, but he was sure it was just the January wind. And then a moment later, he heard it again, and he turned and looked toward the window and his own reflection.

But where his own reflection should have been, he saw, looking back at him, a boy in blue, with lilies on his clothing and long hair to his shoulders, gazing gravely at him.

Oliver caught his breath and his heart felt as though it had raced into his throat. The boy was *there*, where his own reflection should have been—he was looking at him right now with pale, gray-blue eyes, and his body was somehow floating in front of the second-story window. Oliver also saw that he was wearing the kind of ancient cloak that is called a doublet, and that the lilies on it were fleurs-de-lis, the tiny flowers that are the old symbol of the kings of France.

He reached out a hand and rapped against the window lightly with the little golden key.

The boy in blue reached up his hand, too, and touched Oliver's through the glass, just as though he really were Oliver's reflection, and not another person on the other side of the window.

For half a second Oliver thought that he must be the victim of an illusion, and he looked down at his own clothes to be sure that there was nothing there that he could mistake, in a window, for a doublet covered with golden fleurs-de-lis. But he just had on a navy blue T-shirt, as he had thought. He noticed that the boy looked down, too, when Oliver did.

So he is my reflection, Oliver thought to himself, only somehow not.

Oliver raised his head again, and he saw that the boy in blue did the same. This time, though, their eyes met, and locked.

Then the boy stared directly at the little golden key that Oliver had found in the *galette* and his eyes seemed to widen and—Oliver was quite sure of this—his lips formed the beginnings of a wide and relieved smile.

Then the boy began forming words with his lips, though it seemed to take great effort to do it. Oliver pressed his ear against the window to hear what the boy in the blue doublet was saying, but as he did, he saw that the boy— almost as though he didn't want to—pressed *his* head and ear against the window, too, so that it was touching Oliver's, on the other side of the window.

Somehow he *has* to act like my reflection, Oliver thought, even though he isn't. He straightened up again, so that he could look directly at the boy. And this time, the boy moved his lips again.

He heard words, so faint and hollow that they were barely audible; the wind whistled outside, and even the sounds of the dishwasher seemed like a roar, so that Oliver had to strain to hear. Yet now, very faintly, but very clearly, like the church bells that rang on Sunday morning from blocks away but whose chimes you could still hear in the kitchen, Oliver heard a distant, pale, drawling voice—a voice like a flute, no, like a recorder, playing far away—speaking French in a nasal accent that Oliver had never heard before.

"O Roi, reviens chez toi! Retourne dans ton royaume!" the boy said. "O, my king—come home! Return to your kingdom."

And then he said it again; only this time, very slowly, as if moving his lips independently of Oliver was taking great effort. "Come home, my king!"

Then he crooked his finger, and made the beckoning gesture with his finger that means, in every language and at every time, *Come. Come with me.*

The boy held up his hand, and in it was the little pebble with the white mark that Oliver had kicked into the river.

Oliver could see the boy's lips move again, effortfully, too, and once again, only more clearly, thrillingly as though they were reverberating around the dark room, he heard the words again.

"We call you, O King." And then quite clearly, "Come to battle! Bring your sword!"

Come to battle? What sword? Called him *where*?

Oliver was trying to clear his throat enough to ask, as he stared into the deep sad eyes of the apparition of the boy, when suddenly he heard footsteps in the corridor down the hall, and then his father was in the kitchen just behind him.

"Dad. Look!" Oliver finally got the words out, in a strangled voice. He glanced back over his shoulder to summon his father, and then turned again toward the window.

Now there was nothing there except his own reflection, and that of his father, looking over his shoulder.

His father put an arm around him. "The family in the window," he said, and he gave Oliver a quick, absentminded squeeze, and then he went to turn on the radio. He fiddled with the dial, cursing a little under his breath, and in a moment Oliver heard the sounds he usually found so comforting: Big Ben booming, and then the cheerful music that meant the BBC news was about to begin, and then a voice saying, "This is London . . ." But Oliver just sat still and rapt, and stared and stared out the window, wondering what he should do, and where he should go, and who he should tell.

"Dad . . ." Oliver began. His father shushed him with a finger. "The American software entrepreneur Gil Hornshaw has arrived in Paris to begin preparations for a project that he promises to launch one week from today, from a platform within the Eiffel Tower. Details of the project remain a closely guarded secret . . ." the announcer began, in plummy British tones. His father moved closer to the radio to listen.

It was three thirty in the morning when Oliver finally fell asleep. Before he shut his eyes, safe in his own bed, he got up and looked in his father's office. He found his father asleep at his desk, bent down in front of his still-humming computer, the blue-gray light on his face. He was online again, Oliver saw, and he had typed his own name—Tyrone Parker—into a search engine, as though he were looking for himself.

Oliver shut off the computer, but his father remained asleep. He tiptoed back into his own room, still feeling extremely spooked and shaken, and wondering if it had really happened, and if it had, who he should tell, and most of all, wondering why anyone was calling him a king, and asking him to come home.

Chapter Two

More Calling

WHEN HE WOKE, Oliver was still excited, and still a little frightened. Oliver hated ghost stories and scary movies, and he was scared of many other things, particularly of strange diseases and mortal allergies and plane crashes and . . . well, it wasn't that the boy had threatened him. But there was still something menacing just about his being there. The next morning when he started to go into the kitchen to get the croissant and hot chocolate he usually had for breakfast, he found that he could hardly make his feet move back into the kitchen.

It had been exciting, though, to see the boy in the blue doublet speaking to him. Oliver stared at the empty window, now filled only with the gray light of another Paris winter day, and felt a little bit disappointed. What if he had dreamt the entire thing? The one thing he was certain of was that he *had* seen Neige looking up at the window not long before he saw the boy. So what if she had seen him, too?

Skipping his breakfast, he ran down the staircase and into the courtyard to ask her. Neige had a small broom and she was sweeping up behind her mother, cleaning the small flower beds where flowers would bloom when spring came, if it ever did. Neige lived with her mother in three tiny rooms in the ground floor of the building. But she always looked bright, and well pressed, and she wore her hair in a long perfect braid. She was actually quite beautiful, in Oliver's opinion, though it wasn't the kind of beauty that would win a contest, or get her picture in a magazine. She had a blunt nose and a sharp chin. But she also had beautiful large gray eyes, which looked out at you intently, as though you mattered, and a quick, happy smile, which you almost never got to see because, like most French girls, she smiled only when there was something really worth smiling about. Oliver sensed that she did not think there was much to smile about much of the time, especially, lately, not when it came to *him*.

Just then Neige was singing. She had a lovely voice, Oliver thought, and he liked to hear her sing. She was singing the old French song *"Feuilles Mortes,"* which Oliver knew in its American version.

24

"That's a lovely song, Neige," he said politely. "It's called 'Autumn Leaves' in English," he added, in French.

She turned to him.

"It's called 'Dead Leaves' in French," she said, in English. (She had studied English at her school, and Oliver used to help her with her homework, before they had had their argument.)

"'Autumn Leaves' is a prettier title for the song," Oliver suggested.

"Yes. But 'Dead Leaves' is a truer description of the leaves," Neige said, this time in French, and she turned away to continue sweeping.

"Neige, I'm sorry that I said those things . . ." Oliver said miserably. He had been trying to apologize to her for a month. "I didn't mean to be insulting or anything," he ended delicately.

But Neige merely turned back toward him, raised her eyebrows high, and opened her mouth a fraction, as though she were shocked that he had been accusing her of something.

Oliver decided to try a more practical approach. Maybe if he asked her a simple, straightforward question she would speak to him. "Neige, were you looking up at our kitchen window last night?" Then he realized that that could sound insulting, too, if you thought about it too much, so he quickly added, "I mean, I hope you were. Did you see what I saw? The boy at the window . . ."

But then Neige made her mouth into an "O," which

Oliver knew meant only, Oh, you must be very naïve and foolish to think such a thing.

It was the most intense conversation Oliver had ever had without the other person actually saying anything.

But then Neige did say something.

"Oliver," she asked, "did your father remember to leave money for the clochards for Christmas?"

The clochards in Paris are the old men, with long beards and matted hair, who live on the streets. They drink a lot. When Charlie had visited Oliver a year before, he couldn't believe that they were so, well, similar, as if they were a brigade of sloppy soldiers: all the clochards wore long torn coats and had long black beards and, though their faces were smudged and filthy, their eyes were usually coal-black and piercing. Oliver had noticed one just yesterday outside his school, when he had picked out the stone that he kicked home—the unsettling way that the clochard had stared right at him was one of the things that made him choose an imperfect pebble. But why was Neige asking such an odd question?

"I don't know if my father did or not," Oliver paused. "I don't think so. Why?"

Neige just turned away one last time, shrugging her shoulders mightily and raising her eyebrows in exasperation. Then she went on singing. But then she turned, suddenly, and to Oliver's shock, took both his hands.

"Close your eyes," she ordered him, and Oliver did— or, at least, he sort of did, leaving them open just a very tiny bit. He knew that this was not quite honest, but he was curious. "Oh, what can one do / with a boy like you?" she sang, in French. They were the words of a very popular song, but she seemed to mean it personally. And then she sang, almost to herself. "A sword of glass / too fragile to be used / is the only useful weapon / for a boy like you."

A sword of glass too fragile to be used. It seemed vaguely insulting, he thought. But then he merely watched from between his eyelids as she seemed to draw something from inside her sweater, from near her heart, and then brought it up through the neck and pressed whatever it was hard down in Oliver's right hand.

Oliver tried to peek down at it, but all that he could tell was that it was hard and sharp edged and seemed cold, so cold that it was white hot, and seemed to sizzle as she pressed it into his palm.

"Yow!" he cried, in pain. And then he really opened his eyes. But in a flash she had put the thing, whatever it was, back inside her sweater.

"Just a pinch," she said primly, like a doctor giving a shot.

"Why did you do that?" he asked. He felt hurt in his heart and hurt in his hand, too. Was she still *that* angry?

"Look, Neige," he began, and then the words rushed out of him. "I'm very sorry I said that thing about France being a moldy old country. I didn't really mean it or anything. I mean, I live here, too. But you said that thing about American tourists being stupider than cattle marching to the slaughter, which was . . . not a very nice remark, if you think about it at all," he concluded lamely.

Theirs had been one of those stupid arguments where both people say things they don't really mean. At least, *he* hadn't really meant it. They always liked to tease each other about France and America. Sometimes, Oliver would show her his one photograph of himself with Gil Hornshaw, and laugh about how someday he would be the king of a software empire in America while she was still raking leaves, and she would say that she would wait for him to come back to France, bankrupt and ruined, and ready to be civilized again. But this last time . . .

But "Fatter . . ." was all that Neige said.

"Comment?" Oliver said, in French, which means "How's that again?"

"I said they were fatter. I said the American tourists were fatter *and* stupider than cattle being marched into a slaughterhouse."

"Oh," Oliver said.

"Just to be precise," she added.

Oliver didn't know what to say to that.

But, with her back turned again, Neige said—and Oliver's heart lifted as he was sure that he could feel a smile in her words—"Oliver, do remember to wear your crown."

"Why?" Oliver asked again. "Why did you say that? What do you mean?" Was she teasing? Or was she serious?

Then he looked down at the paving of the courtyard. He blinked his eyes, and reached down to pick something up.

It was the pebble that he had kicked home from school and then kicked into the river. It had to be. It had the same strange white marking on it. So it might be true after all. . . .

"Hey, Neige," he called out, holding the pebble up.

But Neige just kept silent and went on sweeping, and a moment later Oliver's mother came downstairs to the court-yard in her Tanglewood sweatshirt and track pants, calling out, "Hey, Ollie, let's get moving before we both get out of shape." Oliver put the pebble in his pocket and went dutifully trotting after her. When he looked down at his hand, he saw that there was branded on it now the very faint mark of a lily.

"Mom, if you were a king, where would you call home?" Oliver panted to catch up with his mother as they walked together to school through the Luxembourg Gardens. Or, rather, Oliver was walking. His mother was running, racing ahead of him, as she always did, even in the Luxembourg Gardens when he was on his way to school.

Oliver's mother ran everywhere. She ran to school; she ran to work. She even ran to the shopping street on the rue Buci when she shopped for dinner. She ran for the exercise, of course, but she also ran because she was a running woman. And also, Oliver suspected in his heart, because running kept her from worrying too much about Oliver and his father. She was such a good runner that she was often accompanied, as she was this morning, by four or five other American women who lived in Paris, and who ran behind her, for inspiration.

"Well, the great kings of France usually had several houses," she replied, taking quick short breaths between her words as she ran. Oliver was dressed for school. He had on gray flannel pants, which itched in the cold air, but you got used to it. He had on a white shirt, and over it a blue blazer. His coat was a blue double-breasted wool coat—the kind that in America is sometimes called a pea jacket—which was handsome but a bit bulky. On his back, he wore a very heavy backpack, with all of the *devoirs* he hadn't done inside it. And on his head he had a black wool cap—the kind of high cap that is often called a toque. All of this made it hard for him to walk quickly, much less run after his mother.

Oliver had dark blond bangs and almond-shaped eyes. He didn't smile often. His expression was usually serious and even intense, but when he did smile or laugh—usually at some absurd thing his father had said—it could take over his body and send his head lolling over to one side as though the laugh were so strong inside that it was tipping him over. But it had been a while since he had found a reason to laugh like that.

It was hard running behind his mother with all that on. "But in Paris they lived mostly at the Louvre," she added.

"You mean the museum?" Oliver asked again, struggling to keep up with his mother, her long hair snapping in the winter breeze.

"Yeah. It was a palace before it was a museum. And then the rest of the time they lived in Versailles—you know, the king's house."

"Sure," Oliver said. He'd been there lots of times with his class. It was immense and breathtaking, and about an hour outside Paris.

Even though Oliver had been up much of the night worrying about the boy at the window, one of the strange things in life is that no matter how much else you have to worry about, you still worry about school.

"Mom," he suddenly asked her, "one word association. I say irony, and you say—?" It was a game they often played.

"Irony," she said, hardly needing to take a breath. "Why, it's . . ." She frowned. Then she stopped and ran in place for a moment or two. "Well, Oliver, it's when—I guess it's when you say one thing and mean something else." She looked at him as he stood there, chewing absentmindedly on his tie. "If I said 'Oliver, you've certainly got the Lance Armstrong spirit this morning,' that would be ironic. Irony's sort of like a mirror image of the thing it seems to be—it's exactly the same but completely reversed." She started running again.

"Oh." He ran some more to catch up with her. "Isn't that sarcasm?"

"Yes, I guess so." She stopped for a moment to think. She panted as she ran in place. "Irony is sarcasm plus time. If I say, 'Oliver, you're on the moon,' that's sarcasm. If you grew up to become a lunar explorer and were on the moon, that would be ironic." And she was off again. The four American women in jogging suits heaved deep breaths and chased after her.

Gasping, Oliver caught up with her at last.

"Mom," he asked, in exasperation more than curiosity, "how do you keep running so well?"

His mother jogged in place. "You just have to make all your physical challenges into mental challenges. You put your lungs inside your mind, and think your way around the path. The same way that you have to make your mental challenges into physical challenges. When you're doing your homework—when you do your homework—just imagine that you're riding your bike, and you just have to push your way through."

She had told him this a million times before, but he never was sure exactly what she meant.

Then she was off again, with her followers behind her. Oliver was worn out. He stopped to pant and look around. He had been playing in the gardens since he was small, and only in the last few months had he really begun to feel that he had outgrown them. It was one of the few places in Paris where he felt at home. Over there were the honeybees in their wooden hives, and there was the playground with its spinning plastic disks. . . .

And there was Monsieur Theodore, the grumpy old balloon seller, already setting up his wares near the marionette theater. He was mumbling to himself as he did it, complaining to no one. Oliver no longer went to the marionette theater, but he still was fascinated by Monsieur Theodore. The odd thing was that he was very skillful in making balloon swords, and took enormous trouble to do it right for each child who paid for one. Oliver did not entirely understand why he went to so much trouble when it made him so unhappy—and even then he got only five francs!—but he did. All day long, winter and summer, from early in the morning until the gardens closed at dusk, he sat by the marionette theater, blowing up balloons and making them into objects and never smiling.

Oliver felt sorry for him—what must it be like to be an old man making balloon swords for ungrateful children?— and so he walked over to him, as his mother continued her track around the Delacroix monument, and he offered him five francs. "A sword, please?" he said.

"It's early for a sword," Monsieur Theodore grumbled. "Why do you need a sword before school?" But he huffed and blew into two green balloons—Oliver liked watching his cheeks puff up, red and raw in the cold winter weather—and expertly twisted them into the perfect shape of a saber, with a hilt to protect your hand and a long swooping blade. Then he handed it to Oliver.

"There," he said. "Imagine. A big child like you wanting a balloon sword."

Oliver very nearly became angry. Why, he was only getting the sword because he felt sorry for him, and now here Monsieur Theodore was, looking back at Oliver and feeling sorry for him! But Oliver took it anyway, and handed him the five-franc piece.

He waved good-bye to his mother and took the crowded bus across the river to school.

It was the usual eight-hour nightmare. For one thing, he absentmindedly had kept the balloon sword that he had bought from Monsieur Theodore in his hand when he arrived in class—just the way that he had kept the crown on his head the night before without remembering that he had it on—and that had really given his schoolmates something to laugh about. He had put it down, and popped it, trying to make everyone laugh. But it hadn't helped.

Having arrived at school with the balloon sword helped make even *l'escrime* class, which he had once enjoyed, become a disaster. *L'escrime* is the French word for fencing, which is the sport of fighting with swords. It sounds cool, and Oliver had once actually been pretty good at it. But now they had risen to a new level of fencing, where you had to describe out loud what you were doing while you were doing it. He had put on his white padded suit and his mesh-cage mask, and he had had to fight two boys. He even tried out a *flèche* in his match with Louis Legrand, the biggest and most obnoxious boy in the fifth *primaire*. A *flèche* means an "arrow," and it is a way of jumping off your front foot, thrusting at your opponent as you leap, and then landing on his other side. It is an extremely difficult move, and Oliver did it well, just nicking Louis's vest as he went by, which ought to have scored a point.

But Monsieur Fileul, the fencing teacher, had cried out instantly, "Analyze the conversation!" which means, Say what you are doing in the fencing match. (An exchange of blows in a fencing match is called a conversation.) And

Oliver couldn't remember what he'd done—he could *remember* it, of course, but he couldn't remember the names of all the different bits. He even forgot that his *flèche* had been a *flèche*, and Monsieur Fileul was so angry that he said, "Oliver! You have become stupid and lazy." Oliver had muttered, almost to himself, "I can't think fencing. I just *do* fencing. I just hit." As soon as the words were out of his mouth he regretted them.

Monsieur Fileul had been furious. He turned on Oliver, and actually hit him over the head with his foil. He hit him with the blunt side, but it still hurt. "You turn a *balestra* into a *flèche*, and then you shrug at me like a . . . like an American boxer! 'I just hit'! We are not fighting here! We are fencing!"

"Tell him to fight with his balloon sword," Louis had said, laughing at him. It twisted his face into an ugly, fat grimace. "He came to school today . . . with a balloon sword! It was so *cute*," he jeered.

Oliver gulped as he got his regular clothes on. Louis watched him with a smug, self-satisfied smile. It was hard enough to fight with Louis, much less analyze it, too. It was like stirring up a beehive and writing an encyclopedia article about honey at the same time.

Then rhetoric class at two o'clock had been, if anything, even worse. Oliver, of course, had not finished his *devoirs* the night before, and French homework is extremely hard to fake.

Finally, Monsieur Jordan was so fed up with him that he

turned to him. "Oliver," he said, "I used to tell the other professors that you were not at all stupid, and merely shy. Now I realize," he went on thoughtfully, "that though I was right, they had reason on their side, too: you are actually shy *and* stupid. It is an interesting combination." Then he had given Oliver a paper to write within two weeks. "Write about . . . irony and metaphor in the rhetoric of Molière! And make it superb or you will fail the course, the year, and probably your life!" he demanded, and Oliver's heart sank. Molière, he knew, was a famous French author, who had written comedies back in the seventeenth century. Everybody said they were funny, but Oliver wasn't sure that they really were.

Shy and stupid! Metaphor and irony! Fight and think! At the end of the school day Oliver felt as discouraged as he ever had. Irony and metaphor—Oliver didn't even know what the words meant! And he had to explain them!

Then, the worst thing of all happened. Among all his professors, there was only one whom Oliver really liked: Madame Sonia, who taught French. (It is odd that you would teach French in a French school to children who already speak it, but French is a particular language that must be spoken in particular ways.) She was kind and tall and young, and really very pretty. She actually reminded Oliver of his own mother, though she was, of course, much stiller.

Today as he was coming from Monsieur Jordan's rhetoric class, he saw her inside an empty classroom, fixing her makeup with a compact—one of those little makeup cases women have with powder on one side and a mirror on the other. She smiled at him, weakly, and beckoned him inside.

"Oliver," she said to him fondly. "How go your struggles with the French educational system?" She smiled. She knew how much he hated rhetoric, and, these days, fencing, too, and Oliver understood that, though she couldn't say so, secretly she sympathized with him.

He smiled back. "Well," he began, "it hasn't been the *best* of days. You see—"

While he spoke she was busying herself with her compact, putting the last touches of fresh powder on her face. Oliver didn't mind; he liked it when women did things like that. He took a breath before he continued, and then saw that Madame Sonia had now looked up from the mirror in her compact. She was staring right at him.

Oliver swallowed hard. There was something wrong with her. Oliver couldn't say what it was, but something in her face, or on her face, had changed, completely. Before Oliver could search her face for the trouble, she spoke, and her voice was nothing like her normal voice. It had changed, too, and was now a deep, suave, and silvery growl.

"Keep far away from the sword, boy," she said, jutting her neck out and almost spitting at him. "Do not meddle in things beyond your understanding."

Oliver shrank away and stared at her. Was she joking? No, her mouth was fixed, and hard, and her eyes . . . that was it. There was something about her eyes.

"Keep away from the king's sword, boy," she hissed.

But then she looked at Oliver again, and burst into tears, and, to his shock, she flung her little compact right across the room—Oliver could hear the crack as the mirror broke when it hit the blackboard—and buried her face in her hands. Oliver could hear her weeping.

He might have walked over and comforted her, but it is hard to comfort someone who has just hissed threats at you. And a teacher is a teacher, after all. Instead, he fled down the hall and out of the school.

Coming home from school, as Oliver crossed the Pont Royal bridge in the gray light, he turned the incidents of the last twenty-four hours over and over in his head.

The night before, a strange boy had floated up to his window and told him to get a sword. Two women, one small, one tall, had both been very insistent about—a sword. Neige had hinted that he ought to have it.

He stopped in the middle of the bridge, with the cars running behind him, and looked out across the winter city. Over his shoulder, on the other side of the bridge, was the Eiffel Tower, which, tonight like so often throughout the winter, was only half visible, its head lost in the hanging gray clouds. He had the gold-paper crown in his back pocket. Neige might have been teasing him, he knew, but she might have known something, too. The mark on his hand was proof of that.

Oliver watched as workmen, looking small as insects from this distance, raced on the lower girders, hanging from scaffolds at the ends of long ropes as they attached what looked like small lights on the great frame. At the very top of the tower, a high probing new antenna had been attached, reaching up, golden, into the dark violet winter sky. And on the front of the tower, right by the observation platform, there had been for a week now something very strange: a giant poster of a mouth, set in a crooked smile. It was the symbol of QuantumLeap, the huge software company, and the smile was the famous crooked smile of the great Gil Hornshaw.

"It's obviously a giant antenna for a new television station," one woman was saying to her husband, as they stood together on the bridge, with their small dachshund on a leash, looking up at the beautiful tower.

"That is surely in error, my dear," her husband said from beneath his white mustache. "Just the opposite is taking place. The antenna will be a parking place for giant zeppelin balloons, which will take us for no charge from one side of the Atlantic to the other. This is an obvious American scheme to encourage us to retire in their country."

"You, my dear husband, are a fool," the old woman said, kindly. "Obviously, this project has an electronic significance. This theory of the zeppelins is too absurd to consider."

They went on arguing and gesturing as they looked at the lights being attached to the tower. Their little dog looked up, too, and he even barked, as though he knew better than either of them.

He probably did, Oliver thought. Oliver looked away from the tower and the poster of the giant smile and the workmen, and sighed. Whatever he might be planning in Paris, Gil was certainly smart. If he were here, he might be able to solve the riddles that had come Oliver's way since yesterday evening.

That night, Oliver's parents had tickets to a concert at the Sainte-Chapelle, a medieval church on an island in the middle of the Seine, with stained-glass windows that rise from floor to ceiling, so that the entire chilly old building seems to be made of colored glass.

The ancient music droned a bit, and so Oliver stared at the windows and tried to figure out what stories they were telling. But stories in stained-glass windows tend to be a bit hard to follow at night.

Oliver turned back and looked at his mother and father. His mother was listening seriously. But his father, who usually loved music, and even to make up songs, seemed bored and distracted. His mother was biting her lip, as she always did.

That night, at home, he went back to the window and looked out. Nothing—no boy. He looked down into the courtyard.

Neige, he was sure of it, was staring up at the window, and beside her was a dark figure wrapped in a long overcoat. Oliver, after his talk with Madame Sonia, was beginning to doubt the motives of even the people he liked most.

He looked down at his palm, and saw the fleur-de-lis, the little lily flower, that Neige had imprinted there. Was she trying to sort of, well, brand him? A chill ran through

him. For some reason, the fear made him feel more determined. All right then, he thought, he would go to the nearest king's house that he could find.

"Mom," Oliver said early on Saturday morning. "I, uh, have
to go to Zinedaine's house today to study." He had thought
of telling his mother that he was going to the Louvre,
because of course, like all mothers, she would have loved it
if he had the idea of going to a museum. But then, he had
reflected, she would insist on going with him, and holding
his hand, and telling him all the funny things he had said
about the pictures when he was little, and if you are setting
out to search for something you haven't seen before that
may be a matter of life and death, the last thing you need is
a mother in full goopy mode. So he had decided to tell her
an encouraging lie.

"But it's Saturday, Ollie," she said, surprised, but also
a bit pleased. "You never do schoolwork on Saturdays."

"Well," he went on, "we've decided to put in extra
effort on our *devoirs* this weekend so . . ."

He shrugged, and left the sentence open-ended. Then
he kissed his mother good-bye, and a short while later was
back across the Pont Royal, with the gold-paper crown and
the pebble with the white mark in his pocket, staring at the
vast courtyard of the Louvre Museum. He was wearing his
standard outfit, except for his wool hat. He had left that at
home, just in case he really *was* a king, and would have to
wear his crown to impress people.

One of the problems with visiting the Louvre is that there are always endless long lines in front of the big glass entrance pavilion called the Pyramide. "In summer they bake like sinners, and in winter they freeze like paupers," Monsieur Jordan had said once about the tourists, with gloomy satisfaction. Actually, it had been while they were looking at some Americans waiting in line at the Louvre that Neige had spoken so disdainfully, and Oliver had made his rude reply.

Fortunately, Oliver knew a good shortcut into the Louvre. You just had to go all the way round to the rue de Rivoli, where there is an entrance to something called the Carrousel du Louvre, which is a group of nice stores all kept underground—"like a mall" Charlie Gronek had said, his eyes glowing, when he had come to visit Oliver; it was his absolutely favorite part of Paris. Down among the stores, Oliver knew, there was a kind of back entrance into the Louvre. The line is much shorter there, and anyway, it's warm. Also, if you pretend to be a member of an American school class who has gotten lost from his group, the guards will sometimes whisk you right in, without making you stand in line at all, tut-tutting at you for being such a fool.

Oliver spent the day in the Louvre, searching for—what, he wasn't sure. He ran up the stairs to the Richelieu pavilion, where the old crowns of the kings of France were kept. The Louvre is a very big place, and in certain areas it is extremely crowded. If you go to look at the *Mona Lisa*, for instance, you will probably hardly be able to see it at all, because it is covered with glass, and will be surrounded by people who are taking videos of each other standing in front of it. All you will see is their reflections. But there are large parts of the Louvre where no one—well, hardly anyone—ever goes: vast halls of old Belgian tapestries and long corridors of ugly old Dutch paintings. And rooms and rooms of old swords and armor. In those places, you can always be alone.

Oliver stared into the vitrines, which are what the glass cases are called, and looked at his own reflection. He walked past case after case of shining armor, gleaming smugly at him. Then he saw them, just as he had remembered: the swords of the kings of France. Old bronze swords and slim foils and sabers blackened by time.

And there, right in the middle of the display of sharp iron and steel, was a single short sword, shorter than the others, made entirely of glass. Even its handle, neatly curlicued and inviting, was made of pure transparent crystal. Oliver walked over and stared at it. It was dazzling. As the light passed through it, it sent little prisms and diamonds of light out onto the wooden floor of the museum.

But what possible use could a sword made out of glass serve in a battle? He bent down to read the label:

"Ceremonial Hunting Sword. C. 1600. French? Crystal. This exceptional artifact, made by artisans unknown around the beginning of the seventeenth century, is the subject of scholarly controversy. Although no one knows its function, it was presumably used in ritual actions, since its extreme fragility prevents it from any extended use . . ."

But that didn't tell Oliver anything, really. Well, here he

was, and here it was. . . . Or something like it. What should
he do now? He had better do something, he thought. Looking
around the room to see if anyone was watching, he snatched
the gold paper crown out of his back pocket and thrust it on
his head. Then he stared into the glass case, hoping that his
own reflection would once again become another boy.

Nothing—then laughter, really loud laughter, coming at
him from across the room. The spirits of the kings of
France were laughing with delight at his joining them! But
then the laughter continued, and took on a definitely nasty
tone, and as Oliver looked over his shoulder he saw a group
of schoolgirls—American, from the look and sound of them,
all around his age—looking at him, nudging each other, and
watching him. He had missed them somehow; he hadn't
thought to look behind him. He realized how foolish he must
have looked, snatching the crown out of his back pocket and
putting it on, as though he thought he *belonged* here, and so
he pulled the crown off his head and turned away.

Then the guard came over, and told him in French,
please not to touch, and Oliver explained that he wasn't
touching anything, but that is not an argument you can ever
win with a guard. The American girls laughed even more,
as the guard continued his rounds, and left the room.

Oliver was so embarrassed that he didn't know what to
do, but he had to do something so he didn't look like a complete idiot. He leaned on the glass case that held the glass
sword. He tried to look completely nonchalant. The girls
giggled again.

He reached into his pocket and felt the little pebble there inside it. He took it out and, having nothing else to do, he leaned over, trying to look as carefree as he could, as he carelessly tossed the little pebble from hand to hand. The girls giggled even more. Then, with an angry impulse very unusual for him, he took the crown out of his pocket and placed it on his head. Let them laugh!

And suddenly a sound began to fill the room. It was very quiet at first, like the hum of a distant wave, only one with a deep bass drumbeat at its heart. The hum became a thrum, and then became a roar, growing in volume and force moment by moment, until the room began to shake and then to tremble, as though the sound were a storm and the room a frail boat in its grip. It seemed to be breaking right on top of him, with a repeated, deep throbbing, thrumming pulse set inside it. Oliver looked around in fear. The sound had set the suits of armor to trembling and shaking. Helmets fell.

And then there was a splintering crack, and the glass cases all around the room began to explode. One by one, the cases broke in a cascade of splintered glass and wood. Oliver stepped back and covered his head with his arms, trying to protect himself from the flying, splintered glass shards.

The American girls screamed in terror and ran from the room.

Oliver could never entirely explain what he did next. As the thrumming sound rose, and the glass cases exploded, he saw that everything glass inside them was exploding, too, the vases and crystals and even the windows in this wing in the

Louvre. And he saw that the penetrating wave of force was approaching the glass sword. Instead of shrinking back, Oliver leaped forward and grabbed it, daring the splintering force.

Suddenly, there was silence. He held the sword briefly. It was heavy, but supple in his hand. As he pulled it out, it struck against the edge of the vitrine.

But now here came the guards, two of them, racing across the herringbone parquet toward him. He held out the sword, panic-stricken, meaning to offer it back to them. But they skidded to a stop, their eyes alarmed. Why? Oh! They thought he was threatening them with it. How silly. He walked as quickly as he could over to them, sword out for them to take.

But as one of the guards took the sword from Oliver's hand, the horrible hum began again, half as loud as before, but quickly building back up to its apex. It was *him*, somehow—it was Oliver's hand on the sword that kept the sound away.

Without even thinking about what he was doing, Oliver snatched the sword back from the guard's hand. The hum stopped. The guards looked at him for a moment, dumbfounded by the onset of the noise, and now its sudden end. Oliver used the moment of surprise to do the only thing he could think of doing, and that was to run.

Boom, clatter, he raced down the stairs, the crystal sword suddenly feeling heavy beneath his coat. He swallowed hard. Up above he could hear the rush of the army of museum guards, and two of the American girls screaming.

"Watch for the boy with the crown!" he heard one cry.

A moment later, he found himself back in the great hall of the Louvre, filled as usual with hundreds of schoolchildren. Oliver quickly placed himself among them. He snatched off the gold paper crown, so that the pursuing police wouldn't be able to identify him. But as soon as he did, the sound began again, the horrible explosive hum! And the moment he put the crown back on his head, it stopped.

So it wasn't just his hand on the sword that ended the sound—it was his hand on the sword while he wore the crown from the cake. But with the crown on his head they would identify him. There was only one thing to do. He reached out, snatched the woolen beret from the head of a nearby boy, and put it on over his crown.

"My hat!" the boy cried out, but Oliver ducked down low and lost himself among the schoolchildren and a few moments later, rushing down to the back entrance to the Louvre, he was outside. Back behind him, he could still hear cries of "The sword!" and "The boy in the crown!" and "My hat!" in one great loud confusion.

He hugged the glass sword to him beneath his coat. Well, as his mother would say, was this a net gain or a net loss? He had a sword too fragile to be used. That was certain. And he could see why Madame Sonia had warned him away from the Louvre. That sound!

His heart fell as he walked back home across the Pont Royal. In the space of two days, he had become a world-class museum thief, and he had managed to alienate every one of his teachers. And something was searching for him with a horrible otherworldly noise.

He stopped on the bridge taking the glass sword from his coat quickly, and then fitting it inside his sleeve, to hide it. The winter's evening traffic of cars and walkers went by, the exhaust filling the air. Several Parisians were looking up at the Eiffel Tower, where the work continued under Gil's enormous grin.

Oliver sighed. Then he looked back down sadly into the muddy-green water below the bridge. If he looked hard, he could just see his own reflection, rippling in the wake of a long green barge.

And as the barge passed, the ripples began to increase, and his image broke even more, and when it ought to have settled back, *he* was there again. The boy in the blue doublet! Only now he was everywhere!

It was exactly as if the river were a kaleidoscope, and someone had placed the boy's face inside it, and turned the tube or given it a shake: everywhere Oliver looked up and down the muddy river Seine as it flowed under the bridges and divided in two at Notre Dame, everywhere, he saw the face of the boy in the blue doublet, repeated a thousand times. Each boy rested inside his own little watery diamond, which shimmered and danced, and all stared up at him again, from the water of the Seine. Oliver was so startled that he tried to shout, but nothing came out.

And then the boy—all the boys together, though Oliver thought there was just one he was seeing over and over—

made the same beckoning gesture with his finger, and Oliver heard the same ghostly, plaintive voice crying out, faint but clear through the noise of the traffic. Only now the countless boys all said it together, in the single loudest whisper that Oliver had ever heard: "O, King of window and water. You have your sword at your side at last! Now, come home to your court!"

King of window and water! Sword at your side! Oliver had found the right sword after all. It wasn't late, and he couldn't have fallen asleep—not here, not on the Pont Royal. Someone was calling him King, and someone was calling him home.

He wanted to pull the glass sword from inside his sleeve and wave it, to show them what he had now. But that might be dangerous . . . so instead Oliver took off the stolen beret, quickly showed the hidden crown, and jumped up and down, trying to get the boys' attention. But their images soon passed from the river, and Oliver was left alone to leap and shout and be watched with alarm and disapproval by all the Parisians passing by on the bridge. A woman walked right up to him shook her finger at him, and then walked on.

King of window and water! What did *that* mean? Yesterday the boy had called him King when he was looking in a window, and today he had called him King when he was looking in the water . . . maybe if he kept looking in, oh, inkwells or dinner plates, then he would become king of those, too. It would be an easy way to become more and more powerful, Oliver thought. . . .

Before he went upstairs to his apartment, Oliver hid the sword in the *cave* of their building. The *cave* (you pronounce the word with a short "a," like the "a" in "bat") was like a little locker that stood in the basement of their building. His father used to keep bottles of wine down there, but for the past year or so he hadn't. There was nothing in the *cave* now except spiderwebs and dust and old bottles and tarpaulins that they had once used to cover the furniture while the apartment was repainted.

It was not completely safe in here, he thought with a feeling of guilt, as he began to cover it with the old, oily cloth again, but no one went down there much, and the truth was that he was a little scared to keep the glass sword in his own room. What if the police showed up? If it was in the *cave*, at least he could pretend that he didn't know where it had come from. He knew that the right thing to do was to bring it back to the Louvre, but it is easier to know what the right thing to do is than it is to do the right thing. Anyway, the boy in the blue doublet *wanted* him to get the glass sword, and surely that was the kind of request you just had to obey.

Oliver looked at the sword one last time before he covered it with the tarpaulin. It was bright, clear, and still light as a feather. Yesterday he had held a child's balloon sword, and now he had this beautiful glass one. It might be stolen, but it was still wonderful to look at.

He picked it up again. The sharp edge of the sword, he saw as he examined it, was covered with small deep nicks and grooves, like scars from previous battles. It even had, he saw with wonder, a deep crimson stain on its very edge. Someone had *fought* with this sword. But that was impossible. He hefted it. It was much too light to fight with. Why, it was as delicate as one of the crystal champagne glasses that his mother took out for company. If you struck it on anything, it would obviously shatter into a thousand pieces. In what time, and in what world, could it have ever really been used in battle?

He looked at it more closely. There, etched on the glass, was a round face surrounded by rays. The sign of the Sun King! So it must have come from the Sun King's court . . .

No, he hadn't dreamt up the boy. And he certainly hadn't imagined this sword, or that sound in the museum. A boy of some kind of strange origin was calling him a king, and telling him to come back to his own house, and to use his own sword, and two women had urged him on and one had warned him away. And all of it pointed one way and one way only: to Versailles and the palace there.

There was a mysterious purpose and a strange task in his life now—that was clear. He held his hand up to look more closely at the fleur-de-lis that Neige had painfully embossed on his palm. But it had already faded, and, as he held it up, he could see just the outline of the little flower. It was odd, he thought, as he went back up the stairs to his apartment, to be in love with a girl at once so musical and so heavily armed.

Chapter Three

In the King's House

"MOM," OLIVER sighed, and tried to make it impressive. "I'm going to have to go *back* to Zinedaine's house today to study," he explained the next morning over breakfast, as he drank his café au lait, coffee heavily diluted with hot milk. "We need to—uh—we need to work harder on our rhetoric papers."

"It's Sunday, Oliver," his mother said. "You don't have to do *devoirs* on Sunday, do you?" Oliver could tell, though, that, once again, she looked slightly pleased.

While they spoke, Oliver's father was reading the news-paper. "This thing about the theft at the Louvre might make a good piece," he muttered. Oliver's heart sank. He looked at the headline: "Crystal Sword Taken. Violent Robbery in Broad Daylight."

"The security guards say that it was taken by a violent teenage psychopath," his father told them. "They always say that a crook has a German accent."

Oliver felt a little better. His father turned more pages. "Hey, look at this! They have a full page on Gil Hornshaw's arrival next week. About how he's taking over the Eiffel Tower to launch this new thing of his. Well, everyone has that news, I guess. But they don't have the big story."

"What big story?" Oliver asked.

"No one is supposed to know, Ollie. He's keeping it a secret."

"Do you know, Dad?"

"I think I *may* know, Oliver. It really is a big story, if I'm right. A big, big story. Gil hasn't even told me exactly yet, and he says he still has a problem to solve. They're working round the clock back in Seattle."

"Well, what *is* it, Ty?" his mother asked.

"I'll tell you when I know, Angelica," was all he said, and then he closed the paper, asked for more coffee, and went back into his office. Oliver watched his mother's eyes as she saw him walk away.

"Anyway, Mom, I have that rhetoric paper to do. Also, I think I'd better pack a lunch, too," Oliver said.

"Doesn't Zinedaine's mother give you lunch?" Oliver's mother asked. She was still looking after his father.

"Well. She does and she doesn't," Oliver replied. He had learned that answers like that—answers that read the same from front to back and from back to front, so to speak—were very good at pacifying his mother.

Before he left, he sneaked downstairs, into the cave, and, in the darkness, groped for the glass sword. Yes, there it was. He held it up and then with great difficulty, managed to fit it under his navy blue pea coat, with the hilt pressed up under his shoulder and the body of the sword fitting stiffly along his left side. It was an uncomfortable but effective way of hiding it.

Oliver walked down the rue du Pré-aux-Clercs, and then turned decisively left, away from Zinedaine's house. He was going, alone, to Versailles, the great country retreat of the royalty of France, the château of châteaux, the king's house. If the people who were calling him King were anywhere, Oliver knew, they would be, they *must* be, there.

Oliver had never taken a train trip by himself before. Charlie Gronek, he knew, was always setting off by himself on overnight bike trips, even though he was only thirteen, a year older than Oliver. The farthest Oliver had ever gone by himself was on the metro to the edge of Paris. So when he arrived on the platform of the train station that would take him to Versailles he felt excited and a little scared. Coffee and train travel will do that for you.

The trip from Paris-Invalides to Versailles takes only

about twenty-five minutes, but, like all train trips, it felt longer than it was. There is something about a train in winter, Oliver thought, that always makes the minutes go by more slowly. You could feel the cold outside on the window-pane, even though it was hot in the train. All the while, the short glass sword, stiff against the inside of his navy blue coat, seemed to prod him like a guilty conscience.

A policeman had walked up and down the cars, and he had looked sternly for a moment at Oliver. Oliver had shrunk a little inside. What if they had his description from the American girls at the Louvre? He tried to look as innocent and stupid as he could, and the policeman walked away. Sometimes, there were advantages to looking stupid and shy, Oliver thought.

After the train had pulled up at Versailles station and everyone piled out, Oliver trudged up the hill toward the château. It was a depressing place as you approached it, Oliver thought. At the top of what looked like a big hill of gravel, there was the back of a big ugly brick house, and a statue of a man on horseback. Oliver plodded up the gravel hill, walked past the ugly statue of the man on horseback, bought his ticket from the bad-tempered lady at the gate, walked around to the other side of the huge brick building, and then his heart rose, as it always did, when he looked out at the gardens of Versailles.

Oliver saw a long, great lawn—longer and, even in winter, greener than any he had ever seen elsewhere, sweeping down in terraced steps toward a long silver canal. Then more stairs, with trimmed hedges all around, and then another fountain set down on the next level, this one with a golden statue inside it—a man in a chariot led by snorting horses that seemed to rise up from the sea. The lawns ran as far as the eye could see down toward the long silver canal of water, with two tall and graceful willows waving at its end. And off the great green carpet and the long silver canal, he could make out charming smaller gardens, like rooms, boxed in by tall poplars, with alleyways and little paths that disappear into little groves and mazes. Everywhere his head turned there were statues of nude gods and nymphs, and when he looked the other way, mazes and hidden grottos beckoned him on. The countless windows of the châteaux glittered a little even in the dim winter sun, and the light fell in silver rays, too, on the canal; and as Oliver gazed out over the gardens of Versailles he felt sure in his heart that if the boy in the blue doublet was calling him to be a king of windows and water, he would find him here.

As Oliver gazed out at the gardens and fountains, he tried hard to remember everything he had been taught about Versailles when he had come here with his class. (One problem with French history is that all the kings are called Louis, and you can tell them apart only by their numbers and the style of furniture they liked, which is easy if you are good at remembering the way chairs look and not easy if, like Oliver, you are not.) He was pretty sure that he remembered that it was the fourteenth Louis—or Louis XIV, as they called him at school—who had had his gardener, André Le Nôtre, build the gardens of Versailles back in the seventeenth century, the century that the French call the *Grand Siècle*: the Great Century. Try as he might, though, as Oliver tried to remember more, it all turned into a big jumble of more King Louises and their musicians and their chairs and their mistresses and the sarcastic, witty guys who kept them company. Then, when the French Revolution arrived, the royal court cleared out—some went into exile, some to the guillotine.

Oliver made his way into the enormous château, past great silent groups of Japanese visitors, who were listening intently to the guides, and great noisy groups of American visitors, who were all talking to each other. (He had to go through a metal detector of course, but the sword, being glass, set off no alarms.)

There were the king's apartments, and here were the queen's apartments—and yet, he knew that none of these were the places where he would find the boy. And so he quietly slipped away from the crowd, and finally was at his destination: the great Hall of Mirrors.

It was a huge but gracious ballroom, lined from floor to ceiling with silvery mirrors in golden frames on three walls. On the far wall a row of windows stood. A guide was giving a lecture to a group of tourists there, and Oliver slipped over and listened.

"Here, we are at la Galerie des Glaces—the Hall of Mirrors," the guide announced, "built in the year 1678 by King Louis the Fourteenth. Never before had so many mirrors been brought into one place. Under the direction of Fontenelle, the king's minister, all of the king's essential business took place here! Great balls were held; treaties signed; wars concluded in solemn majesty—and all reflected back and forth, from one side to another, in an infinity of majesty!" he ended pompously.

And then all the tourists stood and gaped at the endless reflections that are always produced when one wall of mirrors reflects another—so that as they looked there seemed to be an infinite number of tourists, all nested one inside another into the endless distance—and then they snapped photographs of themselves caught in the infinity of reflections, and then turned to go on into the next room.

Oliver remained behind. All alone in the great hall, where the gold-framed mirrors ran from floor to ceiling, he peered into one of the great walls of mirrors, searching for the blue boy . . . nothing.

He stepped closer and held his hand out. To his shock, the mirrors felt cold—icy cold, so cold that they were hot. . . .

And then suddenly the same deep ominous thrumming sound that he had heard at the Louvre, the sound like a wave rushing up upon you, began to fill the room. The whooshing hum, and underneath it the steady, deep beating sound, growing in strength and terror. It came from deep within the mirror, Oliver was sure of it. Yesterday it must have come from within the suits of shiny armor in the Louvre! And then

Oliver thought that he could see, deep within the reflections, a host of dark red eyes, hundreds of them, bright like a horde of cats. In terror, but still recalling what had worked before, he reached into his back pocket and put the gold paper crown on his head.

But then, from the other side of the room, where the long row of matching windows ran, came a long, gentle whisper, like a breeze, or a clarinet, and a sudden stillness spread over the great room.

"You really shouldn't frighten them like that, Your Majesty," said a melodious voice.

Startled, Oliver turned back and looked over his shoulder at the row of windows.

It was the boy again! He was slipping from window to window, as though he were running on an invisible track outside the corridor, in midair.

Me frighten *them*, Oliver thought. But before he could speak, the boy was smiling.

"It's very brave, of course, confronting them like that," the boy said now, skipping from inside one window to the next, "but I'm sure the other wraiths will tell you that it is wiser to wait."

By now, Oliver was becoming accustomed to the boy's appearances, so he simply walked up to the window and waved. Only this time, the boy, instead of speaking, reached a hand out of the window—a full, real-life three-dimensional hand, only somehow watery—and pulled Oliver into the window with him.

Oliver craned around and realized that something had happened to him.

"There you *are*," the boy in blue said, in a kind of drawling old-fashioned French that was pleasing to the ear, though a little hard to understand. "Oh, you've come! I've got you here at last. They'll all be so pleased."

"Who?" Oliver asked. "Who will be pleased?"

"All of them. You know. Those Whose Backs Were Turned. The court."

"And your king?" Oliver ventured. If there really was a king, he had to clear up the confusion.

"Well, the king. Well, he . . ." The boy's voice trailed off.

"I see," said Oliver, who didn't. "And who are you?"

"My name is François, and I'm a window wraith, and I've been sent to bring you home."

"What's a window wraith?"

"It's someone who once lived in the ordinary world who lives now in a window, and makes reflections of the people who pass by and look in."

"You mean you *are* a ghost?!" Oliver asked, suddenly feeling a little terrified.

"Just the opposite, actually. You see, ghosts come from another world and haunt you, but window wraiths *are* the world. We're the memory of the world. We're here for good. *You're* the ones who come and go like ghosts. *You* haunt us."

François seemed to notice the incomprehension on

Oliver's face, and, as they wafted along in—well, where were they? Neither here nor there, it seemed, just . . . lost, in midair—he went on, "When you look into a window, what you see is not you—or not entirely you. It's really a window wraith, looking back at you. There's a window wraith inside every old window. We live inside windows, and look back at you the way you'd like to look, not quite the way you really look, but with something extra—to make you look a little bit better."

"How do you mean, a bit better?"

"Well, no one really wants to look *just* the way they do. So we mingle our looks with yours and improve things just a bit—we look back at you the way you'd like to look. That's why people prefer the way they look in a window to the way they look in a mirror. Have you ever noticed the way that someone—let's say a lovely woman walking down the street— will adjust her hat or her hair in a window? And then walk away smiling, looking happy? Well, that's because the window wraith adds a little something extra for her."

Oddly enough, Oliver had seen his mother do exactly that many times. As he stopped to consider the matter, the boy pulled him a little farther down, so that they came out of the cloud they had been lost in and were just floating directly above the beautiful gardens of Versailles.

"But even though you say you're not ghosts, you're in the afterlife," Oliver insisted.

"No, no. This is not the afterlife. We are in the *life-after*."

"Not the afterlife but the life-after?" Oliver echoed. It was difficult to float and be exasperated at the same time. "What's the difference?"

"In an afterlife you no longer have the cares and worries of living. In the life-after, you are finished with your life, but not with its problems. You have just as much work to do as you always did. There are wars to fight and a king to follow, and evil—well, there is work to do. You have to work for your not-living, if you follow me."

"If you're a reflection, then why can I see you? And if you've been a wraith for so long, why do you look my age?"

"Wraiths always remain as old as they were when they looked into their window with the keenest longing. We don't age, though we do get more brittle. And you can see me because I'm a messenger wraith. You see, wraiths are creatures of water and windows. We can jump from window to window, and we can swim in water. But we have no neutral medium; there's no straight path in the world that we can follow, the way that you can walk on a road from place to place. So most of the old wraiths are stuck here. They can only float a few feet from window to window. It's so dull!" François shook his head in frustration.

"But a few of us younger wraiths have found ways to get from windows to water and water to windows, and go where we want to go, more or less. We leap from puddle to splash, and even from inside sewers to the rear windows of cars, and, if you're clever enough and quick enough, you can generally get where you want to go."

"Is that how you found me?" Oliver asked.

"Yes!" François said happily. "First, I dived into that fountain there"—he gestured below them—"and then I swam quite a long way, until I was near Paris, and then I went down into the sewers, and fell into a passing pipe . . . and then I found my way back into the river—and that's when I saw you, kicking the homing stone across the river! I was so excited! Only the king has the homing stone. It's well known."

"The homing stone?" Oliver asked.

François looked puzzled. "Yes, you know, your stone. The one that always leads you home when you kick it. *You* know the saying: If the King in the Window is lost in the maze or the world, the stone will lead him home."

"Oh, yes, of course," Oliver said, not wanting for once in his life to seem stupid. "That saying."

"It's such a famous saying!" François laughed.

"It's so . . . *known,*" Oliver agreed. So that was why the stone had zipped across the water toward Oliver's side of the river. It was showing him the way home. He was pleased to find out, though secretly a little disappointed that he hadn't been that strong a kicker.

"And so I watched you, and got to the riverbank, and hid myself in the rear window of a car, and then jumped into a puddle—almost didn't make it, actually—and rose up the drainpipe into the courtyard of your building, and got into your window. There was a wraith there, but he was very sleepy. . . ."

Oliver shivered. It sounded like the life of a wet rat.

"And then I saw you, and then I saw you had even left the homing stone in the courtyard, as a sign. And there you were, wearing the king's crown, and holding the—well, you know what—and then declaring yourself! It was wonderful!"

"Uh—I think there may be a small misunderstanding . . ." Oliver began. But before he could go on the boy started to land.

"Of course, it's good for you," the boy said, ignoring him. "But it's even better for me. Racine keeps threatening to send me over to be the wraith in a tall building in a new world. He thinks all my leaping from puddles to windows in Paris is extremely dangerous and reckless. Which, frankly, it is. Last year my friend Hyacinth didn't quite make the leap on a dry day and he just . . . shriveled up." François shrugged. "But who could stay here and just wait in the windows and talk all night, the way the rest of them do? We need action, and I acted and, well, here you are! The king! And now here *we* are."

He looked down from on high at the gardens, covered with fallen leaves, and then he said quietly, almost to himself: "It is the most beautiful big place in the world. There are many more beautiful places that are smaller, and there are bigger places but they are not beautiful. I have loved it here ever since I was a page boy for the Sun King, so long ago, before I was taken over to the other side of the windows."

And then François seemed to pull Oliver right down toward the ground, at the back windows of the Petit Trianon—a kind of little getaway house that Louis the XV built so that he could escape from the big château. François pulled Oliver down out of the sky with him, and together they landed on its roof.

"Now, remember," François said. "Don't let them keep on talking beyond the reasonable limit. They love to talk. And listen: make them tell you everything they can about . . . him."

François was very insistent for a courtier, Oliver thought.

"Who?" he asked.

François looked troubled. "You know. Him. The One with None." He almost mumbled the name. "The Master of Mirrors. He is the one thing they would rather not talk about—but the one thing you *must* hear about. So ask! Act as if you already know it all, and they'll tell you everything."

Oliver saw that there was a large skylight, looking down onto the upper floor onto a kind of ballroom. Peering into the skylight, Oliver could see the outlines of the room. And then as he somehow floated through it, there was just behind it—*and* just in front of it—a roomful of pale courtiers, all transparent as glass, and all bowing down to him.

Chapter Four

The War of the Mirrors and Windows

"GREETINGS, Your Majesty, the new King in the Window!" a wraith in a long white wig, with a fixed but kindly smile, called out to Oliver as he landed within the ballroom of the Petit Trianon.

Oliver was stunned, of course, and a little frightened. He thought that it was up to him to say something.

He heard beautiful music all around, the gentle sawing of old violins and wooden flutes, while just outside the pavilion he saw that a kind of fountain sprayed water all around,

leaping up high along the glass walls. It gave a misty soft-
ness to the cold air, and for once the dark French winter
seemed somehow to have retreated in the face of music and
warmth.

But before Oliver could speak the transparent wraith in
the white wig had begun to greet him more formally.

"Welcome, Your Majesty!" he said. "Greetings, our
much-sought-for and too-long-lost dauphin. You are the
King in the Window—long may you shine!" And they all
lowered themselves. They couldn't bow, really, being made
of glass, but they twisted in the sunlight, and turned themselves at an angle to the sun, and formed a half circle,
and, through their liquid glass bodies, the light of the sun
refracted in a beautiful rainbow on the floor of the pavilion.

Oliver saw that their bodies were absolutely clear, and
yet liquid too, as though made of very soft crystal. Their
clothes seemed almost to be infused inside their bodies, like
tea in water. Yet all of them wore long white powdered wigs,
with curls that fell to their shoulders. In comparison with
their pale and gentle bodies, it seemed as though the wigs
were likely to topple them over and make them break.

But what was most remarkable about them, Oliver saw
as the wraiths slowly straightened, was their eyes. Their eyes
at first seemed to be made of little shards of glittering glass,
but then Oliver saw that they were as bright and glowing as
jewels, and that each wraith's eyes were a slightly different
cast. One had bright ruby eyes, and the next had eyes as
green and glowing as emeralds, and several had pale bright

blue sapphires. Their eyes were so bright that they shone even here in this sunny glass building. It was almost disconcerting.

Then, very formally, they stepped aside. A row of wraiths in pale gray uniforms stepped forward next, pulling behind them, on silk ribbons, what looked like little toy cannons of colored glass. At a nod from the smiling wraith, they solemnly fired off their cannons, and Oliver winced, expecting smoke and a roar—but nothing came out except clear bubbles, each one lit by a rainbow highlight, which rose toward the roof. Oliver was ready to laugh, but he recognized that he was being paid a tribute, and he tried to look extremely serious.

Four more wraiths stepped up and they fought a quick, formal fencing match. They were very expert—"*Flèche*, parry, thrust," Oliver found himself muttering under his breath, keeping track of the conversation—but their foils, he saw, were simply long balloons, like the one Monsieur Theodore had made for him Friday morning. It was really quite ridiculous. Then the row of military-looking wraiths moved forward again, and this time they held what looked like old-fashioned muskets on their shoulders. They spun them, marched ahead very expertly, and fired in the air. But all that came out was a fine spray of water. Water pistols! Oliver thought—how funny. But the wraiths cringed at the sound, and stepped back, gingerly, as though they were both frightened and impressed.

"We are the servants of the window—and you are now

our king!" the kind wraith said as he concluded the ceremony. (His eyes were of a light, almost afternoon-sky blue.) Oliver remained on the brink of laughing at the solemnity with which they went through their maneuvers with the balloons and the bubbles and the feathers. But there was nothing remotely funny or lighthearted about the expressions on the their faces.

"All hail the King in the Window!" they cried, as Oliver looked down to see his clothing covered with light and rainbows, and once again they bowed.

François, instead of floating to the ground, had remained hovering in midair, so that the toes of his pointed slippers were right at Oliver's eye level. But now he slipped down just enough to whisper into Oliver's ear.

"Better tell them to rise," François said impatiently. "They'll go on bowing and rising for hours. They like it."

"Uh—rise, O wraiths," Oliver said at last. But then he was so confused that he said, "Um, what exactly is it that I am king of?"

They didn't seem fazed by the question.

"King of window and of water. As you know! King of all things glass and glassy!" said the most severe-looking of the wraiths. His eyes glowed a dark rich green.

Just the mention of glass seemed to set the other wraiths off into a kind of ecstasy.

"Glass! Transparent, liquid and yet solid," cried one opal-eyed wraith. "It transmits the light of the world in and yet keeps the cold out! Turn it into a telescope, and it extends the philosopher's vision unto the very heavens; make it a microscope, and it lets him see the microbes as they dance!"

And then a wraith with the harp closed his eyes and sang: "Begin with sand / then heat it up / and soon you'll have / a crystal cup . . ."

Oliver knew that that was true. Glass was made by heating sand until it melted and then cooled transparently. He had learned that in school.

Now the first wraith, the nice one with the white wig and the amused smile and the blue eyes, resumed the tale. "In plain French: we are the window wraiths of Versailles—keepers of the wisdom of glass, and the guardians of the Window-Way." He stepped closer, and almost whispered. "My friends tend to be a bit fancy when they describe things. I prefer the plain truth. You may call me Molière."

Molière! Oliver thought. This was the honest-to-God real Molière! Why, writing that essay was going to be a piece of pastry now! Then he felt ashamed of himself for thinking so selfishly at such a serious moment, and he tried to quiet his mind and listen.

"The man tending the glass flowers is the gardener Monsieur Le Nôtre, and, oh, well, you'll get to know the rest of us as you rule," he explained to Oliver. "You must forgive my colleagues if they become carried away by the thought of glass. We have the enthusiasm for glass that fish might have for the ocean, or poets for French. It is our medium."

"Why are they so crazy about glass?" Oliver asked.

"Why are we so in love with glass? Why, it couldn't be clearer!" Molière exclaimed.

He paused, while Oliver gaped at him, and a slightly disagreeable look crossed the kind wraith's features.

"Laugh!" François said suddenly, once again descending helpfully to Oliver's ear level. "It's a joke."

"A mere play on words," Molière said, his whole transparent body coloring slightly red. Oliver hurriedly laughed the kind of very artificial laugh that you laugh when you are trying to act as though something is funny. Then he cleared his throat. "Well, you see, there's a small problem . . . ," he began. "I'm not the King in the Window. Or any other kind of king, actually. I'm a boy, an American boy who lives in Paris, so . . ."

"Don't go there!" a voice said keenly. It was François, of course, once again diving toward Oliver's ear. "Don't go there!"

But of course the wraiths had heard what Oliver had said, and some of them looked concerned. Their bright eyes even seemed to dull for a moment.

"Oh, that is always the way," Molière said gently, waving away the other wraiths' worries with his hand. "The King in the Window is always found, not made, after the old king vanishes."

Oliver was still sure that there was a misunderstanding, but he couldn't think of exactly how to explain it without disappointing them terribly, and anyway it was fun to be treated as a king, at least for one Sunday afternoon, and so he said, "I still don't understand. What are you? What are window wraiths? If I'm your king"—if only for a moment, he thought to himself—"then at least I should know who I'm king of."

"That's better. Get them going about themselves. They like that," François murmured from his perch above and alongside Oliver, nudging Oliver's ear hard with his elbow. "Just don't let them go on *too* long."

Molière smiled again, and the wraiths gathered closer. Some of them hovered, gracefully, above Molière as he spoke. They knew what he was going to say but everyone likes to hear why they are special, and how they came to be that way.

"You see, Your Majesty, the Grand Siècle," Molière declared, spinning gracefully around to gesture at the whole of the châteaux and gardens, "was the great age of poetry . . ." He bowed toward the very severe-looking wraith with the green eyes. (It must be Racine! Oliver thought to himself, recognizing the great poet and dramatist from a bust he had seen in the hall at school.) "The great age of music . . ." He bowed again toward the wraith with the harp. "The great age of the garden . . ." He bowed this time to a wraith carrying a spade. "And yes," he added quickly, "the greatest age of sandwich dressings." Molière turned his head to one particularly tall and solemn wraith who was holding a wire whisk as though it were a scepter and a copper pot as though it were an orb, and the two wraiths exchanged deep and comforting bows. Oliver shifted uneasily. Sandwich dressing?

Then all the other wraiths—there must have been fifty of them, by Oliver's quick count—crowded around Molière and looked on expectantly, as though they were waiting for their praise, too. Molière recommenced. "In short, it had what every great age must have—greatness." He bowed to the other wraiths, wrapping them all up in a single compliment. They looked vaguely disappointed, but allowed him to continue. Oliver liked him for being so kind to the other wraiths.

"But above all, it was the great age of glass. Glass begins as a liquid, and before our day, glass had to be blown, vessel by vessel and pane by pane, by the glassblowers of Venice. To have a window to look out of was itself a great feat known only to the wealthy. But then during the Christmas of 1688, the great Thevart, working in his glassworks at Saint-Germain-des-Pres in Paris, right at the rue du Bac and the rue de Bellechasse—"

"But that's right where I live!" Oliver cried. "I mean, that's my neighborhood."

The wraiths looked at each other uncertainly. But Molière said brightly. "Is it? One more good sign."

But before he could speak again, Racine interrupted. "For it was there that the new way of casting glass in great unbroken sheets was invented, and with that invention the great age of the window was upon us. Five feet high! Nine feet high! The size of the pure rectangles of window glass that Thevart could cast grew apace with every month. The king's counselor Colbert formed the Royal Company of Glass, and put Thevart at its head—and soon the great cast sheets of French glass feared no rival even from the blown glass of Venice." Racine's eyes glowed bright with remembered pride.

"A civilization grew up around the city with windows as their hearths," he went on. "Paris for the first time was filled with shops, and the beautiful things people desired were brought out for them to gaze at and long for. Versailles, palace of pleasure, had more windows than any hall in human history. And everywhere men looked *through* windows, rather than *at* them, and their reflections came back like a little gift.

"And in time the great secret was unlocked to the Wise. It was *not* the windows alone, but the wraiths within them, that gave to glass its grace. It was not the glass, but what was within the glass that mattered—as though we had confused the dancer with the dance, the hat with the head inside it, the bread with the butter, the . . . the . . ."

"The salmon with the mayonnaise?" suggested one of the other wraiths eagerly, but Racine merely shook his head and looked fierce.

"As though we had confused . . . the flag with the wind, the sock with the foot, the . . . the . . ." he went on looking ever more uncertain.

All the wraiths looked on with an expression of polite concern as Racine struggled to conclude. "When he gets engaged in a metaphor, you must let him have his head, until he comes to the end of it," Molière whispered gravely in one of Oliver's ears.

"It can take *days,*" François muttered in his other ear.

But Racine seemed unable to find the right concluding image, and so Molière, after waiting patiently for him to finish, gently took over. "What my great friend is trying to say is that it is the wraiths within the windows that make window reflections so pleasing to look at."

"And if you look through a window with longing, you, too, will someday return to it." Now Racine's voice, as it rose again, became murmuring and full of joy, and Oliver could actually see the things he was talking about within his glass body as though the images in Racine's mind were suddenly visible.

"Imagine all the people looking in their windows, searching for their joy through the lens of their longing! The small boy staring at a train in a toy store window. The woman wanting a hat in the window of Christian Dior; a hungry man staring in the window of the pâtissier who desires a *mille-feuilles* that he denies himself . . ."

Oliver seemed to see the people as Racine named each one: the little boy looking into a department store on Christmas Eve on a chilly Parisian boulevard, and the middle-aged lady in her gray suit staring at the hat, and the fat man desiring his pastry, all of them filled with longing as they stared into windows. . . .

Racine's speech might be very rhetorical, Oliver thought—very fancy and full of metaphors—but it was also extremely affecting, and for the first time Oliver could really see the *point* of rhetoric. It dressed up ordinary things in fancy paper, and then let you unwrap them in your mind, like presents.

Racine shut his eyes and paused, and then his chant continued. "Just think about all the people looking out! The lonely bachelor staring out the window of his study at the children playing in the field below . . . the longing lover peering through the window where the beauties flow . . . the museum guard staring out at the busy street . . ."

And once again Oliver could see with Racine all the lonely people, the sad old man and the unhappy lover and the rest, all looking out of windows at the things they longed for. He reached out to touch them, but his hand passed right through them.

"You have only to take a single glance through a window at a single thing," Molière concluded, and the images seemed to fade in front of Oliver's eyes at the wise wraith's plain voice, returning his attention to the sky-lit room and the wraiths around him. "But if the glance is full enough with feeling, if when you look you long for it with all your heart, and think, If only I had that . . . if I only was there," he declaimed. "Then, when your first life is over, you will return to that window, and become its wraith, and then your duty will be to reflect back the best self of the next person who comes and looks into it."

"We looked into all of the windows of Versailles with the high purposes of love—" Racine said.

"And sometimes with the low purposes of very hot

passion—" Molière added honestly, his glass body reddening again a little.

"And so *all* of the windows at Versailles belong to us, and we belong to all of these windows," Racine concluded, and bowed low. "It's why we can float so easily between them," he added, more practically.

At that very moment, as it happened, small, girlish voices could be heard approaching the Petit Trianon. Two schoolgirls in uniform emerged from the woods. They must have run away from their school group, Oliver thought. He knew the type. The wraiths looked annoyed at the interruption, but at a nod from Molière, Oliver watched as François and another of the younger wraiths together approached the windows—and then went right inside them, becoming ghostly, transparent, flat shapes within the windows.

They got there just in the nick of time, it seemed, just as the schoolgirls outside turned to look in the windows. Oliver watched as the girls saw themselves in their reflections and then peered past their reflections into the ballroom, and walked away, happily giggling.

Then Oliver was startled to see that for half a second the wraiths' faces were still a composite of their own grave and sober visages and the lively faces of the schoolgirls that they had just been reflecting. It was a lovely muddle, Oliver thought, of old and new, boy and girl, serious and happy, youth and child.

"So you're really sort of *reflections*," he said, a bit pleased with himself. "Of course. That's why I went to look for you in the Hall of Mirrors," he added, a little proudly. After all, he *had* figured that much out, and he expected them to applaud his intelligence.

Instead, the moment that he mentioned the word "mirrors" the entire court, all fifty or so of them, gave out a gasp and a cry of woe, and moaned in unison.

"The Hall of Mirrors!" cried Racine. "Had we but known! All of the calamities of our order descended from the moment that we built it."

"But aren't windows and mirrors the same, or nearly so?" Oliver asked.

"Your Majesty," Molière explained, drawing close to Oliver, "your reflection in a mirror and your reflection in a window may seem to be alike, but they are really as different as two things can be. Look into a window with desire, and some day you will become your longing. But look too long into a mirror—and you put your very soul at risk!"

"But isn't a mirror just a sheet of glass with silver applied to its back?" Oliver asked. He knew that from school.

"Yes," Molière agreed dubiously. "Only that, and so much worse than that. In one way, a mirror *is* just hard metal applied to the back of a sheet of glass. Just a bit of tin and quicksilver applied to the back of a sheet of glass. That's all, but—"

"But then what is ice but water turned crystal?" Racine interjected. "Yet ice freezes where water feeds, and ice kills where water gives life. It is the same with windows and mirrors. In the mirror, all is frozen, and everything is reversed. Everything! Do you hear me? Everything! The beautiful mingling becomes an icy twin . . . Yet none knew this, at first. We were blind."

"Well, not blind, we were busy looking through windows, so . . ." Molière corrected him.

"*A figure of speech!*" Racine cried, as though he were very offended. He went on. "It was only after the great age of windows that the mirror-maker—that is to say, mirrors—came to Paris." He flushed throughout his entire glass body. What exactly was he blushing about, Oliver wondered?

"Soon, the great works at Saint-Gobain were turning the great sheets of glass into great sheets of mirror, in the famous four steps: polishing, buffing, sanding, and silvering. And ours became a time of mirrors as great as it was a time of windows. Colbert turned the Royal Company of Glass into the Royal Company of Glass and Mirrors—until at last he had built the great Hall of Mirrors itself, the Galerie des Glaces. The night of its dawning in 1680 was a great night indeed."

"How well I recall it. The glitter! The glamour!" one more wraith chimed in nostalgically.

"Not glitter and glamour!" Racine corrected him sternly. "Pure beauty. An infinity of reflections, beauty sandwiched between glass and metal, beauty staring at beauty!"

"Well, it *was* quite glittering. If not exactly glamorous," Molière said carefully.

"Oh, gosh." Now François, who had been whisking up and down doing tricks just below the glass ceiling, was suddenly beside Oliver's ear again. "Don't let them get started on whether it was glittering or glamorous. That could take *days*."

Racine had already picked up the thread of his story. "But then we learned—learned too late, the terrible lesson. One by one, the courtiers stared into the mirrors, and their eyes went dead, and we realized, with horror, that they had lost their souls! For he was on the other side of the mirrors and—" Suddenly Racine stopped himself, and his suave and lucid speech stumbled.

"Who?" Oliver asked.

Molière and Racine looked uneasily at each other, their crystal eyes suddenly glistening with something that looked almost like tears.

François nudged Oliver with his foot, frantically. "Ask them again! Mention the name! Force them!"

"Do you mean . . ." Then Oliver remembered the name. "Do you mean the . . . the . . . Master of Mirrors? The One with None?"

A cry of horror and disdain rose from the assembled wraiths—the kind of stage cry you hear sometimes in very old-fashioned plays.

"You know of him already?" Molière asked with some surprise, and Racine mumbled only, "Ah, *Magister Speculorum*." That was Latin, Oliver recognized. But he wasn't sure just what it meant.

"Well, not exactly, but—" Oliver began.

"Ah, then. He is nothing." Racine said quickly.

"That is, he is *something*," Molière admitted, looking guiltily at Racine.

"But—he is nothing," the other wraith insisted.

"And yet, somehow something. Definitely something. I mean, he exists," Molière allowed.

Oliver was confused by the sudden display of nervousness in these elegant characters, and so he just blurted out the next important question. "Are you frightened of him?"

"Are we frightened of him?" the two wraiths asked together, and then all the other wraiths laughed at the same time. But it was not the kind of pleasant laugh that sounds like a deep roar expelled in delight. It was the kind of laugh that sounds like a cross between a horse whinnying and the cough of a man on the metro whom you cross the car to avoid. And Oliver noticed that, even as they laughed, the wraiths tightened their grip on their muskets and balloon swords. So they *were* frightened of him.

"But what is he?" Oliver asked.

"Think of him . . ." Molière said after a moment of meditation.

"Think of him as a sprite! An . . . an imp! A lovable scamp!" said the wraith who had mentioned the glamour and the glitter. (He had very pale red eyes, Oliver noticed now.)

"Yes. Why, you could think of him as a welcome respite from too much warmth!"

"You could think of him as a measuring rod," another wraith put in.

"You could even think of him as a challenge!" one more said encouragingly.

Oliver paused. "I *could* think of him that way," he agreed. "All those ways. But before I *think* of him that way, I need to know if he *is* that way."

"Well, no," Molière admitted. "But you *could* think of him that way. It might help."

"Think of him . . . think of him," said Racine at last, "as an age-old opponent, a pleasure to trade blows with—"

"He fences!" Oliver said, surprised. "We're supposed to have a fencing match?"

"You fence! I mean, Your Majesty is a swordsman!" Racine looked marginally more cheerful than he had so far. "Well, that *is* good." And he looked at François again and gave a slight nod of approval.

Well, I sort of fence, Oliver wanted to say, remembering how it had gone at school on Friday afternoon.

"Sabers or foils?" François asked him eagerly.

And because Oliver really *was* sensitive, and had seen the slight expression of disappointment that had risen in their eyes at the sight of so, well, unheroic a new king, he said simply: "I fight with neither. I fight with this."

From inside his coat, he drew out the short glass sword.

Oliver was hoping that brandishing it would have an effect—but an effect like the one it had was even more than he was hoping for.

"The king's sword! The king's sword!" the wraiths all cried. "Against all hope the king's sword returns to us!" they declared, very theatrically.

"Against all hope . . . Why, it's been in the museum for a century. I've told them that a hundred times," François grumbled into Oliver's ear. "They need to believe that everything is so mysterious and dramatic!"

But Molière was more businesslike. "If you have the king's sword," he said simply, "then you are armed for the king's enemy. It is the Master of Mirrors—he who controls and directs from behind the mirrors, who steals souls and takes slaves. He was hiding within the mirrors in the great hall and he looked out and took the souls of all the aristocrats."

"Save for Those Whose Backs Were Turned," Racine said, taking over the story, "who, despite their duties to please their king rather than to gaze on his magnificence, were spared the infinite horror of a fate worse than death, though oddly comprising it. . . ."

"He means that only those of us who worked for a living in show business with our faces turned to the king and our backsides turned to the mirrors got away," Molière explained.

"We pursued the muses, instead of the mirrors," Racine said with dignity.

"Well, we were too busy working to spend any time looking into the mirrors, actually," said Molière breezily. "But it comes to the same thing."

Oliver was enjoying hearing the two wraiths say the same thing in completely reversed ways, but he wanted them to get to the point. But before he could ask them what exactly the Master of Mirrors was doing, and where he lived, the two wraiths were telling the story of how they had been spared being enslaved by the Master of Mirrors.

"Only Those Whose Backs Were Turned survived to become window wraiths," Molière explained. "On the nights of the great balls, we were the musicians and the singers and playwrights. There was Monsieur Charpentier, the composer—"

So that was the wraith with the harp, Oliver thought.

"And Monsieur Le Nôtre the gardener—"

And that was the name of the wraith with the shears in his hand!

"And then there were the watchmakers, like Monsieur Thuret, over there"—a short stocky wraith, his hands filled with watch springs, bowed elegantly to Oliver. "And the code-breakers, like the Rossignols over there—" Now Molière pointed to two fraternal-looking wraiths, who were busy poring over a sheet of ciphers; they barely glanced up at Oliver, but raised their eyebrows respectfully. "Most of the courtiers lost their souls within the mirrors. They are trapped in them still. Only Monsieur le Richelieu survives from among the aristocrats."

Now Molière looked at the tall, severe wraith with the wire whisk and the copper pot, who bowed low at the mention.

"He was in charge of the king's entertainment, and so he never looked up at the mirrors. You see," he whispered to Oliver, "he is a very great figure. He is the man who invented mayonnaise!"

"The man who invented mayonnaise!" Oliver repeated. It didn't sound like a very great accomplishment, but obviously the wraiths thought it was.

"Yes, and busy regulating his egg yolks, he never looked into the mirrors. The others did, and they are caught."

"Taste this!" Richelieu ordered, thrusting the copper pot at him. Oliver did. It tasted like, well, like mayonnaise, but was extremely lemony. Far too lemony. Richelieu looked at him inquiringly.

"It's good. It's very good," Oliver said politely. "It may have just a touch too much lemon."

"I knew it! I knew it!" Richelieu said, with despair in his voice. "But what could I do? It has been centuries since I have had an outside taster. I keep adding a touch of lemon, and the touches add up."

"Oh yes," said Oliver. "So the mirrors were like, uh, cunning traps, sort of like a glue trap for mice?"

There was a silence. "I wish the king would stop using such terrible metaphors," Racine said at last. "His metaphors and conceits are so plebeian. So coarse."

"You ought to say, 'The mirrors are like a snare set for the wild deer in Arcadia,'" François said, hovering in Oliver's ear and for the first time actually placing a hand on his shoulder—it felt oddly wet, but warm. "Something like that, in that manner. That's what they like. Rather than like mice caught in glue, I mean."

"It was pungent," said Molière encouragingly. "The image of mice in glue. It was pungent."

"Yes. It was pungent. But it was coarse," said Racine firmly.

"Of course, the Master of Mirrors is nothing like a glue trap—"

"Excuse me," Oliver said, his head swimming with windows and longing and mirrors and souls and undeserved insults to his style of speech, but determined to get to the point. "But why are you telling me all this? You still haven't told me where the master is, or what he's planning. And why is he called the One with None? None of what?" The window wraiths might live outside time, but he had an RER train to catch to get home. Whether he was a king or not, his parents thought he was at Zinedaine's house on the rue du Faubourg Poissonière.

The wraiths looked at him strangely. "Well, you are the King in the Window, of course," Molière said at last, a little lamely. "And plainly the time has come for you to take your glass sword and win the final battle of the great war of windows and mirrors." They looked at him as though this was so obvious that it was a little embarrassing for them to have to point it out.

But the look on Oliver's face must have been so vacant that Racine felt compelled to add something more. "For these many centuries since, Your Majesty, a great and secret war has been fought between windows and mirrors for the souls of men, and at the head of all has always been a king in the window and his great opponent, the Master of Mirrors—the One with None. Sometimes the window wraiths have held the upper hand; sometimes the slaves of the mirror have seduced their souls. But always he was safe behind his mirrors, and we were safe here in Versailles. But now, we are . . . breaking."

"Breaking?" Oliver asked hesitantly. "You mean, like, falling off things?"

"No," and Molière shook his head decisively. "He is breaking us. Somehow, our ancient enemy has new strength to make himself felt as a presence in the world. And he is growing strong again. This year alone we have lost a hundred wraiths in Paris! And then we lost our king!"

"How did you lose your king?" Oliver asked. It was a worrying question.

"Oh," Racine said. "He graced us with his shining and imperial presence, but then, to our infinite grief, it became impossible for us to locate his corporeal body or intellectual spirit."

This sentence was so fancy that it took Oliver a moment or two to work it out and realize that it just meant "He got lost," and by the time he had worked it out, Molière had already gone on.

"Every year—every day!—there seem to be more mirrors in the world, and more souls lost! And every year—almost every day—another wraith is broken, and another window left without its grace. If we continue to break in this manner, soon, very soon, there will be no wraiths left—no wraiths, no windows, no longings held in glass, no beautiful mingling of the present and the past. All that will be left to show mankind their faces are the icy mirrors and their terrible master, stealing faces—and entrapping souls. The final battle is upon us, whether we choose to fight it now or not."

And Charpentier, the musical wraith, struck his harp, and sang simply: "The breaking / is making / us weep." All the other wraiths in the circle applauded politely.

"Sire, a busload of visitors arrives! We must man the windows!" cried François, who had been scouting near the windows.

"Yes, yes," Molière said. "To the glass, everyone. Your Majesty, you know your charge. It is the most desperate one that any King in the Window has had, since the first King in the Window drove the master into the Way. Find out how the Master of Mirrors has increased his strength, discover his strategy—"

"And his tactics!" added Racine.

"And then—?" Oliver asked.

Molière looked puzzled. "And then? Why then, defeat him, of course."

The wraiths began to disperse, flying up and down and around, to all the windows of the Petit Trianon, getting ready to greet the new visitors with improved and augmented reflections.

"Wait, wait," Oliver cried, but apparently even an

order from their king was less important than the wraiths' doing their duty in the windows. Oliver was almost speechless with shock at what they had told him. His head was buzzing with questions. Could it really be that, because of a silly misunderstanding, they were expecting *Oliver* to fight for them? He couldn't begin to do it.

Apparently Racine was having similar thoughts. At least, he was looking with uncomfortable intensity at Oliver as the other wraiths slipped their transparent bodies effortlessly into the ballroom window. And Oliver, perking up his ears, heard him muttering to François.

"François," Racine asked, even more sharply than before. "You are sure? You are very sure about . . . this boy? If you have made an error . . ."

Apparently, François was frightened of Racine, because he said quickly: "Well, sir, the stone, the crown, the ring, the right time. Then he took the sword, and then—*he said it,*" François said, and they shrugged, and looked at Oliver a little woefully.

Racine just glanced at him coldly. Molière looked at him hopefully.

Oliver was never sure why he said what he said next. After all, he knew perfectly well that he had eaten the wrong *galette* by accident, and that the stone was just a stone that someone had placed in his way by chance, and that the sword had come into his hand in a panic, and what he had said about being the King in the Window on Epiphany had been a sort of bitter joke.

But he hated the suspicious way that Racine was looking at him, and he liked François and didn't want to see him get in trouble, and he was impressed by what Moliére had told him, and then, well, he liked being a king, even a ridiculous one with an impossible task.

"Of course they were right," he called to them, and he tried to put as much coldness in his voice as he could. "All the signs say so." Which at least, he thought, wasn't a total lie. If the signs pointed toward him, it wasn't his fault if the signs were wrong.

A small warm smile crossed Molière's lips.

"Very good then, Your Majesty. You will take charge of this business, won't you?" he said. "We place it *entirely* in your hands. If anyone troubles you, tell them that you are now the King in the Window, and that your wraiths have complete confidence in you."

"And of course, if I need your help," Oliver said confidently, "I can always stare into a welcoming window, and you'll come to assist me."

But Molière and the other wraiths looked very puzzled.

"Need our help? You mean—call on us for assistance?" Molière asked, as though it were the oddest request he had ever heard.

"Well, yes," Oliver said. "I mean, am I supposed to fight this battle by myself?"

"The king is brave / the king's alone / the king does all / and never phones," Charpentier sang.

The other wraiths laughed and nodded approvingly, and

Oliver was beginning to get the sense that they really *did* expect him to do it all by himself. He looked around wildly—of course, all they had were bubble cannons and water pistols and balloon swords, but, still. It was their fight, too, wasn't it, even more than his?

Molière looked at him again. He was obviously trying to be kind.

"Oh, yes. If you need assistance, *help* of some kind—well, you understand, of course, that we have no neutral medium, no way to go from windows to water and back again, save by . . . leaping . . . which gets harder and harder as we become more and more glasslike and brittle." He looked hard at Oliver, as though he wanted this clearly understood.

"But for help, you might, you might . . . ask the witty woman," he said, frowning. "Yes," he repeated, pleased with himself, "by all means. Search for the witty woman, and she will be *sure* to help. And that will be all the assistance you shall need," Molière concluded, and he smiled elegantly, as though that was, entirely, that.

They've got an awful lot of confidence in their king, Oliver thought. If they only knew . . . and then he looked at Racine, and Racine didn't smile, but at least he didn't say anything more. He just stared darkly at Oliver, and turned away. Within seconds, the wraiths were back at their windows, and they began to slowly fade from Oliver's vision as they retreated into their windows to mingle with the walkers. Oliver took his crown off, slipped it into his back pocket and soon the Petit Trianon was filled with a mob of tourists, taking photographs and listening to tour guides. Oliver was quickly lost among them.

And then something terrible happened. From out of nowhere, it seemed the hum, the beat and hum, rose before them, more rapidly than ever, reaching its ugly, ear-numbing climax. Where was it coming from? Oliver thought desperately, and, looking around the hall, he thought he saw some stranger with his back turned, and a small shard of mirror glinting in his hand. But the search was costly, because, before Oliver could reach into his back pocket and put the paper crown on to stop the noise, as he had done before, one of the windows burst horribly, and Oliver heard, he was sure of it, a faint gasp of sorrow and horror from the window wraiths within their windows.

Oliver looked up. A clattering sound filled his ears, and he saw that Charpentier's harp lay now on the marble floor, while the window above had been shattered into a thousand pieces. The shards were tiny and jagged, but within them one could just see pale color, which Oliver knew now was the shattered body of the gentle and musical wraith. Tears came into his eyes, unbidden. And for a moment the wraiths within their windows blazed bright in his eyesight again.

Molière looked at him, his face more worried than ever. His smile was suddenly gone. The wraiths were like pigeons being preyed on by a hawk, evil and bright-eyed, Oliver thought, and they were helpless to save themselves. They looked at him, a child, as children look at a father, expecting him to do something to save them all, because they thought he was their king.

Boy, I've really messed that up, Oliver said to himself. *I should have just said, "No, sorry, you've got the wrong man, or boy," and gone home for good. Now they're trusting me to figure out why they're all being broken, and expecting me to stop it. They want me to save their, well, whatever you call it when they've already had their lives, and I'm not really the king of anything.*

Oliver walked back through the beautiful twilight at Versailles, avoiding the Hall of Mirrors, and took the four o'clock train home.

He came into the courtyard of his building. There in the streetlight, reassuringly, was his mother, wrapped in her long winter coat—but beside her were two policemen, in beige raincoats, looking grave and sober, and one had his notebook out, writing down carefully everything that was said to him.

There was no way Oliver could avoid them as he entered the courtyard of the building. Trying not to let the sword poke him in the shoulder, he went up close to his mother, and made an effort to look very young.

"Oh, Ollie!" his mother cried. "I'm so glad to see you. You see," she said to the detectives, "here he is, home safe from a day of studying. Just as I said. Oliver, these two nice men are looking for that sword some awful person stole from the Louvre yesterday, and they say that someone was seen holding what looked like a sword on the Pont

Royal, and they're checking all the buildings in the *quartier*."

That didn't sound very plausible to Oliver. He doubted that they would check every building; they probably had a more specific description in mind. But he swallowed hard and said, "Wow! How interesting," and tried to look not just young but movingly innocent.

"Listen, my boy," one of the detectives said, staring out over his bushy mustache. He had extremely suspicious eyes. "Have you seen anything? Heard anything? Even just children playing?"

Oliver tried to look as though he were thinking hard. "No," he said at last. "I wish I could . . . No, sir, nothing comes to mind."

"Have you visited the Louvre lately?" the other policeman demanded. The two men were trying to throw him off balance, Oliver realized, treating him kindly one moment and sharply the next.

Oliver simply raised his eyebrows and shook his head. He found himself swallowing hard, and trying not to show it. The glass sword seemed to be pressing so urgently against his side that he was amazed that the detectives couldn't see its outline against his coat. He tried to keep his arm clutched tight to his chest, but he was aware that the posture must make him look very suspicious. And he was sure that the sword would stick out and be visible if he moved so much as an inch.

"Well," Oliver said, but his voice came out much higher even than it should have.

Suddenly, he heard loud singing outside the courtyard. And someone was pounding on it.

A moment later, two clochards, in long frayed coats, and with even longer beards, were suddenly inside.

They began to dance. One grabbed Oliver around the middle and began to waltz crazily with him, and the other began to dance with the detectives, to their great annoyance.

"A Christmas dance!" cried one clochard. "A dance for the king!"

Did he say "king" or "kings"? Oliver wondered, as he felt his arms pressed tight around him. The clochard waltzed him around, holding him tight. As Oliver whirled, he saw the other with his arms around the detectives, and he saw the detectives, in disgust, trying to pull free. . . .

Then, as suddenly as the clochards had come, they were gone, racing out through the gate and up the street, leaving Oliver sprawled on the pavement. One of the detectives followed them briefly, crying out an official threat—"You are contravening the law of France!" he said— but then he came back. Oliver got up, dusted himself off, and felt inside his coat . . .

The sword was gone! Had it fallen on the ground? Oliver looked down desperately for broken glass. No, it was gone. The clochard must somehow have taken it.

The two detectives looked harder than ever at Oliver. One of them walked over and, Oliver was sure of it, bumped him hard to see if the sword would fall out. But Oliver, very coolly and kinglike, merely removed his coat, yawned, and held it out to the detective to hold. The detective looked at him angrily, and turning away from him, asked Oliver's mother to please inform them if she had any more information, and then he looked hard at Oliver and told him to remain wise, which is a French way of warning young people. He actually walked all the way around him, staring hard—was Oliver imagining it, or was he actually trying to see what Oliver had in his back pocket?—and Oliver tried to stare back, and then just looked away.

"What a silly business!" his mother said, after the detectives had gone, as Oliver walked up the stairs, out of breath and his heart pounding, wondering which was worse—that he had almost been arrested for stealing a precious artifact from the Louvre, or that the precious artifact that he actually *had* stolen from the Louvre had been stolen from him?

After dinner with his mother—his father was away again working on his Gil Hornshaw article—Oliver went downstairs to the courtyard to find Neige, and see if he could at least tell her what had happened. But there was no one in the icy courtyard save for the bitter wind. The light was on in Neige's room, and he tried knocking at the window.

She appeared quickly at the window, but held her finger to her lips, meaning, "Don't say a word!" and then she closed her curtain, leaving Oliver cold and alone outside. He trudged back up the stairs, took his bath, and read his book by the window—only this time no one came to greet him—and then he went to his room, to think over the day's extremely peculiar events.

Before he went to bed, he stared in the mirror that hung above his dresser. Well, it certainly didn't feel as if anything much was at risk when he looked . . .

Suddenly, a hand shot out of the mirror and seized Oliver by the throat—a hand in a leather gauntlet and chain mail. Soon it was a whole forearm, shooting out snakelike from Oliver's mirror, trying to pull him in.

Oliver tried to cry out in terror. He was being pulled inexorably toward his mirror. From inside the mirror, he could just see, behind his own reflection, the dim image of a dark helmeted head, with reddish eyes gleaming out at him, and once again the heartbeat hum rose, only this time a low, smooth voice resonated through it.

"Do not meddle in what concerns you not," said the voice. "Do not meddle, boy. The master has you . . ."

As Oliver fought, trying desperately to pull the strong scaly fingers from his throat, struggling to breathe as the hand tightened on his neck, just as suddenly as the gloved hand had shot out from the mirror, something silver flew by Oliver's ear. It struck the surface of the mirror and then somehow flew inside it. An arrow! It broke the surface of the mirror as though it were water and then penetrated deep inside, leaving the mirror whole, like a pond after a diver has leaped in.

There was a terrible cry from inside the mirror, and then the gloved hand fell limp and released him. The arm just as suddenly shot back inside the mirror and disappeared, as though it were on the end of a spring.

Oliver turned, gasping and choking for breath. In his bedroom window, he could just make out the faint image of an archer, a bow in his hand and a quiver on his shoulder, sternly watching the flight of his shot. He remained visible long enough for Oliver to see that he wore what looked like a long coat, or doublet, and that he had a bushy, dark beard. It must be one of the window wraiths' bowmen, watching over him from the window! Oliver waved gratefully, but the image of the archer wavered and was already gone.

Oliver ran out of his room and slammed the door behind him. He ran down the corridor and into his father's office. His father was working on his computer. He turned toward Oliver.

"Dad," he began, "you won't believe what's happening. You see, two nights ago, on Epiphany, a boy came to the kitchen window and—"

"Uh-huh, Ollie," his father said, turning back to his computer and, bathed in the silver glow, still staring at the screen.

Oliver gave up. It was no good. His father was absorbed in his work—he might hear but he would never really *listen*—and his mother, well, if he told his mother, he'd never get out of the house again. Then what would the wraiths do?

He walked slowly back to his bedroom door. It was still shut tight. Oliver remembered the horrible terror of having that hand around his throat, and it was all that he could do to open the door to his own bedroom again. But at last he did, remembering that, at least, there was an archer at the window. His hands shook as he turned the knob and almost refused to work for him, but he felt safe once he was inside again—and relieved that he had been able to do something at least a little bit brave, even if it was only going back to his own room.

Trembling a little, he took the mirror down, keeping his head away from it all the time, and turned it toward the wall. To steady his nerves, he decided to send an e-mail to Charlie Gronek.

"Dear Charlie: I'm fine. Fencing class was okay. The chess move is QXE4. I think that's checkmate. Recently, I've also become the king of a secret phantom army that lives within windows for all eternity. Hope you had a great Christmas. Send me the Super Bowl tape when they play, will you? Best, your friend, Oliver."

Well, Oliver thought as he climbed into bed, apparently I am caught in a war between some kind of evil knights who live in the dresser mirror and the king's bowmen who are standing guard in my bedroom window. The wisest thing, he decided as he settled into bed, pulling the covers over his head—he felt safe enough, with the archer apparently waiting in the window, but he still felt safer with something over his head—was to stay away from shiny surfaces for the time being. Of course, he thought, as he fell asleep, it was certainly going to present a problem brushing his teeth in the morning.

Chapter Five

The World and the Way

ON MONDAY morning, when Oliver woke up, he knew, more surely than ever, that what he needed was an ally, a confidante. There were archers in his window and stranglers in his mirror and a glass sword that he had stolen from the Louvre had been stolen from him, and a hideous hum kept appearing from nowhere and exploding glass when it did, and a host of charming and useless window wraiths out at Versailles were counting on him to . . . well, to save the world, or something like that. *And* he was now a major art thief, suspected by the Paris police and—worst of all, in a way—he still owed his professor that two-week paper on rhetoric and irony in Molière.

He needed a friend. He needed someone who knew about the seventeenth century—the Grand Siècle—and about the kings of France, someone who knew history, and who wasn't afraid to think big. . . .

"Look for the witty woman!" Molière had whispered when he had asked for help. Okay. Who might she be?

He went down the hallway to tell his mother without getting her *too* excited. (He could just hear her saying, "Oliver, it's a wonderful story. You ought to write it down, and maybe we'll act it out with the puppets.") But on his way, a better idea struck him suddenly. He sought out his father.

"Dad. Word association. I say 'witty woman.' You say?"

His father paused. "Why, Lucy Pearson, I suppose," he said hesitantly. "I mean, she's mean and malicious and altogether horrible, but I guess she's witty. Remember when I did that last profile of her? What a character."

Mrs. Pearson! Lucy Pearson! Of course. She was, well, about a hundred years old, Oliver knew, and she came originally from England. She was one of three scandalous sisters, and then she had gone to live with some very weird-looking French guy with a mustache. She wrote books, always about the Grand Siècle. Whenever a new one came out, his father would go to interview her, and she would say mean things about people.

"Do you, uh, have her number, Dad?" Oliver asked. "I—uh—I need to talk to her about this school project I have." That was sort of true, at least.

His father didn't turn his head, but his voice sounded shocked. "Her number? You don't want to call her, Ollie. Believe me, she eats Americans alive. For breakfast. And then has a couple of Australians for a between-meals snack. And she hates children with a passion."

"I'm not really a child," Oliver objected.

"Tell *her* that. Hey, give me some time. I've got to get this Gil Hornshaw piece ready. They're already beginning to set their equipment up on the Eiffel Tower."

"Has he solved the problem?" Oliver remembered to ask.

But his father seemed confused. "What problem?" he said.

"The problem he was having with—whatever the thing is he's coming to Paris to launch."

But Oliver's father only stared at the screen, and didn't answer.

"Dad," Oliver said. He was a very persistent questioner. "What's a quantum leap?"

"A quantum leap? It just means . . . a great big leap, a huge unexpected leap from one condition to another. It comes from the quanta—the tiny particles—inside atoms. One moment they're whizzing around in one orbit and the next—boom!—they're in a completely different one. Why?"

"Because isn't that what Gil Hornshaw says his new project will be—a quantum leap in computing? Why does he say that?"

In the past, his father would have taken the bait, and gotten into a very good conversation about the meaning of words and the possibilities of the project. But now he just shrugged and said something that sounded like "Mnnnphh."

"See you later," Oliver said at last, and went back to his room.

How *was* he going to approach Lucy Pearson? he wondered. He couldn't just call her up and start spilling all the beans about the window wraiths. On the other hand, he couldn't wait until she happened to come over some night, and then try to corner her in the living room before dinner. What could he do?

"Oliver." His mother was in the living room now, and she sounded worried. Oliver looked up. Uh-oh. She looked even more worried than she sounded.

"Yeah, Mom?" Oliver said.

"Oliver, I just spoke to Zinedaine's mother and she said . . . she said . . . that you weren't there once this weekend."

Oh my God, Oliver thought. I should have seen that coming.

"Well, Mom, I didn't want to tell you but I—uh—I've been working on an independent study project with, uh"—he couldn't think of a name!—"uh, with Mrs. Lucy Pearson."

"You and Mrs. Pearson!"

"Yes, it's, uh, on metaphor and irony in the work of Molière!" Well, that part at least was true. "I wanted to surprise you," he added.

The nice thing about mothers, especially goopy ones, is that they always want to believe the best about their children. Oliver's mother, who should have been suspicious, melted immediately when he told her that he was working on a research project with a famous writer.

"Oh, Ollie," she said. "Good for you!"

Oliver's heart sank. Now he would *have* to ask Mrs. Pearson out. For one good thing about lies is that if you tell a lie you often then have no choice except to try and turn it into a truth. Now that he had said he knew Lucy Pearson, the only thing he could do was actually get to know her. But what could he say to make her want to meet him without biting his head off? Everyone has a weakness, Molière had said—but what was hers? He tried to think. He remembered that his father had once said that she lived at home on nothing but champagne and caviar and baked potatoes, but that she would kill her own first-born child for a fine meal at a great restaurant.

So he would have to ask her out to dinner.

He found her number at last in his parents' big green leather address book: PEARSON, MRS. LUCY. He took the white, cordless phone from its cradle in the front hall, brought it into his room, and shut the door. Then he sat down on his bed and dialed the number. Oliver was scared—

he hated making difficult phone calls, and he always avoided them when he could. But what choice did he have? It was still so early, though—not yet eight o'clock. He knew that older people often rose very early. He prayed that she was one of them.

"*Oui, oui,*" a voice answered, in French, but with a silvery, tinny British accent. It didn't sound sleepy, exactly, but quite annoyed. "What is it that you want?"

Well, that was direct. Oliver swallowed hard. "Mrs. Pearson, you probably don't remember me . . ."

"Then why are you bothering me at this impossible hour?"

"I'm Oliver Parker, the son of Tyrone Parker . . . and I wondered if, I just wondered if . . ." He got it out in a rush: "I wondered if you might be free to join me for an intimate dinner tonight," he said. "Just the two of us." It didn't sound as suave as he had hoped it would, but he had managed to say it.

At least she didn't laugh. Or say anything more. Or even ask him what this was in reference to. He could just hear her flipping pages in a book. "I'm rather busy, I'm afraid," she said.

"It's really important," he said. "I was thinking"— Oliver tried desperately to think of the name of a famous restaurant. Oh, yes, he had heard his father mention this one. "I was wondering if you might be amused by dinner at Le Grand Véfour." There. Now *that* must sound suave.

Just like that, she said, "Oh. Well . . . in that case. Will you reserve or shall I?" Her tone became one small half-shade pleasanter.

"Oh, allow me," Oliver said, and so it was settled. Oliver looked at the clock. It was not yet eight o'clock.

All day long at school, Oliver was in an even more anxious and distracted state than usual. He was worrying about the wraiths, he was worrying about the hand in the mirror, he was worrying that Madame Sonia would make the connection between Oliver and the stolen sword and he was worrying about how to pay for a three-star dinner. When he called in between classes to make the reservation, he had to sneak out of school and run down the street to the closest café, and call from the little phone booth there. It was hot inside, and his nervousness made him even hotter. At first the man who answered the phone said, disdainfully, that there wasn't a table, but then he explained that his guest was Madame Pearson, and the man perked up and said, wait, he would see, and then he announced that there would be a table for two persons at nine. So late! And Oliver thought of asking what the average price for a fine meal was at Le Grand Véfour but, after hearing the sound of the maître d's voice, thought better of it.

He was so distracted at school, in fact, that when Monsieur de Montenay, his literature teacher, asked him to compare the style of Racine and Molière, Oliver said, absentmindedly, "Oh, well, one has blue eyes and one has green. And one explains simply what the other says rhetorically." And Monsieur de Montenay had said, with his eyebrows raised toward the ceiling, "And how do you know that!" And Oliver had said, reasonably, "Because I listened," and then Monsieur de Montenay had really blown up at him and called him a sarcastic know-everything. Of course, Oliver hadn't meant one bit to seem like a know-it-all. Just the opposite. He wasn't a know-it-all. That was just . . . all he knew.

So that night, Oliver was waiting for Mrs. Pearson exactly at nine, in the restaurant at the end of the Palais Royal, with a heavy heart and an anxious wallet. He had told his mother he was going to meet with Mrs. Pearson to work on their research project together, but he hadn't specified just when or where. But his mother had insisted on walking him over to the nearest bus stop and said she would be back to pick him up there at ten thirty. This meant that he would have to hurry back from dinner at Le Grand Véfour.

The Palais Royal, like so many things in Paris, has a misleading name, since it isn't a palace, and nobody royal lives there. In fact, it is a small enclosed garden near the Louvre. On a winter night, like this night, it is dark and even a little scary. But at one end of the park, through the skeleton-like outlines of the bare trees blowing in the wind, warm lights glow through orange silk curtains, and that is the Le Grand Véfour restaurant. When Oliver went inside, he shook hands with the maître d', a handsome, smiling man with happy eyes that creased into little slits, and a black double-breasted jacket. He verified Oliver's reservation in a big book, and then showed him to a table near the mirrors, which filled one side of the room.

Oliver had brought with him all the money he had saved: one hundred euros—about a hundred and twenty-five dollars. He knew that Le Grand Véfour was expensive, but surely it couldn't be *that* expensive. Probably if he just ordered steak frites with a glass of flat water, it would be okay. He knew his duty as a host, and that he would have to tell Mrs. Pearson to order anything she wanted. But maybe he could steer her a bit—say something like "The steak frites is very good here." And maybe she wouldn't be that hungry. Old people often weren't.

Oliver looked around. Along both walls ran long plush banquettes, upholstered in dusty-rose velvet, and gold plaques, with the names of famous people who had eaten at the restaurant, were screwed discreetly into the wooden moldings on the tops of the banquettes. A Monday night in winter even at a very great restaurant is always calmer than any other kind of night, and so Oliver was able to enjoy the slightly hushed aura of the room and watch the waiters as they hovered, like elegant penguins, passing from table to table.

At last Lucy Pearson came in. She was wearing a cream-beige suit with long sleeves. Underneath, she had on a simple silk blouse, with a single string of pearls around her throat. Her hair was piled up high, and even though she was much more simply dressed than most of the nervous and anxious-looking American women all around, the waiters all began to bow and scrape with a vengeance. She ignored them all, and, spying Oliver, swept toward the table.

Oliver stood up to greet her.

"Bring us a bottle of the Billecart rosé," she said, firmly to the maître d', almost before her seat had hit the banquette.

"Now, we need to take about five minutes to quiz each other tediously," she said to Oliver. "Five minutes to be tiresome with each other. You're looking well. How are things?"

"Oh, fine, thank you."

Mrs. Pearson looked at him keenly. "You notice how we greet each other with lies?" she said, "I say you're looking well, whereas you're actually looking quite peaked. You claim everything is fine, whereas if everything were fine you wouldn't have insisted on this last-minute assignation. Lies. Nothing but lies. What a liar you are!"

"Well, I'm sorry but . . ."

"About the lies? Don't be. They're the mark of civility. There's nothing so coarse as an ill-timed truth. I didn't say, What a *liar* you are! I said, *What* a liar you are! It was praise."

The waiter brought the champagne, and gravely showed Mrs. Pearson the bottle, wrapped in a napkin. "Open it and leave it here, on the table, where we can enjoy it," she ordered him. "This is Monsieur Parker, author of the leading wine drinkers guide in America, read exclusively by millionaires. Do not be misled by his youth. Despite his years, he possesses the third-best palate in America." A "palate," Oliver knew, is what a great wine taster is supposed to have. "It is his youth," Mrs. Pearson went on, "that gives him such sound judgment. He tastes the wine and spits it out. With a mind unsullied and untempted by intoxication, he arrives at a true estimate of its quality."

The wine waiter looked at Oliver with renewed respect, and bowed and poured his glass very full. Oliver picked up the glass. He had never drunk champagne before.

"Now," Mrs. Pearson said to the waiter, "do not run back and forth refilling our glasses. We will help ourselves. When we wish for an elaborate servile ritual on your part, we will tell you. In fifteen minutes, we will ask you to bring us a plate of foie gras, and after that we will review this sumptuous menu, and make our choices. Now, my friend and I wish to be left alone."

Lucy Pearson took a small sip of her champagne, and another, and then finished the glass in a single swallow. "I always feel guilty, swilling champagne in a place like this. All the poor people in the world and so on," she said, looking contentedly around at the beautiful room.

Oliver watched her. She certainly didn't *look* as if she felt guilty about all the poor people. Then she reached down to her place setting, took from her purse a white silver spoon, and placed it, stem down, into the top of the champagne bottle, so that the round, spoon part was sticking out the top.

"This is a useful trick," she said to Oliver. "It is the *only* sure way to preserve the bubbles. My sister Lelia showed it to me. It was all she knew in life and, really, all she needed to know."

Oliver nodded, but he was beginning to turn pale. He could only imagine what that bottle of champagne must cost. He wondered if the restaurant needed someone to wash dishes.

"Now, Oliver," Mrs. Pearson went on, "we could spend most of the next fifteen minutes making polite small talk. How is school, how do you find French classes, how go your parents? You could reply in kind: How is my new book progressing? Do I often visit London, how do I find the weather? Am I likely to die soon, old as I look? Or we could omit all that, and you could tell me the entire story, whatever it is, that has led you to brave having a rendezvous with such an unpleasant elderly person in such an overpriced boîte."

So Oliver swallowed hard—he was still thinking about the price of the champagne—and then just told her everything: the boy in the window, and the trip to Versailles, and the court, and Molière, and the lost souls in the mirror. He tried to tell her everything down to the tiniest detail. He even told about the metaphors. All the while, Mrs. Pearson sipped her rose-colored champagne, and listened hard. Like many cold and austere people, she was a surprisingly good listener; she nodded intently at the weirdest parts and raised her eyebrows intelligently at the conversations.

"And so, well, I thought, I'd better call you," Oliver concluded, "because my father used to say that you know everything about—about all that time and everything. And because he also said that you were the wittiest woman he knew." He hadn't, really, but Oliver thought it might be diplomatic to say it anyway.

Mrs. Pearson was silent. She reached down and took her spoon out of the champagne, and poured herself another glass. The waiter, hovering nearby, saw her do it and he raced over to help, but she waved him away. She took a long drink, and, quite suddenly, she took the champagne bottle from its bucket, and smashed it, hard, against one of the legs of the table.

The bottle exploded—Oliver almost jumped out of his skin at the sound, sure that the hand in the mirror was back—and pink champagne soaked the carpet at their feet. Waiters scurried, maître d's arrived, apologies were made, and laps dried with napkins—it was odd, Oliver thought, that no one seemed to have noticed that *she* had broken the bottle. Mrs. Pearson told the attendants that the banquette was now too wet to sit on, which it really wasn't, and, after some icy looks on her part and some sorrowful ones on theirs, the two were moved across the room to a table by the windows, looking out onto the darkened arcades and gardens. A new bottle of the champagne sat in a new bucket alongside them.

"Oliver," she said, once they were alone again, "I thought it best for us to remove ourselves from the vicinity of those mirrors." She gestured across the room to where they had been sitting. "You never know who may be looking out."

Oliver shuddered.

"Yes, the window wraiths," Mrs. Pearson went on,

pensively. "We find the outlines of the story in La Fontaine, for example, and there are hints of it in Fontenelle. I don't doubt it. I don't doubt it at all. It would explain a lot, Oliver. The sightings, for instance: in 1924, two American women visited Versailles, and came upon a strange and ghostly procession on the grounds, like a very damp fête. They have since been discounted, with references to costume pageants held in the period. But their account has never really been disproved. Then there is the account, suppressed by the authorities, of how, during the great meeting of the Western heads of state in 1982, several people heard urgent whispering from inside the window. This was discounted, too, since it was an American president who made the claim, seconded by an Italian president. Had it been made by the French president, things might have been different. But I don't doubt the essentials of what you tell me. In fact, I've been expecting to hear something like it for some time. The Wise and the Witty know all about the window wraiths, of course, but we did not know they were quite so dense at Versailles. It is a consequence of the fact that Versailles has been kept intact for so long. This would, as they say, have given the window wraiths a chance to propagate and thrive."

"Like mold on old bread, you mean," Oliver said.

Mrs. Pearson stared at him. "I see what they mean about your figures of speech. Your similes are pungent, but inelegant. I doubt that your metaphors are much better."

"What's the difference?"

"A metaphor is when you describe one thing using the

example of something else. A simile is when you specify that one thing is like another. If I say there's a frightened rabbit sitting opposite me, I'd be using a metaphor. If I said you were like a frightened rabbit, that is a simile. A simile is a literal truth, or can be. A metaphor is a kind of lie, though a lie that tells a truth."

"Like irony is a truth that tells a lie?" Oliver asked, remembering what his mother had said.

"Not at all a stupid remark, Oliver." She looked at him keenly. "You will have to pay attention to these things now, Oliver. The world into which you have been plunged cares terribly about forms of address, figures of speech, rhetorical correctness, and poetic niceties of all kinds. Plain speech will get you nowhere. Elaborate rhetoric is the thing for you. Now then," she said, looking at him keenly, "you *do* look like a frightened rabbit. . . . But then you have reason to."

"How do you mean?" Oliver felt as if he'd swallowed ice. "Who is this Master of Mirrors? And why is he called the One with None? The wraiths just implied that he was vulgar and coarse, rather than really, well, dangerous."

"When intelligent people are challenged by something evil, they often try to convince each other that it is merely squalid," Mrs. Pearson sighed. "You see, Oliver, I'm afraid that your friends have not been—well, completely straightforward with you. This is, I'm afraid, a national weakness of this most elegant and amusing race we find ourselves among, our friends the French. Lie? Not them, oh, never. But they will never be completely straightforward with you if it does not suit their purposes. 'Is the lease for three years?' 'Oh, yes,' they say, not telling you that it is *only* for three years. 'Is the scarf washable?' Yes, of course—but not in *water*. That sort of thing."

She paused and took another sip of champagne. Then she leaned forward intently. "Your new friends, I believe, have given you the impression that the Master of Mirrors is a kind of cartoon villain, a bogeyman, easily defeated by a bright young boy. I'm afraid that it is much worse than that. He is very old, very strong, very powerful, and he and his slaves are, I am afraid, entirely evil."

Oliver felt a terrible shiver running through his body.

"The man you saw last night—the hand that reached for you—belonged to one of his servants, I fear."

"The Master of Mirrors? Is he human?" Oliver asked.

"Was human, once, I think. Or perhaps not. No one really knows where he came from or who—or what—he is. It was four hundred years ago when a strange character appeared in Paris. Did he come from Venice with a new secret of glass-making? Perhaps. From the East? Perhaps. Or perhaps from much farther away even than that. Whoever he was, he called himself the Magister Speculorum—the Master of Mirrors—and he came to Paris, to this very place, the Palais Royal. He was eloquent and secretive and he made mirrors the likes of which the world had never seen. You must understand, Oliver, that in the Grand Siècle, the Great Century, glass goods—mirrors and windows—were as exciting and new and powerful as all of these computing devices and so on are today."

A thought came to Oliver suddenly. "You might say that glass was on the cutting edge of technology?" he said.

Mrs. Pearson looked appalled. "Oliver, if you intend to take up my time with small wordplay, I will find a better way to use my evening."

Oliver apologized, but secretly he felt rather proud that he had made a pun, even as small a one as that. Perhaps he could fit in with the wraiths after all.

"His workshop in the Palais Royal became legendary!" Mrs. Pearson continued. "He made mirrors that went from floor to ceiling, from wall to wall, from one room to the next, in a dazzle of silver, and he offered them for free! And he made mirrors as small and finely tuned as pianos, and gave those away as well. Great leaps in knowledge were now possible: telescopes, microscopes, shaving! For the first time, men could see every pore on their own faces, and women every ribbon on their own clothes, and the world was dazzled by its own reflection—at first. The Wise, of course, were glad because they thought that every new mirror opened another door onto the Way."

"The way? Which way?" Oliver asked. But Mrs. Pearson went on as though she hadn't heard him.

"What no one knew is that the mirrors the Master of Mirrors made had something more, and worse, to them. If you looked at them for too long, you lost your soul."

"Your soul? How did you lose it?"

"He took it. The Master of Mirrors and his slaves were secretly lying in wait on the other side, and snatched men's souls as they gazed at themselves. It is not the mirrors themselves that trap human souls, Oliver. It is the soul-stealers who live within them, who work for their terrible master. They trap men's souls, yes, and women's, too, and then deliver them to their master, who devours them."

"Devours souls!" Oliver cried.

"Like a great black spider within a web, the Master of Mirrors lures people in by their vanity. If your soul is strong and the longing in your heart for something lovely is keen, then you *might* survive even a lifetime of looking. But if your soul is weak—then, sooner or later, the Master of Mirrors sees you from the other side, and his soul-stealers take possession of your soul for all eternity. Shall we order dinner?" she asked suddenly, seizing her menu happily. Oliver was startled. She summoned the waiter over with a quiet lift of her eyebrows.

"For many years," she resumed, "the Master of Mirrors grew in power and strength. It was he who made the mirrors for the great hall in Versailles. And no one understood that he was on both sides at once—making mirrors in the world, trapping souls on the other side. Soon, there was not a mirror in all Europe or Asia that was free from his presence. And he made a pact with the king's intelligent and ambitious counselor, the great Colbert. They formed the French Royal Company of Windows and Mirrors."

"Racine told me about him," Oliver said.

"But then, at last, toward the end of the Grand Siècle, the great century, the first King in the Window appeared. He was a boy like you Oliver, a prince of the realm."

"He was Louis the Fourteenth?" Oliver asked.

"No, no. Louis was the king *outside* the window. The first King Luc was the King *in* the Window, and he was brought up in secret by the Wise, deep in a secret apartment in the cellar of Versailles. He grew wise off on his own, a quiet, secret, watchful presence. The Wise, who had learned last the truth about the master, taught him carefully and raised him well, and then at last he went as king into the Way, and was strong enough to confront the Master of Mirrors."

"The way? What way? You keep talking about some way. What way was he in?"

"Not the way, Oliver. The *Way*."

"I don't get it," Oliver said. He knew that this was a rude way of saying, "I don't understand," but it is understandable that when you really don't get something, you say so.

Before she could answer him, the elegant maître d' and the waiter were beside them.

Mrs. Pearson sighed. "We *had* better order," she said. Oliver looked at his menu. The prices were so alarming that he didn't know what exactly to do, and most of the dishes, though they sounded delicious, also seemed extremely complicated. For instance, there was lamb, which Oliver liked very much, in a sauce made of coffee beans and juniper berries, which he liked very much, too, but not usually together and not usually with lamb.

Mrs. Pearson didn't even open her menu. She simply told the waiter that she would have some caviar to start, and then a breast of chicken with truffles. "It is the only healthy meal one can eat in a place like this," she said to Oliver.

Terrified, Oliver nodded to the waiter that he would have the same. His mind by now was so filled with fear—and wonder, too, but mostly fear—that he had even forgotten about the price. And, as always happens, he was grateful that someone else had been so decisive about ordering dinner.

Mrs. Pearson sighed. The candlelight that rose from their table, and from every other table in the room, cast its flickering golden light on her face. For the first time, Oliver had a moment to study her. She must have been very beautiful once, he decided. She had a long, slender face that might almost have seemed unpleasantly horselike had it not been for the delicate elegance of her nose and the slender almonds of her eyes. Her hair had long ago gone gray, of course, but it was not the dead cold gray of the very old but a kind of silver and gold, which glimmered high on her head in the candlelight. For a moment, Oliver actually felt immensely happy to be dining with this formidable woman, however biting she might sometimes be.

Then, as she spoke again, more softly than she had before, the whole beautiful room seemed to become darker, and the candlelight within it dimmer and more flickering.

The beautiful nymphs with long hair and little else who were pictured on the painted glass panels that lined the upper register of the gleaming room seemed almost to be leaning down and staring at them—seemed almost to be shivering as they wrapped their long hair around themselves for warmth. The waiters and other diners seemed to recede silently into the background, and Oliver felt for a moment almost as if he were alone with Mrs. Pearson in a plush and warmly lit velvet and enamel cave. He drew his chair closer to her.

"Oliver, what I am about to tell you is known only to a very few, and those only very wise or very witty, which you are not, and most of *them* have forgotten," Mrs. Pearson said, leaning slightly toward him, so that the dusky rose smell of her perfume filled his senses. "But as you have become the King in the Window—and you have, we must accept it, there have been bizarre choices before, though none quite so bizarre as this—you should be told, I suppose." She paused.

"Oliver, the World we see around us every day is only one half of the universe as it really is. The other half lies on the other side of the mirrors, and it is called the Way. It is a kind of labyrinth whose entrances and exits can be found on the other side of every mirror. When you are looking at a reflection in a mirror, you are really looking from the World into the Way—but most of us can't enter it. Only the Wise once could."

"Who are these Wise?" Oliver interrupted. "I mean, is that a metaphor for, like, every wise guy? Or is it a description?"

"The Wise are an order, mostly secret, of those who know of the Way and how to use it. To know your way in and out of the Way was what it meant to be Wise."

"Did the Master of Mirrors make the Way?" Oliver asked.

"Oh, no. It is much older even than he is. But he hid in it to steal souls, until at last the first King in the Window was strong enough to pursue him into the other side of the mirrors, and capture him. The Master of Mirrors was led back into the World and imprisoned. He was the one you have heard of, you see, as the Man in the Iron Mask."

"The Man in the Iron Mask?" Of course, Oliver had heard many stories about this legendary French prisoner, who had been locked away in a secret prison during the Grand Siècle, and always made to wear a locked metal mask.

"Yes. You see no one has ever understood the point of the mask. It was not to prevent others from seeing him. It was *to prevent him from seeing himself.* Had he been able to look into a mirror, if only for a moment, he could have called the other soul-stealers to his aid. He was kept away, and his soul-stealers without him were afraid.

"And the young King in the Window felt free to wander in the Way. He even built a small chapel there, a kind of retreat, where he would go with his most trusted friends to experience the other side. It was said to be beautifully decorated, with rich tapestries and amazing paintings and was, somehow, outside time itself.

"But then, feeling secure, the other king—Louis, in the

World—very foolishly built a hall of mirrors of his own, the one we see even today at Versailles.

"The soul-stealers still lay in wait in the Way, on the other side of the mirrors, and they were still loyal to their master. One by one, they took the souls of the aristocrats of Versailles. And they, too, became slaves. At last, the soul-stealers realized that their master was still alive, and found where he was kept, and ordered their slaves to release their master from his prison. On a fateful Epiphany night, they carried him back inside the mirrors—but he was still locked into the mask that the first King in the Window had put on him, and as long as he remains in it, he can live only on one side of the mirrors at a time, and send his messengers out to steal men's souls. He can read the faces of others, but he cannot show his own, and this keeps him locked on the other side.

"The Way has been fouled and corrupted by him, though. It is called the Mirror-Maze now. The first King in the Window was driven out, and his little chapel was routed from the Way. It is said that some of his beautiful furnishings were pulled back through into the World, though I have never seen them. The Master of Mirrors still lurks there, taking souls and plotting his revenge."

"Why didn't the wraiths tell me this?" *If they had*, he was thinking, *I might have been clearer about the mistake.*

"Oh, they would have, eventually. But they didn't want to frighten you more than was absolutely necessary. And telling all at once is not their style. They are French before they are anything else."

"How do you know all this, Mrs. Pearson? Are you one of the . . . Wise? And why are you telling me?"

"No, no." She looked slightly nettled, and then she said proudly, "I am merely one of the Witty." Oliver tried to laugh politely, thinking that it was a joke. But she glared at him. "It is a simple fact. I come from a family of Witty. The Witty are not the Wise. The Wise are an order of those who have seen the Way, while the Witty are an order of those who have read about it in books and old papers."

"So the Wise are, uh, superior to the Witty?" Oliver asked.

"No, the Wise are *not* superior to the Witty," Mrs. Pearson said, and the eyebrows went up again, "anymore than someone who has been bitten by a shark is superior to someone who has read about people being bitten by sharks. They merely have different types of experience, and one of them has, at least, not been bitten. Why am I telling you secrets not normally shared with the less-than-instantly-appealing offspring of American journalists?" She shrugged and made a face. "Someone said once, 'The Wise are silent when it is better to speak, and the Witty speak when it is better to remain silent.' It was not a particularly witty remark, so it doubtless was made by one of the Wise."

"But who am I to lead a war of window wraiths? What do they really want me to do?"

"That part seems obvious, *that* seems plain enough, anyway. They want you to lead them in a war of reconquest, defeat the Master of Mirrors, cleanse the Way, rout his army of soul-stealers, and imprison him so that he can never escape again. End the Great War of the Mirrors and Windows, restore the kingship, so that once again we have a king in *and* out of the window, set off fireworks, and generally bring back the Golden Age and the Grand Siècle. How old did you say you were?"

"Twelve," Oliver replied.

"Any fighting experience?"

"No."

"Well . . . you're not the most obvious choice. But I see your virtues: loyalty; freshness; the untutored, try-anything outlook; and . . ." She paused.

"Go on," he said.

"Well, you were all they could find, Oliver. The King in the Window is always chosen by signs rather than by merit. And you were wearing a crown. And on Epiphany night, in the presence of a window, you did *say* that you were the king."

"But I was just, you know, joking—I mean, not joking, but sort of saying it because kingly was the *last* thing I felt like . . ."

"You were being ironic."

"I was?"

"Yes. At an unfortunate moment to be so. Still, they have taken you for their king, and foolish as that might be, there's no going back on it."

At this moment, the waiters arrived with the first courses and, with many flourishes and complicated explanations, placed them before them. Mrs. Pearson looked with immense pleasure at her circle of dark black fish eggs, which she ate, one by one, like pearls, with a silver spoon.

"*You* must have had some thoughts about what to do," she said, as one by one she bit down on her caviar.

"Well," he said at last. He had thought about it, a little. "I was thinking that since they picked me, then I must have, like, this sort of instinct inside me that would let me, uh, lead and all and that I shouldn't really *think* too much. You know, trust my instincts. Get beyond my conscious mind, get in touch with the universe, go beyond, like, logic, and use the force . . ." Oliver trailed off weakly.

Mrs. Pearson's eyes were like blue ice. Oliver could tell that she was struggling to contain her emotions. "You . . . find . . . yourself in a confrontation with absolute evil, and you . . . are . . . planning . . . not . . . to . . . think?"

Oliver had never heard words said so slowly, with so much outrage.

"Well . . . I . . ." Oliver stumbled.

"Craft, strategy, cunning tactics: *thought.* That is all that allows good to triumph. Renounce reason and you're lost. Rely on your 'inner sense,' and you will make a mess of everything. Thinking is your only hope. Start thinking now and never stop. Outwit the evildoer! Learn to tell the difference between sound argument and slippery rhetoric. Discriminate between the Received Idea and the Enduring Truth; between the odd and the strange; the selfish and the self-centered; the childish and the childlike; between metaphors and ironies, riddles and paradoxes. Think, and if you can't think, read. And if you can't read—why, then think some more! Discriminate, adjudicate, split hairs, dispute priorities, but think, *think*! It is your only hope."

Oliver was shocked by her vehemence. She even took the spoon out of the champagne bottle and brandished it at him as she spoke, and only at the end of her assault realized that she might be losing bubbles and put it back in.

"If you can't think, read, and if you can't read, think!" she repeated and poured herself one more glass of the rose-colored champagne and drained it dry. "Your mind has windows and mirrors. Use them! Hold a sentence up to the mirror in your mind and see what it looks like reversed! Look at a thought through the windows of your mind and see how it changes at different times of the day! Think!"

"The problem," Oliver gulped, "the problem is that I don't think I'm very good at thinking. I don't know how to think. Where do I begin?"

"Begin? Begin thinking? Why, you begin thinking by . . . thinking. About something. You'll figure something out, you'll see something that the rest of the world hasn't, or you'll know something before anyone else does, something perhaps no larger than a snail's horn—and the feeling of wealth that you will feel at that moment, if that moment ever arrives for you, will be better than any other feeling you have ever had."

That was encouraging, at least. So Oliver said, "Mrs. Pearson, don't you think I might be, you know, sort of the right person, after all—I mean, maybe I must have oh, a secret family history that makes me really, you know, the rightful King in the Window."

"You? Not a chance. Pure, comic case of mistaken identity on a cosmic scale. Wrong stone, wrong window, wrong crown. That's all. *And* the wishful thinking of phantoms secluded from the World for centuries: they needed a king, saw you, and made a desperate leap. You are who you always were, and not one bit special. Which means that you are now first on the death list of the soul-stealers. . . ."

Oliver gulped. "Couldn't you lie to me about that?"

"It is civilized to tell small lies. But not to tell someone that he is the first on the death list of the dread Master of Mirrors? *That* would be impolite."

The main courses arrived. Their breast of chicken came in a copper casserole, and when the waiter lifted the cover, a powerful, dark smell of truffles rose from the table.

"So there isn't anything I can do to actually help myself? Aside from thinking, I mean," Oliver added quickly.

Mrs. Pearson paused. "Well, there is one thing. I wouldn't call it a thing, actually. More just a vague rumor heard from time to time that will probably be of no help at all." She began calmly eating, inhaling deeply the pungent aroma.

"What is it?"

"It?" she looked up. "Oh. It. Well, it has been said—not often, and who knows how truthfully—but it has been said that two true mirrors from the great glassworks survived and were kept free from the fouling hand of the master."

"What's a true mirror?" Oliver asked.

"A mirror that shows things as they really are," she said. "Or so one supposes. It's also said that those two mirrors can allow you into the Mirror-Maze without his knowing that you've entered."

"Great!" At last some practical action was being proposed. "But where can I find them?"

"Find them? What in the world makes you think that you can find them?" she said, very cheerfully. "One of them belonged to a soothsayer named Luc Gauric and was last seen at Versailles at the end of the eighteenth century, just before the Revolution."

"And the other?" Oliver asked.

But Mrs. Pearson only went on with her elegant eating. Oliver could tell from the ferociousness of her silence that there was no sense in asking her about the other true mirror.

At last she inhaled deeply. "Oliver!" she said, almost gaily. "It seems that you have been plunged from your innocent pastimes into a pivotal part in the culminating and climactic episode of the Great War of the Window Wraiths. All you have to do is . . . save the world! I, for one, shall watch your conduct with considerable interest. You may soar to the sun. Or all your hopes and existence may be dashed into a thousand pieces."

"Oh," said Oliver. He thought for a moment. "Is that a metaphor?"

"No," she answered. "For your sake I wish it were."

"Mrs. Pearson, will you, please, help me?" Oliver asked. He was feeling frightened, and she seemed to know so much.

Mrs. Pearson nodded. "Oliver, you have just done the right thing. When you need help from a superior person, it is best just to ask her, plaintively and even with spaniel-like importuning. Yes, I will help you, as best I can," she finished grandly. "Courage, Oliver. Do not be downcast." For Oliver's face had fallen, as had the green beans from his fork, as he realized the scale of his responsibility. "I have begun to . . ."

"To respect me?" Oliver finished her sentence hopefully. "My father says that is more important—"

"No, no not to respect you," she said peevishly. "Certainly not to respect you. What is respect? Attila the Hun was respected by every Hun. And by every non-Hun, too."

"But then why? Why will you help me?"

For the first time since he had known her—which, granted, was only an hour—he saw a different Mrs. Pearson. Her face in the candlelight became drawn and pensive. "Why? Because—because I owe a debt to someone involved in this business."

"A big debt?"

"No. A *little* debt, you might call it, but a very important one, all the same. A little family debt. A deep yet little debt. I only hope," she added, more softly, "that I will know when the time is ripe to pay it back at last."

Mrs. Pearson's mentioning the time caused Oliver to look at his watch. It was already a quarter past ten! Better hurry! So before anyone could order dessert, he called for the *addition* and the maître d' brought it in a little red-velvet booklet, on a silver platter.

Oliver opened it and gasped: dinner cost almost six hundred euros—more than five times all his savings in the world! But before he could think what to do, Mrs. Pearson snatched the bill away, handed it to the maître d', and said to him, rising from her seat, "Send it to my home tomorrow. I will give him a check." And she swept Oliver out of the restaurant.

"Of course, we could have paid it now," she said to him as they stood outside the glowing restaurant in the cold, dark garden. "But to be paid at once only increases their insolence. Better to send them running in pursuit of their little bill. Remember, Oliver, those rules for three-star dining: a spoon in the champagne, and have them send the bill. Perhaps you will write me checks in weekly installments."

Oliver stared at her.

"Well, surely you didn't think that *I* was going to pay for that lavish dinner," said Mrs. Pearson, her eyebrows rising straight up like a peacock's tail. "And provide free advice? You have a very strange notion of entertaining. Obviously, now that you are a king, you must live like a king, and that means borrowing money. You can repay the balance over the next few months."

So, painfully, Oliver dug out his money, and handed it to Mrs. Pearson.

"Well, that's less than half. I'll expect the rest in install-ments. You may live like royalty now, Oliver, but I live only on royalties, and few enough of those," Mrs. Pearson har-rumphed, and pocketed the money. "A very small witticism from a very great wit, but then it is very late," she added, "and my company is uninspiring."

For a moment, Oliver hardly cared.

As they stood outside the glowing restaurant in the cold, dark garden, seeing the outlines of the bare winter trees, stretching away in their neat rows, waiting for sum-mer, the crucial question suddenly came back to him.

"What is a soul, exactly?" he asked Mrs. Pearson. "If I'm going to fight for them, at least I ought to know what they are."

Mrs. Pearson stopped and thought for a moment.

"A soul, Oliver . . ." she began. Then she stopped abruptly, and she did something strange. She reached into her pocketbook, and from inside it she took her silver cham-pagne spoon—the one that she had used to preserve the bub-bles in the bottle. She held it up almost absentmindedly into the smoky winter night.

"Look, Oliver," she whispered, and her voice seemed very different than it had all night, full of soft mystery and wonder. "Do you see the way that the entire Palais Royal fits into the bowl of my little spoon? That's the amazing thing about reflections, Oliver. Great vast things fit into small and tiny spaces. Only, look! It's upside down."

Oliver got on his tiptoes and peered at the spoon. It was an old silver spoon, polished bright, with the initials "LL" engraved on it. He could see the whole of the Palais Royal garden reflected in its little bowl. But it was all upside down—the long rows of naked trees and the long rows of iron fences, and the beautiful glowing lights that marched like soldiers along the space between the pavements and the garden, all reflected upside down and curving. A whole variant of the normal universe right inside the little spoon!

The mirror! Oliver looked at Mrs. Pearson, and suddenly a wave of fear overcame him. Why was she so nonchalant about a mirror after everything she had told him? Her face, as light from the lamps of the Palais Royal reflected up from the bowl of her curving spoon, suddenly looked wild, and a little dangerous. What if . . .

But then Mrs. Pearson abruptly put the spoon back in her bag, and, for the first time that night, she smiled at him. It was not the kind of smile that is called a warm or a winning smile—just a quick flash of tolerant pity, really—but a smile it was, all the same.

"I shouldn't worry about souls if I were you," she said. "After we have finished fighting comes knowing what it was we fought for," she said, and her voice was once again brittle and sharp and amused. "All you need to know is that the energy of souls is so intense that it keeps the world alight."

"I *would* worry about the mirror of Luc Gauric, however. Sooner or later, you will have to go hunt the Master of Mirrors in his lair, in a gruesome, bloody, and doubtless losing battle, and the only way to do it is to find a true mirror to use as a secret back door."

"Do you think I can find it in Paris?" he asked.

"I'm sure I haven't the slightest idea," she responded, and she turned on her heel and headed into the shadows down the long arcade of the Palais Royal. Oliver could hear her high heels clacking across the pavement.

Oliver brooded on this as he ran back across the bridge, up the street, and down the boulevard, to be at the bus stop at ten thirty. When his mother came to pick him up, she asked him why he was breathing so hard, but he passed it off with something about the excitement of his schoolwork.

Later that evening, Oliver did a very brave and very foolish thing. He dug out his old armor from his old play chest—gold-colored plastic armor with an embossed dragon in the center of the breast plate—and put it on, and he clasped his own sword gently by the pommel so that its point rested on the ground, and, trying to look as soulful as he could, he took a deep breath and stepped right in front of the long mirror in his parents' room.

"I am here," he said softly, "and I am not afraid."

He was sure that he heard a hiss, coming from the other side, but this time it was muted, and Oliver was sure that there was at least a note of uncertainty and doubt inside the snarl. But then he heard sudden, intense sighing.

He spun around, and saw that it was his mother, watching him from the door of the bedroom. She ran over and kissed him. "Oliver, it's so wonderful to see you in your armor again, my knight," she said.

Before he went to bed, he took his armor off and brushed his teeth with his back turned to the mirror. (It was one thing to be brave, another thing to be foolish.) Then he took a basin of water from the kitchen and put it under his bed: he could look into it to brush his teeth in the morning. He gazed into the water, hoping to see a friend, but there were only ripples, and he went to bed. Well, he thought, it had been a good night. He had learned what he must do, and who he was up against, and he had shown himself to the enemy. He had also made a very useful, though extremely expensive, ally.

Something woke him in the middle of sleep. Gloved hands had begun to massage his temples.

Two fingers pressed down, harder, a little harder, but that was too hard. . . . And then suddenly he felt more fingers pressing down alongside them. He quickly opened his eyes, but could see only two enormous gloved hands, pressing down on his forehead, slipping around his head like a tightening vise. They were back! With a violent turn, Oliver twisted, trying to throw himself off the bed.

"Hey! Sorry! Chill," said a voice. "Take a chill pill, Ollie. It's only me."

Oliver looked up. There, in his bedroom, dressed in a down jacket and heavy muffler and fur-lined leather gloves, was Charlie Gronek of Allendale, New Jersey.

Chapter Six

The Missing Mirror

"CHARLIE!" Oliver cried. "What are you doing here?"

"Got your e-mail, old pal," said Charlie. "And I thought I better get to Paris pronto. My mom's got insane frequent flier miles and she always wants me to visit you. So I said that I'd do a special project on the big Hornshaw project here—you know, this weird 'quantum leap'—they *die* for special-project reports at my school—and so here I am," Charlie added. He yawned. "I got here in the middle of the night, and your mom said I could surprise you. Now what's this sword and sorcery stuff you're heated up about? Can I play?"

"Charlie, it's not a game. I'm afraid it's desperately serious."

"Serious games are the only kind of game I like."

So Oliver gave Charlie the same rundown that he had given to Mrs. Pearson, only he tried to make this version shorter and more to the point.

When he was finished, Charlie looked at him in a friendly—in fact, in a slightly too friendly—manner.

"Oliver," he said, "if that's, like, your reality, cool. Your parents are like, also really supportive about this?"

"I haven't told them."

Charlie looked as if he was repressing a smile.

"Charlie, this is serious. Anyway, what does 'supportive' mean?"

For a second Charlie looked lost. "It's—uh—it's an American word that means, sort of, you may be nuts but you have a right to be nuts in your own way. Hey, *I* like your thinking on this, Ollie. We had to do something like it for credit in symbolic archetype class—that's what they used to call English, but Randi decided to change it. Now we do archetypal symbolic information analysis. I mean, we each had to create our own myth, and draw our own mandala and everything. And then we had to, like, analyze everybody's archetypes. Personally, I'm thinking of becoming a Buddhist. They worship lettuce."

"Charlie, you don't understand. This is desperately serious. This is real."

"Hey, Ollie," Charlie said reprovingly, and he held up a finger solemnly. "Like the Beatles said, nothing is real."

"This is real."

"On the other hand," said Charlie Gronek, settling down with a pillow on Oliver's bed, "they also said although she feels as if she's in a play, she is anyway. Which is different."

"Charlie, this has absolutely nothing to do with the Beatles."

"Oliver, sooner or later everything has something to do with the Beatles." Charlie reflected for a moment. "Okay. I can't see any fun for me in *not* believing you. And if I do believe you—why, it could be fun. So I believe you, Ollie."

Oliver was unhappy, and he threw himself back down on his bed.

"That's not really believing me, Charlie. Believing me for fun is not the same thing as believing me."

"Well, maybe that's the way we believe things in America. Anyway, no one else believes you right now, so you might as well take my kind of believing. Have you tried searching the 'Net for scat?"

"Scat?"

"You know. Clues, significant droppings, signs. Have you searched the 'Net for scat?"

"What do you mean? This war between windows and mirrors is all either really old, or really, well, supernatural.

I don't think doing an Internet search is going to help." He paused. "Well, there is this mirror that Mrs. Pearson said I should look for. The mirror of Luc Gauric. But I doubt you could find anything about it on the Internet. She didn't seem to think that I could find it anywhere."

Charlie shrugged. "Hey, you never know," he said. "One guy in my class, he did a search for something about Egyptian hieroglyphs and he found six hundred pages. An all hieroglyph hub. He got kicked out of school—apparently the hieroglyphs he copied spelled out something really, well, Egyptian, if you know what I mean—but he showed you could find anything. *This* isn't as old as that."

And almost before Oliver knew what he was doing, Charlie had his computer out of his backback and had flipped it open and turned it on.

"Hey, that's great," he said. "I don't even have to log on. There's some kind of wi-fi hotspot right here in your room! Did you set that up?"

Ollie shrugged in confusion. "There is? No—I mean, sometimes I use my Dad's computer to search for stuff, but he doesn't really like me to do it. I don't have anything here . . ."

Charlie raised his eyebrows. "Weird. Well, it's true. Some kind of wi-fi hotspot right around here? Internet café or something?" Oliver didn't think there was—the café nearest to their house didn't even have a telephone—but he just watched as Charlie continued to work.

Oliver had always thought of Charlie as someone who was very impressive in his own way—he could skate and was a skateboarder, and he wasn't intimidated by anything—but he had never thought of him as, well, intelligent, exactly. But he was smacking the keys on his keyboard and setting it up with smooth expertise.

"Okay, Ollie. What's the French word for mirror? And for window?"

Oliver paused. "Well, it's complicated," he said at last. "A mirror is a *miroir*. But it can also be a *glace*. And a window is a *fenêtre*. But it's also a *vitrine*. I guess there are so many words because they are so important . . ." His voice trailed off. There was something significant there, if he could only *think* of it clearly. But thinking, even trying to think, was so tiring.

Charlie had already punched in the words and was scanning the pages that came up on his screen with an expert frown. "Not that . . . not that . . . that's no use, we don't want to buy a mirror . . . nothing there . . . nothing there . . . Hey, Ollie, look at this. Could this be something?"

Oliver peered over Charlie's shoulder. There was a page covered with fine type, as though it had been scanned in from a very old and scholarly book. Oliver translated aloud:

"'In antiquity, well, olden times, mirrors were among the most frequent instruments of soothsayers and sorcerers. From the twelfth to the seventeenth centuries, the wise condemned those who sought knowledge of the future through hydromancy (divination by water), crystallomancy (by crystal balls), or, worst of all, by catoptromancy (divination by mirrors)—'"

"What's divination?" Charlie asked. "And say that last word again."

"Divination? It just means foretelling the future. And I think you pronounce it"—he looked at the word again, and then said, slowly—"CAT-opt-romance-y. Think of a cat who's opting for romance, and add a 'y.'"

"Very clever, Ollie," Charlie said approvingly. "Almost sounds like me, because I *am* a cat who's opting for romance. Being a king is polishing up your wit."

"There's more, Charlie. It goes on. 'Even the notorious Nostradamus insisted that his prophecies were only what he had gained, "from the other side of the mirror." And the great seer Luc Gauric kept what he called a "mirror of truth" in his apartments in Versailles until . . .' Then—gee, that's strange."

For as Oliver read on, the entire page of text on the computer screen began to fade in front of his eyes, bit by bit, and shade by shade, and then it began to break up, as though someone were scrambling it until, within five seconds, it could no longer be seen.

Charlie took over the keyboard, and began to work every back door and trick he knew. But it was no use. The page was gone.

"Oliver, this is so weird. It's not just the page that's gone. There's no record of it. No cache of it or anything. And it was just a page from a library in Paris . . . but it's like it's vanished right off the Web." He shrugged. "Maybe it's something to do with this wi-fi hotspot you're sitting on.

Anyway, it's a start. That truthful mirror. Where should we look?"

Oliver had actually been thinking about just this question, and so now he said, "Well, I think probably the window wraiths know something about it."

"Wouldn't they have told you?"

"Mrs. Pearson explained to me that they don't like to tell you too much at once. They're very, well, French, that way. I think maybe I need to go back to Versailles and order them to tell me, or something, being the king and all," he concluded. He admitted that it sounded like a pretty lame plan.

"Okay," Charlie said. "Then we'll go to Versailles in the morning and search. I've got a few more days before the Hornshaw project opens and I'll have to hang out around the Eiffel Tower."

Oliver sighed. "Well, it's not a very good plan, I know. Searching for a mirror in Versailles is like, well—"

"Like searching for a needle in a haystack?"

"No, it's more like searching for hay in a haystack. There are so many mirrors there, and if he sees me in one of them . . ." Oliver blanched. He could still feel that hand on his throat.

"Well, but he hasn't seen *me*, and he doesn't know about me. As far as he knows, I'm just one more dumb American kid. At least it's a plan."

Oliver couldn't very well argue with that. "Charlie, you're great at these computer things," Oliver said.

Charlie smiled. "'You're a slave to screens,' my mom

always says. But she doesn't see how much I get from them. Maybe some kids just sit there dumbed-out in front of them, but not me."

Before they went to sleep, Charlie emptied his pockets. Oliver marveled at the treasures they contained: a Discman, a Walkman, and an iPod. Why, Charlie had a GameBoy and a miniature DVD player and a cell phone that worked on two continents . . .

"Of course, we have all those things in France—my dad has two cell phones—but my mom doesn't encourage them and neither does my school. She says they're addictive," Oliver explained, when Charlie asked him why his gizmo cupboard was, so to speak, so bare.

"Well, I don't know how you manage without them," Charlie said.

Oliver shrugged. "I read," he said.

Charlie shrugged, and then he pressed Oliver to see if he could remember anything else that Mrs. Pearson had told him about the two true mirrors.

Oliver was practicing the King's Sign, the two-winged bird shadow puppet. He held his hands together by the thumbs, and tried to make the shadow of the bird's feathered wings.

"What's that supposed to be?" Charlie asked him.

Oliver sighed. "It's supposed to be the King's Sign. A big noble bird about to take off. Only it doesn't really look much like it. Believe me, I know."

Charlie looked at him. "Uh, Ollie. GameCube?

PlayStation 2? Other entertainment possibilities that may be out there in the new millennium?"

"I like doing shadow puppets," Oliver said stubbornly. "There's something sort of challenging about them. Though I admit that this one doesn't look that hot."

"This mirror, Ollie. Does it have, like, a name on it?"

"I don't know," Oliver admitted.

"Is it, like, made of gold or glowing uranium or something?"

"I don't think so. It's just a mirror. A loyal mirror."

"I would work on this detail a little, Ollie. I mean, maybe if—"

"Charlie! It's *true,*" Oliver said, feeling a little desperate. "It's a true mirror."

"True to who?" Charlie asked.

Oliver thought. "Well, to me, I guess. I mean, to the King in the Window."

"You mean, like, it shows you as you really are?" Charlie asked.

"I guess."

"You mean, like, a truly pathetic twelve-year-old head case?"

But Oliver just rolled over and went back to sleep.

So on that Tuesday morning—which was, if you are taking the trouble to map Oliver's story on a calendar, as you might, Tuesday, January the eleventh—Oliver set off for Versailles again, only this time with Charlie.

Oliver had told his mother that he was going to take Charlie to school with him—"It will be good for him to experience a really structured educational experience," Oliver had said, trying to sound very knowing—but really he knew that if he was to accomplish his tasks, he would have to skip school for the entire day and take Charlie with him. This may not sound like much, but for Oliver, who had never skipped school in his life, it was as large and daring an act as he could imagine. And he shuddered when he also imagined the consequences. None of his classmates, so far as he knew, had ever just walked off and gone somewhere else when they were supposed to be in school, and though his excuse was actually quite impressive and even sort of scholarly in its way—"I have become the leader of the greatest group of French artists still in existence"—he very much doubted that it would impress his teachers. They believed in school, and now.

Neige was in the courtyard, sweeping up and singing softly to herself, as she always did before she went to school. Oliver nodded at her in as friendly a way as he could. Charlie looked at her and then said, a little too loudly, to Oliver, "Hey, who's the French babe? She is *sweet*. You two really, uh, close?"

Oliver tried desperately to quiet him down. "Shhh, Charlie!" he said. "She speaks perfectly good English." Which was true, although Oliver was never sure just how much English Neige understood: more than you thought or less than you imagined.

But Charlie ignored him. "I mean, I even like the

whole broom thing she's doing. It's very sort of witchy, but also kind of sweet." And he began to sing some kind of American song about a witchy woman riding her broom on Halloween, which Oliver suspected was very inappropriate.

"Charlie! Quiet!" he said sharply, and now Charlie looked at him.

"You really do like her, don't you?" he said, and his smile was suddenly amused.

Oliver tried to hustle him out of the courtyard, all the while looking back at Neige a little desperately, hoping to see some warm, forgiving light in her eyes. But she just stared at Charlie as though he were some slightly disgusting animal, like a horned toad. Then she turned back to her sweeping, and began to sing to herself again.

As the two boys clicked open the great door of the courtyard, Oliver saw, to his horror, that the two policemen from the previous night were hovering at the end of the street, collars turned up, and muttering. Oliver's heart leaped. What if they followed him? But Oliver and Charlie walked up the street and away from them, and Oliver saw that, though the more suspicious of the two scribbled something in his notebook, they remained where they were. What were they expecting? Or looking for?

They got on the train at Invalides station and went down the aisle searching for a seat.

"Hello, Your Majesty," a voice said. Oliver started. It was Mrs. Pearson! She was waiting for them, seated already, looking, Oliver had to admit it, very elegant in some kind of dark chestnut cape-coat with a crepe scarf in pale gray around her neck.

"Mrs. Pearson," Oliver said. "What brought you here?"

"Why, Oliver, I *reasoned*," she said calmly. "I thought. As I would still advise you to do. I knew that after our conversation last night, you would immediately go in search of the mirror of Luc Gauric, and I knew that, if you thought about it at all, you would know that the best place to start would be the Hall of Mirrors in Versailles. Then I knew that, given a choice between your duties as a scholar and your responsibilities as a king, you would follow your responsibilities. And it was a moment's work to calculate the likely train you would take after you had lied to your mother about going to school. A useful lesson for you, Oliver, in the way that just a little thought can help you to intercept, at the decisive moment, your friends—or, some day, your enemies," she added darkly. "So here I am, and here you are, and now who in the name of all that is elegant is this?" she finished, looking at Charlie Gronek.

Oliver could see why she was startled. Charlie Gronek had on his San Jose Sharks team jacket, which was about three sizes too big for him (according to Oliver's mother) and had a huge embroidered image of a shark with his jaws open breaking into a hockey stick, and a wool cap pulled down over his eyes. Mrs. Pearson continued to read the jacket up and down as though it were, well, a special message from the Master of Mirrors. (Oliver, of course, had on his usual uniform of gray pants and a blue jacket, as all French schoolboys wear.)

Oliver introduced Charlie to Mrs. Pearson, and Mrs. Pearson to Charlie, and they shook hands. Oliver explained to Mrs. Pearson what he and Charlie had discovered the night before. But there was something even more frigid about her than usual—was it that Oliver had told Charlie about the window wraiths and their war, or was it just Charlie's jacket?—and she was very tight-lipped.

"How will we know it is the mirror of Luc Gauric, even if we find it?" Oliver asked her.

"I'm sure I have no idea," she said, and she went on reading a small book that she had brought with her. Her hands were wrapped tight around it, and she seemed not to be reading it so much as searching it, flipping the pages for something. Oliver could see, through her fingers, the title: *De l'autre côté du miroir*—the other side of the mirror. What was this?

Well, of course . . . it must be some sort of super-secret guide to soul-saving spells or something. Oliver ought to ask her what it was, and read it, too, he realized.

"Hey," Charlie whispered to him. "Are you sure that your friend Mary Poppins here is really on your side? I'm getting like a major ice flow coming my way."

"Oh, I'm sure," Oliver whispered back quickly. "She knows everything, and she told me the truth about everything. She's one of the Witty."

"Huh?"

"They're an order—like of monks, only thirstier. There's the Wise, like Molière. And there's the Witty."

"The Witty, huh? More like the Weird," Charlie snickered, as Mrs. Pearson stared into her book.

"The Weird, as it *quite* happens," she said suddenly, closing her book with a snap that made Oliver jump—"are a Celtic order. They specialize in filthy limericks and cannibalism. If I *were* one of the Weird"—she looked appraisingly at Charlie—"by now, I probably would have cut you open, eaten your liver raw, drained your blood, thrown your carcass out of the window, and made up a rhyme just to celebrate the excellence of the meal. As it happens, I am *not* one of the Weird. But nor am I one of the deaf." She raised her eyebrows, opened her book again, and resumed her reading.

Charlie, Oliver noted, raised his eyebrows back, but there was really no raising your eyebrows at Mrs. Pearson, so he just said, "Sorry. Cool. Whatever."

Oliver was thinking. "Mrs. Pearson," he said at last, "the Wise and the Witty and the Weird. Are there any other 'W' type groups I should know about?"

"No. The Wise and the Witty are the two orders who will concern you most, save the Watchful, of course."

" 'Save the Watchful'?" Oliver repeated her words. He was puzzled.

"I used 'save' in the old-fashioned sense. I mean, *except for* the Watchful."

"Who are they?"

She shrugged. "Well, actually, no one really knows, precisely. But there is an ancient tradition that the Watchful were supposed to come to the aid of the Wise and the Witty and the wraiths at the moment when the Master of Mirrors escaped back into the Way. But they failed the call, and ever since, they have lived in darkness. Not even the Wise any longer are sure exactly who they were, or where they are now."

"Then we'll just have to *watch* for them, won't we?" Oliver said. He couldn't explain why—he was a thief and a truant and a false king, after all—but he was feeling extremely absorbed, and therefore happy.

"That is not a witty remark," Mrs. Pearson reproved him. "Merely a waggish one." Oliver didn't think it was worthwhile to ask the difference.

Soon, they were at Versailles, and, after climbing the hill to the château—Mrs. Pearson had wanted to take a taxi—Oliver decided to go back to the Petit Trianon. Secretly, he was a little worried that the window wraiths might be shy about appearing to such a gang—if he were a window wraith, he thought, he would be a little shy about meeting Charlie Gronek and Mrs. Pearson on the same day after four hundred years of hiding in a windowpane—so he thought that perhaps he would go first to the skylight and look for them, and then call the rest forward.

Nothing happened. Oliver settled down to wait, as the rays of the morning sun passed through the windows and cast a soft, diffused light on him. Downstairs, he could hear Mrs. Pearson giving Charlie a long, bilingual lecture on the history of Versailles. After a while, Oliver got fed up waiting, and decided to take a walk along the sandy paths outside.

Charlie joined him, while Mrs. Pearson waited. Suddenly Charlie looked around, over his shoulder.

"Hey, we got company," he muttered.

"We do?" Oliver said politely, looking around and putting his hand out in greeting.

Charlie sighed. "Oliver, in the movies when someone says 'We got company' or 'Looks like we got company' it doesn't mean, Get out the tea service, we've got company. It means, We're being followed."

"We are?" Oliver said.

"Yeah, I think so. Sort of something flitting in the distance behind us. But it looked like it was carrying some kind of weapon—not a sword, something bulkier."

A wraith! Oliver thought. But why would one of them be carrying a weapon? And why wouldn't it approach? He turned around, and just in time saw the shadowy figure disappearing behind a tree. He looked again. Yes, there it was; something blue and washy looking. Wait, it was François, he was sure of it! But why was he hiding? Then Oliver looked again, and this time he was sure that he saw five or six wraithlike faces, pale and dreamy, peeking out from behind the leaves of the well-trimmed tree.

Well, if he was to be a king, he had better act like one. So Oliver stepped boldly forward.

"Come out of there!" he said firmly. "And now. It's difficult for me to make these trips, you know," he added. "And I don't intend to go on making them if you won't cooperate."

Actually, he was thrilled to see François—he had half

begun to doubt if there really *were* window wraiths—but he thought it best to continue in the role of a haughty monarch. It seemed to be the only kind of character they understood, or respected.

One by one, the wraiths sheepishly peeled away from their hiding place, and very shyly floated over in the direction of Oliver and Charlie.

"Ah, sorry, Prince of the Blood," François said, as he approached. "Our deep apologies. You see, we took the morning off to play *jeu de paume*. And we wondered—who are they?" Oliver realized that the "weapon" he was carrying was a tennis racket.

Then, slowly, Oliver could see the rest of the court beginning to appear behind him, in that odd, crinkly, now-you-see-them-now-you-don't way that they had, all looking a little hot and out of breath and all carrying tennis rackets.

Oliver knew from school that *jeu de paume* was the name for an early kind of tennis that aristocrats liked to play in the seventeenth century. But he decided to continue seeming more arrogant than he felt.

"Amusing yourselves, were you?" he went on. "While I'm out being throttled by your enemies, you are busy playing racket sports? Is this the—"

Now Molière looked up. "Oh," he said. "You have engaged in combat with the mirror-men? Are they defeated then? We've been waiting for word."

"Are they defeated?" Oliver said sarcastically. "No, of course they're not defeated. We haven't even begun to fight,

I don't know where or how . . ." But watching the faces of the court droop as he mumbled these words, Oliver had a sudden realization. *They're helpless,* he said to himself. *They don't know how to fight a battle or mend a cloth or do anything other than amuse one another.* They were Those Whose Backs Were Turned. Musicians and players and gardeners and pages and playwrights. They had been loyal to their king once, and they were still loyal to the King in the Window now, and they assumed that once their king had acted, everything would be all right. It was admirable, in its way. They were looking to Oliver to lead and, well, he had better lead.

So as Charlie gaped and Mrs. Pearson came near, watching quizzically, Oliver gathered himself together and, trying to remember to be extremely metaphorical and rhetorical, he said: "My friends, the battle will soon be joined, and, uh, the winged eagles of the windows will, uh, throw stones at the, uh, silver fortresses of their enemies. Or something," he ended. Then an inspiration struck him. "I've chosen my marshals, and I have brought them with me. That is who 'they' are," he said. In French armies, a marshal is a kind of super-general. "I mean, I have scoured the ranks of today's heroes to find those who are most worthy to serve our cause."

A murmur went up around the court. The marshals had been chosen! Great military leaders! This was more like it! This was something that they understood!

"Yes, they have gathered here at Versailles even today, each putting down his or her normal military cares for the duration of this war." Oliver was trying to think quickly: his

and took Mrs. Pearson's and Charlie's hands, too, and led them forward, and in a moment all of them were floating out above the gardens of Versailles, being gently supported by the courtiers, and chatting away as though they had done this many times before. Within moments, Oliver could hear Charlie giving advice to François about his backhand in tennis, and could see that Mrs. Pearson was taking notes of a conversation she was having with one of the gentlemen of the court. ("And then Madame Montespan did *what*, do you say?" he could hear Mrs. Pearson asking. She loved four hundred-year-old gossip.)

"Where are we going?" Oliver asked Molière, who was leading him along in midair.

"To the Etoile, of course. The King in the Window always receives his arms in the Etoile," Molière said, as he pulled Oliver along in the chilly air. "Now that you have your marshals, you must be armed for battle. Though we don't have the mirror of Luc Gauric, we still have the rest of the king's weapons of war," he added proudly.

Well, this was more like it, Oliver thought. Weapons of war! Shining armor and strong spears and so on . . .

They wafted out across the gardens, and followed Molière's route. Oliver felt the breath leave his body at the splendor of it.

Down they flew around the Obelisk Grove, which contains an island in the shape of a quadrilobate rectangle, and a ring of reeds with 231 jets of water, the tallest a hundred feet high. Then they flew out over the Fountain of Latona, with its horseshoe-shaped slopes decorated with twenty-two statues in white marble, showing the Four Abductions, the Four Seasons, the Four Elements, the Four Times of Day, the Four Temperaments of Man, the Four Poetic Forms, and the Four Continents.

They arrived at last at the Etoile, or Star—a hidden little grove with a star pattern radiating out from its center in narrow gravel paths. Molière brought him down gently into the center. Oliver sat down, with Mrs. Pearson on one side of him, and Molière on the other. And then Charlie arrived, on the arm of François.

But as he looked around, Oliver saw Racine staring at Charlie's jacket and hat with what looked like almost open disgust.

"Marshal, indeed," Oliver heard him mutter.

Oliver decided that he had better do something to increase Charlie's prestige. He remembered what Mrs. Pearson had told him about how easily impressed the court was by fine speeches and special awards and honors.

And so he walked over to Charlie as, one by one, the other wraiths arrived, and said grandly, "Marshal Gronek is more than a great general. He is, by ancient royal decree, the, uh, the . . . Keeper of the Key!"

"What?" Charlie asked. But Oliver took out the little golden key from the Epiphany cake and very solemnly gave it to him. Charlie, catching on, took the impressive-looking key and put it gravely in his pocket.

The wraiths looked suitably impressed, and even Racine seemed to grumble a word or two of approval. But he noticed a worried look on Molière's face as he did it. Still, Oliver was feeling quite pleased with himself. He was ordering people around and elevating his friends with honors and awards—it was all quite kingly.

Molière turned to him. All around them, the window wraiths were looking on expectantly.

"Before he is given his arms, your Majesty, it is the custom for the King in the Window to make a speech," he said to Oliver.

"Oh, well . . ." said Oliver. Suddenly he felt much less kingly. Although he was struggling to be rhetorical, he didn't know if he actually could make a speech. "Could I just say a few quietly sincere words, and then you could give me the weapons?"

Molière looked shocked. "A few quiet, sincere words! Why, no! Before he is armed, a true king must always make a speech composed of several highly colorful lies." He looked with dismay at Mrs. Pearson. "Has the King not learned to lie yet, Madame?"

"Oh, dear me, yes. He's *very* well begun in lying. Very well begun, indeed. A very gifted natural liar, really. Now, Oliver, that is a good thing, for, as Molière says, as King of Windows and Water, you will have to lie very often."

"I will?" he said, rather shocked. "My father always taught me that lying was the worst possible thing a leader could do."

"It is," Mrs. Pearson agreed. "But he was thinking of black lies. There are so many other colors, and some of them are necessary ornaments to the majestic palette," she said, and she came over and gently took Oliver by the elbow, leading him to a small bench in the circle, and gesturing to Molière to join them.

"Are you saying that white lies are okay?" Oliver asked as he sat down, with Molière and Mrs. Pearson clustered on either side. He saw that the rest of the window wraiths had drawn back discreetly, and had even begun to hover a foot or two above the ground, asking polite questions of Charlie, whom they now were calling Key Keeper. "Like when you told the waiters last night that I was a wine expert and the rest—those were white lies, weren't they?"

"No, those were *red* lies, the color of the Michelin guide to restaurants that American tourists carry about. A red lie is one in which everyone finds a commercial benefit. After all, last night everyone benefited—you were not made responsible for the extravagance of my indulgences, and the restaurant had the privilege of indulging my extravagances."

"But if there are white lies, red lies and black lies . . ."

"And there are black-and-white lies, the lies one tells authors, as for instance when *you* told *me* that you had read all my books!" Oliver blushed furiously, but she went on. "Oh, there are so many more colorful ones than that! There is the pink lie, told to a small child to avoid hurting his feelings: '*Everyone* is going to sleep now, darling, not just you.' And the violet lie told to a beautiful aging woman: 'Darling, are you mad? You don't look a day older.' Another kindness—of a kind."

Oliver was beginning to enjoy this. He thought for a moment. "What's a magenta lie?" he asked.

"Well, magenta is the color of wine, so that is the kind of lie you tell to a hostess about her food. "My dear, the kidneys and cauliflower were simply wonderful. It's just that I am under doctor's orders to eat nothing but custard apples.""

"A crimson lie?"

"A lie the color of blood, told to a general or coach, a brave lie. 'It doesn't hurt a bit,'" Mrs. Pearson said promptly.

"Okay. A gray lie?"

"Oh, obviously, the kind told to a lawyer or accountant, who wear dark gray suits. A dark gray lie is the kind you tell to your tax adviser," Mrs. Pearson said, *very* darkly. "And a silver lie is the lie you tell to a soldier—silver because soldiers once wore armor. 'Your country will never forget your sacrifice!' That sort of thing."

Oliver thought. "Is there a golden lie?" he asked

"Ah! A golden lie. That is the greatest and most valuable lie of all." She stopped. She came to Oliver's side and whispered strongly to him: "But now *you* must lie a bit, before you're armed. Apparently it's the tradition. Just say something untrue in an elegant way, or else they will not have confidence in their king when they give him his weapons."

Oliver cleared his throat, stepped back into the center of the star-shaped enclosure, and looked out over the gathering of wraiths in the beautiful, bosky, leaf-filled garden.

"My people, I mean, my nonpeople, my friends: I wish

to say that I—that I have the same confidence in your wisdom that you have in my courage," he said at last. It wasn't a lie exactly: he *did* have the same confidence in their wisdom as they had in his courage, which was to say, not very much at all. But at least it was saying something untrue in an elegant way.

His words seemed to satisfy the wraiths. At least, Racine and Le Nôtre now came together around him. They held out a small wooden box.

"You have your sword," Molière said very seriously. *No, I don't,* Oliver thought. *I don't even know where it is,* he added, to himself, and his stomach did little somersaults. "And now you shall have your wand, and no king since the first king has been armed with sword *and* wand."

Sword and wand, Oliver thought, and his heart leaped up a little in his chest. This was more like it. Even if the glass sword was useless—and a vagrant on the street had stolen it, anyway—a wand might be, well, the kind of thing magicians use. He looked up excitedly. He knew what Mrs. Pearson had said about magic, but still . . .

"We give to you your wand, Your Majesty," Richelieu said very solemnly. "And we give it with pride."

Oliver opened the little lacquered box. Inside, there was a short wooden stick, like a Popsicle stick, and on its end a wooden circle. A wand? What kind of wand was this? It certainly wasn't a sorcerer's wand. Though come to think of it he certainly had seen something like it before. Next to it was a little bottle, with clear, soapy-looking liquid inside.

Oliver took the little wand and the bottle out and held them up dubiously. What were they? Could they really be what they seemed to be? He didn't know what to say.

"The wand," Molière said encouragingly. And then whispered breathlessly, "Your bubble wand!"

"What?" Oliver asked.

"It makes bubbles," Molière said, very seriously, and he bowed deep, as though begging a favor, and held out his hands, as if to demonstrate. Oliver gave him the two objects. Very cautiously, as though he were handling some terribly explosive substance, Molière opened the top of the bottle and dipped in the wand. He held it up: a thin film of soap had formed on the surface. Then he waved it—sure enough, a stream of bubbles flew through the air.

Oliver looked around helplessly. But the circle of wraiths seemed deeply impressed, almost frightened, by the flight of bubbles through the chill smoky air.

"Bubbles, your majesty," Richelieu said deeply. "It is your . . . bubble wand!" And he took the wand from Molière, dipped it in the bottle, and waved into being some more bubbles of his own.

Oliver had certainly played in the park with bubbles and bubble wands just like this one many times when he was younger, dipping in the wand and waving it to make the bubbles. But it was hardly what he expected for a king in his court.

"Are they, uh, magic bubbles?" he asked, hoping against hope that they would do something. But the little bubbles flew off across Versailles, popping after a few seconds of existence, just like all the other bubbles he had ever made.

Racine looked puzzled. "Magic? I know nothing of magic," he said. "They are *bubbles,* Your Majesty. True and tested and timeworn bubbles. And the reservoir of soap is there, and it is deep." He stirred it with his finger, to show Oliver, and then withdrew it and dried it carefully, almost with fear.

Oliver didn't know what to say. The wraiths were helpless, certainly, but were they crazy, too?

Well, in for a glass sword, in for a bubble wand, Oliver supposed. And so he simply bowed deep, and put the bubble wand and liquid soap in the pockets of his gray flannel pants.

"And for you, Madame Le Marechal," Molière now said, turning toward Mrs. Pearson, "we have—the great firearm of the king's right hand!"

"It was always given to the King in the Window's chief adviser," Molière explained.

Well, a firearm . . . that had to be more useful. And with great care Molière and Racine unlatched a long wooden box and drew from it an old-fashioned gold and silver pistol.

"Now, you must be extremely careful with this in battle," Racine said. "It's lethal."

He held it up toward the sky and pulled the trigger. A short spurt of water rose from the top, and then drizzled to the ground. He pulled the trigger again (Molière shut his gleaming eyes and turned away, Oliver noticed) and this time a slightly higher spout of water shot up, three or four inches high, and then dribbled down again.

"You see," said Racine, his eyes alight with the gleam of battle, as Molière also turned back to look admiringly at the pistol. "Water."

They're *nuts,* Oliver thought—a bubble wand for me and a water pistol for Mrs. Pearson. But there seemed no point in telling them so, and Mrs. Pearson was accepting the pistol with a deep bow and many thanks, so Oliver merely turned to find Charlie and start for home.

So: now he was armed—with a useless sword and a bubble wand. And actually, he didn't even have the sword. And he hadn't told his subjects that he'd lost it. What kind of lie was that? he wondered. Then it came to him. A transparent one, obviously.

All the way home on the train, everyone was silent. After great excitement—and actually meeting the window wraiths of Versailles had been exciting, even to Mrs. Pearson—it is normal to be a bit subdued. Charlie just shut his eyes, exhausted, and snored gently on the seat. Mrs. Pearson read from her book.

As the train rolled, Oliver tried to sort through all that he had learned, and all that he still didn't understand. He reviewed the essential points in his mind: The wraiths were an ancient race of artists and aristocrats who lived in windows, and had to spend their lives making reflections. They were kind and tended to be extremely rhetorical—except for

Molière, who had some common sense. But they were foolish, or seemed that way. For some bizarre reason, they believed that toys were useful weapons and that a glass sword that would obviously shatter the moment you tried to use it was the most dangerous sabre in the world. The wraiths were locked into their windows (except for the few days around Epiphany, and when they flew between windows at Versailles) but the other side, the Master of Mirrors slaves, seemed able to move freely from mirror to mirror. They were *much* more mobile, which was dangerous. Water was the wraiths' friendly medium (which didn't help much, unless it really flooded). There were also two true mirrors that were outside the Master of Mirrors' control and had never been contaminated by him, and if Oliver could find them—well, that would be good, but why exactly? And what made a mirror "true"?

But then his head filled with so many other thoughts. Who had fought with the glass sword and how? And where? Why had the wraiths given him a child's old bubble wand, and treated it as though it were a ticking bomb? Why had Neige pressed the figure of the fleur-de-lis into his hand, and how had the little pebble he had kicked into the river come back into the courtyard? And then there were red and magenta and the unknown golden lies, and Mrs. Pearson's champagne spoon with the Palais Royal upside down in it, not to mention the brutal, questioning faces of the policemen and the furious face of his rhetoric teacher . . . and, oh my God, he still hadn't started that paper! And he had been absent from school, and without even a bad excuse!

Oliver looked again at the title of the book in Mrs. Pearson's hand.

The Other Side of the Mirror? As they left the train, he decided that he should really ask her about it now. He was sure that this book must have some of the secrets they needed to find and defeat the Master of Mirrors.

"Mrs. Pearson, will you tell me what's in your book? Why is it important?" he asked, over the rattle of the arriving and departing trains.

And then she held it up, and Oliver saw the rest of the title: *Et tous que Alice a trouvé là.* And All That Alice Found There.

He laughed! Why, the little book that Mrs. Pearson had been poring through as though it were a vast secret text was just a French translation of *Through the Looking Glass and What Alice Found There.* It had been Oliver's favorite book when he was a little bit younger, but still . . .

Of course, almost everyone has read these wonderful books, which were written long ago by the great Charles Dodgson under the alias of Lewis Carroll, and which tell the story of a young girl named Alice, who enters a strange world underground, and then an even stranger one that she finds through the looking glass in her living room. Oliver's parents had given him a set of tapes of a fine actor reading the "Alice" books, and, often, he would listen to them at night in the darkness of his room. Oliver was an insomniac, and the combination of the strange, funny dialogue and the lulling sound of the reader's voice always helped him go to sleep.

"Why are you laughing, Oliver?" Mrs. Pearson asked him, standing in the twilight of the railroad station

"It's just, well, a children's book. I mean, I like it and everything but . . . I guess it's sort of relevant right now, isn't it?" he added diplomatically, seeing the look forming on Mrs. Pearson's face.

Mrs. Pearson held the book out, and Oliver took it, and, as he did, the book fell open to the first two illustrations by Sir John Tenniel, which show Alice pushing her way through the looking glass, and then her arriving on the other side.

Mrs. Pearson smiled as he gave the book back to her. She said, "This book was very important to my sisters and me when we were children. When I left to live in France, all that they would say to me was 'What's the French for fiddle-dee-dee?' which, as you recall, is what the Red Queen demands of Alice . . ."

"And Alice says 'Fiddle-dee-dee's not English!' and the Queen says, 'Whoever said it was?' I like that bit, too." Oliver finished for her. He thought for a moment. A strange but enticing suspicion was beginning to grow in his mind.

"Why did you come to live in France, Mrs. Pearson?" he asked.

Her eyes took on a faraway look. "Oh, I married a man" was all she said.

"But then why does it say 'LL' on your champagne spoon? Why not LP?"

"Because . . . Oliver, don't you know it's very rude to ask personal questions?"

Oliver felt a bit abashed. But then he remembered that that was a quote from *Alice*, too. Was she sending him a signal? Could it be that . . .

He thought that it would be a good idea to turn the subject back to *Alice*, but a thought was slowly growing in his mind. "I wish it were nice on the other side of the mirrors—funny, I mean, the way it is in the book."

"Nice?" Mrs. Pearson said. "Is it really so nice in the book? I wonder. If—" But then she broke off.

"What would it be like, to be on the other side of the mirrors?" Oliver persisted. "I suppose everything would be reversed, the way it is in *Alice*. Left would be right, and right would be left, just the way it is when you look in a mirror."

But Mrs. Pearson only looked at him, and then she said, "Yes. Turned right around, everything would be, wouldn't it?" Was she trying to tell him something?

Then she turned to walk back to her house on the little street called the rue Monsieur, over near the great golden dome of the Invalides.

Oliver and Charlie trudged home, with Oliver rehearsing the lies he would have to tell his mother about where he had been. What color were those fibs you told your mother about school, when really you were trying to save the world?

As they approached the boulevard, they heard a kind of whooshing, rushing sound. Charlie stopped, and his ears seemed to twitch with excitement.

"Skaters!" he said. "In-line skaters? In Paris?" he could hardly contain himself.

"Yes. They always come out in packs after dinner. They—" But before Oliver could finish his explanation, Charlie was dashing up the street toward the sound. Oliver looked after him, and thought of following him, but he was so tired and, well, he was pretty certain that Charlie could look after himself. He could probably even end up on skates himself even if he didn't have a word of French.

As Oliver came into the courtyard of his own home, he heard the lovely quiet crooning that he had always been so glad to hear. Neige—and she was singing again. Neige! He looked back down at his palm, where the lily was now only barely visible as a trace, a memory. Even Neige would be impressed by what he had done today, by all he had learned and said. Secretly, Oliver was a little disappointed that his new friends were not all that impressed by him.

"Neige," he said, and he began to explain to her, in a rush, about the mirrors and the window wraiths and the Master of Mirrors and his quest. "You see," he sighed. "We're searching for the mirror of Luc Gauric, Neige." He felt rather proud of his knowledge. She was staring up at him, even as she went on singing. She must be quite impressed, he thought, to stare like that.

He went on. "You see, Neige. It's this sort of old, old magical mirror that lets you enter a mysterious maze and . . ."

"I know what it is," Neige said calmly. "It's in my room."

Chapter Seven

Soul Samurai

OLIVER WAS too shocked to speak.

"In your room?" he repeated at last.

"You seem surprised. Why? Because I'm a girl? Because I'm the *gardienne's* daughter?" She was mocking him, he knew, and he felt himself turning red. "Oh, Oliver, for a king you look past more than you see into."

"I'm sorry, Neige," he said at last. "I just didn't think—" He paused. "How do you know I'm a king?"

"How do I know? How do I see it, you mean. I am a

crystallomancer. I see into glass, and use my crystal to fight the master." She reached inside her sweater once again, and pulled out a silver chain. At its end, Oliver saw, there glistened a crystal—a long, jagged, clear, and narrow rock. That must have been what she had used to make the mark on his hand. "But you looked right past us," she said almost angrily. "We were poor and servile and you never guessed."

Oliver sighed again at his own stupidity. "Can I see it, at least? The mirror, I mean?" he asked.

Neige looked back and forth in the courtyard. "Yes. Well, come in quickly. I'll show it to you. Since, for good or ill, you are the King in the Window. . . ." She shook her head with wonder.

Neige's room was hardly a room at all. It was simply the back part of the living room, with a curtain pulled in front, and a loft bed above for Neige to sleep in. All over there were glass and crystal balls. On the wall below her bed, Neige had pinned up photographs of strange, clear-eyed women.

"Who are they?" Oliver asked.

"Shhh. Portraits of crystallomancers," Neige said.

She opened the drawer underneath the loft bed, and pulled out something wrapped in a paisley shawl, like a gypsy's shawl. She carefully unwrapped it and handed it to Oliver.

"There," she said. "The mirror of Luc Gauric."

Oliver took it in his hands as though it were as fragile as a butterfly. In fact, it looked like a butterfly. It was the oddest-looking mirror that he had ever seen. Where most mirrors are flat plates of silvered glass, the mirror of Luc Gauric had two mirrors side by side, each one placed at a forty-degree angle, and facing each other, so that they formed a V like a butterfly as it closes its wings. But when Oliver looked carefully at it he saw that there was no dividing line between the two mirrors. They were a single swooping piece of silver. Oliver cautiously looked into it.

At first, Oliver was frightened to look into the mirror. But then he recalled that it was supposed to be a *true* mirror, so cautiously, he did. "It looks normal," he said, a bit disappointed. He looked again. "Only weird somehow . . ."

"Look again," said Neige. "The mirror on either wing cancels out the reversal of the other, and concentrates the image in the center. The image you see in it is a true one. . . ."

"This is one of the two true mirrors," Oliver said. He wanted Neige to know that he wasn't a complete idiot.

But she didn't seem impressed. "Yes, the wraiths of Versailles were supposed to protect this one, but when the master's slaves broke the old king, they forgot to watch it—" She sighed and shook her head. "Idiots," she hissed.

Oliver was rather shocked to hear his new friends and followers, the window wraiths, being spoken of so derisively.

"How did *you* get this mirror, Neige?" he asked. She didn't answer. Oliver looked again into the two-winged mirror. And this time he noticed that he did look strange. What was it? Something . . . oh, yes! The part in his hair was not on the right side! That is, it *was* on the right side—that is, on the left side where it really was, instead of being reversed as it would have been in a normal mirror. He raised his hand to touch his part.

"Oh, I see," he said. "This is a true mirror because it doesn't reverse things. My right side is still on the right side, and my left on my left. That's interesting, but everything else looks about the same as—"

Neige snatched the mirror away from his hand and quickly hid it under the bedclothes. Her mother, Madame Farrad, had just come into the kitchen, and was bending over her pots. She looked down, inhaled deeply the aromas rising from the stockpot, and then turned and stared hard at the children. Oliver looked at her and tried to nod in a friendly way.

She was as unsmiling as she always was. She turned back down to her pots.

Oliver saw Neige carefully reach down and disentangle the mirror from under her covers. She held it down low in front of Oliver. "Look again," she whispered. "Look at my mother's face in the mirror."

Oliver gazed again into the mirror of Luc Gauric. Over his shoulder, he saw the same scene: Neige's mother among her pots, grumbling as she cooked. But now, as he looked into the mirror, she stood and looked in his direction, and Oliver held up the mirror cautiously and watched her in the mirror of Luc Gauric as she moved behind his back.

And in the mirror, he saw that in the center of her forehead there was only a single enormous eye.

He looked again. Yes, she had no other feature: no

second eye, or nose, or even a mouth. Just one enormous staring eye.

He nearly dropped the mirror with shock. Neige took his hand.

"You see?" she whispered. "My mother is a catoptro-mancer, and she has stared in mirrors so long that they have taken from her every feature save one single eye. We can see it only in the Gauric mirror."

"Does everyone look like that in this mirror?"

"No. But everyone in the mirror of Luc Gauric has the face that they have made. It shows their soul-state without illusions."

Oliver quickly turned around and stole a glance at Neige's mother without the mirror. Yes, she looked normal, two-eyed, if ugly. Now he took the mirror again and held it up so that it reflected the scene behind him, and his heart once again skipped a beat as he stared into it. Only one grotesque eye in the center of her forehead!

Now Neige's mother was putting on her overcoat and scarf. "Neige!" she called out. "I am going to the butcher's. Mind the house." They heard the door open and close.

Neige looked around. "*Bien.* Quick. Give me the key. We must get it safe alongside the sword before the master finds out."

"Can the mirror show the, well, the state of everyone's soul?"

"Yes, of course." Neige hesitated. "You must understand . . . Come, quickly." She tucked the mirror under her coat. "While she's gone. Come, I will show you."

Together the two children went out the great doors to the courtyard, which made a sharp distinctive click as they exited. They were out on the little gray street, and a few moments later, in the midst of the pedestrians on the great wintry boulevard Saint-Germain.

"Look at the people all around you," said Neige, and Oliver did. It was the usual winter crowd at night on the boulevard Saint-Germain: elderly couples with small dogs in their winter coats, stern and elegant-looking women, a policeman in his uniform looking dour, even a mother pushing a baby to sleep in a carriage.

"Now, look," said Neige. Oliver looked down into the mirror of Luc Gauric. He gasped. The scene was the same— but the face of every walker on the street had been transformed. The elderly couple had a single mouth, shared between them, binding them together. The elegant woman had no mouth at all, and no nose, only two vast eyes staring out from her face. The policeman was one large enormous nose, and the mother and child—well, the mother had four eyes and the child four mouths! Everywhere he looked in the true mirror he saw reflected in it faces that looked like horrible cartoons.

"You see?" Neige said. "People missing eyes who have looked too long at themselves, people missing noses who are wine lovers. Some people, like the mother and baby, gaining new ones, but mostly people losing their faces. To find someone with a full face is passingly rare. So rare, Your Majesty."

"Have they all lost their souls?"

"You can't tell. Each feature they have lost weakens the tie of the soul inside. But souls gone for good? You can see *that* only on the other side of the mirrors."

Oliver felt, once again, how near he had always been to so many secret and horrible truths, without knowing it.

"Quick, we must hurry home before my mother knows the mirror is gone," Neige said.

He looked at her seriously. "Neige, I don't—I mean, why are you on my side? Your mother is a catoptromancer . . . I mean, why do you want to help me?" he added falteringly; and inside he thought, *She doesn't, really.*

"I told you. Because I am a crystallomancer. I let you see my crystal, because you *are* the king. I divine through glass and water, not mirrors and ice. You may have noticed that all the wraiths are men, and that they are all fools."

"Well, not all . . ." Oliver protested.

"Yes. All disorganized, confused, well-intentioned, talkative, pleasure-loving *fools.*"

"Well, no," Oliver protested. "Some of them are pretty clever . . ."

"They are fools," Neige repeated with disgust. "Those Whose Backs Were Turned, indeed. Those Whose Eyes Were Shut Tight is more like it. Thinking that *they* are the keepers of the window way; thinking that their protected little existence at the king's house is what keeps souls safe. If it were not for the crystallomancers, they would all have been broken long ago."

"It must be pretty weird," Oliver persisted. "Living in a house with someone on the other side."

Neige shrugged. "Well, not so weird. The usual mother-daughter business, really; one utterly evil, one completely good. Anyway, it's no weirder than your situation."

"What do you mean? My father's a nice man, and I get along great with my mom, if it weren't for having to catch up to her all the time," Oliver said. But Neige just stared at him and seemed about to say something, but then she didn't.

"Quick," she said. "I've been thinking. We must get the mirror safe to a hiding place. With those detectives hanging about, it isn't safe in my room anymore. Who knows which side the police are on?" She charged down the boulevard, walking away from the street they lived on.

"Where are we going, Neige?" Oliver asked.

"To the quarries," Neige said shortly. She led Oliver, looking around all the time, as they slipped down into the Paris metro. The Paris metro is a subway like any other, which stretches across the city, but it is very old, and was built so long ago that it feels cramped and cozy.

They got onto the last car of the silent metro. There was only an old clochard, spread out across three seats, snoring, but Oliver noticed that he had one eye half-open from time to time, as though sizing them up. It made him uneasy. Neige spent the whole ride clutching the well-wrapped mirror tight to her bosom, keeping it near to her crystal, as though that alone would make them safer. What if . . . At last, after a half hour, they arrived at the Clignancourt metro stop.

When they emerged into the black winter night, Neige took him by the hand, and led him down and away from the metro station. Now Oliver knew where they were going: to the Puces—the flea market of Saint-Ouen, a kind of maze of small shops selling old antiquities. His mother liked to go there. But he had certainly never been at night.

The lamps on the streets made small puddles of golden light in the winter mist.

Neige led him by the hand to a small rug shop at the very edge of the flea market, and knocked twice. The door opened from inside. They stepped in. But no one was there.

Neige fell to her knees and searched with her hands along the dusty floorboards. At last she seemed to find what she was looking for, and she pulled at something on the floor until Oliver heard a single decisive click. Neige pulled, and a trapdoor rose on a hinge from within the floor.

Oliver peered in. A ladder led downward into what seemed like perfect darkness. Oliver felt the cold air of a deep cavern around him. "Is it safe?" he asked. But Neige only snorted and began to descend. Oliver came after her.

He found himself in an immense, cool, low-ceilinged stone cavern, like a huge room lined with neat limestone boulders. Torches and flashlights flickered through the darkness.

The walls, Oliver could see, were hung with what looked like ancient, threadbare tapestries, showing strange scenes of war. The air was cold but surprisingly dry. Then, as Oliver's eyes adjusted, he saw a semicircle of grim look-ing men in long, torn overcoats and long beards and smudged faces staring at him. Clochards! Oliver shrank back. He recognized at once the clochard who had been out-side his school, the one on the bridge, and then even the one they had just seen on the metro that night—had Neige led him into a trap? Now the clochards were approaching him, grim and unsmiling. He turned to look wildly at Neige. Could she have betrayed him into these sinister hands? What a fool he had been for a king!

But now the oldest and grimiest of the clochards was approaching him with hand outstretched, and then, to Oliver's shock, he reached out, hugged him, and kissed him smackingly on both cheeks.

"All hail the King in the Window," he said gruffly. "We go on our knees to no man. But a new king deserves his trib-ute." He laughed.

"Who are you?" Oliver blubbered. "Why are you . . . ?"

"The clochards are your protectors," Neige answered firmly, and Oliver watched her, a small, neat, hooded figure striding confidently among the forbidding-looking men, and then settling in front of their half circle with her hands on her hips. "The crystallomancers and the clochards are the only *really* reliable people in this whole business," Neige said. "They have not let you out of their sight since that first night. I put the sign of the lily on your palm so that they would know who you are."

"But I thought . . . the clochards were just, you know, drunks."

"*That* is what you are *supposed* to think. The clochards of Paris are an ancient order, too, as old as the Wise or the Witty or the Wraiths for that matter, and far more efficient. They actually *work*. They work in alliance with the crystallomancers. Every year, the crystallomancers of Paris wander through the popular quarters, finding bright and determined lads who will devote themselves to the fight against the master and his soul-stealers.

"When they choose to join, on that day, they take a vow never again to look in a mirror. They are the bravest and most fetid of all the good orders—they *never* bathe or shave or change their clothes, so that they are never even tempted for a minute to look into a mirror. They have given up all thought about their appearance. If they looked in a mirror even once, they might damage their souls, and they refuse."

"Even once—?"

"Each time you look into a mirror, even for a moment, there is always the chance that the master will see you, and the sinews of your soul will weaken, however little." Now the clochard who had hugged Oliver was speaking, in a deep, well-soaked voice, the kind of voice that is produced by years of sleeping on steps outdoors and having only cognac to drink. "The clochards are the only men who *never* look, not once, and never allow themselves to be tempted. We are freer from his poison than any men alive. And we are the safest guardians of all treasures," he added meaningfully.

"They are the samurai of the soul wars," Neige concluded passionately. She smiled fondly at the leader, and fell to kiss his hand. "Incorruptible, if a bit malodorous. Good, but stinky. They have been protecting you since this business began."

"We have very strong souls, and very dirty faces," their leader laughed gruffly. "We avoid *all* temptations. No new clothes, no soap and water, no women to court—nothing that would ever tempt a man to wonder how he looks and go to see himself. Well, it's not so bad, is it, boys? Bah!"

"So I see. . . ." Oliver said, and then realized that it was the wrong thing to say.

" 'Twas I, Gilles the Uncorrupted, who put the homing stone of the king in your way to kick home. Bah," said one of the clochards, this one with a particularly long and matted beard, and then he, too, clutched Oliver by the shoulders and kissed him strongly on one cheek and then the other. The aroma was, well, a bit intense.

"And it was I who sneaked in before those ridiculous cops and brought your sword safe away!" another particularly smudged and filthy one announced, and from within the confines of his greatcoat he brought out the glass sword that Oliver had stolen from the Louvre!

"My sword! I mean, the sword," Oliver said in confusion. "I mean, wow. You took it that night."

The clochard with the sword nodded as he held the glass sword up to the flickering light. "Of course. We are always around, and always watching, and no one watches us, because they think we are merely drunk and lost. We are invisible men in a visible city."

Oliver, looking at his knee-length beard and tattered coat, suddenly realized that he had been the archer at the window.

"But I always thought that the clochards were, you know, homeless and miserable."

The clochards drew themselves up and seemed offended.

"Not us," said their leader at last. "We *care* for the truly homeless, for the drunken and poor and addicted and miserable of this sad city. We go among them, and they are our charges. When they are broken, we bring them here to the quarries." He jerked his head over at a dimly lit corner of the quarries.

Squinting his eyes, Oliver could see that there was a row of cots and blankets spread out, and on them were the real miserables of the city, sleeping peacefully under the watchful eye of the clochards.

The watchful eye . . . "Are you the forgotten Watchful ones?" Oliver blurted out.

But Gilles merely shook his head sadly. "No, Your Majesty. I wish that we were. We search for the true Watchful. But we are your servants, and the servants of all who fight the mirrors."

And so Oliver winced as, one by one, the clochards stepped forward toward him, and each one first seized him by the shoulders and then kissed him violently on either cheek.

"What do you mean you gave me the stone?" Oliver

said, when at last the procession of kisses were finished. "And where are we?"

"We are deep in the ancient quarries of Paris, where all the stone of the city comes from. It is the one safe place; not a single shiny surface." Oliver had heard of these limestone quarries often before—the other boys in his school would tell awestruck tales of the hidden wonders of the great Cavern X, the largest and oldest of them all—and knew that they were deeper even than the catacombs where tourists go. He had often wondered what they would be like.

"Why? Why did you want me to have the king's stone, and be mistaken for the king?" Oliver asked. But before the clochard could speak, Neige had already answered.

"*I* made you king, Oliver. When the Master of Mirrors' men broke the old king, they had one of the wraiths nearby, waiting to steal the key and the mirror."

"One of the wraiths!" Oliver cried.

Neige nodded grimly. "I'm afraid so. There's a spy there. But it was a dangerous time for them. The clochards and crystallomancers were watching, and even the younger wraiths, too, were out looking for their new king. So the spy passed the key to my mother in our *galette*, and delivered the mirror in the dead of night."

"But you took it from her?"

"She had it under her bed. As far as *she* knows, it's still there. The plan was for my mother to deliver both key and mirror to the master when he . . . when he . . ." Neige's voice faltered. "When he called her back inside."

"How do you know that?" Oliver asked.

"I can hear her talking to . . . them . . . in my crystal." She fondled the icicle of glass that hung around her throat. "Well, I wasn't worried." She brightened. "Unfortunately, the banal mix-up at the bakery meant that the key ended up in *your* hands. Of all people! I was frantic with worry, but then I considered it through that afternoon, and I thought, well . . . why not?"

"Why not!" Gilles's laughter echoed through the cavern. It made Oliver feel more than a little unkingly, to be laughed at in quite this way.

"Why not? Let the American boy be taken for the new King in the Window. It wasn't the best plan, but it was the only plan I could make. I had Gilles put the homing stone in your way outside your school—of course, I've watched you kick those pebbles home for years—and then I told my mother I had accidentally switched the cakes. And when I finally looked up that night and saw what was happening—"

"You in the window, she means, with the key and crown and François the wraith-messenger rising up to meet you," another clochard explained. "You see, I, Serge the Smelly, was there, too." So he had been the shadowy presence in the courtyard.

"I thought: well done again, Neige! The wraiths have their king, the key has a guardian, and the unfortunate lonely boy has something to do with himself," she added.

Oliver was stunned. It was a little bit shattering to find out that, instead of impressing Neige with his new kingship, she had actually arranged it, and that he had merely been her stooge.

"But if you have the true mirror then—then that means that the king, that I, can walk into the other side. Right?" he asked.

Neige shook her head impatiently. "No—not a bit of it. You need more than just the mirror. You need . . . Here. Come and look."

Neige led him over to the high stone wall where the ancient tapestries hung. "Serge, some light!" she called out. Serge began to walk toward them, drawing a flashlight from his cloak.

"No, no," she said. "Shine it from there. It's better." And she drew her crystal up into the light as Serge turned on the little flashlight.

The light, passing through Neige's crystal, seemed to focus and brighten a hundred times over. Now Oliver could make out clearly the faded images on the old tapestries. They were in the high, noble style of the Grand Siècle, and showed a figure, surrounded by awestruck followers, performing great deeds in high style. As his eyes adjusted to the light, he saw, with a thrill, that the central figure in the dim, woven scenes was a crowned youth—a boy, really—armed with a short glass sword, stabbing at a strange ghostly creature. The first King in the Window! It must be.

"There," Neige whispered. "These tapestries come from the oldest room at Versailles. The clochards saved them after the Revolution. They're priceless! They're the only record we have of the acts of the first King in the Window. There he is, enthroned with his four great possessions: the crown, the key, and the two true mirrors. And there you see him—holding his two great weapons, the wooden wand and the glass sword!"

But before Oliver could figure out how he fought with the wooden wand—a thing he was very curious about—Neige had dragged him over to the next tapestry. "Now, there—you see? There, he's bending down and rubbing some other shiny thing on the front of the true mirror. But what is it?" Oliver bent down to see what it was the king was using, but the tapestry was worn and threadbare in just that place.

He reached out to touch the tapestry, and, as he did, he noticed that tiny bits and shards of broken glass had adhered to its surface. He pulled his hand away. Now the tiny shards of glass were on his palm, too. He looked at them closely. They were colored—tiny bits of yellow and blue and red glass.

"It's clear, though," Neige went on. "The only way to use the mirror is to touch it first with something, some kind of mirror, I think. Now, look on the back of the true mirror."

She unwrapped it again, and carefully handed it to him. He turned it over. On its wooden back was carved, in an old-fashioned hand, the words *"Utilisez Uniquement la Glace Habitée. Perfection exigez."*

"'Only use a lived-in mirror,'" Oliver translated. "'Perfection demanded.' It must mean that you have to place a regular, reversing mirror of exactly the same size and shape as the true mirror above it to let you enter the other side. Don't you think?"

"We've tried that," Neige said. "It doesn't work. But there must be a way. If only we could understand . . ." She turned toward the leading clochard. "Serge, I need your help. I need you to keep this safe just until tomorrow night, when we will pass it back inside. To the other queen. It isn't safe with me now." She held out the mirror, wrapped in her shawl.

But all of the clochards stepped back uneasily.

"Please, ma'am. We can't," Serge said, his head down. "Even for you."

Neige stopped. "You mean even wrapped and bound? Even for a night? I told you, I'll take it to her tomorrow."

"Even if she were here herself. The temptation is too great for our legion. It would be like leaving a beautiful woman in a house full of monks. They might resist, but then . . . they might not . . ."

"But what can I—"

"Give it to me," the clochard called Gilles said suddenly. "Bah! I am not afraid. I have not washed or bathed or thought of looking at myself for two decades now. I am beyond temptation."

"Gilles! You are a filthy fellow after my own heart," Serge, the chief, said, looking at him fondly. "But there's none of us can't be tempted—"

"Not me. Not now. Not ever." said Gilles, and he spat on the stone floor, and held out his smudged hands for the wrapped true mirror. He put his thumbs in his hideously tattered overcoat and threw his head back proudly.

Neige looked uncertainly at Serge, but he merely shrugged, and so she handed the mirror to Gilles. "Keep it safe. I will be back for it tomorrow," she said, and she turned toward Oliver. "We will have to put it under the keeping of the old queen. Now, quick. Where are you keeping the key? Let's have it!"

"Uh—the key? You mean that little golden key? From the *galette*?"

"Yes. Of course. The key is the key to, well, *everything*. Give it to me, quick! . . . If he ever gets his hands on it, the master will be free!"

So that was the you-know-what! Oliver realized. The little key! But why did it matter so much?

"Quick. Where is it? They have the sword safe. They can keep the key safe, too."

Oliver paused. "Well, actually, Neige, this afternoon I gave it to Charlie." And he weakly described how he had given the key to Charlie in order to impress the wraiths.

"You gave the key to that other American boy. The dolt? The dimwit?" (Of course, Neige used the French terms, but they were even more insulting than these equivalents.) Neige was almost hissing at him, incredulously. "And the wraiths didn't stop you?"

"Molière said something about the key being important, but I assumed he meant, you know, as a symbol of kingship or something. And I guess he assumed that I knew what I was doing . . ." Oliver's voice faltered.

Now Neige merely sighed. But it was a long and deep and pained sigh.

"Hey, glass girl," Serge, the chief of the clochards, said. "This—let's be honest—this is a serious problem. He will kill for the sword. And he will kill for the crown. And he will kill for the mirror. But the One with None will do *anything* for the key." What could be worse than killing, Oliver wondered.

"I know, Serge . . ." Neige said weakly. "All right. Where did you leave him? The other American, I mean."

"He went Rollerblading. In-line skating. With the skaters."

"Well, then," Neige said, "you had better find him." She stared at Oliver and he started tentatively for the door. She sighed again. "Oh, all right. I'll come with you. And Serge, you and one of your best men come with to help us search. These Americans—you know, he's probably gliding somewhere on his skates in the sewers, with the ordure splashing up around his feet and one of those idiotic grins on his face." Neige sounded exasperated. Oliver thought that she was being unfair, to both Charlie and Americans generally, but, seeing as that he had lost the sword *and* the key, he could hardly say anything in return.

Before they could leave, the remaining clochards had to give a last ritual salute to their new king. Oliver steeled himself for the assault, and welcomed his new soldiers. At least, he reflected, grimacing as one by one the aromatic clochards came forward, took his shoulders, and kissed his cheeks, at least he couldn't any longer really call himself lonely.

Chapter Eight

Ice and Crystals

NEIGE AND Oliver and the two clochards raced across Paris, searching for Charlie among the skaters. Packs of in-line skaters fill the Paris streets at night, gliding from the column in the Bastille to the lion in the Place Denfert-Rochereau. Approaching midnight, the sound of the in-line skaters whooshing along the boulevards was so loud that it sounded like water—like a wave or flood washing through the city.

Neige and Oliver thought that they had found him on

the boulevard Montmartre—but it turned out to be merely another American boy in a Sharks jacket, who was pretty annoyed to be stopped.

Then they spotted a boy in a hockey jacket on the boulevard Montmartre—but it turned out to be a Romanian girl who had bought the jacket on her last visit to San Jose. It was apparently a popular jacket.

At last Oliver, worried and disappointed, stopped at a café on the boulevard Saint-Germain called Le Bizuth. He stepped inside, sat down at a table, and ordered them an Orangina. He rubbed his eyes. What a long day it had been, he thought. He noticed a crowd, a group of handsome-looking young women skaters. They were clustered around someone at the bar, laughing and giggling with delight as they listened to someone. It must be someone like Louis Legrand, he thought, someone who was sure of himself and fluent and, well, kingly. Not like him . . .

The crowd of girl skaters broke at last and headed, in one ensemble *swoosh*, for the door. The boy they had been crowding around had stayed at the bar to savor his drink. Oliver blinked. It was Charlie! Charlie, who had been surrounded by all the girls, completely accepted already and without a word of French.

"Charlie," Oliver cried. "Where's the key?"

"Whoa, Your Majesty," Charlie said. "How're the ghosts? Broken any good windows lately?"

"Charlie! The key! That little key I gave you this morning at Versailles. Do you still have it?" Oliver demanded urgently. Neige glared at Charlie as if she wanted to throw him, skates and all, under a taxi.

"Yeah, sure. It's in my pocket." Charlie said, and Oliver breathed a deep sigh of relief. "Why can't you get ice cubes in this town?" Charlie asked with annoyance. He had ordered a Coca-Cola, and apparently it had been brought to him at room temperature. This is the normal thing in Paris, but it was irksome to Charlie, as it is to most Americans who visit the city.

"I mean, this is warm," he went on, making a face.

"Des glaçons, Monsieur," Oliver said to the waiter, which means "ice cubes, sir." "Charlie, quick, give me the key," he repeated.

Charlie nodded, meaning, Let me just have a quick drink. The waiter brought a tall glass with precisely four ice cubes in it to Charlie Gronek, who dropped them into his drink carefully, one after another. They were small, rounded, hollow ice cubes, of the kind you find in France, nothing like those big, lazy American chunks. They hit the soda with what Oliver, in the back of his mind, thought was a strangely loud and clear fizz.

"Tastes weird," Charlie said, "Here, Ollie, have a sip, while I look for it. What's the big deal about it anyway?"

Oliver took a sip. It seemed fine to him, and he passed it back to Charlie.

"Well, you see—" he began, pausing, because he really wasn't sure *what* the big deal was about the key.

But then Neige cried out. "CHARLIE!" and Oliver started and looked up quickly.

At the zinc counter, Charlie Gronek was being sucked alive into his own ice.

His eyes were wide with terror, and his tongue was being pulled out like taffy, stuck tight to the topmost ice cube. As his tongue was tugged into the glass, it seemed to grow smaller, too, as though it were being seen through the wrong end of a telescope. Before Oliver could think, Charlie's chin and mouth followed his tongue into the glass: tapering horribly as they were pulled in, and then shrinking suddenly as they passed the rim. Now his whole head was being sucked inexorably in, his neck distending and then snapping into the ice cube like an elastic band. Then his whole torso suddenly seemed to elongate toward the suddenly boiling brown liquid.

Oliver cried out, and he and Serge reached out with both hands to pull his friend back from the suction of the glass. But no matter how hard they pulled, Charlie was still sucked inexorably into his Coke. Even as Neige pulled on the back of his shirt, his shoulders seemed to become toothpaste as they moved slowly, inch by inch, into the glass. Now, kneaded and misshapen, they were through, and, for a horrible moment, Oliver could see his friend's face trapped inside the next, lower ice cube, while his shoulders and sweater were inside the upper one, as he was pulled down into the ice. For a horrible moment Charlie was held head first, almost perfectly perpendicular, with his sneakers dangling helplessly above the glass, like a sinking ship about to go down. Now, as Charlie struggled to escape, his middle body stuck, like a tree planted in a vase too small for it. Then, with a sudden loud crack, the rest of his body went through, and his legs slipped out of Oliver's grasping clutching hands, into the glass. Neige let out a scream, and Oliver fell toward the counter in despair.

Breathing hard, furious and scared, Oliver picked up the glass into which Charlie had disappeared, and stared into it. For a horrible moment, he thought that he could see a tiny Charlie, hardly more than a wriggling pinprick of blue and black color at the very center of the ice cube, with two other clear cubes above and below.

Glace habitée. So that's what it meant. It wasn't a lived-in mirror at all that they had to find . . . that wasn't it at all.

It was *living ice.*

And it was living ice that might yet open the back door of the true mirror.

"Quick," he said to Neige and Serge, picking up the glass and clutching it to him. "They don't know it, but it's our chance. Neige, if we apply the living ice to the Gauric mirror, we can follow Charlie into the other side," Oliver said excitedly.

But Neige was white. "They wouldn't have done this if they thought we still had the Gauric mirror safe. It would be too dangerous for them. They must have—broken it."

"How could they? We left it with the clochards only a moment ago," Oliver said quickly.

"Back to the quarries. Quick!"

"But that's all the way on the other side of Paris! You'll never get there before the ice melts," Serge said.

Oliver simply snatched the silk scarf that Neige wore around her throat, wrapped the ice cubes in it, and rushed out of the café and into the street. The waiter held out a hand to hold him as he brushed by, but Oliver did not stop. Together, the boy and girl rushed out into the street.

"Tell all the others that the key is missing!" Neige cried to the two clochards.

Oliver held his hand out for a taxi. He had always been timid about hailing a taxi in the middle of the street. In Paris, the normal thing is to line up in an orderly and logical way at a taxi station on a corner. But now he had no choice, and he found himself planted in the middle of the boulevard, putting his body almost directly in front of an oncoming taxi.

"*Arrête,*" he cried—"Stop!"—and the driver did. Oliver was amazed—he had stopped! He was beginning to suspect that kingship was in part a matter of believing that you were one. He opened the back door and pulled Neige in beside him.

"Go to the Saint-Ouen flea market," he said, "and drive as fast as you can."

The driver shrugged and made a French face. "Did you want me to be arrested, my child?" he began, but Oliver looked him square in the eye and said, "Drive. I said, *drive.*" And, a little bit to Oliver's shock, the driver actually shut up and drove.

Oliver could just feel, beneath the layers of silk in Neige's handkerchief, the four little lumps of ice—but the handkerchief was already growing damp, and then still damper. Quickly, Oliver rolled down the window to let more cold air from the gray winter night into the cab.

So that was it, he thought. There was nothing to do but try to get to the true mirror before the living ice melted.

Then, as they came out of the tunnel at the Châtelet, into the traffic on the boulevard du Temple, Oliver heard it— a police siren, making the two-note up and down sound of all French police sirens. He drew a breath. Maybe it was just an ambulance, taking someone to the hospital . . . but it drew relentlessly closer and closer. No, there was no doubt—they were pulling over the taxi that Oliver and Neige had taken.

Now, two men were getting out of the car behind them. The blue light from the top of their black car swept through the dark Paris night. Oliver recognized them at once. The detectives! They must have been watching him and thought he was on his way to where the glass sword was hidden.

"Any plan, Your Majesty?" Neige asked.

Oliver stared out of the window at the approaching detectives, and then back at the handkerchief in his hand. What *was* he going to do? He had to think. What to do?

"Well, I have one," Neige said calmly. "Go when I go." And she quickly pushed open the door of the taxi, fell to the ground, and rose again to stand upright, only now holding her crystal up toward the blue light.

The flashing blue light on the roof of the black car caught in Neige's crystal like sunlight in a prism, and seemed to flash right out across the night sky, illuminating the dark cobblestone street like a flare, and blinding the two policemen. They threw their hands up to protect their eyes from the sudden blaze of light, and as they did Oliver spilled out of the taxi on the other side and raced around to take Neige's hand. She pulled him down a small alley on the other side of the car.

"My fare!" the taxi driver shouted after the two children, but they were gone. Oliver quickly looked back, and saw that the two detectives were already recovering. They had on dark glasses, Oliver saw, as though they were ready to protect themselves against the light. Now they were back in their car, and Oliver heard the motor race and the car quickly turned down the alley after them.

Neige pulled him along the alley, where an old clochard seemed to be sound asleep at one end. As their footsteps approached him, Oliver was stunned to see him quickly rise to his feet, nod to Neige, and plant his great bulk directly in front of the oncoming car. The car squealed to a stop inches short of his unmoving beard.

Neige kept her hold on Oliver's hand, and tore around into the next street. Oliver saw that they were on the edge of the Place de Clichy, one of the great and usually crowded squares of Paris. The lights of the brasseries and hotels were still on, and their signs cast orange light on the dark pavement. Oliver was so startled to see where he was that he didn't see the chestnut roaster directly in front of him. In the great squares of Paris in winter there are chestnut roasters. They wear navy blue sweatshirts and roast their chestnuts on what look like overturned tin drums. A fire burns at the center, and the roaster keeps the chestnuts scattered around the rim, roasting without burning all through the night.

As Oliver turned the corner, he tripped over a chestnut roaster in the Place de Clichy, and as he stumbled forward, the handkerchief leaped out of his hand onto the red-hot brazier.

"Oliver!" Neige cried now, pointing at his hand.

Without stopping to think, he pulled himself onto his knee and, without looking, desperately reached back up onto the surface. His hand came down on the brazier, and the burn was so intense that for a moment it felt cold, then shocking, then seared his hand, and shot with pain like electricity up his arm. But he reached out again, and found the wet parcel, and grabbed it to him. His hand was already throbbing with pain. The knotted handkerchief was wet, and he clutched it desperately—and felt four little nubs of hardness inside, all that remained of the ice, but still there. On his palm, he saw quickly, the king's mark that Neige had put there days before now glowed brightly, as though alive.

He looked down. He saw that the ice was melting right through the handkerchief, and beginning to drip down onto the sidewalk.

Frantically, Oliver looked around. Then he had an inspiration. The only thing that could keep the ice cold was more ice. He dashed up the boulevard, searching for what he knew had to be there, an *ecalier des fruits de mer*—a seafood stall. Like many of the brasseries of Paris, the great brasserie Wepler's kept a stall of fresh seafood on the street, to seduce clients into coming inside to dine, even after midnight. Guarded by a very cold-looking Portuguese man in an apron, stamping his feet, the seafood—the pink-and-white langoustines and the tiny little clams and the small gray shrimp—was displayed up above on a tilted metal shelf, with ice below and lemons lining it, for decoration. Dark cedar baskets of oysters fronted the seafood stalls, plump with the glistening shells.

Standing in front of the red-faced oysterman, Oliver gasped for breath. "Ice, sir, I'd like to buy some ice."

The red-faced man looked at him suspiciously.

"Go away," he said, turning back to commune with his bushels of oysters. "I don't sell ice."

"I just need ice. I'll pay anything," Oliver insisted.

The oysterman looked back over his shoulder disdainfully. "Go away. Do I resemble an iceman? I don't sell ice," he repeated.

Oliver was ready to fall to his knees in tears.

"Oysters, we want to buy oysters." said Neige, catching up with Oliver, even more out of breath than he was.

Reluctantly, turning around slowly—even a Parisian oysterman can't absolutely refuse to sell oysters to a willing oyster buyer—he stared down at her. "What kind?" he said. "You're too young for oysters. Anyway, I have orders to fill for the clients."

"*Lots* of oysters. A dozen *plats*," said Oliver, blessing his father for having taught him how to order.

Reluctantly—it was too large an order to sneer away—

the oysterman turned back toward his bushels, and began to pick out the oysters. After he had twelve laid out in front of him, he gave the children half a loaf of bread. You are always given bread with oysters in Paris. Then he reached down with his knife to open them.

"No, we want to take them out," Neige said. "Don't open them." The oysterman raised his eyebrows.

"Now, give us . . ." Oliver began, and his hand itself was beginning to become damp from the melting *glace habitée* in Neige's scarf. Neige shot him a look as sharp as a dagger, and threw her chin in the direction of a café across the street. He looked over his shoulder. Yes, the two detectives were back— searching the grand café, going from table to table.

But then Neige shot him another, calmer look. She knew that everything depended on being offhand.

Swallowing hard, she said, "We have to take them home to my father. Oh, and he insists on shaved ice to keep them cold."

The oysterman paused. Oliver, from long experience, knew what was going on in his head. If he insisted now that he didn't sell ice, he wouldn't simply be asserting his superiority over a couple of children. He would actually be insulting Neige's father's system of oyster-management, even though he didn't actually know Neige's father (and even though Neige's father didn't, in fact, like oysters, because she didn't have a father).

It was irresistible. At last, the oysterman, grumbling to himself, inserted his shovel into the packed crushed ice, and reluctantly held a scoop of ice out to them.

"I don't have plastic bags," he added quickly. "This isn't a hardware store."

Quickly, Neige tore the scarf from around Oliver's throat, and held it out to him. He dumped the ice inside. She quickly handed it to Oliver. He held it tight. It felt blessedly cold, stinging his burned hand. He wrapped the ice inside it even tighter, and then placed it like a cushion around the melting ice in the scarf. *Having to buy ice to keep ice cold—now that was an irony.*

With his other hand, he emptied out his pockets of all the euros and change he could find inside and tossed it at the oysterman, praying that it would be enough. Not waiting to find out, they turned and raced away toward the metro entrance, in the very center of the square.

Neige and Oliver pushed through the traffic, dodging cars, Neige holding the Styrofoam plate of oysters in front of them, Oliver clutching the little double-wrapped package of plain ice, with its precious little cargo of inhabited ice inside. His other hand still felt scorched, but for the moment he prayed that ice and adrenaline would keep him going. The sound of their running footsteps could be heard right across the square in the quiet of midnight—and, sure enough, the two detectives looking around unhappily across the street heard them, and now were running after them.

"I can't run with this," Neige gasped, as they arrived, horns blazing behind them, on the central island of the Place de Clichy. She nodded with her chin at the Styrofoam platter the oysters rested on.

"Just leave it . . ." Oliver was saying. Then he noticed a Parisian *gendarme,* a police officer, staring down at them from a few feet away.

Without thinking, Oliver began to stuff the oysters into his jacket pockets, until they bulged, and then he picked up the five remaining oysters, and, unable to think of another method, slipped them under the top of his wool toque, the pointy French hat Charlie always made fun of, where they snuggled uncomfortably on top of his head.

For one horrible moment, the policeman stepped in front of him, obviously trying to recall whether there might be an obscure law forbidding those under the age of eighteen from transporting concealed shellfish on a public conveyance. But, unable to bring it immediately to mind, he sighed, and stepped aside. Oliver and Neige dashed down the stairs.

As he passed through the turnstiles, Oliver was sure that he could hear footsteps coming after him. They rushed into the tube-shaped metro station. There! The last train was waiting for them—and they ran inside the doors. As the train began to pull away, Oliver saw the two detectives, in their raincoats and mustaches, racing down the steps. But they were safe, the doors had shut, and Oliver and Neige, cringing together on the seat, drew a breath. The last thing Oliver saw as the metro pulled from the station were the faces of the two detectives, and he saw that the sunglasses they were wearing had mirrors for lenses, reflecting the station around them.

The train pulled at last into the Clignancourt stop, and

Oliver and Neige ran toward the little carpet shop where they had begun the evening's adventure—only now they were running, racing desperately down the streets toward it. Out in the cold night, running down, down, the winding *alles,* trying desperately to remember the right path. Oliver kept expecting to hear the sound of the detective's car, or the hard steps of their running feet. But he and Neige seemed to be utterly alone; perhaps the two men hadn't known what stop they were going to or . . . There—yes, there it was.

And then they were inside—on his knees, sobbing, was Gilles, the clochard without vanity who had promised to keep the mirror safe.

He looked up, saw them, and looked away, terrified.

"I had to look. . . . I had to try it," they heard him muttering. "And he saw me. He tempted me. He said that I could see my mother in the mirror if I only looked again. And when I looked again, the American was behind me, and he grabbed the mirror from me—"

Oliver and Neige stared into the little shop.

"He took it from me—and he smashed it. I grabbed the pieces from him when he went to flee, but that is all I have." Now Gilles was weeping. "I have only the shards left."

"Did those detectives do this?" Oliver asked.

Neige shook her head. "No. They could not have got here in time. He sent one of his slaves. He knows each man's weakness, and what he dreams of seeing in the mirror," Neige said, almost to herself. "Even Gilles. He saw

Gilles, saw where the mirror was, and sent one of his human slaves to smash it. Another American, it seems."

"There's nothing we can do now," Oliver said glumly, looking at the horrible shattered shards of the one true mirror that Gilles was weeping over.

"No, Oliver," Neige said wildly, "we still have to try."

"Try what?" he said despairingly. He looked around. "There's nothing to be done," he said. "It's broken. Remember it said, 'Perfection Demanded?'"

"A perfect fragment might still work," Neige said. "We have to try!" she cried, and she grabbed the handkerchief from his hand.

Kneeling, she discarded the outer cloth full of the oysterman's ice, and then carefully unwrapped the inner core. Four tiny, jagged little nubs of ice were still whole. Quickly, she picked out five or six especially tiny mirror shards, and lay them alongside the ice.

"He may have outwitted himself," she muttered. "He is clever, but he is not wise, Oliver. The slave he sent may have been told that we had living ice that fit the mirror, and must have thought our ice was smooth and large—a block. So he smashed them so that the ice wouldn't fit. They might not have known that the living ice that we have would *only* fit a fragment of the true mirror. . . ."

Oliver saw what she was after, and he, too, began frantically to search the broken shards for possible matches. In a half minute they had ten.

"This one's close," Oliver said urgently, picking up one

jagged fragment. He pressed it against the ice. Nothing.

"Perfection is a process," Neige said calmly. "Watch."

From deep inside her sweater she once again withdrew the long chain and the little prism. She looked over her shoulder, searching for something.

"It's so dark," she said at last, desperately. "Damn the winter here . . . no light at all—but there! One ray is all I need."

Through the dark winter, a single pale beam of moonlight entered the little rug shop and danced across the broken mirrors.

Neige turned to position herself out of the little beam. Then she placed the broken mirror right in its way, and raised her crystal above it.

The single faint beam of moonlight was caught in the lens and, as it emerged, became a bright and burning ray—the quiet moonlight was now white and hot and cutting.

"Yes, yes, we can," Neige said. "We can't cut the ice. But we can trim the mirror."

Carefully, she traced the edges of the mirror with the white-hot beam of crystallized moonlight. In astonishment, Oliver watched them burn away. He had seen boys burn paper with magnifying glasses, of course, in the summer in America. But he had never imagined someone burning away the edges of a mirror with moonlight. . . .

"You're good at this," he said encouragingly.

"Never done it before in my life," she said. "But I've heard about it from my mother." Carefully, exquisitely, painfully, she etched away the edges of the shard of mirror, following the lines of the ice with her eyes, trying to make them match, keeping the single beam of faint moonlight centered precisely in her crystal.

Then Oliver heard them. The unmistakable, relentless running footsteps of the detectives. They were approaching the little shop. They couldn't be more than a half block away.

"Hurry!" he said to Neige. The steps thundered down on them.

"There," she said at last. "A perfect fit."

Without a pause, Neige reached down and placed the ice upon the mirror. Immediately, the shard of broken mirror began to glow, as if from inside, like a diamond, and then to smoke. For a moment it seemed to be made of gauze, of silk, like a veil, waving, beckoning them in.

"It's too small to enter," Oliver said fearfully.

"It seems to adjust to fit you. Remember Charlie?" she said. Oliver shuddered. Drawing a deep breath, she placed her finger on the little wet sandwich of ice and glass.

At first nothing. And then her finger elongated, looking beautifully elegant at first, then grotesquely distended, and then the perfectly matched ice and glass fragment began to pull her inside. Quickly she was sucked in, but she didn't cry out, only smiled, with a desperate act of courage, and beckoned Oliver on with her other hand, holding it out for him to take.

Now the bright light of the detectives' powerful flashlights were illuminating the little shop, turning it into a harsh white glare.

"Stop!" cried one dark and guttural voice.

Oliver shut his eyes and grabbed her hand, and began to feel himself being stretched taut and pulled, as though by a tide, into the tiny sandwich of ice and mirror. Once, as a boy, he had been caught, terrified, in an undertow on the beach when he was with his parents on an ocean holiday in America. This was like that, he thought in one frightened moment, only ten times stronger, and he could not even see a horizon, or his parents on the beach.

Now his wrist, his forearm, his elbow were inside—now they were both inside. Now the shoulders, how much farther would they go? It was like being born, but the wrong way round, he thought. The suction drew him deep deep down, as he and Neige were sucked inside—like water racing around a sink, and then being pulled down a drain. In ten seconds, they were gone, vanished into the little wet scrap of mirror and ice.

As they pushed through the ice, Oliver could see nothing but darkness. But then he felt his body begin to swell, and expand, returning to its natural shape and size, only with every nerve and fiber in his body somehow newly awake, and stirring. He opened his eyes and looked around. Neige's hand was still firm in his. He looked at her. Her eyes were opening, too. They were safe, but, as they looked around, he knew where they were.

Oliver and Neige were alone, and on the other side of the mirrors.

Chapter Nine

In the Mirror-Maze

THEY WERE lying in a long corridor, with great picture windows on either side.

It looked a bit like one of the galleries in the Louvre, Oliver thought, as he rose to his feet. He looked down, and saw that the floor was made of wooden parquet, laid in a herringbone pattern. It felt oddly light and springy.

The only light came from the windows, which weren't really windows, Oliver slowly realized—more like big glowing television screens or tapestries. He looked up at them. Each one showed a giant human face, staring directly out, doing nothing. It was like being in a hall of giant television screens, each one broadcasting a single moving face.

Oliver looked down at his hand in the light of the glowing screens. Things looked sharper, clearer, *wirier* here than they were in the real world. Oliver looked at Neige's hand, too, as she got first to her knees and then slowly rose to brush off her clothes and take his hand. Even in the dim light, there was detail, but too much detail. It was like looking at things in a giant magnifying mirror, where every pore and abrasion on your skin suddenly comes forward.

One of the faces now seemed to look directly at Oliver, and then he raised a hand. It was a man's face—a middle-aged man, looking weary, and bearded and . . . empty somehow. Oliver thought that the giant was watching them, threatening them as he raised his hand, and he pushed Neige back against the far wall into the darkness.

He can't see us, Oliver then realized, with relief, as he saw the giant look right past them. What *were* these faces, he wondered, gods or watchers or knights . . . ?

But then he saw that all the giant held in his hand was a can of . . . a can of *shaving cream*. He pressed the nozzle and applied the cream to his face. Then he brought up a razor and began to shave.

"It's a bathroom mirror! It's just the other side of a bathroom mirror. Only it's magnified twenty times," Oliver whispered to Neige. "They're *all* mirrors," Neige whispered back. "They must be the backs of every mirror in the world."

Oliver looked down the endless corridor and realized that Neige was right. All of the giant faces belonged to people peering into mirrors, immensely magnified, and unaware that they were being watched. As his eyes adjusted to the scale and to the faces, he saw that they came from all over the world. There were Indian women placing single dots on their foreheads; American women applying lipstick; African men adjusting their tunics, and Englishmen adjusting their bow ties. Over there was what looked like a clown, unsmiling, applying his white makeup—Oliver could sense the bright pulse of the naked lightbulbs on the dressing room mirror—and then there was a sad, rich-looking woman adjusting her tiara, as though about to go out to a ball.

Every mirror in the world opened onto these corridors, Oliver thought, no matter where it is! No matter how small or how unimportant, he realized, one side of every mirror looks at you . . . and the other side of it faces onto this dark corridor.

Then, as they looked up at the unseeing faces, Oliver and Neige found that they were being *pulled* along the corridors, gently but firmly, as though by a giant magnet. As soon as they began to use their feet, they were pushed or pulled, moved along, and always in one direction, down the corridor of mirrors. No matter how they struggled, their feet would move—slide, really—only in one direction. Oliver stopped walking and found that he could stand still for a moment—but he couldn't reverse the way he was going. It was as if they were on an invisible conveyor belt, pulling them inexorably toward some unseen destination.

Oliver's throat was dry, but he wanted to say something to Neige.

"Neige," he said, "do you realize where we are? Do you see what *they* are? Why, they're . . ."

"Yes, of course!" Neige whispered. "Don't make a sound! We're on the other side. Just watch!"

Even if it had been safe to speak, Oliver would soon have been unable to. He was too startled, and shocked, by everything he saw around him. So he and Neige simply passed down the corridor, silent and looking up.

Oliver was spellbound by the gallery of giant heads looking past them as they glided by. It was like being on some horrible ride in the haunted house in some terrible amusement park. They could see great new corridors, just like those in the Louvre, radiating from their own at strange angles as Oliver and Neige surfed helplessly past. But all the corridors were filled with huge human faces, their lips moving silently, their faces often staring down, their brows tensed—the other sides of all the mirrors in the world. Women applied makeup, men shaved, children brushed their teeth, or just stared ahead. One man was staring straight ahead into the mirror, rubbing his chin, drawing closer and closer to the mirror's surface. His face looked bored, unhappy, and then his eyes seemed to slide away from his own attention, and he looked blankly, neutrally, into the mirror.

At that very moment, something sprang from the darkness and slithered right up the face of the giant image, the backside of the mirror. Oliver suppressed a cry and he and Neige stood still in the shadows, feeling their feet tugging them down the hallway, but managing to hold on to the edge of one of the mirror frames to stay still.

In the slowing light that radiated from the mirror-image, Oliver could see that the beast, whatever it was, had long flippers in place of hands and arms, which he used like suction cups to mount the mirror. Using some kind of sticky web that he sprayed from one flipper, the strange, seal-like creature quickly drew a map of lines around the unhappy man's enormous face.

The pattern of lines all centered on a space just between the sad man's eyes, a space that was quickly outlined with a black circle—a bull's-eye! Then the creature turned its face, and Oliver saw that it had two long and sharpened tusks, spotted with blood; slowly, almost delicately, the creature tapped with a needle-sharp tusk against the circle it had drawn between the staring man's eyes.

Almost instantly, two lines of thin gray thread seemed to shoot from the other side of the corridor, and then a silver spike at the end of the two lines, like a harpoon, struck between the man's eyes, although he seemed not to feel its presence.

Now, from the shadows, not far from where they were hiding, a second creature emerged; Oliver and Neige pressed themselves harder against the wall. The new specter was clean-shaven, and ugly, and he wore a small white hat and a long apron, like a butcher's. He pulled, with a horrible grunt, on the two lines that extended from inside his victim's skull, wound them tight, and guided something down from within the man's forehead. It slid down the rope into the watcher's gloved hands. It was a round object, wet and gray and rimmed with blood, and with what seemed like an emerald glowing at its center. He held it up and tossed it, chuckling, into a kind of dark black velvet-covered box.

Oliver squinted. What could it have been? What could it be?

Then he saw the duo emerge into the center of the corridor, holding their trophy. Instead of floating, like the window wraiths, they seemed to glide down the dark corridor, a bare six inches above the floor. Oliver soon heard a kind of *whoosh* echoing down the empty corridors, and a second team appeared. Another "seal" and another "butcher," as Oliver now thought of them, one like a hideous flapping, tusked sea-creature, only talkative, and his partner, the harpooner, in a strange white apron. Each team held a dark box.

Oliver and Neige clung harder to the edges of the frame to keep from being pulled forward, praying not to be seen.

"How was the hunting?" the second seal asked.

"Not too good," said the butcher from the first team.

"Vanity is not enough," his companion added. "Two I've been working on gave way at last. But the Americans are giving us less and less."

"I had the French government corridors, and then some offices in New York," said the other butcher. "I did well. Sixty souls." He held up his little velvet-covered box.

"He will not be pleased," said the first seal. "We need to increase the numbers. He keeps saying that so many are needed."

"Then work must be done on the other side."

Neige poked Oliver sharply. Now, she spoke. "We'll have to follow them," she whispered to Oliver insistently. "They must have Charlie."

"Listen," said the first seal. "There is a report from the eighteenth corridor. Strangers may have entered the maze."

"Where?" the second seal demanded. "They came in through the ice, too?"

"No, worse. They found the old back door that should have been destroyed last night by one of the Outsiders. They were driven in though. The master felt them enter. Still they must be caught, have their souls stripped out, and sent back out. Tonight is the night, remember. The One with None has promised to show himself at last!"

"Quiet!" growled the other butcher. "You know better than to call him that! He hates it! It must never be used."

And then they were gone, gliding down along their corridor.

Oliver didn't know what to do. He held on to the edge of the mirror frame, to keep from being swept down the corridor. It was like trying to hold on in a very high, invisible wind.

Then Oliver thought again of why they had come. He thought of Charlie, alone and captive in this maze of mirrors.

"Well," Oliver said at last, turning his face toward Neige, and speaking for what felt like the first time in his life with complete firmness. "We have to press on, whatever else happens, and find Charlie."

Somehow the thought of his friend in captivity, instead of making him more afraid, made him feel much less afraid. Using his mind to decide to do something, he found, released him from his fears. Making a plan to do something dangerous made him feel safer than waiting for something dangerous to happen. He had to follow the soul-stealers and find Charlie Gronek.

"But we can't control which we way we go," Neige whispered to him again. "If we allow ourselves to be swept away by this . . . force . . . I can't figure out how we will ever get out again."

"Well, I suppose wherever . . . this . . . moving walkway or whatever it is, is going is to the place where whatever is going to happen is going to happen," Oliver said, after a pause. "So if we just let ourselves be taken wherever it's going, we should find out . . . whatever it is."

"Well, there's no denying that," Neige said, and her eyes flashed as they did so often when she was exasperated with Oliver. "Is that the best plan you can make? We should just let ourselves be pulled along like luggage on a conveyor belt?"

Oliver was annoyed. "Now, listen," he whispered fiercely. "You heard what they said about the Outsiders coming in for a council of war? The Outsiders must be people, people whose, well"—he found his voice faltering—"people whose souls they've taken. If we can mix among them, maybe we can slip into the castle, or dungeon, or lair, or whatever it is at the center of this maze, and find Charlie, if he's there. Do you have a better plan?"

Her bright eyes softened just a touch.

But "No, I don't have any better plan," was all she said, and she took his hand, and together they let go and found themselves beginning to glide inexorably down the corridor, neither one knowing where they were going or where they would end up.

Whatever it was that was pulling them along, Oliver was starting to think of as a slow but irresistible natural force, as *the flow*. By holding on to the handrails and edges they could halt it for a moment or two. But then the flow would still pull at them irresistibly and they would find themselves flowing back along the corridor. It was as if space itself, on this side of the mirrors, moved only in one direction, and pulled you along with it.

For at least an hour, they slipped noiselessly along the walls and tried to stay in the shadowy recesses of the Mirror-Maze, pulled forward down the corridors and around corners, relentlessly, by this flow. In the frames all around them, the giant faces went about their mundane business of cleaning and wiping and brushing and just looking, never knowing that only millimeters away an army of black knights, soul-stealers, were keeping watch for a moment of weakness, like whalers scanning the oceans for their giant prey.

"How do you think they know when a soul is ready to be taken?" Oliver whispered to Neige as they surfed past. They looked up and saw an Asian woman, staring intently down into a blue glow.

Neige didn't answer at first. "I think it's the eyes," she said at last. "I think it must be the light in their eyes—"

But even as she said the words, a strange sound began to fill the hall—a deep, thrumming drumbeat, filling the corridors with its trembling vibration.

Then, as the drumbeat grew louder, some of the faces at the mirror seemed to push forward as though butting with their heads right through the mirrors into the space where Oliver and Neige were standing. There was no sound of breaking glass, though. Instead, the heads seemed to push through the mirrors as though the mirrors were mist, and then the heads, as they emerged on the other side—Oliver's side—as he watched in horror, were once again normal-sized. Then the hands of the soulless ones pushed through, and then their bodies, elongating like taffy as they were pulled through, and then they were there, right in front of him. Hard objects seemed, well, squishy and mutable here in the maze, he thought. People changed sizes, became fluid in shape, as they slipped in and out of the mirrors just as he and Neige had when they broke through the membrane of ice and mirror.

These were the Outsiders, Oliver thought, as he and Neige held on to the rail along the wall. One by one, as if by instinct, the new arrivals coalesced into chevron-shaped squads of eleven members, and, like Oliver and Neige, seemed to be pulled toward some destination at the center of the maze.

Oliver turned to whisper to Neige as he studied the faces of the Soulless. They were from every part of the world, solemn and stricken faces from Europe and Africa and Asia. But, Oliver was sure of this, there were no children among them. There were even faces that he recognized. There was Madame Sonia! His teacher was marching forward like a listless zombie. That was why she had warned him. . . . But something he saw as he looked back and forth from Madame Sonia to Neige shocked him.

"Oh, Neige," he almost cried out. Then he stopped himself and whispered. "Your eyes!"

He had been looking at Madame Sonia and the rest of the Soulless Ones and he realized what had been so strange about Madame Sonia's face—could it have been only four days ago that she had tried to warn him? Her eyes were dead and flat, *all* of their eyes were dead and flat as blackboards. Neige's eyes, always so quick to brighten and flash in anger or mischief, by comparison seemed so bright that they looked like shining flashlights in a midnight alley.

Neige and Oliver followed in the darkness of the shadows as the phalanxes of Outsiders marched dolefully through the corridors, and as they marched they were joined and bordered by strange legions of drummers, dressed like knights of the Grand Siècle, with sharp pointed helmets, and bearing snare drums nearly as large as their lower bodies.

They beat a steady rhythm as they drove the legions of the Soulless forward. The deep thudding heartbeat persisted and seemed to shake the walls around them.

At last, Oliver and Neige came to a series of high stone doors, placed in a semicircle, which seemed to open onto some kind of hall or cavern. Oliver could feel an ice-cold wind blowing from inside it into the corridor.

Now a great voice began to resonate in the halls, above the sound of the beating drum.

"You have answered the assembly," the deep voice said, "and you are here. The great day has arrived. Tonight the crystal-gazers join us. Tonight you will see the Master of Mirrors and Lord of Ice as he really is, at last."

"Crystal-gazers?" Oliver whispered to Neige. "But you're a crystal-gazer!" Suddenly fear crept over Oliver like a cold wave. What if Neige was . . .

But Neige frowned and furrowed her brow. "Crystal-gazers? No crystallomancer would ever join the One with None."

Then Oliver and Neige stopped whispering, for twelve leaders had stepped forward from the twelve phalanxes that waited by the gates. The leader of the phalanx that Oliver was following stepped forward and turned to address the captives behind him.

As he did, Oliver's heart stopped, and tears rushed into his eyes. For he was looking into the soulless eyes and face of his own father.

Chapter Ten

The Master of Mirrors

WHEN TERRIBLE things happen to us in life, on either side of the mirrors, our first thoughts are to get our balance back by thinking of something trivial that is just to one side of the real tragedy. And so now Oliver, seeing his father in this procession of the Soulless, thought first of mirrors. My father never looks in mirrors, he thought to himself. He never even adjusts his *tie*. It's always off to one side, when he wears one. He never looks in mirrors. He seems to spend all day, every day, working.

And only then did the real pain of it strike him, not in the head but in that place just below the heart, where the worst pains of life strike us. However it had happened, it was true, as true as anything else he was experiencing in this waking nightmare. His father! His father enslaved in this dark nighttime procession on the other side of the mirrors. Soulless and entrapped! Could his soul really be gone for good, sitting wrapped up in a velvet box in the back of the Master of Mirrors's lair?

Then, as Oliver simply thought about his father's past, to his shock he suddenly *saw* scenes from his father's life, right before his eyes, like a moving hologram, a three-dimensional movie. They were scenes as quick and blurred and jumpy as when you run a video on fast forward, but clear and vivid and three-dimensional, too—absolutely real, as though Oliver were standing within them.

He saw his father as a young man, meeting his mother, his mouth turned up in joy and his eyes alight. And then his father with a baby in a hospital room who must have been Oliver himself. Then his father with his mother getting on a plane (they must be going to Paris, Oliver thought) and then his father with Oliver, walking him to school and kicking a pebble home and answering his questions, worried but happy still. Watching, Oliver tried to reach out to him, wanting to take a kick at the stone himself. . . .

And then he saw his father bending over something, his face suddenly furrowed and unhappy, and talking to someone on a cell phone outside their apartment, late at night.

Oliver strained forward to listen, but he could hear nothing—his mind ached suddenly with the effort, a physical pain more intense even than the strain he had felt in his knees while he was fencing. Then his mind gave way like an over-stressed muscle, and the image passed.

Now the flow was taking him and Neige away, along with the lines of soulless slaves pulling them toward the cavern. He shook his head to relieve the ache. What was this force that moved them so inexorably wherever it wanted to take them? And how was it possible that he could see the past just by thinking about it?

They were being pulled right through the carved entrances. Oliver felt the stone, ice-cold beneath his feet, seeming to radiate iciness even through his shoes. As his eyes became accustomed to the interior, he saw that the light inside came from hard, mirrored sconces filled with great blocks of ice, which somehow glittered as bright as diamonds and cast a hard searching light all over the room.

In this cavern, though, the flow, instead of pulling them all forward in one direction, seemed to send them turning, very slowly, right around the room, as though the floor of the cavern was rotating.

A high stone platform stood at the center of the cavern. It looked like a scaffold, or a stage, and all of the Soulless gazed up at it. High on the scaffold was an armless white throne, and seated on it was a strange figure in a suit of shining silver armor. His short legs dangled over the edge of the throne, but his armor was polished bright, glaring and flaring in the diamond-light, and with his two small hands he seemed almost to be conducting the Soulless as though they were his orchestra.

The Soulless, as they were pulled into place by the flow, looked up at the directing hands of this strange figure and began breathing together, deeply and loudly. Their breaths rose and fell, at first apart, then, like the woodwinds in an orchestra as they finish tuning and begin to play, growing together and slowly gathering in volume and force.

Then Oliver heard, above this steady keening breathing sound, another sound, a thousand individual thumps, and then this sound, too, grew unified and louder, as though it were being conducted, like music, into a single beat.

Heartbeats! Oliver realized that the sounds he was hearing were the heartbeats of the Soulless. Their breaths rose and fell in unison, swelling as they did, and then the single unified heartbeat rose through the rising and falling breaths. . . .

It was the sound! The horrible hum that had destroyed the glass cases in the Louvre and had broken Charpentier. This was what it was, and where it came from. It was the sound of the breaths and heartbeats of all the Soulless, gathered together into one violent force sent out into the World—the sound of all the lost souls breathing while their hearts beat in a single rhythm together.

As the flow pulled them around the room, Oliver saw that the suit of shining armor was not surmounted by a great shining helmet, as one would have expected. Instead, the short creature, whatever it was, had an enormous head, which seemed likely to topple it over from its sheer size, and its head was locked within a grim iron-and-leather mask, with two narrow slits for his eyes, and encircled by rusting iron strands. Around its throat it was held by a thick black iron band, with a strong lock in place behind.

The Man in the Iron Mask! Then this was the Master of Mirrors, Oliver thought. Just as Mrs. Pearson had said! And he had been forced to wear this mask for centuries!

Now the hum and thump of the Soulless grew even louder in volume as three of the soul-stealers mounted the steps that ran to the high scaffold. Oliver and Neige saw that one of them held a small black box in his hand, like the soul-holding boxes Oliver had seen them put souls in. They took positions circling the masked man, and one reached into the box—and took out the golden key from Oliver's Epiphany cake, lifting it high toward the ceiling.

The key! Oliver churned with anger and frustration, as the huge, pumpkin-headed figure in the shining suit of armor stopped conducting, allowed himself to fall from his chair, and suavely took the key from his servant.

"I have suffered for you, all of these centuries, and now at last my suffering has been repaid," the voice resonated from within the mask, as he held the key up. It was, to Oliver's shock, a kind, smooth voice. "Now I shall be free. The new mirrors have opened to the world, and more and more of mankind can be saved from their horrible affliction of desire."

He reached around, inserted the key in the lock that held the iron band and mask in place, and turned it. It made a grinding noise, and then a sharp, decisive *click!*

There was a grumbling of hinges and a creaking of rusted latches. He reached up and, waving away his slaves, began to pull open the front of his mask himself. One by one he undid the latches and stays that the lock had held in place for so long.

The leather-and-iron mask slowly opened on its hinges, separating into two halves, like a cantaloupe being pulled apart. The mask came open, and a puff of brown dust flew from it . . .

A moan of pleasure, as of one released from a great burden, rose from the masked head . . . as it felt, for the first time in centuries, cool air on its face. The moan could be heard even over the ever-mounting hum and heartbeat of the Soulless. They watched as the mask opened fully at last, and the huge hands threw it aside, and the face inside was unveiled to them.

The great head turned slowly to gaze, unmasked, at all of his servants, the harpooners and soul-stealers and knights and the great crowd of soulless slaves.

And as it did, Oliver saw that it had no face at all.

Where his face should have been there was nothing. It was a blank wall of pure unbroken skin, with flesh as smooth and round as an egg or a polished stone.

"The One with None," Neige whispered weakly, as she stared up at the blank-faced master. "He stared too long into the mirrors! There is nothing left of his face!"

The vast smooth head was without mouth or nose or eyes or ears, perfectly blank, standing still as his slaves rotated around him, staring up in wonder. Yet Oliver somehow knew that he could see and could certainly speak, as though he sensed everything through the white shell of his face. Oh, don't let him see me and Neige hidden in the corner! Oliver thought, as he bowed his head down, so that the Master of Mirrors could not see his eyes, and signaled to Neige to do the same.

What an idiot he was! His teachers were right. He *was* stupid. Like a fool he had casually given the key to Charlie at Versailles in order to impress the wraiths, and then, neat as a move in chess, they had snatched Charlie off the board and taken his prize. The key was the trust of the King in the Window, had been so for centuries, to keep the mask from ever being unlocked. And now Oliver had handed it right to the Master of Mirrors, and allowed him to unlock his mask, and show his non-face for the first time in centuries. . . .

The voice of the Master of Mirrors rose, even though he had no mouth. Oliver expected the voice of evil to be harsh and grating and deeply resonant. Instead, it was as suave and insinuating as velvet, and as clear and hard as ice, and as serious and frightening as death.

"At last you see me whole," he said, "and gaze on my perfection. Tomorrow, you will go out into the World and prepare for the last battle. The old King in the Window is dead. The new king has given me the key and become my servant. The new mirrors are everywhere. You have nothing left to fear in the Way or in the World."

Liar! Oliver wanted to yell. I never gave you the key, and I'm not your servant. But now, the great blank head turned as though to survey his slowly turning audience. The Soulless gazed back at their master silently.

"Be glad!" the Master of Mirrors said, and his voice was kind and mild. "You are the only free creatures in all the cosmos. The terrible burden of wanting that sat inside you, burning like a coal in your brain—it is gone! The horrible pain of longing and desire—gone!" And he reached his small hands to open the box that he kept by the side of his throne. Inside were the hundreds of glittering diamond and ruby souls that the soul-stealers had taken that day. He held them up and showed them to the slaves.

"Do you see? You have been released from this parasite, this tumor, that filled your life with the pain of longing and wanting. And now you are free! You are at one with one another. You no longer stare in windows and beg for your release from desires. You are safe with me on the other side. No longings. No self. Each free from wanting. Feel the lightness of your liberty!"

Their breathing eased and their heartbeats thumped. But Oliver looked around, and all he saw was how entirely the light had gone out of their eyes. Their bodies still belonged to them, but their souls were in the hands of the Master of Mirrors.

"We are the only free people in the cosmos," the master went on, his blank face radiating sound. "We are free from wanting. We have no selves. We have no me, no you. There is no duality. There is only us, one great unbroken consciousness. All of us one."

And then, quite suddenly, his blank face became a real face—a large, normal face, a harmless face with chubby cheeks and spectacles. Was that what he really looked like?

But then his face changed abruptly into a woman's face, long and beautiful; and then melted into another man's face, this one Asian with a long mustache; and then again, now an old man's face; and again, an old woman's; and again and again and again! Faster and faster, faces came and went on the One with None. At last a blur of features crossed the face as his slaves fell silent. "We are one!" he cried.

But Oliver understood. The Master of Mirrors had no face of his own—but now that he was unmasked he could take over all of their faces!

Oliver quietly took Neige's hand, looking again at his father, staring blankly up at the master.

Neige turned toward him. "We must get out. Before he sees us!"

"I don't think we can. This, thing, this gluey thing, keeps us here."

She shook her head. "No. This force, whatever it is, if it flows in, must flow out, too. Next time we turn toward the gate that we came in, try to push your way out there."

"We are one!" the master said again. "And we are free.

And soon the oldest way will be opened again, and I shall be set free to rejoin you in the World and go among all the blessed mirrors, old and new, as today I have set myself free to share your faces!"

What did he mean? Oliver wondered. Why could he control them from the Way at a distance, but he could not yet cross back into the World? And what else did he need besides the key to complete his escape?

Oliver watched the great blank face until the turning flow brought them around once again to the door, hoping that he could somehow find enough spring in his step to escape. But as they turned, and he tried to break free of the flow—nothing happened. It was as though they were both nailed to the floor.

At that very moment, the Master of Mirrors turned toward them. Oliver's heart went into his mouth as he did— and it was as if he could feel the master inside his head, trying to pry it open like the fishmonger on the Place de Clichy had opened his oysters. But then the master was looking past them, toward a group of soul-stealers standing in the rear. Another moment and he might have had the King in the Window as his servant, Oliver thought . . . but the master's desires were somewhere else.

"The time has come to bring the two queens in, and to find a young queen, too," the master said. "Go. Bring them here to me. And then find *her*—and bring her here to me as well," he intoned, and the soul-stealers standing all around Oliver and Neige turned toward the gates.

What two queens? Oliver wondered. Who could they be? But before he could whisper to Neige, she was speaking.

"He has . . . *her?*" Neige said, almost to herself, and Oliver saw that she almost turned white with fear as she said it. "He can't have her!" she said.

"Who is *she?*" Oliver whispered back.

But then the Master of Mirrors nodded once, heavily, in their direction—and as he did it was as if the flow that held that group of soul-stealers in place had changed and no longer moved in a circle, but was pushing them instead toward the door—as if they had been set out on a small stream, tugging away from a great river. As silently as they could, Neige and Oliver slipped behind them, unnoticed, and followed the flow out the door.

Now they were back out in one of the corridors, being pulled along, trying to elude the glare of the mirrors. But where was Charlie? Oliver thought hard, desperately, trying to imagine what had happened when they brought Charlie into the maze. When did they bring him here? Where did they take him?

It did no good—but then his heart jumped. For as he pressed his mind to think about Charlie, he suddenly *saw* Charlie right before his eyes, as though someone were once again projecting a moving three-dimensional image in the air in front of him.

There was Charlie, right there, struggling and kicking, wearing his San Jose Sharks jacket and with his in-line skates around his shoulders. Two soul-stealers were dragging him down another long corridor, but this one had only small doors lining it with barred windows. Oliver's eyes were still open, and the image was just like the one he had seen as his father's past, only it wasn't as much work. He didn't have to, well, use his mental muscles that hard. Could this mean that what he was seeing now was closer in time, nearer to him and so required less mind power?

Then the vision disappeared. But Oliver knew, at least, that he had been looking at the past—looking directly at the moment, how many hours ago was it now?—when Charlie had been kidnapped. And looking directly at the place where he had been taken.

"Neige, I know where they took him," Oliver whispered excitedly. "I saw it."

"How do you know?" she said.

"I thought hard about it—and I just, I just *saw* what had happened tonight. I saw the moment when they took him away! It was like I could see into the past. Try it. Think as though you were running."

Neige closed her eyes, too, and she frowned, as though thinking hard. "I see it too!" she cried, as the flow continued to pull them along the corridor. "I see it, too. They're dragging him into some kind of cell. When was it? How can we see it? And, now, oh, Oliver, now I see us waiting outside the room until the guards come out. It's . . . just moments away from happening. I can tell. I can see it!" She opened her eyes again, and they glowed.

But suddenly, Neige pointed down one small,

approaching hall. "It's there! It's those rooms! That's where they took him."

Oliver looked. In front of them was the same row of small doors with barred windows that Oliver had seen, too. It was the same door that he had seen a moment before in his vision! The door that they had dragged Charlie Gronek through! Only now it was closed, and the corridor was dark and silent.

But would this force, whatever it was, propel them past it? At first they seemed to continue to be tugged down the same corridor—but now, no, he thought hard about Charlie and they were making a turn, being pulled along down this darkened hall. It *wanted* them to go there. Safe or dangerous? All Oliver knew was that it was happening. They surfed toward the door, and, as they came up on it, took hold of the door frame, and peered inside the barred window.

In the dark and gloom, they could just make out two guards, seated on stools by a grumbling fireplace. No, it wasn't a fireplace after all it was an . . . iceplace. What was flickering inside it were chips and pieces of ice and diamonds, giving off that same hard clear light that had lit up the cavern.

And between them, on the floor, bound, his face just visible in the dim and flickering light of the fire, was Charlie Gronek himself.

"We found him!" Neige whispered to Oliver. "We saw him, and we found him! I've never seen so clearly even in my crystal."

"Ahhr, it's hot in here. Thank God for the ice," one of the guards was saying. He rubbed his hands in the light of the ice. "Have you knifed out his soul yet?" he went on, with horrible casualness, to the other, gesturing at poor Charlie.

These guards seemed rougher than the other soul-stealers, Oliver thought. They were fat, for one thing, sloppy and ugly, and they wore odd, schoolboylike striped shirts; a kind of jailer's uniform, Oliver guessed. What was even stranger, though, were their weapons. Each one had a long ostrich feather—could that be right? Yes, it was, absurd though it seemed—dangling from his belt, and what looked like an overstuffed pillow in a holster.

"No. The master wants to take the soul of this one. By himself with his own blunt knife. But I think the One with None will be disappointed. This one doesn't have a soul," he said, kicking Charlie, "just a mess of old bawdiness. When you shine the searchlight in his eyes, all you see inside are a lot of loud drinking songs with half-dressed wenches . . . No longings in this one."

"Those are *music videos,*" Charlie said impatiently, "and quit looking in my mind." Oliver was thrilled. Charlie still had fight left in him.

"What do we do?" whispered Neige. Oliver stopped to think.

"Wait!" Neige went on. "One of them will come out in a moment. I saw that, very clearly. And I saw it without my crystal to help, either!"

They waited for what seemed like an eternity—though

it was probably only five minutes—until at last Oliver heard a loud impressive groan coming from somewhere farther back in the room.

"It's the old man acting up again," said one of the knights wearily.

"Why do we have to stay here with him? We are the only ones kept from the unmasking," said the other.

"Because the master trusts us."

"Listen to him moan! Oh, will you go out and get his dinner? I'll look in on him and stay here with this one," he said, and he kicked Charlie again.

A moment later, one of the two guards emerged from the door. He turned as though to lock it with a large key, and then, thank goodness, shrugged, as though thinking, Why bother? and was pulled away by the flow. He had left the door one useful crack open. Oliver looked inside the cell, and saw that the second guard had stepped away from Charlie toward the inner room, where the groan had come from.

Well, that had reduced the odds, Oliver thought. But what to do now? "What have I got in my pocket?" Oliver whispered to himself.

Well, what *did* he have? He felt inside the pocket of his coat. He had the pebble that he had kicked home—that had kicked *him* home, actually—on Epiphany night, and the bubble wand and the bottle of soap that the wraiths had given him. Fat lot of use all *that* was . . . crazy wraiths . . . He could kick the pebble at the guard, he supposed, and then blow bubbles at him, and that would do absolutely no good at all. If he had the glass sword, perhaps—but even that, which at least looked as if it might be useful, would probably shatter as soon as he used it. . . .

Wait a second, he thought. Inside the room there was Charlie's San Jose Sharks jacket. There must be something in that. Charlie always had so many . . . things. Electronic gizmos and iPods and Discmans . . . And there were his skates . . . . Oliver gestured toward Neige, and together they pulled themselves around the door frame.

As soon as they were inside the room the force—the flow—stopped. For a half moment Oliver was almost sick as the constant push forward, which he had by now become used to, halted. It took him a moment to recover his equilibrium, and as he did, he turned toward Charlie, bound and sick-looking on the floor.

Before Charlie could call out, Neige had clapped a hand over his mouth. Charlie's eyes were alive with delight and relief.

Not even stopping to say hello to Charlie, Oliver went at once across to the table where Charlie's jacket and skates had been thrown by the guards. The contents of his pockets were spilled out and thrown around. They had obviously gone through his things, to find the golden key, and had then left everything else in a heap.

Well, they were no use . . . or were they? Suddenly, the beginnings of a plan began to form in Oliver's head. He had an idea—he actually had an idea! Yes, there it was— Charlie's Discman, right next to his cell phone. And

Charlie's—what did you call it?—oh, yes, his Game Boy. He took out the Discman and turned it on, and then turned the volume up as high as he could; the sounds of the Beatles singing "Birthday"—loud, happy rock music—came through. Then he turned on the Game Boy. It was set on some kind of American football game, and, giving a shrug to Neige, he slipped outside with her, holding tight to the door frame again to avoid being swept away by the flow.

The fat guard rushed back from wherever he had been in the back, startled at the noise from the Discman. He took his long feather from his belt and raised it, threateningly, and approached the two little machines. You could hear the music, like a thin tinny buzz, rising from the headphones. Would he have the sense to put them on? Oliver remembered what his mother had said when she had refused to buy him one: "It's like an addiction, those things. . . . Kids just put them on and disappear inside. It would make you withdraw from all interaction with your peers."

The fat guard in the striped shirt picked up the headphones and slipped them on. He listened, fascinated. Charlie, Oliver saw, was watching, too, his eyes wide open and alert. At first taken aback, the guard was soon lost within the headphones. Now he looked down at the little flashing lights on the Game Boy, the moving figures. He reached down and pressed a button, and the little moving figures stopped and then changed directions. With a sigh, he sat down, and peered deeper into the Game Boy as the music from the earphones moved deeper into his head. He was lost.

"My mother always says those things are worse than drugs," Oliver whispered to Neige.

Together they tiptoed carefully behind the completely absorbed soul-stealer. Charlie's eyes flashed with gratitude as they approached, and, holding fingers up to their lips to remind him again not to exclaim, Oliver and Neige together carefully rolled him toward the corner. Oliver untied his hands and ankles.

"Oh, wow, am I glad to see you," Charlie whispered with heartfelt emotion. Then suddenly he checked himself and said, very coolly, "Hey—what took you so long?"

"What do you mean, what took us so long?" Oliver said. "It's a miracle we're here at all."

"I know. But it's just what you *say* when you're in a desperate spot and you get rescued. Hey, what took you so long?"

"Oh," said Oliver. He was, as usual, impressed by Charlie's knowledge of the rhetoric of adventures, but not sure how useful it actually was.

So Oliver just said "Shhhh," as quietly as he could. "We have to figure a way out." He glanced at the back room. "Is there a way out through there?" he asked.

"I don't think so. It's just another cell, kind of. I know they've got somebody big in there," Charlie whispered intensely.

"Who?" Oliver said.

"The famous wudyacallit, seer," said Charlie.

Oliver wasn't sure what to do. They should flee, yes,

but flee where? How would they find a way out of this maze? What if the flow just pushed them back toward the center, and the Master of Mirrors? He had to decide. The other guard would be back soon. . . .

"Let's run," Charlie said.

"No," Oliver said strongly. "We can't. There's this . . . force in the halls here, that drags us along wherever it wants us to go. If there's someone important back there, I should find out what he knows, and how he can help us. Maybe he knows how to defeat the flow."

"Good, Your Majesty," Neige said, sounding just a touch warmer than she had since they had crossed over. "I'll stay here and watch for the other guard."

"Oliver," Charlie whispered fiercely, "what CD was in my Discman?"

"Uh—the Beatles. *The White Album*, I think."

"Yeah, but the first disc or the second?"

"The second, I think. The one that begins with 'Birthday.' "

"You realize what that means, don't you?"

"What?"

"'Revolution 9' is on that side. The Yoko electric noise thing."

"So?"

"*Nobody* can listen to 'Revolution 9'! It's a universal listener-repellent. Even if he's deep in a video game, as soon as it starts, he'll take off the headphones. We have only about fifteen minutes."

Oliver nodded, and walked by himself into the hidden room.

It was lit by the light of a single candle. Sitting there, all alone was, an old man, in a long robe with a fur-lined collar, and a long white beard. He wore a long filthy gown, and Oliver saw that encrusted in it were old straw and gold beads and, all over, little bits and shards of broken colored glass. He sat on a stone bed, and around his ankle was a balloon.

A seer? Oliver had a guess ready. "You must be Nostradamus," Oliver said, haltingly.

"And you are . . ." The old man squinted, and his eyes took on a faraway look. "Oliver," said Nostradamus at last.

It wasn't entirely surprising that Oliver knew who Nostradamus was. Unlike Molière or Racine or any of the other great figures of French history, Nostradamus was not someone you talked about a lot at the Ecole Fontenelle, but there was still no denying his existence. He had lived in the century before the Grand Siècle and he had published a big book of vague, cryptic prophecies, which people in the Grand Siècle had struggled to interpret. People are still trying.

"How do you know about me?" Oliver asked.

"Oh, I still see things. If *you* had spent five hundred years in here seeing things, why then you would see things, too. I heard your name. You know," said Nostradamus, sitting down. "I do have a gift of prophecy." He stopped, and muttered to himself, "I do have the gift. More or less."

"Can you help me?" Oliver asked. "We're lost in the maze and can't get out."

"Well, travel into the future and see your way out," the old man said calmly.

"I can't travel into the future," Oliver replied angrily.

"Oh, *everyone* travels into the future here. You probably saw something that just happened, or was just about to happen, to a friend of yours."

"Yes, that's right! I—"

"Well, *that* part's easy here. Ever since I first came in here, so many centuries ago, I could see that. Everyone here can."

"Why?" Oliver's curiosity was suddenly aroused. He knew that they had no time to waste, but he also sensed that this encounter with Nostradamus might not be wasted time. He asked urgently, "Why can they? And what is that . . . flow . . . that won't let you walk in two directions?"

"That's just a question of time," the old man said. It didn't seem like much of an answer to Oliver. The old man stared off into the distance.

"And so, you see, I went back into the world, and told everyone about the wonderful things I could see in the future, and they were so impressed. Because, you see, I *did* see *some* futures very clearly."

"Did you come in through the king's way? I mean, with a true mirror and living ice and all?" Oliver asked.

"Oh, no! I came in long before the king's way opened. I entered by the very oldest way, and I could see the future all around me—things that would happen to myself, and to my friends. Saw them all."

"But you said everyone here can do that—"

"But that, you see, was all that I could see," he went on, as though Oliver had not said anything. "And when people say they want you to tell the future, they don't mean what is just about to happen, or what will happen in the very long run, or what will happen in the next five minutes to someone they don't know. By 'knowing the future' they mean knowing *what will happen in the next three years to them.* Now, that's a very, very tiny part of the future—but for some reason it's all they care about."

"Do you know how to get out of here?" Oliver asked urgently.

"So then—and only then—I, ah, lied," the old man went on, as though Oliver were not even there.

Oliver was growing desperate with the vague old man's meanderings. Couldn't he say something useful? "But I did see them."

"See what?" Oliver asked.

"See *them,* I mean, when they were brand-new, and he was just inventing them, just beginning the plan. And I saw the plan, when I saw . . . *them,* and then he saw me—and here I am," he added, quietly. The old man suddenly looked terrified. "But I can't tell you the plan! I can't tell you what they are! For terrible things will happen if I do. So don't ask! He placed the mirror-curse on me."

"What's the mirror-curse?"

"Reversal, reversal, reversal. When I tell the truth, no one believes me! And so I am condemned to tell it in riddles that no one can understand."

Then Oliver had an idea. "I'll make a deal with you," he said. "Just tell me what you know that might be useful to me—tell it in riddles, if you have to—and I promise to do everything I can to help you get away from him. Or them. Or whatever it is that frightens you."

He looked up peevishly at Oliver. "But how will you get back in? Once you've gone you'll have no reason to come back to get me."

"Oh, yes," said Oliver quietly, "I will have a reason."

Nostradamus looked at him oddly. "Your father, you mean," he said at last. "*That* I saw. It was very near. Riddles, you said? I will give you riddles—but I warn you, you won't understand them. That is the nature of the curse. Perhaps at least that is better than truths that you won't believe."

The old man leaned closer. "Listen! The most important thing is this—the Oldest Way of All is still open! But you can find it only in the great glass windows that all the world looks at, and no one can ever look through."

Oliver was bewildered. "How can you look at a window and not look through it?" he asked. He had expected riddles, but this was more like gibberish.

"Learn this, too," the old man went on, raising his finger high, as though he were enjoying the attention. Oliver was getting restless. What was going on in the outer room? When would the guard stop being entranced by the Discman? "There is another great army of aid you can call on at a moment of need," the old man went on. "They are the Watchful."

"Yes," said Oliver eagerly. "I have heard of them. How can I find them?"

Nostradamus stared ahead. "They long ago refused the call of the Wise, and they have a debt to pay. But on the night that the King's Sign flies at last, the Watchful will leave men's sides and return to their side."

"What does that mean?" asked Oliver frantically. "How can they do both?"

"Know this, too. I have seen three things that are cool and warm at the same time. When The King in the Window knows all three, then the empire of the Master of Mirrors may end. But—the king will have to turn the world inside out, in order to leave the master wrong side up, and he must lose the World in order to save it."

More nonsense, Oliver thought. But he tried desperately to remember it all: the Watchful and the walking in the light and the world inside out.

Then he remembered the question that Molière had told him about.

"The wraiths dream of what they call a 'neutral medium,' a road to travel on that would let them move freely in the world. They can't form an army until they find it. Is there one? Have you ever seen that?"

"There is no neutral medium," the old man said. He pressed his thumbs to his eyes in thought, "Save Neige, of course! Her crystal's falling!" he said at last.

Neige! Was Neige in danger? Where had her crystal fallen to? He had better go back outside . . . and just then

Oliver did indeed hear a commotion in the outer room.

The old man looked at him calmly. "I can see—I can see *running,* in your future," Nostradamus said, kindly.

Now Oliver could hear the voice of the guard who had put on Charlie's Discman.

"Number nine, number nine . . ." he was chanting, in English, dolefully. "Number nine."

"What are you *saying?*" he heard the querulous voice of the other fat guard, the one who had left the door open, now. Where were Charlie and Neige?

"The magic—it was such magical music," said the Guard of the Headphones. "Such beautiful music. But then the voice enters, and calls a chant: 'Number Nine, Number Nine . . .'" he shrieked.

Now the other guard spoke more sharply—almost viciously—"This belonged to the boy we took! Why did you use it?"

"I don't know," the first knight said stumblingly, "I don't know—I thought one of the Outsiders left it . . ."

"Idiot! The Soulless don't care for music! It is one of the signs. The Outsiders cannot have brought it. It must be the young ones, the intruders. Quick, return to the Great Hall, assemble ten knights, bring them back quickly. Hunt them down and kill them. Now at least we have their scent."

Oliver stopped breathing. He looked around for a weapon. Then he noticed something odd. Nostradamus was wearing a sword, long, sharp and glinting in the dank light. How strange! Why would they let a prisoner keep a sword? But at least it would provide Oliver with a weapon.

"Your sword. May I have it, please?" Oliver whispered politely.

Nostradamus shrugged, drew the sword from its sheath, and handed it to Oliver.

It was far heavier than Oliver had expected. It almost dragged his arm down. But then he felt its edge, bright and cold. It was as sharp as a butcher's knife. *This* would be of some use, anyway, whatever became of the old man's riddles.

Outside now he could hear the guards calling to each other. "NUMBER NINE! NUMBER NINE! NUMBER NINE!" They must have somehow plugged the tape into a broadcast system—the guards, Oliver understood, must have believed that there was a message in the song, a spell like the one they had called out from the podium inside the great hall.

Oliver had one last question he had to put to Nostradamus. He leaned forward toward the doddering old man.

"My father . . . my father . . ." he said. "Is there no way I can win back his soul?"

"Oh," said Nostradamus. "Ah. I understand." He reflected. "In all my travels, I have heard that there is only one way," the old man said softly. "And I have heard that it is very easy, but it is also very hard. For to take back a soul you must look in the one mirror that is also an open window, the one window that is also a perfect mirror. If your father sees his reflection there, his soul can be restored to him.

But"—Nostradamus held up a warning finger—"while he must look only at himself in the mirror, he must never take his gaze from what the window shows of the world beyond."

Oliver grimaced. It was hopeless—but it was all he had.

He took the old man's hand. "Thank you. And I will be back." Then he thought of one more thing. "Uh. How can I find a way out of here?"

The old man shrugged. "Why, use the king's way home, of course." Then he added, more intensely, "Do you promise to come back for me?"

"Yes," Oliver said, "I promise." He took Nostradamus's sword in his hand, and gulped hard.

"Yes," said the old prophet, "I know you will come back. I *see* that you will."

Oliver sprang into the outer room. No one was there. He ran out to the corridor, clutching the bright steel sword. But where were Neige and Charlie? He looked up and down the corridor wildly, keeping his feet planted so that the flow could not pull him away. Wait—what was that at the end of the corridor, so long it seemed almost miles away? It was Charlie! And he was gliding away on his in-line skates, with Neige holding on tight to his waist as though he were the engine of a train.

The two guards were chasing after him, too. But Charlie's skates gave him greater speed and flexibility. He dodged and ducked the two guards as, quite ridiculously Oliver thought, they chased after him with their long feathers.

Good for Charlie! It was as if he were surfing the flow, while the two guards were merely splashing helplessly in it.

Oliver knew exactly what to do. He was the king, and he must take the king's path home.

He took the pebble from his pocket and let it drop to the floor. Before the pebble struck the floor, Oliver kicked it with all his might.

The pebble flew down the corridor, like a punted football, turning over and over—and then, to Oliver's delight, it seemed to stop in midair, almost as if it were thinking, and then decisively dove down one of the open corridors that ran from the main hallway.

"That way's home!" Oliver shouted to Neige and Charlie. "Follow the pebble home!"

Charlie turned his head, saw where the pebble was going, and quickly turned on his skates and raced after it, with Neige careening behind him. Would the flow let them go where the homing stone led? Yes it would! The stone must have powers to lead you home even in the face of the flow.

Charlie and Neige were following it as quickly as they could. Oliver watched them disappear around the corner. He pushed himself into the flow to join them. Suddenly from the windows that lined either side of the corridor, soul-stealers leaped out, three of them, each carrying a long, silly-looking feather. Yet their eyes were grim.

Now that he was unmasked and could inhabit their bodies, the Master of Mirrors must be able to send his slaves in and out of the mirrors freely, Oliver realized. Before I gave him the key, he could only reach out at you. Now they could *leap* out at you. . . .

He felt the sword's edge again. This *was* good, and the moment they were upon him, he slashed fiercely at the first of the guards with his heavy steel weapon, striking him squarely in the center of his chest.

But the sword struck with a strange, soft, squishy sound, and then the hard weapon seemed to droop and melt in Oliver's hand as he slashed away with it, furiously and futilely, until at last it was bending over as though it were made of butter.

The master's guardsmen laughed, and then the three of them, feathers ready, slashed down at Oliver.

Oliver looked down at the sword in his hand, now bent right over like a rainbow. No wonder they had let Nostradamus have this! But he had no time to think how something so hard could become so soft—because he was dodging and rolling to avoid being cut to pieces by the guards' fluttering feathers.

For these feathers were not like feathers at all. Even though their plumes waved gently in the air, when they struck they were as heavy as iron—and they were razor-sharp!

They cut scraps from Oliver's clothing as he frantically tumbled and turned. Anywhere a feather touched, the fabric of his shirt ripped open. Once, he even felt the unbearably sharp edge scraping the flesh of his stomach. . . .

He turned his head, quickly. There were three of them, red eyes glowing, panting, and more behind. He would be cut to pieces!

But suddenly there was Charlie, grabbing Oliver by the scruff of the neck, and pulling him away, turning, breathing hard, as he flew on his skates down the corridor, surfing with the flow.

"We followed the stone, but Neige wouldn't let you go—" Charlie shouted. The guards were racing down the corridor after them, feathers raised.

"I just *thought* my way back to where you were. I thought of you and you were there," Neige said, looking a little dazed. "But now how will we find our way home?"

"I've got it," said Charlie, and he opened his palm. He held the homing stone in his hand. "I caught it in midair. Kick it, Ollie, I mean, Your Majesty."

And once again Oliver gave the king's pebble a decisive kick down the corridor, and once again it rose, stopped, seemed to look, and flew down a hallway in the maze.

"It *always* knows the way home," Oliver said with delight, and then the three of them raced down the corridor, following the homing stone of the king. Oliver had his hands centered on Neige's waist, who was holding on to Charlie, and the three of them went rushing down the corridors of the Mirror-Maze like a very short, uncertain and shaky train.

There was a flash, like a sudden burst of light, from the giant mirror-backs that lined the corridor. For a moment, the huge sad faces that looked blindly down and out at the Mirror-Maze were gone, and all was black.

Then a moment later, *he* was there. The Master of Mirrors's face was in every mirror, staring out at them, blank and pitiless and penetrating. The mirrors glowed with his evil presence. Up and down every corridor, only the face-less face of the One with None looked out at them, watching their desperate flight.

Now more soul-stealers were pouring out of the mirrors. It seemed as if there were hundreds of them, sent by the master, who must be able to see where Oliver and his friends were. Now they were just behind him. Oliver watched in terror as one of them reached down and took something from the ground. What was it? A rubber band . . . he pulled it back and it flew through the air. Oliver was relieved—it was just a rubber band!—when he felt a sharp pain, and reaching back instinctively, his hand came back from his ear, wet. He looked at it. It was covered with blood. My God, had a rubber band cut off his ear?

Oliver turned his head quickly and saw one of the knights stooping again. Something soft, like bubble gum, was in his hand, and now—but Oliver ducked his head quickly, and the spinning gum embedded itself in the wood of the floor beneath his feet.

The soul-stealers glided grimly after them, snarling and relentless. Oliver could hear Charlie's breathing become short, and could feel the strain in his muscles.

If only Oliver had a weapon, a way to fight! He reached

into his jacket as they sped along. But all he had was the bubble pipe and soap that Molière had given him. And they were supposed to be the king's weapons!

Desperately, hopelessly, not knowing what else to do, Oliver dipped the wand into the soap. Still holding on tight to Neige with one hand, with the other he managed to blow a stream of small soap bubbles just as the guards seemed about to fall on them.

The soul-stealers, seeing the bubbles coming, threw their hands up desperately to protect their faces. A look of panic filled their eyes, and they tried to stop their forward progress and dodge the bubbles, falling backward.

But the bubbles gracefully drifted toward them—and then struck the three armed creatures with the force of small cannonballs, each one exploding with a loud deep boom as it struck the pursuing demons, driving right through their chain mail, leaving great gaping wounds in their armor, sending them spinning backward in grotesque twists, and then leaving them lifeless on the floor of the Mirror-Maze.

Oliver stared, his mouth open. The soap bubbles had done *that*? But he had no time to feel relieved, for now he could hear still more soul-stealers running toward him down the corridor. He turned. There were at least fifty of them.

Oliver stood up straight, and, as Charlie's skates surfed the flow and pulled them gently down the corridors of mirrors, he began to blow more bubbles down toward their pursuers.

It was like having a small cannon in his hand. The bubbles flew down the hallway, as if they were seeking out their enemies, only to bowl the soul-stealers over with the force of a grenade, exploding in sharp fragments as they bounced off walls and knocked down the knights. Only the mirrors themselves seemed safe; the bubbles bounced right off them. The pursuing knights stopped in disarray, as the bubbles floated and tore through their ranks. Oliver dipped his wand back in his soap. But it was almost empty. He scraped hard against the bottom of the soap bottle. Hardly any left . . . what to do, where could they go?

The Master of Mirrors's blank face still stared down at him from every mirror, and Oliver was sure that he could sense rage in his blank and imperturbable features.

Where was the king's pebble, the homing stone? Oliver thought frantically. He looked around him.

"It's there!" Neige cried, clutching Charlie's waist with one hand while pointing with the other.

Yes, there it was, just ahead of them—it was hovering before a double-mirror, a mirror twice the size of all the others he had seen. This must be the way home.

Now he and Charlie and Neige sped toward it, pushed by the flow, the exhausted Charlie gliding along on his skates.

And then he saw not the master's, but Mrs. Pearson's face at the large mirror where the homing stone hovered. Yes, Mrs. Pearson was there, wearing—could it be?—a white slip, and she was holding the water pistol that the wraiths had given her.

They had to get inside the mirror. Oliver reached out to grasp Mrs. Pearson's hand. But quickly, from every other mirror around it, more soul-stealers leaped out from in front of the master's face, tens and then hundreds of them, all in black armor and carrying long sharp feathers at their sides.

Oliver looked up desperately at Mrs. Pearson. The soul-stealers were reaching out for his throat, grasping his legs . . . and in the double-mirror, he saw Mrs. Pearson turn forthrightly and level her water pistol at the mirror and fire. A little stream of water emerged from the barrel of the pistol as Oliver watched helplessly.

The short squirt of water passed through the mirror and emerged on the other side—right where Oliver was engulfed by the soul-stealers—as a sizzling plume of white-hot flame. Oliver felt the heat on his cheek as the water was transformed into a streak of fire as it crossed over   through the mirror.

The flames struck the corps of soul-stealers who surrounded Oliver, so white-hot that even their armor began to melt away. Oliver heard howls of pain and wonder as the flame forced them back down the corridor. But he was safe. Mrs. Pearson had very good aim. She peered out, seeming to search to see just what she had been able to do. Then she held her hand out, and it passed right through the mirror, reaching toward Oliver. More soul-stealers emerged from the corridor of mirrors, but they held back, fearful, frightened of Mrs. Pearson's water pistol–flame thrower. Oliver reached out for Mrs. Pearson's hand again.

Now, far down at the end of the corridor, more soul-stealers appeared somehow double-quick, surfing the flow, with the giant, curtained chair held in their midst. They came toward Neige, feathers high.

"Quick, take the lady's hand," Neige cried to Oliver, and then she turned, and pulled from inside her sweater the feather that she must have taken from the guard who had listened to the Beatles, and parried the first knight, knocking the even longer feather from his hand with a single deft move (Oliver knew she took *l'escrime,* fencing, every Tuesday and Thursday). Before the other could get his weapon drawn, she had turned and, spinning her body around, had sliced off his head, hacking at the neck, in one terrible, devastating, feathery blow.

Instead of bleeding, the decapitated knight simply emptied out, like a burst balloon, with a rush of hot air escaping above, and then everything else, head and armor and body and sword, quickly turning into gray ash. The second knight turned and, looking in horror at his vanished neighbor, and then at the brave young girl with the feather, ran back down the corridor.

"The young queen!" now the voice of the master rose again from all the giant mirrors. "She will be the new queen for the new mirrors! The young queen. Take her!"

Neige looked at Oliver in puzzlement and wonder.

The knights charged again toward Oliver. From every mirror back Oliver saw the face of the Master of Mirrors glowing more powerfully than ever, and then the hum of the breath of the Soulless began to rise, and their single heart-beat, beating in unison, filled the corridors.

Oliver felt paralyzed for a moment by the sound. And then the Master of Mirrors, peering out of every mirror, turned his head and—Oliver could feel it, even if the master had no eyes to see with—fixed his eyeless gaze on Neige.

"Neige, come with me," Oliver urged, pulling at her elbow. But Neige seemed overcome, almost hypnotized, by his huge, faceless, fleshy presence.

"Come," said the great blank face, gently. "Come. Who is to be master?" And then his hand came up within every mirror frame, and Oliver saw that he held Neige's crystal, and let it catch and intensify the dim light of the corridor, so that a thousand bright beams were cast directly at her.

"There it is!" Neige cried out. "My crystal! I must have dropped it! I cannot lose it." She pulled her arm free from Oliver, and walked, mesmerized, against the flow, toward the great blank head of the Master of Mirrors, reaching out for her crystal. She approached—and almost too quickly to be seen, the Master of Mirrors pulled Neige to him and into the mirror.

A bright explosion of light, sudden darkness—and the Master of Mirrors was gone, and then the old sad faces of the soon-to-be-soulless were all that looked down on the corridor of the Mirror-Maze.

Oliver began to run toward the mirror where the Master had been, but Charlie grabbed his arm.

"Neige!" Oliver cried.

"We have to get out!" Charlie said.

"She came back for me," Oliver said.

"We'll come back for her," Charlie implored him.

Oliver looked up, and to his shock, saw that Charlie was half in, half out of the immense double-mirror—and inside it, Oliver saw six beautiful women trying on clothes, and therefore—there is no other way to explain it—in their underwear, a blaze of lace and black silk and pearly stockings, completely indifferent to the fact that anyone was watching them.

"Neige!" he cried again, but within a moment Mrs. Pearson had him by the wrist, and he was joining the rescued Charlie among the half-dressed ladies.

Oliver turned to the now blank and solid dressing-room mirrors and pounded on them hopelessly. The French ladies in their beautiful underwear merely looked at him with hooded eyes, and went on with their tryings-on. Oliver was back in the World, but he had left Neige and his father behind, and the One with None was, after centuries of imprisonment, unmasked at last.

PART TWO

Chapter Eleven

The Great Reversal

"EVERYTHING is reversed on the other side of the mirrors, Mrs. P. Not just left and right. *Everything.* Hard is soft and soft is hard. Swords melt and bend, and feathers and bubbles slice and explode! Everything is reversed!"

Charlie was flushed with excitement as he explained their adventures to Mrs. Pearson.

"Or a glass sword!" Oliver said.

"What?" Charlie said.

"Or a glass sword," Oliver said again, stirred by how

things were fitting together, even though he dreaded thinking about what might be happening to Neige. "The sword
that always shatters in the World must be the sword that
never breaks in the Way. It must have been made for the
first King in the Window when he went to war in the Way
to capture the master. *All* of the weapons the wraiths have—
the water pistols and soap-bubble blowers and fountain
cannons—are deadly arms of war on the other side. Mrs.
Pearson's water pistol became a flame-thrower when she
fired it through the mirrors. They used all those weapons
long ago in their battles in the Way, and still keep them
now."

"Sure, that's it. Ice is fire, fire's ice, soft is hard, and
hard is soft," Charlie said happily.

It was sometime early on Wednesday morning. The
three of them were sitting, worn out but safe, in Mrs.
Pearson's apartment on the rue Monsieur, surrounded by
her piles of books and her old eighteenth-century prints.

She explained that she had called Oliver's mother to
tell her that their "research project" had run late—"Though
late as this, even *I* hardly expected,"—and that she would see
that Oliver and Charlie got home safely. Mrs. Parker had
been puzzled but, as Mrs. Pearson did not mind saying,
rather cowed by Mrs. Pearson, and she had apparently asked
only what Oliver had had for dinner. Unfortunately, it also
seemed that the director had been calling from the Ecole
Fontenelle all day long, inquiring about Oliver's where-
abouts.

Dully, taking this in, Oliver also noticed that there was something strange about the apartment: there were dust cloths everywhere, covering things, and many other framed objects lined the walls with their backs turned outward. There were even locks on the silverware drawers.

Oliver only half-listened to Charlie. He was thinking, hard. He looked out the window at the courtyard of Mrs. Pearson's building.

"It goes much deeper than that, I think," said Oliver carefully. "Even time and space are reversed on the other side of the mirrors. In the World—our World—time flows only one way, forward. You can't control which way time goes, but you can control which way *you* go in space. But on the other side of the mirrors, space flows only one way. That was the flow we felt, the force that kept us from going backward. It draws you toward that central cavern and then sends you back out again."

"Sure," said Charlie. "That was how you got there and got back out."

Oliver went on: "I think that in the World, time goes one way but *space* goes two ways. In the Way, space goes only one way, but *time* goes two ways, back and forth. Time is all around you, and if you use your mind-muscles—the way you use your body-muscles in the World to move around in space—you can go ahead or behind in time. That's why we could see things that had just happened, like your being taken prisoner, and you could travel right to things that were just about to happen, like me nearly getting killed with feathers."

"Could you see farther back than that? Travel back? In time, I mean?" Mrs. Pearson asked urgently.

"Ye-es. Yes, I think so, but only with a lot of effort." Oliver recalled how he had seen scenes from when his father was young—but he had been so shocked then, and had had to work hard to see those things for only a few seconds. He decided not to mention it. He somehow knew that his father's predicament was for himself alone to know.

"You have to really, really think to go any farther ahead or behind. That's what Nostradamus was trying to tell me. The thing about time travel is that all that anyone thinks of is *time*, and they don't think about the *travel*," he said.

"Okay. But why did the flow, or whatever it was, stop when they pulled us into the cells?" Charlie asked.

"I think— I think," Oliver went on, "that long ago the first people to have made the Way must have made space-proof rooms, just the way we have time-proof rooms."

"Whuddya mean, time-proof rooms? We don't have time-proof rooms."

"Well, they're not really time-proof. Time still goes on. But they *feel* time-proof. I mean . . ." Oliver thought hard, trying to give an example of what he felt so strongly. "Like your own room at night. When we're sleeping, we feel time-proof. Or a nice room in the twilight with a fire in the fireplace. You feel safe from time—there's nothing pressing on you. It's how I used to feel at night when I looked out the kitchen window, before, you know, before François came. So I think that they have flow-proof rooms, too, places where you don't feel the push of space so much. I guess they were built long, long ago, when the Way was open, and the Master of Mirrors just exploits them now to keep his slaves in control."

Mrs. Pearson regarded Oliver with a kind of soft, respectful look. "Oliver," she said, "You are actually, unbelievably, almost, impossible as it is to imagine, *thinking*. I believe you have it. In the World, time is fixed and we move in space. In the Way, space is fixed and you move in time. It would explain so much!"

And she went on to speculate that it would explain that thing called "second-sight"—the way that people had the sense of seeing things that had not yet happened. They had simply stumbled into the Way through an open mirror, and then stumbled back out, and really had seen things but hadn't known how. Why, the reversal of time and space in the Way would explain mysterious disappearances, and travel in time—the Way was probably even the "other way" that the Three Magi had found, and probably the secret passage through time that . . .

Oliver cut her short.

"We have to go back inside! Right away! He wants Neige for something, and I think it's something that's going to happen soon. He wants her for some reason. I heard him say something about the queen of the new mirrors. We have to go back for her. Now!"

"We will," Charlie said. "But we have to get some rest, and figure out how, first."

"No! We need to get back there now," Oliver insisted.

"Even if we are to get back inside the Mirror-Maze, we won't be able to do it the same way as before," Mrs. Pearson said. "The living ice has all melted, I'm afraid, and anyway, they'll be watching for anyone entering by the gate of the true mirror very carefully."

"But if we don't have living ice, and we don't have an open door, how can we get inside?"

"Well, that is the problem, is it not?" Mrs. Pearson said. "And it is ours to solve. And soon, as you say— whatever they intend to do, they intend to do now. I have a partial plan, at least. In fact, I intend to leave this very night! But first we had better get you two boys—I mean, Your Majesty and His Maréchal—home."

Oliver began to protest again that they had to go after Neige, right away, but Mrs. Pearson only held up her hand.

"We need to *think,* we need to think more than ever, coolly and logically, before we act. But, first, quick! Remember: He is *everywhere* now, in every mirror. We cannot risk being seen in any of them. Quick, empty your pockets!"

Oliver began to turn his pockets inside out and examine their contents.

"Well, I don't think there's anything *dangerous* in them. I've got just the wand . . ." He bent down to scrutinize what else he had.

"Don't look!" Mrs. Pearson cried. "Whatever you do don't look! If it *is* a mirrored surface, he could be looking out. One glance and he'll know exactly where you are." She gestured around the apartment. "You can see I've mirror-proofed this flat—I've covered up every shiny surface in this place, from silverware to candlesticks. I've even buried my champagne spoon deep within my pocketbook. We must do everything from touch and memory."

Oliver looked around and he realized that, indeed, all the shiny surfaces in the room, mirrors and plates, had been covered or turned toward the wall.

Charlie was examining his own pockets. "Here are my keys . . ." he said.

"Dangerous!" Mrs. Pearson called out. "Don't look at them! You'll have to let yourself into Oliver's house entirely by feel. Even a glance at your keys and he might see you."

Mrs. Pearson insisted that they not take any chances. ("We must not be seen in any mirrored surface. Not a rearview mirror or a shiny surface.") So as the three of them left her home, they had to inch alongside the walls of the rue, like escaping prisoners scared of being seen by the guards and searchlight.

As they edged nervously along, Oliver noticed what he had never really noticed before, and that is how every city street in the world is divided neatly in half between mirrors and windows, as though a truce line had been declared at the end of a battle. On one side are the windows of shops and restaurants, beckoning people in to buy and eat, and on the other sides there is always the line of parked cars, shiny and shut tight, but covered with mirrors as a battleship is covered with guns.

Charlie, who seemed entirely to have recovered from

being a prisoner in the dungeon of the Master of Mirrors, minutes from having his soul knifed out, scooted ahead on his in-line skates.

"Stay on the safe side!" Mrs. Pearson called after him, and he nodded impatiently, and skated along beside the windows, nodding now and then as though he recognized a wraith inside. She turned toward Oliver. "Parked motor-cars *are* hideous, aren't they?" she said. "Dirty tin boxes!"

They continued to creep along the walls of the street. Oliver waited for her annoyance at the parked cars to subside. "What made you think of going to the dressing-room mirror to bring us home, Mrs. Pearson?" he asked at last.

She shrugged. "I knew that a mirror that had long been encrusted with vanity would be the most permeable to the other side. That was the vainest mirror I could think of—the mirror in the dress department of Christian Dior, where women who have become too rich too late try on clothes that are too elaborate to be too exciting. The rest was obvious. As most things are if you think them through."

"Where are you *going*, Mrs. Pearson? You said you were leaving tonight. Where for?" Oliver whispered intensely.

"I intend to get on a train, right now, tonight, and look backward. I believe that the time has come to use the wisdom of the book to open an old secret door to the Way."

Oliver could sense that Mrs. Pearson was being deliberately mysterious. He had come to understand that she liked being deliberately mysterious.

"What book?" he asked.

"Alice's, of course. *Through the Looking-Glass.* You've noticed me reading it."

"Yes, of course. But what's the point?"

"Oliver, tell me the story of *Through the Looking-Glass*," Mrs. Pearson said, as though they were sitting at home and not pressing their backs nervously against the windows of a Paris shopping street, doing anything to avoid being seen from the shiny surface of a parked Peugeot.

"You know it," Oliver objected.

"Tell it to me, simply and sharply, without the comic bits. It's important."

"Okay," Oliver said. He thought for a moment. He stopped. "Well, there's this young girl, and she pushes her way through a looking glass, a mirror, and on the other side she finds that everything's reversed—at least, handwriting and all is—and there are all these strange characters, chessmen and a, well, a walrus and a carpenter, and Tweedledum and Tweedledee, and she makes these sudden abrupt trips from one place to another, and then she finally finds herself being crowned a queen in this nightmarish banquet hall and then—and then she wakes up . . ."

"Fine. Now, imagine for a moment that a child *had* gone through the mirror, quite by accident, and seen the other side," Mrs. Pearson said. "Would the child know that they were evil things rather than odd things? And if the child had told someone else about it—might that someone else have understood the evil of it, and then to comfort her, he might have made it seem not evil, but merely odd."

"You mean—Alice went through the glass? But she didn't know what she was seeing?"

"Oliver, too many of the details are the same. The feeling of gauze as she entered the mirror, the smokiness, the language. The knights' strange regalia, the samurai helmets on the soul-stealers—if a small girl were struggling to describe them, chessmen might be *exactly* what she would think of. And all the frightening types: the bloated clones in striped shirts, as you describe them—Tweedledum and Tweedledee. The soul-hunters with their knives and their round collection of souls—who else but the Walrus and the Carpenter and the oysters! Imagine if a sensitive child had seen these things."

Oliver thought. "I see what you mean. Even the big masked head, booming words out so softly and strangely . . ."

"Yes—who else does that put you in mind of but Humpty Dumpty? Oh, Lewis Carroll made him seem funny rather than terrifying. But isn't that what a good man would do—a loving friend and a kind Anglican minister? A loving friend would try to make light of it all, turn those images into jokes, and tell her that she had only had a dream. But there's a core of truth still there. And I suspect that he knew there was. I think he knew that what Alice found was really urgent news, and he wanted the World to have it."

"Well, that's certainly interesting. But what does it have to do with us? Practically, I mean."

"It means Alice's window into the Way may still be there, in Oxford, and it may still be open. And the master may not know it."

Oliver shrugged. "But how would we ever know where it is? How would we ever find it? And what makes you think we could go through it?"

Mrs. Pearson paused. The cold wind sliced around them on the dark street. She pulled her shawl tight. For the first time since Oliver had met her, she looked almost old.

"To answer your questions in order. I know where it is because I've seen it. I believe that we could find it again because it is still in the place where I left it. And I am sure that we could go through it, because I already have."

Oliver turned in surprise. Mrs. Pearson had been inside! But then a suspicion that had been growing in his mind spoke up.

"Mrs. Pearson, tell me the truth" he said. "You're related to Alice, aren't you? You're her granddaughter, or grandniece, or something like that. Aren't you?"

Mrs. Pearson pushed flat against the wall, and stared at him with a new esteem. "Oliver! That may be so. But what makes you think that?"

"Your spoon. It has an LL on it. So those must have been your initials before you were married. And you told me at dinner that you owed a *little* debt to someone. Well, that was Alice's real name. Alice Liddell. Alice *Little*. Those were your real initials: LL. Lucy Liddell."

"Oliver! Very impressive. Thought right through like . . . like a thinker! . . . Yes, I am Alice's granddaughter. When I was a girl, growing up, my sisters and I discovered Alice's mirror locked away upstairs—we still lived in the same house, you see—and we passed through it many times. We never went deep into the maze, or the Way. But I know that that mirror was open . . ."

"That's fantastic. I'll go with you."

"No, Oliver. The Way is vast, and the Mirror-Maze is large within it, and there are many paths inside. I shall take a side path. You must confront him at the center. The final battle is at hand."

Oliver's voice became intent. "But what does he *want*? The master. He controls all his slaves already. What does he want?"

"Want? He wants to be out. Why, he wants what any rational person wants. He wants to go back to Paris. For the moment, he is still trapped behind the mirrors. He is searching for some other way to get back into the World."

"But isn't he free now that he doesn't have to wear the mask?"

"Not entirely free, not quite yet. At least, I hope not. As long as the One with None was caught behind his mask, he could not look from the backsides of the mirror into the World. He had to send his slaves out along the mirror-way every night, soul-hunting. Once he was free to unlock his mask—no, Oliver, do not apologize, it hardly helps—he could look out through the mirrors into the World, and he could take over the face of any of his slaves in the Way. But he cannot actually enter the World, and *become* them—take over their bodies and their very selves. Not yet. I suspect that that is what he wants to do now. For once he gets back into the World, he can become whomever he's captured. And then so many—who knows how many—will not only be in thrall to him. They will be him, as if they had been swallowed whole."

Ahead of them, Charlie was skating, in the dark Parisian street.

"But why? *Then* what does he want? Why does he want to get into the World and take over his slaves? It can't just be to get back to Paris."

"Oliver, never underestimate the small causes of great evils," Mrs. Pearson replied. But then she frowned. "I wish I was certain. He wants to leave the Way to take over the World—and he wants to capture the World so that . . ." Mrs. Pearson set her lips and shook her head. "No, I can't see it. Not yet. At least, all we know is that the one thing that stands between him and the World is the King in the Window—and that, my young friend, is you."

Oliver looked down to where Charlie was sliding and gliding on his skates in the moonlight and street light of winter. He felt very small, and very helpless, and nothing at all like a king.

"I leave you here," Mrs. Pearson said at last. "I shall find my way inside, and so must you."

"How?" Oliver asked.

Mrs. Pearson was suddenly just as frosty again as she had been on their first meeting. "How could I possibly know?" she said. "You're the king." She sighed. "It's too soon, too soon. Your education has only just begun. You have only now begun to think. You barely know the color of lies, and what do you know of the shape of dreams, or the speed of wishes? Ah, well."

"Speaking of education, don't worry too much about your school," Mrs. Pearson added dryly. "They are a tad perturbed about your absence. Fortunately, I reassured your mother that you were engaged in this—what did you call it?—special research project under my guidance, and, of course, when she repeated that to your schoolmasters, they must have been *very* impressed."

Oliver nodded, relieved.

Mrs. Pearson turned toward him. "Oliver," she said. "I keep meaning to ask you. What *is* a 'special research project'?"

Oliver suspected that she knew perfectly well, but he said only "Oh. It just means—studying outside of school."

"You mean reading? And talking? And thinking?"

"Well, yes."

"Such a fancy term for such simple things. And doing it on your own? For its own sake?" she asked tartly.

"Yes. Well, you do get a grade in the end."

"Ah. It seems then that my life has been a special research project. I wonder what grade I shall get in the end?"

Oliver suspected that she was being ironic, but she turned away and was gone before he could be sure.

Chapter Twelve

Crumbs and Colored Glass

"OLIVER, WHAT *is* this fascinating research project you're doing with Mrs. Pearson?" his mother asked the next morning. She was in her jogging pants and Tanglewood sweatshirt, doing leg stretches. His father, as far as Oliver knew, was still asleep. Oliver was relieved. He wasn't really ready to see him yet. He knew that he would see his outer shell, but the thought that his inner nut (it was a weird metaphor, Oliver knew, but he couldn't think of a better one) was in the soul-case of the Master of Mirrors . . .

Oliver was trying to think, even as he got dressed for school. What did he know, and what did it mean? He knew that the wraiths had given him a soap-bubble blower and a water pistol because they knew that they would be deadly weapons on the other side, and he knew, too, that Neige had pressed the figure of the fleur-de-lis onto his hand because she was a crystallomancer, and that she and her friends, the clochards, were guarding him. And he knew that there were two true mirrors in the world, which could let the King in the Window in and out of the Way without the Master's knowing—though one was now broken and one was still lost. . . .

But every question solved left another riddle unanswered. What were the "new mirrors" that the Master of Mirrors had spoken of? Why would they be joined with the old mirrors, and why was that so dangerous? And, if Mrs. Pearson was right, what did that have to do with the worse and even more evil project that the Master of Mirrors had in mind?

And then of course, to help him, there were only the three riddles of Nostradamus, which were truths about the future told in ways that—he sighed—no one could ever understand. What was the secret army of the Watchful, who would return to man's side at the moment that they left their sides? What were the three things that were both hot and cold, and what were the windows that everyone looked at but no one could look through?

And then—the weirdest part—how could he possibly turn the universe inside out, *and* turn the Master of Mirrors upside down? It was all hopeless, no matter how long he turned it around and around in his head. And when he shut his eyes, trying to think, he saw always the featureless face of the Master of Mirrors, great and fleshy and blank, staring out at him, cold and powerful, where Oliver was shaky and confused. And then he thought again of Neige . . . and then he thought again of his father, and, instead of becoming clearer, the more he thought, the more lost and frightened he felt.

"Oliver, dear. I asked what this project was that you were working on with Mrs. Pearson," his mother repeated. He had been lost in thought. "And why won't you have some breakfast?" She seemed equally concerned about both questions.

Oliver started, and tried to think what to say.

"Mom," he began, "imagine that the world we live in isn't the only—"

But Charlie was interrupting him. "Yes, Mrs. Parker," he said, in an unctuous, virtuous voice. "The research project Oliver is working on has to do with the theory of the multiverse and its, uh, origins in eighteenth-century French thought."

Oliver stared at him. He had never heard Charlie speak that way before.

"Oh, really?" Oliver's mother had said.

"Yes, the idea that we live in a multiverse, with many parallel realities, first appeared in the theories of the plurality of worlds by the French philosophers of the

Enlightenment," Charlie went on, more matter-of-fact than before.

Oliver looked dumbfounded at Charlie.

"Well, have a good day at school," his mother said, seeming a little puzzled at Charlie's words. "I think it's very nice of you to take Charlie to your school, dear. You'll have to translate for him. Do you remember when you were only three, and Charlie visited us, and you were trying to tell him what stained glass was? And you didn't know the word in English so you said that it was 'No, no, Oliver glass'? Because whenever you stained something we always said, 'No, no, Oliver.'" His mother hummed to herself, and reached over to kiss his head. "No, no, Oliver glass," she repeated, chuckling.

At that point, of course, Oliver wanted to kill his mother—and Charlie was smirking at him so hard, and covering his mouth so obviously as he laughed, that Oliver sort of wanted to kill him, too.

As they left the house, Charlie turned to Oliver. "No, no, Oliver!" he began, but Oliver gave him a look so dark and deadly that Charlie cut it out.

Then Oliver turned to Charlie. "Charlie, when did *you* learn all that stuff you told my mother?"

"Hey. Ollie. I'm not an idiot. I'm just an American." Charlie said. "Now, where are we going?"

"Why didn't you want me to tell my mother the truth?"

"Yeah. Great. 'Mommy, I'm the King in the Window and I spent the last day in an anti-matter universe fighting

giant faceless evil guys with feathers. Oh, Mommy, it was so
. . . exciting.' Like, *that's* really going to help us."

"Yes, I suppose you're right. But what about all that
other stuff? All that business you were telling my mother
about many worlds and universes and so on?"

"Oh, that's all true, I'll tell you later. Hey, I'm still
hungry. Could we get some real breakfast?"

Oliver took a deep breath. By now the two boys were
on the Pont Royal, in the cold gray light of a Paris winter
morning. Paris stretched out on either side of them, to their
right toward the Île de la Cité, the oldest part of Paris,
where the two towers of Notre Dame Cathedral dominate
the sky, gray towers against gray heavens, to their left
toward the Trocadéro and the Eiffel Tower. Charlie, of
course, chose to look at the tower, where the lights of Gil
Hornshaw's great project were still being strung up and
were now being slowly turned on.

"Look at that," Charlie said. "What *can* he be doing?
We gotta get over there and find out! You know him, Ollie.
Let's go right over."

Oliver blew his breath out and watched it steam. Then
he stuck his hands in the pockets of his coat, because he had
forgotten his gloves. "Ouch!" he cried. What had scratched
his hand? He took his right hand out of his pocket and
looked at it. No wonder it had stung. The inside of his
pocket was lined with those little shards of colored glass that
he had picked out of the tapestries of the king in the
clochards' cavern.

And then something about the conversation with his mother struck him again, and he stopped to think. Right there on the little street, in the cold morning, despite his exhaustion and his worries, he stopped to let his mind make pictures and connections. What had she said? He stared at his hand . . . and then out at the cluster of churches on the Île de la Cité . . . and then he turned to Charlie. A possibility bloomed in his mind.

"Charlie, we're not going to my school," he said at last. "Again. God knows what they'll do when they catch me. Skin me alive, probably. We're going to walk over to the Île de la Cité and look inside a church there. A chapel, really. It's about half an hour away. Come on. We can get some more breakfast on the way." He felt almost guilty thinking about breakfast, with Neige trapped in the Way.

"Why?" Charlie asked agreeably.

"You'll see when we get there. I'm probably wrong— but if I'm right, we may be on that right track that Mrs. Pearson said I had to find. First, though, I'm going to have to run back home. Wait here!" Oliver said.

When he came back , five minutes later, he was out of breath and there was a bulge beneath his pea coat.

"We're going to the Sainte-Chapelle. It has the most beautiful stained-glass windows in Paris. And that's saying a lot. And it's got—well, you'll see what it's got."

"Okay. Great. Medieval-type sightseeing. I'll send my mom a postcard. Why, though?"

"Well, because . . . I'll tell you why when we're there.

Now you tell me: what was all that you were talking about with my mom? That stuff about there being many worlds? Is that true? And what does it have to do with us?"

"Wait, and I'll tell you when we sit down. I liked the toast your mom made us, but I could use one of those chocolate bread things," Charlie said. He meant a *pain au chocolat*, a rich pastry filled with dark chocolate that children in France are actually encouraged to have for breakfast.

A few minutes later, Charlie and Oliver were safe and even cozy in a café on the boulevard. They sat by the windows, and Oliver covered all the silverware on the table with napkins, and he wouldn't even let Charlie stir his café au lait with a spoon. He made him use his finger. ("It's gross," Oliver conceded, "but would you rather be gross or soulless?" "Most of the guys at my school are gross *and* soulless," Charlie commented, but then he stirred with his finger.)

And then Oliver, once again, asked Charlie to explain what he had been talking about when he told his mother about the multiverse.

Charlie had the American gift of being ready to talk about anything anywhere he found himself. He munched on his first *pain au chocolat*—he had ordered three—and began to answer Oliver's questions.

"The multiverse?" he said happily. "It's something we studied in school in Rama Rama's class on the Tao of physics."

"The what of what?" asked Oliver.

"It's sort of like the mysterious side of science. Rama Rama used to be called Mr. Kilgerman, and he just taught us chemistry. But then he got his head enlightened when he went on summer vacation in Nepal and he came back as the Rama Rama. But what he teaches is all, like, true. You can read about it in *Scientific American* and everything."

"Well, that's good. But what's the idea?"

"Well, what scientists think is that there may really be many, many, many other worlds alongside this one. They call it the multiverse. Usually, you can only really know it's there when you're watching teeny-tiny little particles. What scientists call 'quantum particles.' You see, when a tiny particle— like the smallest particle of light there is—when you first look at it, it's sort of like . . ."

Charlie saw the confused look on Oliver's face. Then he had an inspiration. He tore a crumb from his *pain au chocolat* "Well, just imagine that this crumb is the particle of light, and I'm flicking it across the table the way I might fire it out of a flashlight or something." And Charlie cocked his thumb and finger, and shot the crumb across the café table.

Oliver watched him. "Okay. I can imagine that."

"But then, all at once, that particle of light seems to spread out like a wave so that suddenly there are a million crumbs, headed for every corner of the table. There are so many that it's like a crashing tsunami of crumbs headed in every direction. More like a wave of water than a lot of individual crumbs." And Charlie actually spilled some of his water across the café table, to give Oliver the idea. The waiter, hearing the splash, turned and gave him a dirty, shocked look.

"So when you hit it it's like a speeding crumb but then when you watch it it's like somebody spilled a glass of water?" Oliver asked, ignoring the waiter. Being a king was giving him the arrogance even to ignore café waiters.

"Yeah, right," said Charlie. "Somehow, that tiny little particle of light sort of spreads out right across the table so that there are a hundred different particles, all headed for different pockets."

Charlie's hands described the action. He paused to eat more chocolate bread. "But then—here's the weird part—a nanosecond later, when you go to look to see where the little speeding crumb has gone, all of it—the whole tiny particle of light—is back in one place on the table, and nowhere else. It's all gone back to being a single crumb."

"So where do the other little bits of crumb go? What happened to the wave?" Oliver asked.

"Well, the cool physicists think that all the other crumbs you saw suddenly disappear are on other café tables in other universes alongside this one, ones that we can't see! There's a gazillion parallel worlds right alongside this one, and that's where the rest of the wave, all the other little crumbs, end up. *That's* the multiverse. There are millions of worlds out there, each one a little different, or a lot different, and the rest of the wave of light rushes into them."

"Are you serious?"

"Completely."

Oliver paused to think about this. It was an idea that seemed pregnant with possibilities. Could you get into the Way *this* way? "How do they get there? I mean, how do the particles get out of this universe into another one?"

Charlie shrugged. "Well, it's as if there are little tiny cracks between universes, and they rush into them."

"You mean, like mice finding the little cracks in the walls between apartments?"

"Yeah. Sort of. You really like those mouse metaphors, don't you, Ollie?"

"Is there any way to communicate between those universes? I mean, could we e-mail our counterparts in the other universe? 'How are your crumbs?' Or, 'How many arms do you have? I've got two. Oh, you've got six?' That kind of thing?"

"Well, no one's figured out a way to go back and forth between universes in the multiverse. But if they ever do, then, sure, you could e-mail one another. If the guys like us in the parallel universe spoke English. But they would probably speak something *like* English or French but not exactly. Maybe Prenglish. Or Brench."

"That's weird, Charlie."

"No weirder than a lot of stuff we call normal. Actually, Ollie, it's really just like this mirrors and windows war we're caught up in. I mean, think about any window reflection"— Charlie gestured out to the solid glass wall that separated the café tables from the street—"and you can see how all the light rays head toward a window. Some of them break up and some of them bounce back and some of them go right through. The ones that bounce back make your reflection, and the ones that go on let you see what's beyond the window. In a way, you're still in the same room you're in, *and* out in the street or garden, too. In a way, every window is a multiverse right here on earth."

"I still think it's weird," Oliver objected. "I mean, there's weird like the window wraiths. And then there's weird like a gazillion worlds alongside our own that you can't see with people in them."

"Ollie, that's what a fish that was living deep in the ocean would think if you told it there was air up above and then a sky above that and then space up above that, and planets up above in space and stars everywhere. He'd say you were crazy. But there is. You're thinking like a fish, Ollie, when you gotta be thinkin' like a king. Think like a crowned head, not like a can of tuna."

But something else was pulling at Oliver's mind, as he turned to look out the window and watched the frosty day go by. He thought about all the other Olivers, or near-Olivers, in the rest of the multiverse. Do they have the same temperament as me, he wondered? Do they like the same things I would? If I could talk to all the other Olivers in the multiverse, would I never be lonely? Is there someone who's just like me right now, going somewhere on the train? Would I be friends with all of them, more than I could be friends with anyone else?

And then, he realized, with a shock, that the feeling of

loneliness that had clung to him like a winter coat almost for as long as he could remember was gone. Neige and Mrs. Pearson, Charlie and Molière—everything was terrible and frightening, but at least he had company.

Then another thought struck him, and he tried to tell it to Charlie.

"But that means that if each world out there in the multiverse is like our world, then it also has a Way on the opposite side of its mirrors, which means that . . . that's its opposite, then—what if you . . ."

There was something hard and difficult to reason his way through, but he knew that it had *something* to do with what might happen to a mirror in the Way, and he couldn't get it. He could sort of *see* the thought, as though it were running just ahead of him. But he couldn't catch the thought yet.

Finally, he gave up with a sigh. They paid the bill. Then they left the café and walked down the boulevard Saint-Germain, packed even on a winter morning with young students hustling to and fro.

But Charlie was staring up at the Eiffel Tower, where the lights of Gil Hornshaw's project were still filling the girders.

"Ollie," he said, "this is so obvious it's ridiculous."

"What, Charlie?"

"*That's* the quantum leap. It's a quantum computer—that's what he's making! Gil Hornshaw is making the world's first quantum computer—"

"What, Charlie?" Oliver asked.

"It's a quantum computer."

"What's that?"

"It's a computer that could work in the entire multiverse. If you could send the little quantum bits out into the multiverse, and then get them back again, you could have the most powerful computer ever engineered. If you had one circuit working in this world, and sending out its little particles simultaneously into all those other worlds, you'd have a gazillion switches working at the same time throughout the cosmos. A quantum computer would be to an ordinary computer what a reflection in a mirror is to a reflection in a window—it would be the same basic idea, but gazillions of times more powerful and focused, and you could do more things with it, just the way that with a mirror you could make telescopes and microscopes."

"And you think that's what he's making?"

"I'd bet anything that's it! What else is big enough? That's why he keeps dropping hints about quantum leaps. That's why it's the name of his company. He's building a quantum computer, and he's going to start it up this week right here in Paris!"

And Charlie looked up, his face alight with wonder, at the glittering tower.

For a moment, Oliver joined him. But then he looked down again.

He sighed. "Charlie, I wish that our fight would lead us into the future and to somebody positive like Gil. It sounds like more fun. But I'm afraid we're going to have to look into the past first, before we can look ahead." And he set his stride forward and walked on.

They arrived at the Place Saint-Michel. There, just on the other side of the Saint-Michel bridge, and right in the middle of the river, lies the Île de la Cité, the oldest settled part of Paris.

And as Oliver looked out from the Place Saint-Michel toward the old island, his breath tightened. Now it was Oliver's turn to see and exclaim.

"Look!" he cried out. Charlie had never heard Oliver use this tone. "Look, Charlie: see the angel?"

"What angel?" Charlie asked, puzzled.

"It all comes together! The windows that can be seen out of but not seen into—that can be looked at but not looked through. Like Nostradamus said. I was right. It must be the Sainte-Chapelle. I think we've found the first answer, Charlie!" Oliver was not usually a very demonstrative person, and for a moment Charlie thought he might have gone a bit crazy from all the pressure of suddenly being a king.

"What are you talking about?"

"We've found it, Charlie! Now we just have to act quickly. Charlie, do you see the angel?"

Now Charlie looked across the river, where Oliver was pointing. Just above the roof of the huge, ugly, depressing, official-looking building peeked a small statue of an angel—high, high up on a spire.

"That's the spire of the Sainte-Chapelle—the most beautiful stained-glass windows in Paris are in it. For centuries it's been completely surrounded by the Palais de Justice. It's a big church, with stained-glass windows, but it's inside the courthouse building, and the walls are so high that you can't see anything but the angel on the spire!"

"So what?"

"Stained glass, Charlie, stained-glass windows. That's the third way, the king's way, the oldest way that the master was looking for. Remember Nostradamus's riddle? What kind of glass window does everyone look at and no one look out of? Why *stained-glass* windows, of course. That's why the tapestry of the first king was covered with shards of colored glass. Someone must have pulled it through a stained-glass window during the retreat from the Way."

Charlie stopped. "Yeah. I get it. That makes sense. There's glass for good, and mirrors for, like, wicked—and then stained glass is some mystical-magical, free-time, good-or-evil, your-call!-thing in between. But what good is it for us? *We* can't just walk through a stained-glass window. . . ."

"Maybe the king can," Oliver said calmly, and kept walking.

"Oliver," Charlie whispered a few moments later, as they mounted stairs. "This is truly, deeply weird. I mean, here we are in this kind of big, official, boring government building, and a semimystical, paranormal ancient church is just stowed away inside it?"

"My father and mother and I always come here when we're going to a concert," Oliver explained. "You see, it's right up the staircase, with all these courts on either side."

They were inside the Palais de Justice, near the Sainte-Chapelle. The hallways were lined with bulletin boards posted with official announcements—an apartment being auctioned by the state, a recruiting poster for the police.

"But then right down here," Oliver was saying, "you cross a little corridor and, well—here we are!"

There they were. A short and dingy corridor had bridged the way between the law and the medieval church. They pulled the big wooden doors open, and they were inside.

It was dark. But there was light enough to see. The chapel did not seem to be an old stone building that had windows—it *was* windows, all windows, with a little stone lace and tracery between them. If the stained-glass windows at the Cathedral of Chartres are the highest and most solemn in all of France, the stained-glass windows of the Sainte-Chapelle are the most sublime. They are fifty feet high, and there are twelve of them, radiating beneath the highest ceiling in France. The entire chapel seems to be made of glass.

Charlie gasped. The high vaulted ceiling seemed almost to be pulling them upward, like a magnet; it seemed to rise that high above them, and the great stone interior—as good in feeling as the stone cavern had felt evil—swept away all around them. For all that the building was stone on the outside, on the inside it seemed to be made of glass.

There were twelve stained-glass windows, radiating in blue and dark red and an occasional patch of amber. They crowned the enormous space and distilled a colored light onto the stone below. Charlie stared at them in wonder. They showed strange scenes from the lives of the saints, and cast a vivid and beautiful blue light across the cold stone floor far below. The dim sunlight passed through them, and then came out in sheets and bolts of colored light, falling down in rays like bales of soft hay.

"Do you see now?" Oliver asked Charlie.

"But if you, I mean, the king, can get in this way, why didn't the wraiths tell you that in the first place?" Charlie asked.

Oliver considered. "I don't know. But I mean, just look up and—oh, my God."

"Hey, Ollie, that's really your spiritual thing you're feeling there? It's a whole new aspect . . ." said Charlie, sounding very impressed.

"I don't mean *God*. I mean, my school!" Oliver whispered fiercely. "My entire class is here!"

Yes, there they were, Monsieur Fileul and Louis Legrand and all the rest, looking up dutifully at the stained-glass windows. Of course, every year, they made a trip—and Oliver should have known that it was today. Maybe he *had* remembered it, unconsciously, and it was what had put Sainte-Chapelle into his head. But for now, they would just have to be sure that no one he knew saw them.

"Charlie, we have to get out of here."

"Oh, yeah. So what? Just tell them that you're on a journey of personal discovery and you'll be back in school when your inner voice calls out for directed study again. That's what *I* would do."

"Charlie! I don't know what it's like to be absent from an American school for three days. If you're absent from a French school for three days, it's like you've murdered somebody. I think they may send me to Devil's Island or something."

"That would chill your personal journey a little," Charlie admitted.

"Yes, it would, Charlie, and—" Oliver's voice stopped and he gulped with shock.

For just at that moment, the crowd of students parted, and Oliver saw that, standing there with Monsieur Fileul, were Madame Sonia and the two detectives who had chased them into the flea market. The two detectives were wearing their mirrored sunglasses. They were showing Monsieur Fileul a photograph and talking very excitedly as their hidden eyes roamed over the chapel floor.

Then Oliver saw that Madame Sonia was among them, sweeping the floor with her dulled eyes as she searched for something—or someone.

"Damn. They must have followed us here from your house," Charlie said. "Now, we *do* have company."

Just at that moment, Louis Legrand, as Oliver's luck would have it, turned his head away from the droning lecture, yawned, and looked directly across the cold stone floor at Oliver and Charlie, even as Oliver tried to shrink down into his scarf and coat.

A decent person would have winked significantly at Oliver, or nodded and kept his mouth shut. But not Louis.

"Look," he cried out, in French, of course. "The American boy!"

And with a single gaze, all of his classmates turned their heads and eyes toward Oliver. Monsieur Fileul gaped, appalled, and then, drawn by a force as powerful as the flow, began to march, and then stride, across the chapel floor toward Oliver and Charlie, with the entire class like a small vicious army behind him. Madame Sonia, unsmiling—almost unrecognizable to Oliver—was by his side.

"What do we do?" Oliver asked.

"Well, you could just walk up to them and tell them that in a caring community every member respects the other's need to follow their own private mission, and then continue on your journey. Or—"

"Or?"

"Or you could threaten them with the sword you're hiding under your pea coat."

"How do you know I have the sword hidden under my pea coat?" Oliver asked.

"It's sticking out of your sleeve," Charlie whispered back. It was, too.

"It's only made of glass," Oliver whispered fiercely.

"They may not notice that for a moment or two." Charlie replied. "If it looks like a duck . . ."

Oliver drew out his glass sword and brandished it— waving it back and forth in a menacing, though rather awkward, gesture. The crowd of pursuers paused for a moment, spellbound and anxious as Oliver waved the glass sword in their faces.

Then the spell was broken. "It's glass!" Louis cried out. "It's just glass."

That *nuisance*! Oliver thought. And the detectives looked at each other and then raced after him again as Oliver and Charlie scrambled across the chapel floor. And soon the whole crowd was only inches away.

"Up there," Charlie cried, and they elbowed their way past a waiting group of nuns to a stone staircase leading up to the narrow balcony that ran just underneath the largest of all the stained-glass windows.

They raced up the hard, winding stairs, while they heard the angry roar of voices below them, Louis and the detectives crying, "There they are!" and Monsieur Fileul echoing them.

They climbed to the top and looked dutifully down. The light from the blue windows shone down in clear blue rays on the floor. Oliver shivered for a moment in the cold church, and gratefully stepped into a beam of warm light that radiated from the blue windows.

"I think the only other way into the other side is through stained glass—these stained-glass windows," Oliver said. "The two true mirrors were the king's back doors into the maze, but stained glass was—I think it must have been like his fire escape. That was how the first king got in and out in secret, and that's what Nostradamus was talking about. So we go through it."

"And if you're wrong, and we go crashing through, breaking a French national treasure and our necks at the same time, what then?"

"It doesn't matter. We have to go back for Neige. She went back for me."

"Okay," said Charlie, holding up his hands in a gesture of surrender. "But how do we go?"

"I don't know." Oliver said, shivering. "This light's so warm to be in . . ."

And Charlie said, "That light's so cool to look at."

And they looked at each other, as the clatter increased on the stairs, and the single blue beam of light was all that they could see to escape on.

An hour's travel through the flat and brown and romantic countryside of Normandy, a quick half hour in darkness in the tunnel, and then a slower journey through the lambs and green hedges of Southern England, and Mrs. Pearson had found her way back to England.

At the Oxford station, she had been freezing cold. She recalled why she had left England, with such glee, so many years ago. It was *always* cold here, not the smoky, enclosing winter-cold of Paris, but a deep, bone-chilling dampness that seemed to penetrate everything and everyone.

It had taken minutes for her to find the house, and then to open the back door with her old key. No one had changed the locks! The house was empty now. Her last sister had died years ago, and the family could never decide what to do with the old place. There was talk of tearing it down, turning into a small museum.

Yes, it had been just as she recalled. The room all covered with white sheets, the mantelpiece above. She had recalled how she and her sisters had slipped into the room, and found the glass key in her mother's drawer, and then slipped into the secret room. But what she could not remember was how they had actually gone into the mirror. It had just happened, then, somehow. One moment they were at the door, and the next moment they were in the mirror. How had they done it?

There was the fireplace and the mirror and even the little clock. It was her grandmother Alice's room, and Alice's mirror! Mrs. Pearson stared straight ahead, and moved forward slowly toward the mirror.

She held out a hand and wiped the dust from its surface, and then she held the dust to her nose and sniffed it. She had passed through this mirror as a child. Could she again?

The blue ray of transmitted sunlight seemed to thicken and steady in front of their eyes as the two boys watched the thing that was both warm and cool. Just behind them, they could hear Monsieur Fileul and the other boys banging up the stairs, shoving past the knot of tourists. The hard click of the detectives' heels on the stairs.

"It seems to be connecting the window and the air—" Charlie said.

"I think it's a ladder, Charlie! I think it's a ladder of light."

"You think it's strong enough to hold us?" Charlie asked dubiously.

"It must be!" Oliver said, and then more weakly, "I *hope* so."

"Okay." Charlie looked up at it. "So you get on first."

Oliver climbed out onto the edge of the balcony. He looked at the beam of light . . . but what if it was just an accident of the day's light? What if it was just blue light? What if he took a step out and then . . . the thought of the cold stone floor rushing up to smash him as he fell filled his head, and he shrank back.

"I just can't do it," Oliver said.

Charlie, beside him, took a deep breath. Now Monsieur Fileul and the other boys had emerged at the top of the stairs. Oliver could hear their yelling and their relentless steps.

Charlie looked down "I can do it, because we have to," he said, and put one foot out onto the beam of light, nervously but surely. "It's solid!" he called out to Oliver, and then he boldly stepped up and placed the other foot upon the beam of blue light. It held him!

The two detectives in their raincoats and mirrored glasses came out of the stairway door, raced out across the balcony, and lunged for Oliver. Just behind them, his entire class looked on, breathless, held back by a glaring Monsieur Fileul.

Just as the detectives reached for Oliver, Charlie pulled him right up by the arm and onto the blue beam of light.

"Come back here!" Monsieur Fileul cried out helplessly, and the two detectives swatted and reached out, frightened to jump on. But the beam of blue light was slippery, and, as Oliver struggled for his balance, he slipped and his glass sword dropped from his hand toward the stone floor below.

For a horrible sickening moment, like the one when you know a disaster is about to take place and are powerless to stop it, Oliver watched his beautiful sword turn and twist in the void. And then—could it be?—its flight had stopped and it was, yes, it was, coming back *toward* him, against gravity, upward.

And then he saw—it was François, in midair, barely visible as a pale glass shape in the blue winter light. François had caught the sword and was bringing it back to him on the beam.

"Here you are, Your Majesty," François said as he politely handed Oliver the sword. Then the young window wraith settled down on the ray of blue light and turned and bowed to Charlie and then, as he had done that first night, he gestured for Oliver to follow him.

Oliver crouched down to get his balance, and so did Charlie, and the two boys crawled up the beam of light, right behind François. Oliver stole a look down, and saw the two detectives muttering into their mobile phones as they watched the boys crawl up the blue beam in the Sainte-Chapelle and Monsieur Fileul impotently shaking his fist and ordering Oliver to come down; Oliver simply ignored them, and then he stopped crouching and walked up the light like a king.

* * *

"You merely have to think your way across," the voice was saying, calmly.

Lucy Pearson turned her head toward the curtained window, and then she remembered. She had always heard that voice, and she had always seen a glimpse of that face. It was the old man, the white-haired old man in the long parlor window. Yes, now she remembered! It had been the voice of the old man urging her on from the window that had helped her through the looking glass. She peered more closely at the window now. There he was, the old wraith in the window, just visible . . .

"It's still very safe. And you can enter by not knocking, you know," the kind, thin, wraithish voice came from the window. Yes, that was what he had always said. Enter by *not* knocking.

But how do you not knock?

"You remember," now it was the breathy voices of her sisters, in unison. "You remember, Lucy. You enter by not knocking. You remember how."

What was it that they used to do? Think. If to knock you tap the door in front of you, then to not knock, you must . . . oh, yes, of course, how silly of her. Now she remembered. She almost laughed; it was so simple. And she lifted her fist and, instead of knocking forward, flicked her fist backward, just short of her nose, three or four times.

And then, yes, the mirror was turning to mist. Now the gauze was parting, and she pushed herself forward, inside.

Chapter Thirteen

A Ladder of Light

OLIVER AND Charlie climbed the beam of light into the tree in the stained-glass window.

"It's easy. You can do it," François said as he danced around them, sometimes on one side sometimes on the other. At last, they were seated—absolutely seated, flat as wraiths, in the upper branches of the big rosette window of the Sainte-Chapelle. As so often in the past week, Oliver was startled to see how normal weird things became even after just a few moments of familiarity. He looked at his pink skin and blue clothes and realized: I am made of color, I am a piece of stained glass.

"What are you doing here?" Charlie asked François at last. "I mean, how did you get in here?"

"You were never supposed to come here!" François said, "It was smart of you to think of it, but it is *extremely* dangerous!"

"Why?"

"Well, the king knows." François looked as puzzled as someone can look while they are flattened within a stained-glass window.

Oliver thought that he had better sound confident, even if he wasn't, so he said, "Obviously. Stained glass is the oldest part of the window way, and it still runs from the windows to the mirrors without obstructions. But only the King in the Window could open it."

This was a new kind of lying, Oliver reflected: pretending to understand why you were able to accomplish something that you *had* actually accomplished, but didn't know how.

"But no King in the Window would ever do it before," François added, looking worried. But then he brightened. "But you are the new king, so I am sure that you have done it for a very good reason."

Why, Oliver wondered, had the other, older, weaker kings all been frightened to enter the old stained glass, the Old Way? What bad thing could happen as a result? Charlie spoke before he could finish the thought.

"Well, which way do we go now?" he asked.

François merely bowed his head. "All we need to do is to turn ourselves around and we will be facing the Way," he said.

"All alone," Charlie added grimly.

But how do you turn around in the middle of a stained-glass window? It was easy for François. He had lived in windows for centuries, and had merely to flip his body from one side to the other, as though he were a playing card.

It took Oliver and Charlie several moments more to do it—it was really less like turning, because their bodies had become entirely flat, and more like slowly jumping from one point to another. (François did it so quickly that it looked like a flip.) But at last he and Charlie were facing away from the interior of the chapel.

But what they saw was not the city of Paris outside the Saint-Chapelle.

Instead, they could see the vast dark endless maze of mirrors stretching away down far below them. And then Oliver saw, looking down on the maze from high above in the stained-glass window, that while most of the maze was covered in smoke, there was a section, very near the edge, that was brightly, almost harshly lit. It looked new.

"This stained-glass window must be the path into the Way from above," Oliver said to himself.

Then, as he looked toward the Mirror-Maze, he felt again as though it were radiating upward, the tug of the flow and that odd capacity in his mind—the sense that he could will himself backward and forward in time, using his mental muscles.

What was this new part of the maze? What was in it? He took a deep breath and, taking Charlie's hand, thought, as hard as he could, of Neige, just as the last time he had been inside he had thought of Charlie—only this time he was willing himself to be inside just moments before, to be with Neige, wherever she was.

And, just by thinking it, without even a chance to say good-bye to François, he suddenly found himself, along with Charlie, back in the halls of the Mirror-Maze.

Neige, he knew, must be near here. She had to be; he had moved his mind in time to be near her. Yet where was she? And why were these halls so different from the ones where he and Neige had wandered before? Those had been dim and dusty and very old, with glimpses of old gilding lit by a glow like candlelight. They had reminded him of dark forgotten corridors in the Louvre or at Versailles. But these new halls were white and antiseptic and very clean, with a strange hospital smell, like alcohol or fresh rubber. The giant faces were inside their screens, just as they had been before, but they had no frames, and seemed to burn out at him with a new brightness.

Once again, the irresistible flow of space pulled them along, under the giant faces. There was something different about these faces, Oliver noticed, as they floated by.

"Hey, it's a little like being on an E-ride at Disney World!" Charlie called out at first, "only with duller attractions." But then he fell silent. Oliver tried to put his finger on what was so different about these huge faces.

They were looking *down*. That was it. Instead of sadly staring out, as most of the faces in the other corridors had, these faces were just as sad, but they all stared down, as if at their own fingers.

"Crystals!" Oliver said suddenly. He had been lost in thought for the past few moments, and now suddenly almost seemed to spring up from the floor. "Crystal-gazers! Soothsayers from the West! Nostradamus means crystal *screens*. Crystal displays. Digital readouts, plasma monitors—*computers*. That's the secret! Those are the new mirrors! The Master of Mirrors has forged an alliance between ancient mirrors and modern screens! He's trying to do to the computer what he did to glass four centuries ago—take it over and make it his own."

"What are you talking about, Ollie?"

"Remember what the wraiths were saying? That something had happened in the past few years that had switched the balance? Well, it's obvious. It was the coming of the 'crystals'—billions and billions of televisions and computers. And he's gotten inside *them*, now, too, just the way that centuries ago he got inside the mirrors!"

"But how can you tell?"

"Look at them!" Oliver by now was practically dancing with excitement as he gestured at the sad, vast faces. "That's what these faces are, Charlie. They're not looking out through mirrors. They're looking down at keyboards.

They're *word processors*, not mirror-gazers. That's why the Master of Mirrors has been able to triple the numbers of his soulless slaves in the past half century, why he's able to break the wraiths, and it's why they're ready to attack. He must be transferring glass and mirror energy into electronic energy. That's why he needed to crown Neige—"

Charlie stared at him. "Of course! You got it!"

"And that must explain why there was that wi-fi hot spot in my room. The wraiths told me that it was where the first plate-glass factory was, and he was making its energy new—sort of modernizing it."

Charlie squinted at him. "But does it mean that all computer screens are evil?"

"I don't think so—I think it's probably just like the mirrors. They could be good and true—but the master is trying to make them bad. Charlie," Oliver said slowly, staring up at the giant faces flowing down, working at keyboards or staring at monitors, "these are the new mirrors." And, he thought to himself, there are so many of them! And I'm the same old king. And Neige, Neige, where was she? How could he find her?

Mrs. Pearson was upstairs in the looking-glass house now. When she was a girl, they had never traveled this far—they had never gone beyond the first room. But now she knew she had to go farther, and so she had ventured deep into the other side, up the stairs, and into the back parlor. She found who she was looking for there, old and frail, but her hair still long and her pinafore still starched.

"You must give it back, you know," Mrs. Pearson was saying.

The old lady had long, long white hair that reached almost to the floor and cascaded around her pinafore. She was seated on a throne.

"I am glad to see you, my dear," the ancient lady said, falteringly. "I want to go home, you know. I have been here so long. When I felt myself about to die, I came back inside, and thought to stay for good in the looking-glass house. And the other children who were lost inside the mirrors came to stay with me."

Behind the rocking chair, where she sat and rocked, were hundreds of small children, with large lost eyes. They looked longingly at Mrs. Pearson. Mrs. Pearson looked again at them, at these wide-eyed and haunted children.

"All of them, in the last centuries, wandered in through an open looking glass. A looking glass is always closed to all hands but the hands of a child, or a grown-up who had once, as a child, passed through," the old woman said. "But if they go outside the house, you know, the master will take them for his slaves. So they stay inside, safe with me. I have the other mirror, you see, which the White Knight gave me. So we are safe."

The lost children stared at Mrs. Pearson with their great sad eyes, standing solemn in their old-fashioned clothes, pinafores and knickerbockers and broad sad ties.

"I will take you home," Mrs. Pearson said. "I will take

you all home. I know the way. But first you must give me the other mirror, so that we can save the new girl, as the knight saved you."

And the long-haired and pale-faced silent children suddenly sighed, and their collective sigh was as long and deep as the wind in willows on a summer evening.

And Alice, old and frail and never-dying, locked behind the mirrors, sighed, held out the true mirror that she had been keeping safe, and gave it to her granddaughter.

Oliver's mind searched for Neige. He floated, drawn along by the flow, among the windows where the screen-gazers stared down. Charlie, alongside him, was looking at them keenly—and then, strangely, he drew his cell phone out of his pocket and began to stab at it.

But Oliver could think only of Neige. He was sure—he could feel her mind, somehow, and he was sure that she was in danger. As he thought of her, he felt the by now familiar pull of his mental muscles drawing him backward and forward in time. There was the moment of vagueness and the *whoosh* of a strange force, and, after a moment of rushing blackness, he found himself, alone, without Charlie, in a new place.

Where was he? He looked around. Then as his eyes became accustomed to the darker light, Oliver's heart leaped with fear as he saw that he was back within the dark cavern at the heart of the maze. But where was he, exactly? Then Oliver realized that he was looking out from within the mirrors that lined the great hall. He was a mirror image within the mirror—that was why he felt so strange. His heart was beating on the wrong side! But he was rooted in place. Neige must be very near.

But this time the scene was different. There was a crowd of soul-stealers—he was hidden within their reflections, he realized—but now there was also a great banquet table at the center of the cavern, and there was the One with None, unmasked, his horrifying featureless face presiding over it! His head turned slowly and he searched out the mirrors, looking at the reflections of his slaves rather than directly at them. . . . He must not move, Oliver realized, or the master would see that he, too, was there, hidden away among the lifeless mirror images.

But now they were bringing in three biers—long stretchers, borne by the soul-stealers, and hidden by veils. They were coming to the center of the cavern and one by one they pulled the curtains away from the three biers and upon them there were three women, three queens: one in red, aged and withered and terrible looking; one in white, young and proud and fearsome, cold. And there in the middle was Neige—Neige herself, looking dazed but determined, and dressed in a robe of silver-blue.

It *was* rather like the last chapter in *Alice,* Oliver thought. Only there was nothing funny about it. The three queens, only two crowned, were placed at the white table. Neige, he knew, was to be the third.

The Master of Mirrors began to speak, nodding his big head in his terrible way.

"Crown the three, crown the three, welcome the three queens. When the young queen has been crowned, we will know that the moment to launch our last battle has begun," he intoned, and the soul-stealers intoned along with him: "Crown the three, crown the three, three queens for one king, three queens for one king, three queens for one realm."

Oliver's blood ran cold, as though his whole body had been invaded by the shivers. Three queens for one king—that must mean that the moment the three queens had been crowned, the One with None would attack the World. But how would he get out?

"One queen for each of the three realms of the mirror: a crown of ice for the Queen of the Ice. A crown of silver for the Queen of the Mirrors. And a new crown of crystals for the Queen of the Crystal Screens."

Oliver looked and saw that the first old queen had a red gown, faceted with mirrors and a crown of shining silver. She must be the Queen of Mirrors. The second was pale, and had a gown of ice and blue silk. Her crown was clear and cold and transparent. She must be the Queen of Ice, oldest of all.

Queen of Mirrors, Queen of Ice . . . And now a third crown stood on the banquet table. It was unlike any that Oliver had ever seen. It seemed alive, as though with electricity or a current of some kind: small, quick, green digits raced up and down its spires. The master picked it up, and seemed ready to place it on the head of Oliver's friend. And then Oliver understood. Neige, a crystallomancer, was to be made the Queen of Crystals, of screens, a new dark queen for a new age.

"We tried to crown the girl-queen in the last century and failed when the priest broke in and saved her. But it was too soon—the crystal world was not yet quite ready. Now is the time."

"O, Queen of Crystals, all who look in your realm will find a glimmer of ice in their eyes. They will be fixed and still and they will all soon belong to me," the Master of Mirrors said, and he brought the glowing, busy crystal crown toward Neige.

His great featureless head turned, right around like an owl's, as he surveyed his domain.

Oliver took a deep, silent breath, and steeled himself. It was suicidal, he knew, but he couldn't just let Neige be turned into a tool of the master. He would have to put his crown on, and break through the mirror, and do . . . something . . . to save her.

But even as he readied himself to break through the mirror and throw himself at the master, come what might, a commotion arose on the other side of the hall. The mirrors on the other side of the cavern suddenly broke open with a sound like a huge, resounding crash and then an oddly musical tinkle. A cry of fear and wonder rose from the massed slaves.

Charlie and the window wraiths of Versailles broke into the room, feathers raised high.

Racine and Molière and Richelieu—and all the rest, burst in, carrying their tennis rackets and feathers and bubble cannons right in the middle of the cavern, their long wigs flying.

How had they gotten in the Mirror-Maze? But before he could even begin to think about the question, Oliver knew that he must join his friends, so he pushed himself out of the mirrors—it was like pressing against a firm skin that suddenly broke—and entered the cavern, his glass sword raised high.

The window wraiths, their feathers and tennis rackets raised, were soon at battle with the soul-stealers as they fought their way toward Neige. The element of surprise was with them, of course, as they attacked and they cut a swath with their feathers through the evil ones and their slaves. How courageous these usually charming wraiths were being, Oliver realized as he raced across the confused cavern toward them.

It was his moment to fight. He raised his sword high above his head. Outside, in the World, the glass weapon had seemed heavy. But here in the Way, when he hefted it high above his head, it felt light and supple, more like a whip or a rapier than a sword.

He found himself almost paralyzed with fear and indecision now. Could he really do this? But then one of the soul-stealers was rushing toward him with a snarl, and, before Oliver could really think, or decide to act, Oliver had turned the glass sword squarely in front of his face, just for protection. The edge caught the charging soul-stealer right in the side of the throat—and to Oliver's shock, the single touch of the glass edge sliced his head from his shoulders as neatly as though Oliver had raised his sword high and slashed it down.

Oliver looked on dumbfounded at the soul-stealer fallen at his feet. But quickly he was in the very center of the battle, and all he could do was thrust and cut and slash with the glass sword, and watch his enemies fall away around him. The glass sword was as whippy in his hand as a riding switch, and everywhere he went he merely had to flex it and the soul-stealers backed off in fear and wonder at the King in the Window's glass saber.

Soon, Molière was near him.

Just at the edge of his vision, Oliver could see Charlie engaged in a desperate fencing match with two of the soul-stealers, while Neige, nearby, was using her crystal to focus the cold ice-light that filled the cavern into chilly beams of destruction, blinding and stunning the enemy. She still had the electronic crown on her head.

"How did you break in?" Oliver shouted out.

"It was easy!" cried Molière. "Your friend Monsieur Charles did it! He gave us the number. The screens are other kinds of mirrors." He held up Charlie's cell phone. "Maréchal Gronek had one phone, and we had the other! We e-mailed ourselves inside."

The wraiths followed Oliver as he slashed and thumped his way toward the table where the three queens had been enthroned. Even in the midst of his own swordplay, Oliver was overwhelmed by the sheer bravery of the wraiths. For all their fragility, they were fighting hard. Even the Duc de Richelieu was flinging mayonnaise from his jar at the soul-stealers. (On this side of the mirror, mayonnaise became a weapon of serious destruction.) Their bodies, so lithe and fragile in the World, were hard and rigid and knife-edged in the Way, and the soul-stealers fled from them in fear.

And now the faceless Master of Mirrors was directly in front of him—and Oliver blindly struck out with the glass sword, and watched in triumph as the blank head of the master came off in one sudden swoop.

"Oh, thank you. That was most refreshing."

Oliver spun around. There was the Master of Mirrors standing, entirely intact, on the other side of the cavern.

"Thank you, Your Majesty" the serene and strange voice repeated. Now, where was he? Then Oliver turned—and there he was again, a mere five feet from him. Whole and unbent.

Then all the faces of the soul-stealers, every face of every one, in the cavern turned white and blank as their master's.

"Do you see . . ." the voice said, almost with amusement. "We are all one."

Oliver realized what the master meant: Why, the master could be any of them at all. He had long ago taken their faces, and their souls, and he could inhabit any of them, or anyone else whose soul he had devoured. But he couldn't leave the Way, could he? Mrs. Pearson had said that the first King in the Window had locked it from behind.

"Stop all this *thinking*," the master now said suavely. "It fills your mind with hungers that will never be fed. Your ambition, your desire for the girl, your longing to be important. Seek serenity." He smiled serenely, though he had no mouth. "Balance is everything. Windows and mirrors in harmony is what the world needs. Equipoise. Peace. No duality. We should be at peace, you and I."

His blank face looked at Oliver's, and it seemed for a moment not empty but inviting. "Come—let us end this now. The window way will remain open; the Mirror-Maze will remain what it is. A window in the living room to look out of and a mirror in the bedroom to look into." He chuckled playfully. "All of this running around with feathers and traveling in time and knocking people on the head with glasses and soap bubbles flying hither and yon? Is that the higher life? Please."

Their minds locked, and for a moment Oliver thought: He's right. What am I doing this for? Someone puts a paper crown on my head, and I imagine that I'm a warrior. Oliver was exhausted—tired of fighting and wanting and thinking and acting and being.

It was Neige's eyes that saved him. He looked across the cavern, and saw that, beneath her strange electronic crown, the light in her eyes was still glowing. Then Oliver remembered the empty look in all those enslaved eyes, the fear that was all that was left when the light in their eyes went out, and he knew better.

And then he heard Neige's voice, sounding just as exasperated with him as she always was.

"Oliver, you idiot!" she was saying. "You've done *exactly* what he wanted you to do."

And even as she spoke, Charlie desperately lashed out at the master with his feather, and a head fell, but then the laugh emerged again from another head—and then another slash, and another laugh.

"Then thank you, Your Majesty," the voice went on, and it was soft and icy and silky and amused. "You were kind enough to give me the key, and have freed me to take any face I choose. Now you have broken the seal, and shown me the way out. *Only* the King in the Window could open the Oldest Way of All, after it had been closed for so long. And now you have. It was kind of you to do it. I sense our oneness," he ended, his cool voice placid as ever.

All the mirrors that lined the far wall of the cavern pivoted, as though on hinges, and as they did Oliver saw that on their other side they were all made of stained glass, thousands of bright and brilliant colors. Then, as though they were being pulled along by a draft of wind, all of the soul-stealers seemed to lift up into the air, and hover there, and then they passed, one by one, right through the opened mirrors that lined the terrible cavern, and away into the World.

Horrified, Oliver could just make out, on the other side of the mirrors, in the World, the glinting color of dazzling stained glass. The stained-glass windows, it was plain, were a secret doorway into the Way—but they were a secret doorway *out* of the Way, too, and Oliver had foolishly opened it.

A terribly cold wind blew through the cavern, as if

someone had opened a window onto the arctic circle.

Oliver and Molière stood there, crestfallen, as the icy wind bit into them. What a king I am, Oliver thought miserably, as he watched them fly out through the open stained-glass windows. It was like playing chess, and he had always been bad at chess. You had to make your move, but think about your opponent's move. Like a fool I gave him the key to unlock his mask, and then like an idiot I opened the Oldest Way, the stained-glass way, and showed him the way back out into the World.

Now, a familiar French voice was ringing by his side.

Neige was beside him now, throwing her crown to the floor in frustration. "If you had waited your turn, I would have had him exactly where I wanted him."

"But Neige, you looked . . ."

As the frozen wind grew in force and seemed to seize every person in the hall, Oliver saw Charlie fighting desperately in the midst of the two evil queens, who laid their thin and bony hands on him and seemed ready to drag him away, out of the cavern. But even as he started to rush toward Charlie, Oliver was knocked right down by the cold wind that encircled the room, and lifted him up, and he knew no more.

Chapter Fourteen

Qualms and Quanta

"IT'S COLD," a voice was saying. "I'm very cold."

Oliver woke up in darkness. For a moment he thought he was still in the cavern of the One with None. But the sound of dripping water was audible somewhere in the distance. . . . Was he back inside the maze, in one of the dungeons?

"Don't worry," said another voice, in French. "Bah, you're the king. Why should you worry?"

It was Serge, chief of the clochards. Oliver recognized

the voice. He slowly rose up on one elbow, and looked around. Yes, he was back in the Cavern X, which the clochards used as their headquarters. He stirred again, and a hand touched his forehead. He jumped, but the touch was warm, and the second hand held a candle. It was Neige, looking anxiously down at him.

"Neige," he said, "where am I? What's happened to you? How did we escape?"

Oliver rose on one elbow.

"Everyone's safe. Charlie and the wraiths, at least," she added darkly. "Charlie fought off the two queens, I used my crystal to blind the rest of the magi, and pulled all of us out through Molière's e-mail with the help of the mailer-demon."

"The mailer-demon?" Oliver asked, rising up on one elbow.

"A lesser sprite who assists the crystallomancers," she said. "A strange but contemporary thought," she added gloomily.

"Where are the wraiths of Versailles?" Oliver asked glumly.

"The path through the stained-glass windows was still open after the master had passed back into the World. The wraiths pursued him through it, but it was too late. By the time we were back in Paris, he had escaped into the World. They are within the windows of Paris now, crowding together."

"Well, at least they can help us fight! They're incredibly brave, Neige—"

"If they had their neutral medium—a path they could walk on—then they could help us fight, when the moment for fighting comes. But until then, here in the World they are locked in their windows again."

"Would it help if it rained?" Oliver asked.

Neige sighed. "Of course not. They would have to go from raindrop to raindrop. It would take forever. The soul-stealers can slide on ice, but between the windows and the water the wraiths are stuck."

Oliver nodded. "So what do we do now?" he asked.

Neige raised her eyebrows. "You're the king," she said simply. Oliver could tell that she was still angry about his upsetting her plan to entice the master into a marriage and then betray him. He had messed it up, it was true. He had been so proud of his sword fighting.

Oliver rubbed his eyes. "What day is it?" he asked.

"Thursday morning, of course," Neige answered shortly. Oliver thought. This afternoon, it would be just a week since he had found the pebble and put on the crown. He had been the King in the Window for a little less than a week—and see where it had gotten them all.

"We fight!" It was Serge, the chief of the clochards, who was speaking now. "What do we do? What do we do? Enough thinking, enough talking . . ." All around him, the other clochards in their long coats nodded in grim approval. Oliver saw that they were having breakfast in a circle, and that they were using only wooden spoons and forks and bowls. They had obviously mirror-proofed the cavern, too.

"And we have the thing we need to fight with. Look here, young Neige," said Gilles. He gingerly reached under his torn and ratty coat, and brought out the two-winged mirror of Luc Gauric, averting his eyes as he handed it to Neige.

Neige took it in wonder. "But this was broken in a thousand pieces on the night that Oliver and I went into the mirrors . . ."

"Nine hundred eighty-seven and one third pieces, to be exact," Gilles said proudly. "And we put it back together."

"But how could you do it?" Neige asked. "You've sworn never to look in any mirror, even a loyal one . . ."

"We didn't look, Miss. We did it all by feel. A cut here and there, but we finished it last night." He held up his hands. They were covered with bandages.

"How good of you! It means we have one true and loyal mirror to help us again," Neige said.

"We barge right in. Find that ice we saw inside—and then, inside! And after him," Serge said.

Neige sighed. "I wish it were that simple," she began to say.

Suddenly, there was a knock on the stone door that led to their quarry. It was a triple knock, the knock that sounds like "shave and a haircut."

It was Charlie. "It's grim up there," Charlie said, pulling off his damp jacket. "Damn grim." He looked over at Oliver. His eyes briefly lit up with pleasure, and then he dampened them again. "Hey, Ollie. Where you been?" he said.

Oliver wasn't offended. He could tell that it was just what you said.

"What's happening? Where is he?" Oliver demanded.

"I don't know. It's weird, though. It's dark, and cold, up there. Plus there's this kind of light that's been sweeping through the city. Like a giant searchlight. The funny thing is that you can't see where it comes from. It just sweeps around all night long, as though it's, well, searching for something up and down streets. It explodes windows. You can hear them breaking all over the city. First this big loud pop and then the crash and tinkle of window . . ."

"It's the Scouring Light," Neige said. "It is what the wraiths fear most. It has not been seen in half a millennium."

"The Scouring Light?"

"What was a sound—the hum—emanating from the Way, can become a light here in the World. He's using it to erase the wraiths from their windows."

"We find him, and we kill him," said Serge bluntly.

"No," Oliver said. "Neige is right. We need a plan. A thought-through strategy."

"I had a plan," Neige said. "It would have been perfect. The moment they had crowned me with the crystal crown, I would instantly have become the queen of all screens—these, oh, computers and video—"

"The queen of video games, too?" Charlie asked. "Hey, the Game-Queen, quite a brand. What was going on in there?"

But Neige just shook her head. "He needs a queen to rule with him for each of the elements he dominates. Queen of Ice, Queen of Mirrors—and then he had tried to make me the Queen of Crystals. He sort of—sort of marries them." She wrinkled her nose. "But I was only pretending to be drugged and obedient. Do you really think that even the One with None could overcome two thousand years of crystallomancers' genes? Please. But then you had to come and rescue me. Thank you."

It occurred to Oliver that the way that Neige said "rescue me" and "thank you" was even more ironic than the way she had previously called him "Your Majesty."

Well, what *was* his plan? Every plan he had made so far had left them in a worse situation than the one before. He had given away the key to the Master of Mirrors's mask, then he had lost Neige, then he had accidentally shown the master the way out of the Mirror-Maze by opening the Old Way, the stained-glass windows . . .

"I don't suppose I could have made a bigger mess of things than I have, could I?" he sighed at last.

"Actually, your thinking was really getting pretty good there on the other side," Charlie said. "The way you got us through the stained glass, and then the way you figured out what the new screens were. I was actually thinking to myself that the pressure of searching for Snow Red here had really given you a brain-wave upgrade."

"Thanks!" Oliver said, a little surprised.

"Of course," Charlie went on, "on the operational, did-it-achieve-the-strategic-target basis, no, it wasn't so hot. By going through the Oldest Way of All, it looks like you broke the seal between the two halves of reality, and let all the evil weird types who were hiding in the Way back into the World. So, no, I guess we can't call it a successful mission. But I suppose there's probably a parallel universe somewhere where you screwed it up even worse than you have in this one. *That* could cheer you up."

Oliver should have been annoyed. But as Oliver listened to Charlie, his mind suddenly leaped—just as Mrs. Pearson had said it might—from Charlie's joke to a new idea.

"Charlie! The parallel universe! That's it!"

"Huh?"

"If you're right that Gil Hornshaw is going to start up the first quantum computer here in Paris, then that explains what the One with None is trying to do. He wants to take it over. That's why he had to break out yesterday. That's why it was so urgent. He's going to try to take over the quantum computer!"

Charlie stopped chewing for a second. "You think so?" he said.

"I'm sure of it. He's going to launch himself as a what-do-you-call-it—a virus or something—inside the quantum computer. If he can get himself inside it, he'll be able to send himself out through the computer screens into every corner of the multiverse, the same way that he can send his face out into every corner of the World through the mirrors. And he'll be all powerful not just in this Way, and not just in this World—but in *every* Way and *every* World throughout the entire cosmos. He'll be Master of All." And no soul will be safe, he thought, silently. Not one.

"And all the universe will become one giant mirror, with his reflection in it," Neige said sadly, almost to herself.

"He'll have, like super-cosmic stickiness," Charlie added.

"Come on, Charlie," Oliver said. "We've got to go and warn Gil."

"You're right. We don't have a moment to lose," Charlie said grimly. But then he lay down on the floor of the cavern and casually picked up a plate of the food that the clochards had been eating.

"Charlie! You said it yourself. We don't have a moment to lose," said Oliver.

Charlie looked up. "Oh, yeah," he said, as he picked himself up off the floor and went toward the exit. "I guess you're right. Sometimes I forget that the things you've got to say really are the things you've got to say."

The streets of Paris were black and slick with the cold winter rain, when Oliver and Charlie rose from the entrance to the quarries. The two boys walked across the fifteenth arrondissement, up toward the river and the Eiffel Tower. It sits at the edge of the Left Bank, right by the shore of the river Seine. Behind it on the Left Bank stretches away the Champ-de-Mars—the field of Mars—a long and beautiful formal park, with a military school closing it off at the other end. Directly across the river, which is very narrow at that point, on the Right Bank, is the Palais de Chaillot—the Chaillot Palace. Just as the New Bridge isn't new, the Palais de Chaillot isn't really a palace. It is a huge smooth concrete plaza, where in-line skaters like to skate. The front of the palace, where it faces on the plaza and looks across the water toward the Eiffel Tower, forms a kind of wall—like a long smooth façade.

The Eiffel Tower was scintillating with Gil Hornshaw's lights from top to bottom, and high above, the QuantumLeap symbol, the immense crooked smile, was lit up in red.

All around the perimeter of the tower, Oliver and Charlie saw as they approached, were an army of Gil Hornshaw's assistants—young men and women, in black suits and skirts. All of them were looking out keenly for intruders, and all of them were sipping coffee—lattes and espressos and soy mochas—from Styrofoam cups. The good smell of hot milk and espresso permeated the air.

Two of the coffee-drinking assistants, spying the boys, came over and one said, in perfect French but with a strong Seattle accent, "I'm afraid you must move on," gesturing with his cup. "Restricted area."

"I need to see Gil Hornshaw," Oliver said urgently.

The two QuantumLeap employees looked at each other and they seemed about to laugh.

"No one sees Gil Hornshaw," one said.

"I can. He'll see *me*," Oliver said. "Please. Just call

upstairs and have someone tell him that Oliver Parker is here."

But they shook their heads politely. "Sorry. Have a latte?" one asked nicely.

Oliver was desperate. But Charlie, to his surprise, said, "Sure. Can you do me a double decaf iced vanilla one?"

The assistant smiled brightly. "Of course," he announced.

"At least it buys us time," Charlie said through the side of his mouth. The assistant instantly returned with the drink.

Then Oliver remembered something. Of course! He had his snapshot of himself with Gil in his wallet, from the last time they had visited his big house in Seattle—the picture that he had liked to show to his classmates, until they got exasperated with him. Oliver dug it out and displayed it to the two suspicious assistants.

They held it up warily. But there was no question. The photograph certainly showed Gil Hornshaw, with his famous crooked smile and V-necked sweater and anxious eyebrows. And his arm was around this very boy.

"Wait here," the male assistant said at last, and he turned back toward the tower, taking the snapshot with him. Oliver saw him engaged in a frantic discussion over his walkie-talkie. At last, he turned back to the two boys.

"You're allowed up. Gil *really* wants to see you," he said, clearly impressed, and he led them under the feet of the enormous tower, toward the yellow elevator cabin that runs up its northeast leg.

From a distance, or in pictures, the Eiffel Tower looks tall and graceful and thin and willowy. But when you are underneath it, you realize how vast and muscular and huge it is. Its four legs seem like the legs of a cosmic elephant. When, at last, Oliver and Charlie came to the restaurant on the platform two thirds of the way up one of the legs, they found it empty—the chairs turned over on the tables, and a snake's nest of cables and wires and connections all around.

And there, sitting unpretentiously up on one of the tables, in his trademark V-neck sweater and jeans and sneakers, with brown-tinted aviator glasses perched on his nose, was Oliver's father's oldest friend, the great Gil Hornshaw. He was leaning forward casually, and his hands were wrapped tight around an enormous, steaming triple latte.

His face seemed to light up with pleasure as the coffee-sipper led Oliver and Charlie toward him, and Oliver felt an enormous rush of relief. At last, someone powerful he could talk to!

"Hey, Ollie," Gil said, flashing his familiar face with its crooked grin. "Hey. Isn't this a gas?" he almost giggled. "Twenty years ago your dad had to show me how to change the clock on a VCR, and now here I am, practically king of France." He laughed again.

Oliver introduced Charlie. Almost as soon as he'd shaken hands, Charlie said, "Mr. Hornshaw, you won't believe how much I admire you. You're my hero. I came all the way here from New Jersey to see what you were going to do here. But I—"

"Listen, I'll make the official announcement tonight with your dad here. But—let me tell you guys now! It's a—"

"It's a quantum computer!" Charlie said. "Right?"

Gil looked both puzzled and a little nettled. "Yeah. That's right. And it's installed right here on the Eiffel Tower. But how the heck did you know?"

"Oh, Charlie here is amazing about tech things," Oliver said proudly. "He just figured it out . . ."

"Because I figured, you know, that anything you did had to be the ultimate of whatever it was," Charlie added quickly. Oliver looked at Charlie. He had never heard him in such an open, enthusiastic, worshipful mood before.

"Okay, then," Gil said, looking at Charlie first with a kind of mistrust, and then with a slowly growing amused respect. His crooked smile once again spread across his face, and he adjusted his tinted glasses. "Okay. Then you've probably also figured out that those lights you see all over the tower are the quantum condensers—sort of like the circuit-chips for the computer."

"You mean that it can project all its computing out into the multiverse, and then bring them back into a mainframe on the tower? Awesome." Charlie stared out at the thousands and thousands of bright twinkling lights that filled the tower. "Like the Beatles say, an across the universe computer. Will you be able to beat anyone at chess, and figure out pi to the last decimal—all in one morning? Figure out the dimensions of the universe?"

"Figure out the dimensions of the universe, and find out

how cancer cells spread and even draw the shape of every snowflake that falls in a blizzard before it starts, if we want to. It's that powerful," Gil said. "I just hope we can use it for good—real good—and make the world a better place." Oliver looked at him and felt hopeful for the first time in days.

"Gil, there's an enormous problem," he spilled out. "You see, the Master of Mirrors escaped from the Way last night with his soul-stealers—from the Way through the stained-glass exit and he's using the Scouring Light to keep the wraiths locked in their windows while he tries to break into your computer—"

"Whoa, slow down, Ollie my man," Gil said, laughing, and reaching out, mussed up Oliver's hair. "The Master of What? The soul-stealers of where? I can tell you're pulled out of shape about something, but tell it to me slow. Whoa! Slow down and tell it to me in order."

Oliver did. Gil, blessedly, was a very good listener, almost as good as Mrs. Pearson, who didn't interrupt and who took everything you said just in the spirit in which you said it. He nodded at the interesting parts of Oliver's story, and grimaced at the bad ones. Oliver had been afraid that Gil would think he was crazy, or joking, or exaggerating. But instead he just looked at him seriously, and said, softly, "Whoa, whoa . . . intense, intense." His assistants watched from a distance, sipping their espressos and cappuccinos in their paper cups, and dipping biscotti into them and then gobbling them in wonder whenever Ollie related a particularly startling episode.

"Ollie, I can't really say I understand what you're say-ing, all of it, but I can tell that it's serious and that, in some way that may be beyond my understanding, it's real," Gil said at last when Oliver was finished. "So I'll tell you this: more than anything else, I've been afraid of someone hack-ing into the quantum computer. If that happened, it would screw up not just this world, but every other world. Galactic multiversal virus. Cosmic spam!"

Charlie laughed, and then Gil leaned forward conspira-torially. "It's only in the last month, really, that we've found a fuel powerful enough to keep the quantum computer tick-ing in every universe at once." He winked. "Now, don't ask me what that is, Charlie. I have to keep some secrets even from *you*."

Gil picked up his latte again, and shook his head rue-fully. "So we've built in every imaginable kind of safeguard, and I've put my very *top* security person on it. But with what you've told me, I'll recheck and redouble all of our security. We're going to turn the thing on at eight o'clock tonight, and by midnight I hope we'll have, well, we'll have found pi and squared the circle and probably reunited the Beatles, too," he laughed, "and be on our way to more. Oh, here she is. Oliver, Charlie—say hello to Lumière DeLuna."

A very tall and beautiful young woman entered the empty restaurant. She was as willowy and elegant as a fash-ion model, with shining silver-blond hair and bee-stung lips and long almond eyes. When she walked across the room, she seemed to coil and uncoil rather than just walk, and her whole face and shining hair, which she kept mounted in a high and soft bun, intertwined with strings of small glowing pearls, seemed to shimmer, as though she were lit by some inner fire. Like everybody else who worked for Gil, she was drinking a tall latte, and she smiled mysteriously at the two boys as she approached.

Gil reached out, chuckling, and mussed up Oliver's hair again. "Now, tell us both. This, uh, friend of yours, Neige. The one with the crystal. I'd like to meet her. I hate the thought of her running around Paris alone. It sounds like she's in danger," Gil said.

Lumière DeLuna seemed to lean forward, too, as though she cared terribly about the fate of the wraiths as well. Charlie stared at her.

Oliver settled his hair back into place where Gil had touched it. Then Oliver paused, and touched the spot again.

Suddenly Oliver spoke up brightly. "Boy, Gil. It must feel pretty exciting to be doing this. I mean—how does it make you feel?"

Gil looked modest. "Oh, it feels really great. You know. I guess I'm still just . . . just a poor computer geek."

"But it must make you feel like something," Oliver probed. Charlie looked at him in puzzlement.

"Oh, I'm just plugging in another gizmo."

"Yes, but, I mean, on a night like this you must feel, well, ninety-stories high!"

Gil frowned. "Well, we *are* ninety-stories high," he said, a puzzled look on his face.

Suddenly Oliver yawned. "Gee—I'm feeling so tired, I've hardly slept at all."

Charlie interjected. "He *is* tired, Gil. The thing is they're—"

But at that moment, Oliver pitched forward from exhaustion, and Gil's latte spilled all over Charlie's lap.

"Yeeow!" Charlie cried.

"Oh, sorry," Oliver said. "We'll just be a second!" The two boys went into the bathroom so that Oliver could help Charlie clean up.

"Boy, are we lucky," Charlie said. "It's awesome. Gil Hornshaw is going to help us and everything. He's built the quantum computer! And he really seemed to get it about the Master of Mirrors and stuff."

"Yes, he really did seem to get it, didn't he?" Oliver said weakly. "But I think I know why."

"What do you mean?" Charlie asked.

"Gil Hornshaw gets it about the Master of Mirrors," Oliver whispered, his shoulders collapsed in despair, "because Gil Hornshaw *is* the Master of Mirrors."

Chapter Fifteen

Light and Shade

"WHAT ARE you talking about?"

"His smile—that smirky sort of smile? *It's on the wrong side of his face.* Compare it with the photograph." He held it up to Charlie. Sure enough, Charlie saw that the man in the photograph, holding the little Oliver on his lap, had his crooked smile on the right side of his face.

Charlie whistled softly. "So you're saying . . ."

"That he forgot to turn the smile around when he crossed over from the Way. Or maybe he can't turn it around; maybe he has to keep the mirror-image face that he stole. But it's him. I'm sure of it. He must have taken Gil's soul a few years ago—it must have been easy, given how much screen-staring Gil did—and once he broke out into the World, he took over Gil's body, too."

"Are you sure? Maybe that side of his mouth is just worn out after all these years of crooked smiling?"

"And his hands are so cold—like ice, Charlie," Oliver went on, ignoring him. "That's why he keeps his hands around that latte all the time—to warm them up so that if he touches a human being to shake hands or something you wouldn't notice. But even so, when he touched my head so *warmly*—even then it was cold. So the second time he did it, I switched coffees on him, to be sure. I took your iced whatever—and after that, then his hands were colder than any ice I've ever felt.

"And then Charlie, this was another thing," Oliver whispered fiercely. "*He couldn't use a metaphor. He couldn't even understand one.* When I was inviting him to make one up and say how he felt, he kept using ironies—sentences that say one thing and mean exactly the opposite. 'I'm just a poor computer geek' when he's the world's richest man, and 'It's just another gizmo' when it's the biggest thing in history. When I threw a metaphor right in his lap, and asked him if he didn't feel ninety-stories high, he didn't even understand what I meant. He could only understand it in a—what does Mrs. Pearson call it?—a literal way. Talking to him was like . . . well, just like staring into a mirror."

"You're crazy, Ollie. Or maybe just tired," Charlie said skeptically.

There was a long silence between the two boys. It was broken only by a sulky and silky voice coming from outside.

"Are you all right, boys?" the voice called out. It must be Lumière DeLuna, Oliver thought.

"Just a minute!" Oliver called out, and then he turned to Charlie and whispered urgently. "Okay. If you don't believe me, just watch what happens."

They walked back onto the platform of the tower.

"You boys okay?" said Gil. His wide crooked smile seemed worried and sympathetic at the same time.

Oliver tried to be as careful as he could. He gulped hard. "Have you seen my dad, Uncle Gil?" he asked.

"Your dad?" he shrugged. "He was here a few hours ago, I think. I imagine he went home to work on that story. I told him, too, about the computer, of course. It ought to be quite a night for him." Was there the faintest hint of a cruel and pointed smile at the corners of his mouth as he said this? "He's finally got a really big exclusive," Gil explained.

"Well, I think I better get home, too, then."

"You bet!" Gil Hornshaw said. "Make sure you take someone with you to watch you, won't you?"

"Oh, I think it's okay."

Gil paused. "Sure, whatever." He went to turn back. He slapped his forehead. "Oh, jeez, I am so absentminded. Yeah, you were going to introduce me to this friend of yours, this, uh, Neige. She sounds like quite a girl." His face,

Oliver was sure of it, was gleaming with interest and desire.

Oliver backed off, toward the elevator. "Oh, okay, Uncle Gil. I'm sure she'd . . . she'd love to meet you."

A supercilious smile broke out over Gil Hornshaw's face. "Yeah. I feel as though I know her already. From your description, I mean. Sure, Ollie," he said. "You'll tell me when you find her, right, won't you?"

"Sure. Sure I'll tell you," he said weakly. "I'll bring her right here."

Gil's smile gleamed. "Okay, old boy. Now give your uncle Gil a big hug and I'll catch you on the flip-flop, old buddy," he said, and he held out his arms. Oliver approached him, and accepted his big, embracing hug. He shrank away after a moment. He *was* icy cold, and he felt his frozen fingers toy with his back pocket. *Reaching for something? The crown?* No, he could feel that was still safe. What was it then? Gil pulled Oliver deeper into the hug, pressing Oliver's head against his icy chest, and Oliver could feel his cold fingers wrap around his back.

And then he abruptly jerked his head upward, striking Gil's head, and knocking his tinted glasses right off.

They fell to the floor, and Gil quickly fumbled to pick them up—but not before Charlie saw his eyes uncovered.

"You're right, Ollie!" Charlie whispered, in shock.

But now Gil had his tinted aviator glasses back on and he was smiling at the boys again.

"Some hug," he said dryly to Oliver.

(Oliver winked just perceptibly at Charlie. Another irony!)

But did Gil know that they had detected him? Oliver sensed that it was important to put any suspicions he had to rest. "Listen, Uncle Gil," he said, trying to sound as enthusiastic as he could. "I'm just so grateful to you for your listening to me. It's just . . . fabulous . . . and I'll come back as soon as I can find Neige so that you can . . . protect her!"

Was there a skeptical look on Gil's face? If there was, all he said, calmly, was "You do that, boys. I'll be so glad to help. The big machine gets turned on at eight o'clock precisely." Now his crooked smile had become a kind of leering smirk.

"Yes, that's right." He turned back toward the console of his computer. "I'll send Lumière to take you down."

"There's no need! We can do it ourselves!" Oliver said, and, before Gil could respond, he grabbed Charlie, and the two boys dashed, waving, out of the room and back into the hall where the elevator doors stood.

They pressed the call button, and waited for the elevator to arrive. But when it did, Oliver pulled Charlie off to one side, let the elevator door close loudly, and then forced him down toward the floor. The two boys crawled as silently as they could back to the small window that looked down from the restaurant platform toward the ground.

Far below them, they saw a row of Gil Hornshaw's assistants, bringing in crates on little handcarts. Many of the crates were open and contained the expected things: keyboards and circuit boards and connecting cords.

But then, as the two boys watched, two of Gil's black-clad assistants wheeled in a velvet-box, ancient looking—the very one that they had seen leave the Way the day before. Another one of the black-clad assistants opened it with a golden key—*the* golden key!—as though to examine its contents.

Oliver and Charlie gasped. Inside the box were the ruby and emerald souls that Oliver and Neige had watched the soul-stealers take when they first entered the Mirror-Maze.

"The souls," Oliver said quietly. "They've brought them here from the other side."

"That's the new fuel. That's how they run the quantum computer," Charlie said. "Soul power! That's the secret."

"Mrs. Pearson said that a soul was the most energetic thing in the universe, that it could keep the entire world alight," Oliver said.

"Sure, a soul is the perfect fuel for the quantum computer. Instead of devouring the souls, he's using them to power it . . ."

"And then will keep feeding it with souls until there are no free ones left," Oliver finished.

Oliver stepped away from the window and carefully made their way back to the facing glass door that opened onto the restaurant.

Oliver peeked in cautiously. Gil was still sitting by the console. But as he turned to address the assistant nearest to him, his smiling, boyish face turned frosty, and grim.

And then his face began to fade, to fade right away, feature by feature, like wax melting, until it was as blank as the face of his true self, the One with None, and he then turned his grim blankness toward Lumière.

"Destroy every window they look into. The glass ghosts may be hiding there. And destroy the boy-king, too. But bring me the girl."

"Have a latte?" she offered. But he looked out—or, rather, pointed out, not having eyes—across the Champ-de-Mars in the winter light.

"Inside out . . . upside down . . . there is nothing in it," Gil muttered to himself through his nonexistent mouth, as though repeating the prophecy. "There is nothing in it." But then he turned toward the assistant.

"When we turn on the computer," he said, "make sure the boy's father's is the first soul to burn as fuel."

"But there are so many . . . I don't know if we . . ." Lumière said weakly.

"Find it. Stay up all night if you have to to find it. Have a latte," said the Master of Mirrors, and he turned away and gazed out across the field of Mars.

"Go. Follow the boy. Find the girl. Bring her to me. I cannot seal my power until she is queen. And smash the glass ghosts!" he said.

Oliver and Charlie watched in horror as Lumière shook out her silver hair, then spun slower and slower, and then faster and faster, her features blending and mixing until at last she became a whirlwind of pure light. She cork-screwed her way off the tower, and flew out, a helix of pure white light, into the Paris twilight.

* * *

"Now what do we do?" Charlie asked, as they walked across the bridge back to the Right Bank. They had crept all the way down the staircase of the Eiffel Tower. "I mean, obviously, we don't let him date Neige . . ."

"Well, at least we lead the light away from where the wraiths really are," Oliver answered.

But, as they crept along the narrow and winding streets in the winter gloom, they saw her—a super-bright, white searchlight, like a giant spinning torch, passed above their heads, glancing across the buildings on the street. Wherever it landed, it seemed brighter than the moon, brighter than the sun itself, revealing everything it touched in pitiless and ugly detail.

The Scouring Light, like a tornado of cold fire, went on, sweeping around the block, searching window by window, for something. It was like a white finger, searching. . . . Oliver and Charlie knelt and pressed themselves hard against the base of the building.

Then it stopped. As it glowed hard, the dim outline of a figure could just be seen within the window and Oliver saw, in horror, the dim two-dimensional figure of a wraith trying to escape and slip out of the window.

But it was too late. A bang rang through the air, and the window exploded, and then, as though for evil measure, all the other windows in the building exploded, too, one after another, in quick succession. All the beautiful French windows—the double windows that open out like doors onto little balconies—from floor to ceiling, all one after another exploded outward in an ear-splitting splinter of glass and wood. Then there was silence, and then the moans of people coming to their missing windows, standing on the little balconies and looking with fear at the sky.

Oliver was shocked and he felt sick. He had been trying to lead the Scouring Light away from the wraiths, and then, accidentally, he had helped them destroy one of his own subjects.

They crossed the rue de Tournon. Oliver saw the searchlight leaning out, sweeping across, in front of them, the end of the rue Bonaparte and going down the rue de Sèvres, past the Bon Marché department store. Then Charlie's cell phone rang, and Charlie pressed it to his ear.

He held it out to Oliver. A thin familiar voice, as though coming from over and across mountains, filled with static and the high-pitched beeps of distance, said, "It's me, Oliver. I'm still inside. I have an army for you. We shall come out. It is outside the maze, but I see mirrors all around. Somewhere in Paris. Please be there."

"This is insanely dangerous," Charlie said. The two boys were standing a short while later in front of the Musée Grévin on the boulevard Montmartre, a street in the middle of the Right Bank.

"I heard her," Oliver said stubbornly. "She said mirrors all around. That means a hall of mirrors or a Mirror-Maze. She wouldn't think of trying to get out of the maze in

Versailles. It's too well guarded. So I could think of only one other place. And this is it."

"What's inside?" Charlie asked.

"It's sort of a wax museum, and sort of a fun house," Oliver explained as he bought two tickets from the little booth out front. "And the most amazing thing inside is the hall of mirrors."

"He'll be looking *right at us,*" Charlie objected, as they mounted the elaborate, gilded but slightly run-down stairs of the strange museum. "He'll see us."

"We have to hope that he's thinking about his new mirrors—the computers—and isn't concentrating on the old ones. It's two o'clock, so he'll be turning that thing on in six hours. I'm sure he's concentrating on it completely. We just have to hope that Mrs. Pearson can break out before he catches them."

If you visit the Musée Grévin someday, you may be amused by the wax figures of famous entertainers that fill the first floor (though you will notice that most of the entertainers were popular long ago) and you may be mildly frightened by the display of horrors (though you will also notice that the red paint that stands for blood has peeled away over the years). But your real destination will be the six-sided hall of mirrors on the third floor. It has been there for more than a hundred years, and the mirrors line a hall filled with strange twisted columns and weird dark figures.

"I suppose the master had this place made to give some of his soul-stealers a way into Paris," Oliver guessed, looking around, and feeling a little chilled as the two boys crowded with the tourists and children and sensation-seekers into the room. It was definitely a creepy sensation, Oliver thought, to be looking into so many mirrors, knowing what was on the other side. But they had to do it—Mrs. Pearson needed their help.

The mirrors in the Musée Grévin face one another, and the reflections bounce on reflections to give the illusion of an infinity of reflections. Oliver and Charlie stared at their own endlessly receding images.

"It's like standing in the multiverse," Charlie said, as he looked at the illusion of endless worlds in which they stood, along with all the other tourists.

"It *is* standing in the multiverse," Oliver mumbled to himself, hardly knowing what the words meant.

"What do you mean?" Charlie asked. But before Oliver could answer, the lights came down, and a strange voice came over the small and tinny loudspeakers. "Take a voyage with us back in time," the voice intoned, and then the lights went down, and everyone stood in pitch darkness. Then a second set of lights came on, on the edges around each mirror, and now the darkened hall of mirrors, and the infinite reflections that bounced from one side of mirrors to the next, were filled with images of man as he had been before he had ever seen a mirror, primitive men around a campfire, staring inside . . . the mirrors ran away in every direction.

Then, suddenly, deep, deep, deep in the reflections Oliver saw, yes, he was sure of it, a tiny figure advancing toward him, and behind the figure he sensed some kind of crowd, almost a hazy nebula of smaller figures.

The cloud of smaller figures came into sharper focus as Oliver watched. Through the dark mirrors he could see them coming. They were children! A mob of long-haired children, and they were running—running out of the mirrors. And the small figure leading them was, yes, he was certain of this, too, it was Mrs. Pearson. He could tell because she had raised her champagne spoon, and was leading the children along with it, as though it were a sword, or scepter. And in her other hand she held something tucked against her chest.

Then Oliver saw why they were running. Behind them, like a pursuing fury, there was a phalanx of soul-stealers, in their striped shirts and long aprons, hunting them down. The Master of Mirrors must have left a guard behind to watch the exits and entrances of his realm in the Way.

Quickly, almost instinctively, Oliver reached into his back pocket and pulled out the gold paper crown, by now dog-eared and creased, and placed it on his head in the dark hall of mirrors.

Mrs. Pearson and the children came running toward him, thousands upon thousands of small rushing children, in smocks and long pinafores and old-fashioned knickers, all converging on the hexagon of mirrors.

Mrs. Pearson's anguished face loomed large in the center of the mirrors, there on every side. The crowd of tourists gasped and cried out.

With a crash of shattering wood and glass, Mrs. Pearson

and the lost children came tumbling into the hall of mirrors at the Musée Grévin, and just behind them were the soul-stealers, reaching out with their harpoons and aiming at them.

And then the soul-stealers, converging on every side onto the center, saw Oliver in his crown and came skidding to a stop. To Oliver's shock, they turned right around, and disappeared back, deep into the mirrors.

Falling and rising and coughing and shaking their heads, Mrs. Pearson and the lost children of the mirrors—their eyes sad, their skin white, their faces long—filled the hall of mirrors. And in her hand Mrs. Pearson clutched a small and bright two-winged mirror.

"Oh, hello, Oliver," she said calmly. "Here's the other true mirror. And here's a new regiment for the battle."

There were not as many lost children as it had seemed at first in the Musée Grévin—they had been multiplied by the mirrors—but still there were nearly a hundred, enough to make a spooky party, a few moments later, in a French café. Oliver and Mrs. Pearson directed them to the tables, and ordered hot chocolate for every one. The pale-faced children sat and sipped their chocolate in silence.

Mrs. Pearson, however, seemed as talkative and as much at ease as she always was in a place with good things to eat and drink. Of all the details that Oliver and Charlie shared with her, the need of Gil Hornshaw's assistants for so much coffee was the one that seemed to fascinate her most.

"Drinking champagne enlivens the soul; coffee merely

simulates it," she went on. "If you have a soul, champagne makes it more soulful; if you don't have one, a latte gives you the illusion that you do. You may write that down," she said loftily to Charlie.

"Sure thing Mrs. P.," Charlie said. But, of course, he didn't write it down.

"Mrs. Pearson, three questions. Who are these kids, what is that mirror, and why did the soul-stealers stop when they saw me?"

Mrs. Pearson sipped her tea. "The kids, as you call them, are the lost children of the Way. They wandered into the Way over the centuries. Just as Alice did, and as I did. They all got out of the Mirror-Maze just as we did—by accident, and without going deep inside or becoming known to the master." She put down her tea. "But then, when their time in the World was over, and they should have been drawn to the windows of their longing, the hold of the Mirror-Maze was still too strong on them. They were drawn back into the Mirror-Maze, and they lived there, in their children's bodies."

"What about Alice, your grandmother?" Oliver asked.

"She was drawn back there, too, even more magnetically—remember, she almost became the master's queen!—and when her time was over, she went back into the mirrors. They have lived furtively on the fringes of the Mirror-Maze for a century. Only when the hold of the master over his maze is destroyed will they be set free to go to the windows where they belong.

"And the mirror is Alice's mirror. It is the one remaining true and loyal mirror. She was given it as she was being crowned, but Lewis Carroll rescued her just in time. But she kept it safe with her forever after. Even the master could not take it from her. And now it is yours."

"The clochards have reassembled the mirror of Luc Gauric," Oliver interrupted. He reached down and carefully touched this second true mirror.

"Then, thanks to my ingenuity and resource, and theirs, you now have, for the first time, two true mirrors—mirrors that are open and faithful and non-reversing. Now, what was the other question?"

"The soul-stealers stopped when . . ."

"Yes, they did. I wish I could say it was because you cut such an imposing figure, so many kings in so many windows. But I suspect it was because they are under orders not to leave the maze until the master returns. Meanwhile, Your Majesty, you have at last collected your army!"

Yes, Oliver thought to himself, looking around the café at all the pale-skinned children drinking their cocoa. And it consists of a hundred or so ghosts armed with soap-shooters, locked inside windows, and a troop of fragrant but dedicated clochards, ready to lead a hundred pale children.

He looked over at Mrs. Pearson. But for some strange reason Mrs. Pearson was merely trifling with her champagne spoon, flicking it from bowl to back as she stared into it.

What was wrong with her? What was the point of it? That was no use. And yet, somehow, somewhere, he also knew that there must be an answer. Nostradamus had said as much. Turn the universe inside out, turn the master upside down, find the other two things both cool and warm, solve . . . oh, solve the riddles, and set the world free. And save his father. His thoughts drifted further and further away. And a force that seemed as irresistible as the flow in the maze pulled him forward.

"Of course, what he's doing now is exactly the same thing that he did in the Grand Siècle," Mrs. Pearson was saying, speaking of the Master of Mirrors. She seemed to have recovered her focus. "Just as he gave away mirrors then until so many were trapped, now he is giving away the power of his quantum computer, and hopes that all will then be trapped within *it*. Same concept, different period. You see, Oliver—Oliver?"

For Oliver had slipped away, and he was at last alone, as kings must be before a battle, and Oliver was, at last, thinking. Or trying to. He had never thought so hard before, and he had no one in the world to help him. Whatever happened now, he knew, he would have to make it happen, and he would have to make it happen with his mind.

He took his pebble with its strange marking out of his front hip pocket.

Oliver felt very lonely, again, after he had not felt lonely for the last exceptional week. He had been frightened recently, but not lonely. He saw now that there are two kinds of loneliness—reflections of each other, actually. One was when you were lonely because you were alone. And the other was when you were lonely because people depended on you, and you couldn't share your worries with them. He had known the first kind of lonely before, but he was the second kind of lonely now.

This must have been the kind of lonely his father had known for so long, he realized—the loneliness of being an adult, filled with cares and worries and preoccupations, and being unable to talk even to your children about them. Well, Oliver was the grown-up now, or at least, he had to think like one. If they were to have a chance—if the entire cosmos were to have a chance—it would be because he could see a way clearly, and see it in his head.

And he was a little frightened, too, of course. He knew that Lumière DeLuna, the Scouring Light, was free, and must be searching for him and for Neige. He had to be very careful.

All around him, Parisians went by in the late afternoon gloom, their quick, worried steps making *click-clack* noises on the hard, wet pavement, taking sudden looks up at the threatening sky. The soft drizzle fell. Oh, why did it never snow in Paris . . . ?

Oliver glanced up at the Eiffel Tower as he came to the Pont Royal. The bright lights of the quantum computer condensers were beginning to glow brighter. And then, somewhere nearby, in all those ancient windows lining the river, the window wraiths of Versailles had taken shelter, but were still prey to the Scouring Light. How could he lead them to victory in the war of the windows?

What had he learned about thinking? Mrs. Pearson and Molière had told him to take sentences seriously and turn things upside down and reverse them—to hold them up in the windows and mirrors of his mind. And all of them had told him always to read when he was uncertain, and to take words and sentences seriously.

Simplify, he thought to himself. Okay, really *use* the windows and mirrors in your mind. What do the wraiths need? They need to advance, but there's no way for them to advance, for they can advance only in a neutral medium, and there is no neutral medium. Nostradamus had said it loud and clear. *There is no neutral medium.*

There is no neutral medium. Re-create the entire scene. Picture it. Oliver did not close his eyes—only people who are pretending to think close their eyes—but he twiddled with his hair and sucked in his cheek as he kicked his pebble along the shadowed streets of Paris.

Far off, he idly noted that through the violet sky a single star began to shine. How odd and lovely, he thought idly . . . you never saw Venus from Paris.

No, don't become distracted. Hold ideas. *See things. See* Nostradamus. Think of everything, remember everything, he said. Recall the scene. He had been prophesying in riddles, and then apologizing for predicting the future in such an enigmatic way. You must call an army to your aid. *If men would return to the light, "they"—someone or other, some army—would return to their sides.* They will need a neutral medium, but there is no neutral medium.

Then Oliver had been about to ask something and he had stopped the conversation. What had he said? Oh, yes: *Save Neige.*

By now, Oliver had kicked his pebble right to the center of the Pont Royal—right to the spot where he had seen François in the water. He looked out over the gray river, and out toward the beautiful tower with its glowing lights of the vast quantum computer. His father's soul would be burned as fuel to energize them. No, no don't think of that . . . think only of the riddles, think only of the answers.

Save Neige. That was what he had said. Though that was a strange prophecy, really, since Neige hadn't even been kidnapped yet.

They will need a neutral medium, and there is no neutral medium. Save Neige, her crystal's falling.

That's what he had said. Oliver could hear the old man's voice. Oliver turned his head and looked up at the gray and violet sky in the cold January light.

There is no neutral medium, save Neige, her crystal's falling.

There *was* something there. Try the mirror in your mind. Try and turn the sentence right around, away from the obvious, to find another meaning hidden backward in the same words. *Neige . . . crystals . . . falling.* How would you reverse a sentence . . . ? Well, maybe from one language to the other. Look at the sentence in French, and then reverse it to see it in French, then in English again.

Now, try the windows of your mind. Look through one window, and see what lies beyond. He put Nostradamus's sentence up in his head, as though he were holding it to a window, and he tried to look at its reflection while still trying to look beyond it. What could he see?

And then it came to him. Oh, boy, was he an idiot. Of course!

And Oliver spun in triumphant satisfaction at the Left Bank end of the Pont Royal, arriving there, and at the answer, simultaneously. He had it! He had solved Nostradamus's first riddle! And all he had to do was to turn it around—the same thing seen the opposite way, the same sentence turned right around. And then see what lies beyond that matters. Mirrors and windows in your mind!

Okay, the next riddle. That thing that Nostradamus had said about light. Well, what exactly had he said? *If men will only walk in the light, they will return to their sides* . . . Who were *they*, though? Angels, muses, fairy godparents? Oliver threw his hands up in exasperation. He was standing on the corner of the rue du Bac and the quay. He looked up again at the sky.

Yes, it was still violet, and yet the small circle of starlight that he had been sure was the planet Venus still shone bright in the night sky, up above the steeples and sloped roofs. If anything it shone more brightly. How lovely, and how strange! He looked again.

The point of light was . . . growing larger. How could a planet in the twilight grow? But then he realized with a sick start . . . that was no planet. It was a light, a light that had been looking down at him, searching for him. And with every moment it grew larger and closer until it was a fireball in the Paris sky.

It was the Scouring Light, she herself, and swooping down at him.

Oliver fell to one side as the Scouring Light attacked. His eyes were blinded by her light, and he dove to the ground. A roaring pain filled his head—had she taken it off? He felt for his scalp. Was it on fire? No—she had missed his head by inches. He could feel his hair singed by the light.

Where had it—she—gone? Oliver heard a hiss of steam over his shoulder. She must have landed in the river. That would stop her for a moment, though, he was sure, for only a moment.

He looked over his shoulder from where he lay, frightened, on the ground. The white light she had cast was still bright on the long, dark, tree-lined quai bringing everything into sharp focus. He raised his hand. Why the bright trail of her light even made his own silhouette against the far wall, across the street, look very large. . . .

Then his heart stopped racing, and he almost laughed.

And then his heart leaped high—for suddenly he saw it all, saw how the riddles of Nostradamus intersected with the mysteries of the multiverse, saw how the eternal battle of mirrors and windows might be brought to an end, saw exactly what he would have to do, and how he would have to do it. He held it as solidly in his mind as he held the pebble in his hand!

Oliver looked up. He was startled to see where he was. He was back at home! He was right on top of the rue du Pré-aux-Clercs! The pebble had led him home, as though it had a will and mind of its own to take him there. He was back on the small slanted street where he lived with his parents.

A figure was coming out of the large door of their building. He heard the familiar *click* and push of the big green door. He looked. It was his father, in his raincoat and scarf. He turned and walked down the street, away from Oliver. At first Oliver thought not to say anything. But he could not help himself.

"Dad," he called out finally, weakly. "Is that you?"

From the end of the street, his face in shadow, he heard his father's voice.

"Hey, Ollie," he said faintly.

Oliver tried to sound as sure as he could. "I'm going to save you, you know, your . . ."

His father laughed. A short, sharp laugh that echoed up and down the cold and empty street.

"There's no saving it," he said. "I lost it to a friend."

Oliver started to walk toward him, but his father held up his hand. "Don't come near," he warned. "He'll . . . he'll see . . ."

"I know all about . . . him," Oliver said. "I saw right through him. I know who he really is, and how he trapped you. He wanted you to—to—" *To get to me*, he wanted to finish by saying.

He pressed on. "The Master of Mirrors must have used his mind in the Way to look forward, and gotten a glimpse through time of me becoming, you know, the King in the Window. That must have been what made him take your soul as a sort of hostage, against me. So he took Gil's, you know, and then your—"

Oliver's father laughed again, more quietly. Then he

said, "No, Oliver. It wasn't that. He didn't need to trap me.
I trapped myself."

"No, Dad, you just looked at a computer screen too
long, too many hours online and at work and . . . you see,
he's making them into mirrors, really, and his mirrors trap
souls and . . ."

"It wasn't the screens, Oliver," his father said at last.
"Those may be the way they get you, but it's not *why* they get
you. Your mother stares at a screen too, and she was never in
danger. The soul-stealers come for you through the screen.
But the soul-*takers* are the repetitions, the procession of work
and worry, the bills you worry over too much each month, the
faces that you forget to long for, the surrender of another
dream to another need. Do that for a lifetime, and the sinews
of your soul get so stretched that all the soul-stealers need to
do is reach in and pull. Hardly a yank—you'll understand
some day, Oliver. But you'll be braver than I was."

And then he turned and walked down the small and
slanting street, toward the river.

Oliver started to run to catch him. But something
stopped him. He could not save his father if he did not first
destroy the Master of Mirrors and his soul-eating machine,
the quantum computer on the Eiffel Tower. To save him, he
would have to leave him first.

"There *is* a way," Oliver cried out, and he hoped that
his father could hear him. Then Oliver turned away from his
father and, pressing his paper crown to his head, raced down
the boulevard toward the metro.

Chapter Sixteen

The Battle of Ice and Water

IT WAS surprisingly hard work, explaining his plan, to Charlie and Mrs. Pearson back inside Cavern X. The clochards were sitting by their small fires, the old tapestries with their scenes of the first king could just be seen along the walls, with the ancient weavings of the sword and wand hardly detectable in the flickering flames. Neige—Neige was nowhere to be found. Charlie had told him that she had left the cavern without telling anyone where she was going.

Oliver was terribly worried about her—she didn't even

know that Gil was searching for her—but he tried not to show it. He stood in the semidarkness, like a professor, trying to explain his idea to his friends and counselors. When you have let an idea come to you, it is hard for other people to trust it. They all nodded at his solution of the riddles, when he explained them, but then the second part of his plan made even Mrs. Pearson scrunch up her forehead.

He tried to be patient. "Look, if we're inside the maze and we look into a true mirror, then things on the other side won't be reversed, will they?"

"No, I would guess not," Mrs. Pearson allowed.

"So: if someone is standing in the Way looking into a true mirror, then nothing on the other side, in the World, will be changed or turned around. That means that the rules that hold in the Way . . ."

"Will also be true in the World. I see that."

"Right. Hard will be soft, soft will be hard; the wraiths' weapons will work just as well here as there. The World will become its own reflection," Oliver's voice grew urgent.

"But the World won't have changed just because we're looking at it through a true mirror," Charlie objected. "If it did, then any time anyone looked through the true mirror from inside the Way, the World would have been reversed. And that's never happened before, has it? I mean, Alice had the true mirror inside there for a century, and the World was always the same. . . ."

"It never happened before because out in the World all the other mirrors were *false* mirrors, *reversing* mirrors,"

Oliver explained. "And they switched everything right back around. The moment you crossed back over into the World, the first mirror the light rays struck turned everything around. . . . It's as if . . ." He looked desperately around the cavern and noticed that Serge was idly clicking on and off a flashlight. He grabbed it from him.

"Look, imagine that I turn this flashlight on inside the Way and then shine it out at the World through the back of a normal mirror, one that's a door into the Mirror-Maze. Are the light rays reversed? Sure. It's a normal mirror. It reverses things on both sides of the Way and the World."

"Now imagine that I shine the flashlight from the Way through the back of a true mirror, a nonreversing mirror, and I walk back into the World through it. Are the light rays reversed? Not yet. But then the first ordinary, reversing mirror that they strike is going to turn them around again—reverse them. So everything's back to normal.

"But now imagine that, for once in all of history, the first reflective surface they strike *doesn't* turn the light rays around? Then what?" He held the flashlight steady and waited.

Charlie considered, and then said slowly, "Well, then, I guess that all the light rays between those two true mirrors—the one in the Way and the one in the World—will be just the way they were to begin with. . . ."

"So if to begin with those light rays were shining in the Way . . ."

"Then they will still be obeying the rules of the Way. . . . And if the second mirror behind reflects everything that's in the first mirror in front—" Charlie continued.

"And if the first true mirror shows the World as though it were the Way . . ." Oliver encouraged him. "And the second true mirror reflects the same thing back to the first mirror without reversing it all—"

"And then it reflects it back again, unreversed . . ."

"And then back again, still unreversed . . ."

"Then everything caught between those two mirrors—"

"Will be just as they would be if you were looking at the World from inside the Way with a true mirror—"

"Which turns the World—"

"Inside out!"

The two boys paused, breathless. And then Charlie picked up the thread again, very quickly.

"Which fulfills the prophecy, allows the wraiths to charge, and means—"

"That all of our weapons will work in the World just as well as they work in the Way. . . ."

"And the battle is ours!"

They stared at each other.

"I'd rather see that done on paper," Mrs. Pearson said.

And so Oliver quickly sketched, with chalk on the wall of the cavern, two little diagrams with stick figures and arrows, the first showing two people passing out of the Way into the World through an ordinary mirror, and then another showing two people looking out from inside the Way through a true mirror, with the second true mirror capturing what they saw and bouncing it back, and a quick funny-looking thing in between that was meant to be the Eiffel Tower between them.

"I get it," Charlie said at last, nodding at the drawing. "I don't believe it, but I get it. It sounds like . . . *too much* thinking . . . if you know what I mean. But it's thinking, that's for sure."

"And here's what it will all add up to," Oliver said. And he drew a third diagram, full of arrows and showing something else happening in the space.

Mrs. Pearson and Charlie crowded around this last drawing, gesturing and gasping in surprise.

"A triumph of pure reason," Mrs. Pearson said at last, decisively, looking at Oliver's final stick-figure diagram. "Or else—"

"Or else what?" asked Oliver.

"Or else a disaster of abstract thought. You can never tell which will be which until you try. And by then it's too late, which is one comfort."

Mrs. Pearson was only being frank, Oliver knew. But he was frustrated. "Trust me. I know this will work. I can't explain why, but it will. All *you* have to think about is leading the skaters, Charlie—and I know you can do that. And all I have to do is visit the Luxembourg Gardens for a few minutes to talk to someone, and it's in the bag." He tried to look rather secretive and knowing as he said it.

The truth was that Oliver *hoped* his plan would work, and *thought* his plan would work, but he didn't *know*, not for sure. Seeing Charlie's face, newly lit with courage, Oliver knew at last what the golden lie was that Mrs. Pearson had promised to tell him about when he was ready. The golden lie was the greatest lie of all—it was the lie you told others about your own courage, in order to make them courageous. And what made it golden, Oliver saw, was that it was shiny, reflective. Your pretending to be brave when you weren't made other people braver than they really were—and their bravery bounced back on you, as Charlie's was doing now, and made *you* brave. The golden lie was the lie of courage when you didn't have it, which meant that you did, which made you brave.

He found his crown on the floor and, tattered and creased as the paper was by now, he put it on. He understood that to be a king at all it is necessary to act like a king even if you do not feel like a king, and that to be a good king you must first accept your crown, and wear it proudly, come what may. Courage is measured in what you do, not how you feel. Everyone is always afraid. The brave, he knew now, just lie about it better than the rest of us.

Oliver found Neige, where he had feared he would find her, on the Champ-de-Mars, striding forcefully toward the Eiffel Tower.

He ran after her. "Neige," he called, "don't go there, don't go to him. I know you think you can, you know, manage him. But you can't."

She turned and looked at him, pale but determined. "I can manage anyone. And if I have to sacrifice myself—well, at least that way I might save many others. My mother's soul, for example."

"Your mother!" Oliver said.

"Yes, of course. My mother may be, well, all the things you know her to be. But she is as much my mother as your father is your father."

"But, Neige, joining him—"

"I would never join him! I would only trick him . . ."

"But you can't trick him! He's too deep and too old and too wise. Listen to me! I have a way that we can rescue your mother, and my father and, well the world. Just listen to me!"

"Oliver, you may have a crown, but—"

"Neige, all we can count on is each other. The Master of Mirrors wants you and he wants to destroy me—and we are all that can save our parents, if they can be saved. Stay away from the tower and the master! Come with me across the bridge, and we can still save them both."

This time Neige said nothing in return.

"At least you're listening to me," Oliver said, trying to get her to smile. "A week ago you weren't speaking to me."

"Just this morning I wasn't speaking to you," she sighed. "But now I will. Tell me your plan, and, if it's a good one, I shall follow your orders. A boy becomes a king when others treat him as one, I think I have read that; and since you must be a king now, or all is lost, we had better start acting as if you were."

It was not exactly the most ringing endorsement that Oliver had ever received, but it was better than nothing.

Oliver bent over, and began to explain his plan, in all its intricacy, to Neige, as he had explained it to Charlie and Mrs. Pearson. And this time, Neige listened.

Neige went to search for the window wraiths who were hiding in the windows of the Palais de Chaillot on the esplanade of the Trocadéro, which faces the Eiffel Tower, across the river Seine. The Trocadéro is a large, smooth plaza, where children love to go skating. On this winter evening, only the determined in-line skaters were still outside.

Inside of the old museum, Neige went to the windows. She held her crystal up and found Molière.

He was wearing a pot on his head, and his feather drooped as he held it up.

"I'm aware that we look funny, my dear," he said, "but this is as dangerous as we can be. Usually the dangerous are unintentionally funny, because they do not see their own pomposity. We wraiths, however, are unintentionally dangerous, because no one really understands our potential."

"His Majesty has a plan. He wants you all to show yourselves, fully armed, at exactly five thirty, as the last rays of the sun disappear," Neige explained. "I'm afraid it's very dangerous; I'm going to illuminate your presence in the windows with my crystal. Be ready to leap aside when he— when the master, I mean—sends out the Scouring Light, of course, but then . . ." And she ran through Oliver's plan quickly.

Molière paused. And thought. "It is a good plan. It is

a *rather* dangerous plan for us, but then I suppose that it must be. You can't make an omelet without breaking eggs, of course, or at least so they tell the omelet-maker. And you can't break eggs without making an omelet. So at least they tell the eggs. Well, we are the eggs in this omelet, and must do it, and hope for the best."

"A very fine metaphor," said Neige. Molière smiled. He knew that this was a generous thing for a serious crystallomancer to say to a word-spinning wraith.

"Well, what time did you say? . . . I am afraid that though a brave army, we are rather a poor army."

"Oliver has a larger army than that. He has the lost children ready and fueled with cocoa, and he has . . . well . . ." and even though she knew that the Master of Mirrors could not hear her, she whispered it anyway. "He has them," she gestured toward the in-line skaters. "They're an army hidden in plain sight." And Molière looked at the skaters, and saw that Charlie Gronek was leading them.

Crouching under the wall of the Trocadéro, Oliver gazed out at the Eiffel Tower, where the lights of the quantum computer were glowing ever more brightly as the machine warmed up, ready for the moment of its launch. They made the tower into a gleaming, jeweled spire, strange and beautiful and ominous.

Oliver looked at his watch. Five thirty exactly. The homecoming hour, when everyone in Paris would be on their way along the dark and lamp-lit streets.

He nodded to Neige, crouching beside him. The moment was here. She rose, and ran across the smooth plaza, dodging the in-line skaters as she did.

Then Neige threw off her hood, and, with the wind blowing strong through her long hair, took off her cloak and lifted her crystal from inside her sweater. She held it up to the last dim rays of the sunlight. The sun, refracted through the prism of her crystal, caught it and sent the light up against the broad window. As it did, the light from Neige's crystal lit the window as surely as if it had been spotlit in a theater.

Within the window, the window wraiths of Versailles appeared, solemnly clutching their feathers and pop-guns and water pistols, etched in pale silhouette against the glass of the great picture window, as forthright and boldly out-lined as they could be. They looked like strange, liquid ghosts, outlined in their window in the gathering gloom. Hundreds of them had gathered, from all over Paris, feeling their way very slowly from old window to old window, there for the last battle. It was pure courage, Oliver realized, as he saw them standing in their comic rows, a high and golden lie. François, he noticed, was in the very first row.

Oliver and the wraiths stood, shivering a little, and wait-ing. First nothing—could the Master of Mirrors not have seen them, and not taken up the chance to destroy his ancient enemies? Could he have refused to take the bait that Oliver had offered him?

But, now, wait—what was that? Yes, high up on the peak of the Eiffel Tower, the bright, blinding point of light appeared. It was Lumière, the Scouring Light, spinning at the apex of the tower, and turning into white-hot spinning light. In the bright light, Oliver could just see the raised arm and blank face of the Master of Mirrors across the river as, like a god throwing a thunderbolt from Mt. Olympus, he sent his Scouring Light across the Seine at the window where the wraiths stood, defying his power. The Scouring Light hurtled down, a blinding light against the darkening sky, falling from on high toward the vulnerable and exposed window wraiths.

They remained unblinking and steady as their doom rushed toward them.

And, as the helium-white helix came diving lethally toward the window, Oliver leaped up and held his hands up to the bright and blinding light. He fell to his knees, and fumbling, brought his hands up, trying to remember the form of the crowned bird, the King's Sign, which he had practiced so long in the little kitchen.

His hands felt very cold and stiff in the winter air, and he lost a precious moment limbering his fingers. O, how to *do* it? It had been a week since he had practiced it, projecting the shadow puppet against the blue-and-white striped curtains in his mother's kitchen. How to do it? Right: hands intertwined, fingers locked, forefinger up—palms out for wings . . . There!

The sign, he was making the sign! In the matchlessly bright glare of the Scouring Light, Oliver made the King's Sign. It cast an immense silhouette against the wall of the Palais de Chaillot visible across Paris.

The Scouring Light came spinning down over Oliver's head, corkscrewing violently down into the wraiths' window, shattering it in a second into a million fragments. The explosion, and then the hissing sound. The wraiths leaped as she arrived, and Oliver saw most of them leap free, floating gracefully into the air, yet some were trapped, and Oliver shuddered at the splintering sound.

But it *had* gone out! The signal they had waited for centuries to see. But had they seen it?

"What did you do?" Neige demanded, rushing toward him as she took cover again.

"I've sent out a signal," Oliver said calmly. " 'If men would walk in the light, they would leave their souls and return to their sides.' "

"Who? Who would return to whose sides?"

"Watch!"

And, at five forty-five in the cold January drizzle, all the shadows of the city of Paris set themselves free, and fled from the sides of men to go to the side of Man, in his battle at the Eiffel Tower.

At first, in the darkening evening, the event was barely noticeable. The head of a walking man's shadow turned sharply to see the King's shadow-sign. Then another shadowy head turned, suddenly free from the enslavement to his walking master. Then one long evening shadow sprang away from the heels of the woman who was casting a forked silhouette on the sidewalk. Then, in a burst of rebellion, all the shadows set themselves free to go to the side of the King in the Window.

A solitary stroller, out on the Quai Voltaire, looked down at his shadow—only to jump with surprise as he saw the shadow slowly turn its head and stretch to look up, toward the wall of the Trocadéro. Along the snaking, winding rue du Bac, the double shadow, cast by lamplight, of two old ladies, walking their dogs, suddenly leaped aside, leaving the startled dogs, and their walkers, behind on the sidewalk.

Shadows of lonely men in small apartments near the Gare du Nord leaped out of the windows and slipped down the façades of their buildings without even saying good-bye to the men in the armchairs. The shadows of waiters in the brasseries exited en masse. They were legless, because the waiters had been wearing long aprons, so these shadows, off on their own, looked like society women in long tube dresses. They crowded one another as they pushed and elbowed to get out of the door.

Thin shadows, fat shadows, chic shadows, and plain shadows, shadows from the Avenue Montaigne carrying the dark silhouettes of hat boxes and shadows from the butchers of La Villete carrying their cleavers—all of the shadows of Paris leaped away from their walkers and danced out onto the sidewalk, and then onto the façades of the apartment houses and stores, all on their own. They went up the sides of the Panthéon; leaped up to the dome of the Institut de France; slipped like black water along the banks of the Seine, passed like hawks across the façades of the apartment buildings.

The shadows were free at last, and answering the call of

Oliver Parker, the King in the Window who had made the sign.

"What's happening?" Neige shouted to Oliver.

"The shadows are breaking free. If we stand in the light, the shadows will return to our sides. That's all it means."

"What means?"

"Nostradamus's riddle. That's who the Watchful are. The Watchful are shadows. They were the third great army—the third outward projection of man, alongside the window reflections and the mirror images—and they ran away when the war first came. They were to answer the call, at the time of the first king, and they failed. They've repented it all these years—that must be why we always feel that shadows are sad and depressed and mysterious, without knowing why—and now their moment has at last come round again."

"But what are they going to do now?"

And Oliver said simply: "I'm not sure, Neige. But I *think* I know. Watch!"

Oliver and Neige, crouching down on the plaza of the Trocadéro, soon saw that the shadows were collecting at the top of the tower, hovering just above its needlelike peak, or balancing precariously on its spire. Thousands, no, there must be tens of thousands, of them, Oliver thought, all melding and merging into one huge gray-black shape.

A cloud! Just as he had hoped and planned! They were losing themselves, combining their shapes into an enormous cloud of shadows. The cloud grew darker and darker, vaster and vaster, as new shadows raced to join it. Soon, it entirely covered what was left of the sun's rays with its darkness.

The familiar drizzle seemed to stop for a moment, as the air turned colder and colder.

And then at last it happened. It began to snow in Paris.

A soft white snow began to fall on the rooftops, lovely and gentle, and the snow quickly began to cover the river and the tower.

Oliver turned to Neige and cried out in triumph. "I was right! I thought it through! I thought it right through! Nostradamus didn't mean *save* Neige. He didn't mean you. He meant your *name*. He meant only that *neige* means 'snow.' When he said 'save neige,' he meant 'There is no neutral medium *except for snow.*' The only neutral medium is snow—that's what lies between water and ice, just the way shadows lie between mirrors and windows. And the only way to make it snow in Paris was to make it cold enough to turn the rain into snow! And the only way to make a cloud to cover the sun was to make a cloud of shadows."

Oliver raised his glass sword high above his head, and the window wraiths, free for the first time in their long history of hiding, landed gently on the falling and drifting snow.

Oliver went to the front of his band and, brandishing his sword, signaled to them.

As the snow fell faster and faster in the cold, it at once blanketed the city, and the blanket of snow was like a quilt, and the city felt warmer even as the cold cloud below feathered it with snow, for snow in a city always begins in the cold, and then makes warmth.

"That's it!" Oliver said. "That's the second thing that

is both cold and warm! Snow in a city!" And then he raised his voice. "Wraiths! You are free to go where you wish! Now. Where do you wish to go?" he cried.

"To the tower! To the end of the Master of Mirrors, to freedom for all!" and they rushed to the edge of the Trocadéro bridge and Oliver, wearing his crown, mounted up on the banister of the bridge.

"Take the machine before he can master the multiverse! Seize him and we'll drive him back into the Way and lock him there forever!" Oliver cried. *And I will retake my father's soul before it's fed to the machine*, he promised himself, with desperate hope.

"Save all souls!" the answering cry went up, and echoed across the palace and the tower. And the window wraiths of Versailles began to charge.

High above on the tower, the Master of Mirrors looked down at the storm of cloud and wraiths and snow below him. Everywhere his eye traveled, the wraiths were advancing along the snow. Within moments, the wraiths seemed to cover the four piers of the lower tower as they stampeded, skimming across the snow. Wave after wave of window wraiths clambered up the sides of the tower, threatening to overwhelm the soul-stealers. And after them came the clochards, clutching the tower's snow slippery girders and wielding their staffs, directing the battle like great officers.

One by one, as the master watched, his army of assistants lost their faces, fading right away. They put down their lattes, and their black clothes became long black chain mail. They were soul-stealers again, no longer in disguise.

"Turn on the quantum computer," cried the Master of Mirrors.

"It's too soon!" His first, frightened assistant tried to stop him as he charged for the console.

"It is the only time," the Master said defiantly. And slowly the tower began to tremble as the soul-stealers threw their switches and the glowing lights of the particle generators in the tower became brighter and brighter.

And then he said, "Now, feed the souls."

Down below, at the base of the tower, the soul-stealers began to feed the energy furnace of the computer with the glowing red and diamond captured souls.

"Hand me the quantum soul-sprayer," he called.

One of the soul-stealers handed him a long black hose. All the other snaking cables and brightly colored wires that were strung up and down the tower flowed into it. At the end of the black hose, a stream of bright energy, like golden snow, overflowed and spat golden spray out at the night sky. It was a pipe of quantum particles, energized by soul power to stream right across the multiverse. The Master of Mirrors held it out, and the spray of particles flung itself over Paris, and then disappeared in every direction.

"I am everywhere at once," the Master of Mirrors exclaimed, "and nowhere at all! The universe is a hall of mirrors, and I am its master."

* * *

Quickly, Oliver clambered to his feet. He knew that he was king, and he would have to lead now.

"For world and windows! Wraiths advance!" he cried. "Save all souls!"

And from the tower there was first silence, and then came the evil answering cry.

"Burn the souls black. Burn them black!"

The wraiths were charging the evil assistants bravely but recklessly. Oliver knew his obligation was to keep his head, and direct the charge.

"Remember the plan," he shouted, struggling to be heard over the falling snow and the charging army. "Remember the plan!"

He did not have to worry. Molière and Racine kept their heads and did not race up the tower. Instead, they pressed ahead to the other side, went behind it, and then, raised themselves on a drifting dune of snow. Clutching Alice's true mirror that Mrs. Pearson had recovered from the Way, they raised it high behind the tower.

Oliver ran back to Neige's side; she and Serge grasped the other true mirror, the mirror of Luc Gauric that the clochards had reassembled.

"Hold the mirror high, Neige," he said. "Our troops are inside the Way looking out at the World through a true mirror."

Neige looked at him, and she seemed more beautiful than ever as she staunchly held the mirror and cleaned the snow from her eyes. "But, Oliver, if that's true then it means, oh, that everything here in the World should become as things are in the Way, hard things soft and oh, my God Oliver, look—"

For as they spoke, two things happened. Mrs. Pearson's army of lost children began to emerge, like floating apparitions, from inside the true mirror. And as they emerged, Monsieur Theodore, the balloon seller from the Luxembourg Gardens, handed each child a trusty balloon sword, to use now that the World was turning inside out. Each of the lost children took a balloon sword, and looked grimly up at the tower where their enemy lay.

And the Eiffel Tower, caught between the two true mirrors, with the snow falling on its iron surface and the wraiths climbing over it with their feathers raised high, had begun to soften, and then, ever so slowly and gracefully, to bend.

The great tall latticework was trembling, just a little—and then Oliver was sure that he could actually feel it beginning to *lean*. Lean forward, toward the river. The tower was tilting, bending as the world between the two true mirrors turned inside out.

And then the tower, which had seemed to be shaking and trembling like a brick lighthouse in the middle of an earthquake, suddenly seemed to find its feet, and it began to sway, gracefully, back and forth, like a dancer, or like a lithe living animal. Its base was like four strong and agile feet, its middle section like a swaying dancer's stomach, its spire like a long neck. It seemed to stretch, bend, sway, and *reach*—like a long-necked giraffe feeding beneath a tree.

Then it suddenly bowed its head, and in a single, graceful, breathtaking arc, the Eiffel Tower bent itself across the river Seine, like a rainbow bridge, its head resting on the plaza of the Trocadéro, its four legs still planted tensely in the earth of the Champ-de-Mars.

And, raising his ancient glass sword high, the King in the Window called for all his armies to charge.

Along with Mrs. Pearson and the lost children armed with the newly powerful balloon swords came Charlie and two hundred in-line skaters from within the true mirror, where they had hidden. Instantly, they were whizzing out from behind the concrete pillars of the Palais de Chaillot, and onto the tower.

"It worked, Ollie. You out-thought the universe itself, and the Master of Mirrors!" Charlie cried.

As the tower bent itself over in an arch of metal, the restaurant platform, with its four circular turrets, became a kind of head. Charlie and his skaters leaped right onto it, using the gentle incline of the esplanade to get their momentum—and then whooshed right up the bowed front half of the folded tower until they arrived at its summit. Then, from that height, they sped down the straight central spine of the tower, swooping down on it as if it were a greased channel.

Their knees bent, their heads low in the snow, they skimmed at up the arc of the tower and then down the other side in a single blinding fall, aiming directly for the platform that now hovered right in the middle of the tower turned bridge, directly over the Seine.

What had been an impregnable position for the master and his minions high up on the tower had now become a vulnerable one. It had been caught in the middle between two onrushing armies—the wraiths climbing from the bottom on their safe cushion of snow, and Charlie and the in-line skaters falling down on them from above.

Now that the world had turned inside out, the weapons of the window wraiths were powerful again. Some of the younger wraiths pulled out the soap-bubble cannons—they looked like transparent pop-guns—and began to fire at the soul-stealers on the tower.

Standing astride the leaning platform, the Master of Mirrors held the pipe of flowing energy produced by the quantum computer. Only the arrogant turn of his head expressed his fury and confusion as the wraiths rushed forward and upward through the falling snow, rushing past their own king in their eagerness to overwhelm their ancient enemy. Beyond them, Oliver could just make out Charlie and his skating companions arriving among the soul-stealers while on the ground below, Molière and Racine still held the true mirror high.

Caught between the two true mirrors, The King in the Window and the Master of Mirrors, faced each other for the first time, alone, high above Paris at the bulge of the bending tower.

Chapter Seventeen

The Cosmic Chase

THE MASTER of Mirrors stared at Oliver. Then he did
a strange thing. He bowed, deep and low, at his rival. Was
he surrendering? Oliver lowered his guard, and his sword,
for only a moment, but it was long enough for the master to
rush right at him, knocking him down.

Oliver fell hard on the girders, the breath knocked out of
him, and heard his glass sword clatter beside him. The master
was on top of him now, clutching his body, as cold as a block of
ice. Oliver felt the Master's long, bitter-cold fingers run across

his body, and then he had his sword back in his hand, and he struck the Master on the back, twice, and hard.

But the Master of Mirrors merely leaped back and stood up again. He pointed the great pipe of the quantum computer, eating souls at one end and spilling quantum energy out across the universe at the other, directly at the true mirror that Racine and Molière held behind him.

"The trouble," the master said, and his voice was still clear and unexcited, "is that though this plan has been quite well executed—the shadows, *quite* clever, the snow, *really* well thought out—still it is a *plan*, a complicated bit of doing. While I am a simple, serene being, and all I need to do . . . is to leap into another world elsewhere, and leave you here among all this noise and excitement and wanting and longing. So I, if you'll allow me, I'll just go—home."

He raised the soul-sprayer and sprayed the golden quantum energy out again at the mirror behind him. The endless reflected images of the Eiffel Tower bending in the snow seemed almost to vibrate as they were struck by the little particles racing through the cracks in matter to all the other worlds. "Oh, yes," he added. "The dust you see here"—he gestured toward the pipe—"why, that's the ash of your father's soul."

And then the Master of Mirrors leaped into the true mirror and raced away across the multiverse, running right into the infinity of images that passed between the two mirrors. And Oliver leaped through the mirror into the infinite reflections after him.

To describe what Oliver experienced then is very difficult, because no one has ever experienced anything at all like it. To imagine it, you must imagine yourself looking into a hall of mirrors, reflecting the same image on and on and on into infinity—and then actually jumping into those reflections and running as fast as you could through the middle of them. There are not many ordinary as-ifs or similes or even metaphors to describe it. You might say that it was as though Oliver were chasing the Master of Mirrors along an invisible tightrope that stretched across the sky, leaping from world to world, through the endless mirror reflections. Or: it was as if he were running down a long hallway of mirrors suspended in the snowy night sky, leaping over the edge of each frame and then racing across the space, and then leaping over the next frame.

Stretched out across the snowy night sky, there was an endless chain of night skies and new worlds beckoning Oliver on—a hundred, no, a thousand, Parises, each off in a world of its own, each like the next, and yet each different. The multiverse had opened up before him, and now he had to chase the master through it.

As the Master of Mirrors leaped and raced ahead of him, Oliver followed, as fast as he could. Breathless, racing through the countless mirrors, when he glanced to either side, he saw that each framed a world unlike the one he had just run across before. There was one world where the Eiffel Tower was bright green with red spots, and another where, as he looked out, he saw that the lost children were just like the lost children in his world, only each one had a mustache, and another where the sky was bright orange and the river Seine a glowing emerald green. There was one world where he had a quick glimpse of a calico tower and a Paris made of glass, only floating on water. All across the great multiverse of the cosmos, the ageless man of infinite faces and no face of his own raced away, and the small boy who had blundered into the throne by accident with a paper crown on his head pursued him.

Faster and faster, the Master of Mirrors led the King in the Window across the cosmos, through one parallel universe after another. Oliver ran—and was glad that he had practiced running so often with his mother. He ran across the night sky as his terrible prey raced and dodged in front of him, and leaped from world to world.

There—could it be—there was the same by now familiar scene, but the Eiffel Tower was upside down, its point planted in the gardens of the Champ-de-Mars, and its feet and large base happy in the sky.

But where was the Master of Mirrors running? What world was he seeking? *Think*. Think like your oldest enemy. Oliver stopped running for a moment to think, and, as he did, he saw that the Master of Mirrors had paused for a moment, too, suspended in the sky, and seemed to be searching for something in his pocket—why?

And then Oliver saw the Master of Mirrors reach inside his pocket and remove the pebble that always found its way home.

The pebble! He had stolen the pebble from Oliver's

pocket when he had rushed at him on the tower. That was what he had been trying to take from him when he was in the guise of Gil Hornshaw. It must work for whoever possessed it, to take that person to his home!

And now the Master of Mirrors kicked it, and the pebble floated up, slowly, slowly, as though picking its world, and then it seemed to fly through the endless reflections, like a football punted high in the air, spinning through the mirrors as it sought its home.

Oliver raced along behind the master. What world was home for the Master of Mirrors—which universe? And then as he ran along Oliver felt an icy air blow on him, and saw, looming ahead of him, a world like no other, showing the by now endlessly duplicated scene of the tower and the river. But in this world, Oliver saw, as he glimpsed it ahead of him, everything was made of hard black ice, and he knew that this must be the cold, parallel universe that the Master of Mirrors had first emerged from, and to which he was now returning.

Oliver wanted to catch the homecoming pebble before it landed in the master's world and brought him home. He sucked the icy air into his lungs, and he tried to lunge ahead. Then he remembered what his mother had always told him: Make all mental tasks into physical tasks, all physical tasks into mental ones. Let your mind rule your body. Oliver did, and as he shut his eyes and imagined himself back, running with his mother, in the Luxembourg Gardens, he felt a new energy infuse his body, and he dove forward in the black sky, making one last, desperate lunge for the pebble.

There! He was ahead of the master, one step ahead.
Oliver reached out with all his might and sent his foot flying
blindly forward and kicked out as hard as he could. Had he
reached his pebble? Yes! He felt it fly away before him, and he
heard the high clear call of the Master of Mirrors as the pebble flew away once again, away from his dark and icy home.

Now where was it going? It spun out across space, but
Oliver knew that it would find its way home—to Oliver's
home, since he had been the last to kick it. And now the
pebble was indeed turning, yawing above him, and then flying out across the dark space.

But the world it catapulted toward in this infinite alley
of reflections didn't look like Oliver's old world at all. In
fact, it looked stranger even than any of the worlds he had
yet seen. What kind of world was this? Now, everything
ahead of him looked shiny but also *long,* as though it had
been pulled taut like taffy, and somehow curved forward
toward Oliver. So strange!

And now the Master of Mirrors, oblivious to the
strange world approaching, raced out ahead of Oliver to
grab the pebble before it fell and send it back toward his
dark home, and he ran across the night sky as fast as he
could, following it, and Oliver watched—winded, now, completely out of breath—as the Master of Mirrors dove toward
the new universe to grab the pebble.

At that very moment, the whole world ahead of them pivoted, very quickly, as though someone had flicked it on a wrist—
the whole scene, the tower and the river and the wraiths swiveled

right around, and then turned upside down. Everything was still long and shiny and distended and misshapen, except—Oliver was sure of it—all of it now upside down.

The Master of Mirrors looked up in horror at the approaching, pivoting, entirely upside-down world, and tried to skid to a stop. But it was too late. He had begun his dive through space already, and Oliver watched with wonder as he saw the Master of Mirrors strike the surface of the new world hard and then flip upside down, dangling helplessly—from the concave surface of Mrs. Pearson's champagne spoon.

That was what the approaching world was! Oliver realized in a flash. That was all that this last world in the great line of the multiverse was! It was the world reflected in Mrs. Pearson's spoon, first back, then front. She had held it up to align it with the infinity of reflections that passed between the two mirrors— and intercepted the Master of Mirrors in his flight.

Then, Oliver, too, dove forward and felt himself sliding down the surface of the spoon. In a moment, the scale of things changed radically, and he seemed for a second immensely large, a giant as huge as all the universe.

And then he felt suddenly small, and he realized that he was just his own normal size again, and that Mrs. Pearson had plucked him with her fingers from her spoon while he was still on its surface, before he had entered deep into the upside-down reflections in its bowl. And now Mrs. Pearson was standing next to him, quite calmly, back in the first world, his world, holding her champagne spoon nonchalantly upward. Inside it, he could see the tiny figure of the Master of Mirrors, upside down, caught, and wriggling furiously.

"A mirror need be only as large as the image it contains," Mrs. Pearson said, holding her spoon up high with its terrible tiny prisoner inside. "I got my spoon up in front of the mirror of Luc Gauric and made sure that the spoon's reflection was in the same line as all the other mirrors, and showed the same image. I lured the homecoming pebble with it, and, when it hurtled home, I intercepted the master with it, nimbly flicking the wrist at the last moment so that he would be trapped in the inverted bowl. Very simple, though, I must say, very effective."

Gasping on the ground before her in the still snowy esplanade of the Trocadéro, having just raced from one end of the cosmos to the other only to find himself home at its end, Oliver could only look in wonder at Mrs. Pearson's spoon, the last mirror in the great cosmic-spanning row of reflections—with the Master of Mirrors now captured inside it.

Up above and beside him, he saw Charlie and the skaters and Neige and the clochards, still leading the battle against the soul-stealers on the bending tower. But he could sense that, without their leader, the soul-stealers were finding the tide of battle had already turned against them, particularly now, as Mrs. Pearson held her spoon high, with the captured master inside it.

And, without quite knowing what he was doing, Oliver seized the spoon from her, and strong words rushed into his mouth, and, so that everyone on the battlefield could hear him, he cried: "Though you be lord of ice and silver, I am king of water and windows. I turned the world inside out, and I turned *you* upside down, and now I claim victory and all your realms for my own! The days of window and water, clarity and light, have at last arrived, and the King in the Window claims his city."

And as Oliver said these words, one by one the lights of the quantum computer on the tower dimmed. . . .

Yet as the lights faded on the tower, the world all around it—the field of Mars, and the bridges, and the plaza of the Troacdéro—began to glow with new light, a thousand new lights, sparkling like the lights on a Christmas tree. And as Oliver looked around, he realized that the new lights were human—the eyes of the assistants of Gil Hornshaw, the soul-stealers who had been loyal to the Master of Mirrors, beginning to shine again. They shone through the dark night like the keen light of a thousand stars in the night sky. The light, slowly growing in intensity, increased, as all the slaves and servants of the master were freed from his power, and their glow was once again the glow of eyes alight with feeling, and the dark winter night of Paris was lit again by the brightest light of all, and that is the light of human longing.

"I mean, get out of here. Go home. Get lost," Oliver muttered, the rhetorical inspiration leaving him just as quickly as it had come. And he let the glass sword fall from his hand.

But then a tiny yet hideous and sarcastic voice came from inside the bowl of the spoon.

"Wise King, Brave King, O, Victorious King! Your father's soul is gone, burned in the great machine. You may be king, but your father is one of the infernal things now. The eyes of my disciples are burning again with attachment and desire and all those other sad things. But your father's soul is burned already, and cannot be recovered."

Oliver fell to one knee and caught his breath, breathing hard in the snow. Could he win the world and still leave his father a slave?

Mrs. Pearson was beside him, seemingly as steady and clever as ever.

"What rhetoric!" she said above the still driving snow as calmly to Oliver as though they were at dinner once again at Le Grand Véfour. "'I am king of water and window!' Well said!"

"But my father!" Oliver said, and, looking at Mrs. Pearson's sad and hopeless face, he realized that she had no plan, no belief, that he could rescue his father.

"It's no good." Mrs. Pearson could barely form the words. "His soul was the first to burn when the master lit the soul-sprayer . . ."

"How long ago did I begin the chase?" Oliver demanded.

Mrs. Pearson looked at her watch. "Seven minutes ago," she said. "It seemed much longer, didn't it, to go right around the multiverse?"

"And are the mirrors still in place? The World is still reversed?"

She nodded, and gestured toward the wraiths who still staunchly held the true mirror aloft, capturing the tower and the palace between them, and Neige and Serge, who held the other true mirror high as ever.

Oliver was tired, exhausted beyond words. But he knew what he had to do. *For to take back a soul you must look in the one mirror that is also an open window, the one window that is also a perfect mirror. If your father sees his reflection there, his soul can be restored to him. But while he must look only at himself in the mirror, he must never take his gaze from what the window shows of the world beyond.*

That was what Nostradamus had told him. And now he knew what it meant.

"If I use my mind, I can go back and forth in time from here, just as I did in the Way," he said to Mrs. Pearson. "If I can go back just seven minutes ago, I'll find my father's soul still intact. And if I can get him back in the World at exactly the moment that I defeat the master, then his soul will return just as the souls of the rest of the master's slaves did. If I go back in time, and find him, and bring him back just in time—why, then, he can have his soul back."

And, amid the still falling snow, Oliver used every mental muscle he possessed to see his father as he must have been only eight minutes before, before his soul had been burned and its ash sprayed out across the multiverse.

Oliver worked, and worked, his eyes shut, his mind hard. To race across the multiverse, he had had to use his mind. Now, to travel back in time, he had to use the muscles of his body. Work, really work, strain, as though he were lifting a great weight directly on his shoulders.

His friends, beside him, tried, too. "Aaargh," Neige cried. She had given her side of the true mirror to Serge to hold, and come to help Oliver. "I can't do it!" And Charlie fell to his knees, clutching his head, worn out at the futile effort.

But then Oliver had an image of his father, quite clearly. But he was not in this world, at all; he was somewhere in the Mirror-Maze.

And in a moment, Oliver was back, deep inside the maze. All around him were the sounds of chaos and battle. Some of the soul-stealers, Oliver saw, had found a way back into their realm. Only here, with the World turned inside out, their weapons were useless. They rushed back, deeper and deeper into the depths of the maze, while the wraiths, eyes wide and pale, pursued them.

Down halls and around corners, Oliver ignored them as he searched for his father. Feathers came slashing down harmlessly on his back; spitballs landed painlessly on his ankles; the cold breath of the soul-stealers hissed past his ears. He could not simply shut his eyes and think his way through time, because the World and the Way were reversed, and once he was inside the Mirror-Maze the rules of the normal World reigned. All he could do was run, and search, and run more, and search again. Up corridors and down halls—would he ever find his father?

And Oliver shut his eyes again, and tried to think his way to óne good memory, something that his father must be thinking about, too, that would open his mind in time to Oliver. Oliver saw himself and his father kicking a pebble home, just as he and the Master of Mirrors had chased the pebble across the multiverse, only now it was a shared activity by a father and son crossing the bridges of Paris, not a race for existence. . . .

And as though the very thought of the homing pebble could lead him back to familiar things, Oliver opened his eyes and saw his father. Crouching in a dark hallway, with a dim light shining on him from an open doorway.

He saw Oliver approaching, and he shrank away.

"I came back inside," he said. "It's safe for my lost sort here."

"It is not safe here. And you are not lost," Oliver said, taking him by the arm and trying to pull him to his feet. "You are not lost. The master is captured, and the world is inside out, and the eyes of the Soulless shine again! If we get back out into the World, you will have your soul again!"

"Too late, too late," his father was saying. "This is my home, now. It's my—it's my self that's gone."

He could not even say the word "soul," Oliver thought to himself.

"But you still have it. And in seven minutes you won't." How to get him back out before time ran out? Oliver again tried to pull his father to his feet. But why wouldn't he look at him? . . . *He must look in the one mirror that is also an open window, the one window that is also a perfect mirror . . .*

Look at him . . .

Look at him.

"Dad," Oliver cried, "look at me. Look me right in the eye." He grabbed his father's face by the chin and forced him to stare at him. They locked eyes, and Oliver saw

387

himself reflected in his father's eyes, and knew that his father must see himself in Oliver's.

"Dad," he said simply, swallowing hard, "just don't look away. Look into my eyes, and never look away."

"What . . ."

"Just don't look away. Look at me, and take my hand."

And his father followed him. Step by step, looking at his father's face in his two hands, forcing him never to stop staring into his eyes, Oliver began to walk backward, with painful slowness, down the corridor. *If I can get to an exit mirror, a safe mirror, and walk backward through it . . . and if he never stops looking,* Oliver thought, *I can save him.*

And his father followed him. As they moved cautiously back down the corridor, Oliver could hear running in the larger main-artery hall outside. The soul-stealers must have realized that their dreadful enemy, the King in the Window, was there—right there, at their mercy, in their maze. And they ran out into the corridor and crowded all around Oliver and his father as they slowly retreated down the dark hall of the Mirror-Maze, staring at each other's eyes.

For of course, out in the World, their master had not yet fallen, and would not fall for another four minutes.

There is nothing harder in all the world than to keep your back turned toward danger as you hear it approaching. The urge to turn around and at least face what was coming at him—as he heard the clatter of the soul-stealers' heels, the banging and chafing of their weapons as they approached, and almost felt their hot breath on the back of his neck—was almost overwhelming. But Oliver knew that his father's soul depended on his never looking away.

"It's okay, Dad," he said, through clenched teeth, "just look at me. Look at me."

"Can I ever be made whole?" his father asked.

"Souls are remade all the time," Oliver said. "I'm sure of it." And somehow, he was.

"Mine is gone," his father said, a desperate sadness in his voice.

"No soul is gone for good," Oliver said firmly. "If you go back in time to the moment when you lost it, it will return to you." He looked his father ever-deeper in the eyes. "You just have to trust me."

His father said nothing, but took Oliver's hand and kept his gaze on him.

Now they were right there, hardly more than a sword's length away, moving backward. What could he do? A horrible pain and then the nothing . . . But there was no way forward except the way backward. He could feel the slow angry growl of the gathering soul-stealers behind him, hardly believing their good luck at having the king at their mercy.

Oliver stiffened, waiting for the fatal blow.

And then there was the slash of a sword—and the soul-stealers turned and cried. For there were Charlie and Neige, eyes ablaze, right alongside him.

"We couldn't go back in time thinking of your father," Neige said, smiling for the first time in months. "The feelings weren't strong enough. But once *you* were back in time, we could get here, by thinking of you."

"Hey, Ollie," said Charlie, raising his sword. And all around him the lunging, grimacing soul-stealers raised their feathers to fight him. Growling and spitting, they came forward with looks of glee and slashed down, in unison.

Nothing happened. The feathers fell limply, lightly touching the children's heads.

Charlie laughed. "You're forgetting, guys," he said to the soul-stealers, "the World and the Way are still inside out, and this little thing"—he held his sword up and waved it threateningly—"can cure your dandruff in one quick slice. Don't come any closer," he said, brandishing the sword. Then he looked over his shoulder at Oliver, who was still holding his father's chin.

"Ollie, old pal," he said, looking at Oliver and his father, and placing a hand on both of their shoulders. "You are *really* into some deep Robert Bly–*Iron John*–type territory here. I mean, if I had even *thought* of something like this for the Reflections unit, I wouldn't be repeating Archetype and Myth next semester. . . ."

"Charlie, don't distract me. Fight!"

"Distract you! I admire you! Don't worry, I'll ride shotgun."

Yet the crowd of soul-stealers came closer, and then one gnashed its teeth.

"We have nothing really sharp, do we?" he said, and then they all advanced, their canine teeth dripping with saliva.

"Back! Back! All of you," a thin and reedy but brave voice cried out. It was Nostradamus. From the far corner of his eye, Oliver could see him stride alongside him, holding the sword that Oliver had taken from him, and dropped after he found it to be useless. The old man held it in shaky hands, but he held it, and the soul-stealers shrank back, and the old man came up closer to Oliver.

"Thank you for coming back for me," said Nostradamus, his eyes full of feeling. "You said you would."

The truth, of course, was that Oliver had completely forgotten about him. But he was glad to see him—and his sword—all the same. So, keeping his eyes locked on his father's, he said, "I did come back here, just as I said I would."

Well, at least that's a blue lie, he thought, a lie that actually is a truth you didn't quite know you were telling.

There was something more important on his mind, though. "We need to be inside for exactly seven minutes, Charlie," he said. "If we go back before then, I'll bump into myself going back in time. We need to re-enter the World just at the moment I jumped in here."

"Got you," Charlie said. "We can keep them at bay that long. I hope."

Back and back they went, Neige and Charlie and Nostradamus leading their way through the Mirror-Maze and keeping the furious but impotent soul-stealers at bay with their swords. And then at last the back of the true mirror loomed before them, and Neige and Charlie and Nostradamus stepped back from the Way into the World, and Oliver and his father, looking into each other's eyes, came out the other side, too, the son pulling the father free.

Chapter Eighteen

Metaphors and Mirrors

"WHAT DO YOU mean, there was nothing magical about it? The Master of Mirrors throws a giant living searchlight across the Trocadéro at twilight, Oliver makes the puppet sign of a crowned bird, the shadows of Paris come loose and make a giant cloud, the cloud of shadows makes snow, the window wraiths are free to travel across the snow. Racine and Molière and Neige and Serge hold up the two true mirrors, and, catching the World in its own unreversed reflection, they turn the World and the Way inside out. The Eiffel Tower becomes soft and flexible, and it bends over and turns itself into a bridge—then I lead an army of in-line skaters up the bridge and down the other side while Oliver here races the Master of Mirrors from one world to another through the multiverse, until he chases him at last upside down into a champagne spoon, and then he leaps back into time to find his father and remake his soul by the force of his own gaze—and you call that *normal!*" Charlie Gronek said to Mrs. Pearson.

It was late on Friday afternoon, just a week and one day since Oliver had first put on the crown and become the king, and he and his friends were back at Versailles. It was warm for a winter afternoon in the country around Paris, and so they were sitting outside, among the bare trees and fallen leaves, at L'Etoile, the star-shaped garden with the fountain of Neptune at its center. The wraiths were celebrating by having a quiet float from pavilion to pavilion. You could see their watery, dreamy, translucent forms in midair, everywhere you looked in the gardens.

"I didn't say it was perfectly *normal*," Mrs. Pearson objected calmly. "I said it was perfectly *logical*. Certainly not normal in the sense of an everyday event, but entirely in sequence once the sequence began. Metaphysics, what you insist on calling magic, Charles, *has* to be strictly logical. Take the melodrama away from the sequence you've just described, and you'll see that it's so. The king makes the sign, the sign calls out the shadows, the shadows make a cloud, the cloud makes snow, the wraiths use the snow as a highway, they overwhelm the soul-stealers, they raise the two true mirrors, the lost children emerge from the Way, the in-line skaters lead the final decisive charge, the World and the Way change places. All as strictly logical as a chess game. One thing leading inevitably to the next, hardly worth getting emotional about. From the moment Oliver—I beg your pardon, His Majesty—thought his way through his plan at the Pont Royal, the rest was as bound to happen as dominoes falling in a row when the first of them is nudged. The rest was mere . . . *activity*." She said "activity" as though it were a slightly dirty word.

"'Action' is what we call it Mrs. P.," said Charlie, "Decisive action is what matters."

It had been an eventful two days. Oliver had brought his father back to his mother. It was good to see them together again. She could obviously sense the spark in his eye, even if she didn't exactly see it.

Oliver had been concerned that it would be a little embarrassing to be with his father, at first. After all, if you have saved your father from having his soul lost, it would be hard for him to tell you to do your *devoirs,* and have real authority when he says it. But Oliver's father had acted as though nothing much had happened—"Oh, it was a weird scene," was all he had said. "Glad to be done with it"—for that is the way it is with fathers, even when you have personally restored their souls to them. They assume that they are as right about life as they always were, and in charge.

He had told Oliver, though, that he and Oliver's

mother had decided to take the family back to New York.

"I just want to go back to writing for myself," he had said. "No more writing profiles of strange friends. And I don't think I'll ever Google myself again." He smiled.

"Oh, it wasn't you," Oliver had asked. "It was the Master of Mirrors, trying to get to me."

"What became of Gil, though?" his father asked. "Is he locked up in the spoon, too?"

"No. I don't think so. When the Master of Mirrors fled back into the spoon, all the faces and bodies he had taken over went back to their original forms. I bet Gil is back safe in Seattle now, soul and all, and doesn't even remember what happened. It's too bad about the quantum computer, though," Oliver went on. "That would have been nice to have, at least."

"Well, I don't know," his father said. "One world at a time. That's enough for people like me. Or even for boy-kings like you."

"It sounds like a song title, Dad," Oliver said. "'One World at a Time.' Maybe you should go back to writing songs."

"Well, maybe when we go back to America, I will," his father had said, and Oliver was glad to hear him sounding positive about music. He was even humming. The music had leaked out of him, and now it was leaking back in.

His mother had cooed over him, of course, and then she had told him that she had fixed everything with his teachers. "That very unpleasant man, Monsieur Fileul, said that he had seen you running with a *voyou* at the Sainte-Chapelle when you should have been at school," his mother said disdainfully. (A *voyou* is a thug; Monsieur Fileul must have meant Charlie.) "And I told him that not only had you been doing a special project with a major scholar, but that you had been a crucial researcher in your dad's friend's quantum computer project, and that if he didn't think that that was more important than finishing some silly homework, then I was going to take you right out of that silly school."

Oliver blanched. He doubted that anyone had spoken that way to M. Fileul before. "What did he say?" he asked weakly.

"He said, 'Oh.' That's always the way with bullies. If you stand up to them, they wilt. You should remember that, Ollie, if you ever find yourself in a conflict with a really big bully—when you grow up, I mean. My darling little King; you looked so sweet the other night with all your armor on. . . . Oh, Oliver, look!" For she had been going through the pockets of his by-now-very-worn-and-ragged pea coat—after all, he had had it on almost without a break for a week, in and out of various worlds and ways—and she had found in it the by-now-torn-but-still-glittering paper crown.

"Your crown! You mean you kept it with you all this week! How *sweet*. Wherever we go in America, Ollie," his mom babbled on, happily, "we'll always have a *galette des rois,* and you'll always get to wear the crown. I mean"—she added hastily, as though he hadn't caught on, even yet—"I'm sure your amazing luck finding the prize in your slice of cake will continue, even outside Paris."

"Mom, didn't Dad tell you about . . . ?" Oliver left the rest of the sentence enticingly wide open. Apparently Oliver's father had decided not to tell his mother that their son had just chased the biggest bully across the multiverse and saved this world and several others. But Oliver only sighed, and his mother asked if he wanted to go to the Luxembourg Gardens and go on the swings, as though he were three, because that is the way it is with mothers, no matter where in the multiverse you find them. They are both goopy and perfect, and there is nothing to be done about it.

The battle at the tower had been treated rather disdainfully in the French press and on French television, which is the normal way in France with anything not organized in advance by the government or by intellectuals as a protest against it. "Unusual Events in the Vicinity of the Champ de Mars. Tourists Involved" had been the headline on the newspaper *Le Monde*.

Charlie assured him that it was better than what would have happened in America. "Back home, it would have been 'Americans Save World from Foreigners Again,'" he said, "and they would have a ticker-tape parade, and then we would have been expected to develop a problem with pills and end up in rehab. Believe me, it's better this way." The Eiffel Tower had sprung back up into place that same night—*boing!*—like a rubber band, as soon as the true mirrors came down.

And yet, for all his victories, Oliver was still feeling, well, funny. The wraiths, on the other hand, seemed perfectly happy. A circle of the Versailles wraiths had descended from their floating and were having lunch. There was a great long table with a white linen tablecloth embroidered with fleurs-de-lis and gold bees, and covered with clear glass plates and clear glass knives and forks. The food was quite solid, though. Roasted chickens with roasted lemons, pheasant in aspic, and baby carrots were just some of the delicious looking dishes that Oliver could see.

When they saw Oliver coming, they all stood or hovered, and clapped, very politely. Oliver bowed slightly. Somewhat to his horror, Racine rose, holding his glass high, preparing to make a toast.

"Friends, wraiths, walkers," he began, "I ask: What has this great and epic battle taught us? That great things make great men? That great men do great acts? Not at all. Small things, my friends, small things: a key, a pebble, a paper crown, an ordinary, unremarkable boy—a boy of no particular qualities or note, a boy like all other boys, a boy less promising even than—"

Oliver felt that was enough of that, and he signaled impatiently. He was still king for a little while longer, at least.

"And what do we find?" Racine continued smoothly, "Such a key unlocks all evil! Such a pebble finds its way across the cosmos to a nimble trap! And such a boy, in such a crown—such a boy becomes such a king as the World and

Way, as windows and wraiths, have never known!" he concluded, and the wraiths broke out in applause.

"We are having a great allegorical painting made," he then explained, "to celebrate your victory. It will show Instructed Metaphor—you—defeating Soulless Irony—the Master—with the help of Comic Irony . . ."

"Meaning Marshall Gronek—"

"And the further aid of Wit—Mrs. Pearson—and Infinite Feminine Capacity—that is, your friend, Neige."

"The whole to be painted in the finest colored mayonnaise!" the Duc de Richelieu added. "Well, I have so much of it," he explained, when Oliver looked puzzled.

Oliver tried to look as if a vast allegorical painting in richly colored mayonnaise was exactly what he wanted for a present. But he had something to tell them, and now was as good a time as any.

"I— I can't be your king," Oliver said. "I'm going home. To New York. I have to . . . abdicate my crown. There aren't any kings in New York, so I'm going to, well, you know, abdicate."

They all stopped eating and stared at him. But then they applauded again—and then, much to his shock, went on eating.

"But what about you?" Oliver was a bit taken aback both by their devotion and by their sudden return to the table. "The window wraiths? Can you manage without a king?"

"We will find a new one. We always have," said Racine. And all the wraiths nodded happily.

"Perhaps this time we will have someone who speaks better French," the Duc de Richelieu added, passing around the mayonnaise.

Oliver was shocked. The ingratitude! But then he realized that they were as brave as lions, and as clannish, meaning as likely to stick together and ignore everyone else, for that is the way it is with highly intelligent French artists, in and out of windows, anywhere in the multiverse we may find them.

Molière, though, came over toward him, almost secretively, and Oliver saw that he held in his hands a manuscript.

"Here, Your Majesty," he said. "An essay I've prepared on the difference between irony and metaphor in my plays, you see. It will put you back in the good graces of your professors." He bowed low.

Oliver took it, held it for a moment, and then handed it back. "I can't take it, my friend," he said simply. "It would be—cheating. And one thing I've learned is that a king can tell a lie, but a king must never cheat." He sighed. "Isn't that ironic."

Molière listened seriously. "No, sir," he said. "It is simply an excellent metaphor for kingship. At least, Your Majesty, you might repeat to your professors all of the things you've learned from me, and, if they ask you your authority for your statements, well . . ." and he smiled.

Then Molière pointed upward and Oliver saw, to his surprise and delight, that, above the silver canal of Le Nôtre's garden, Charlie Gronek and François the wraith were engaged in what looked like competitive floating. François was doing stunts in midair, and Charlie was imitating them on his skateboard, below. They looked very, well, symmetrical, Oliver thought.

Charlie came up to Oliver, standing in the middle of the garden of the white fountain.

"I'll miss you, guy," Charlie said softly.

"Why will you miss me?" Oliver asked, puzzled. "I'm moving back to New York. I'll be an hour away from your house."

"Oliver." Charlie looked more exasperated with his friend than ever. "That's what you say—when the two heroes are going their own ways, one says very softly, 'I'll miss you, guy.' Then there ought to be an explosion, or a pretty girl they've been fighting over comes in, so that they can say 'Why, you miserable . . .' and act like they're about to slug each other or something. Then they look at each other and break into a gale of comradely laughter."

"Oh," said Oliver. "You know, Charlie, from now on I think I'll take my adventures as they actually happen. You know, without any additional dialogue?"

Charlie shrugged. "Suit yourself. It's a slightly childish way to have adventures, though."

Oliver went off one last time to look for Mrs. Pearson. As he searched for her, he was startled to see the clochards all gathered round the edge of the beautiful silver canal. They were staring into it—looking at themselves! It had to be the

first time in years, Oliver imagined. He heard them muttering: "Better than I would have expected." "More beautiful
than I had hoped—no wonder they always look at us, eh?"
Oh, well, Oliver thought. If anyone deserves a moment's
respite after so much fighting, it was these brave and dirty
men. Now, if only they would think about leaping in the
canal for a bath. . . .

He found Mrs. Pearson at last, all alone, her feet up on
a bench, back at L'Etoile. She was sipping a glass of something that looked very much like Billecart Salmon rosé, and
she had a Charvet scarf wrapped around her head and she
was looking thoughtful, which was often, Oliver had learned,
an extremely dangerous thing with her.

"It's strange," Oliver said, as they wrapped their coats
a little tighter around themselves and walked up the smoky,
chilly, and magnificent avenue de Reine, as the fallen leaves
made a soft whooshing sound beneath their shoes. "I've just
sort of saved the world and everything. And I don't feel particularly wonderful. I mean, I'm glad it's saved. The world,
I mean. And I think I would have felt horrible if it hadn't
been saved—"

"If you hadn't saved it, there would have been no feelings to feel," Mrs. Pearson pointed out.

"But I don't feel as good at having saved the world
as I would have felt terrible at having lost it. Do you see
what I mean? I just feel . . . me again, and still just me."

Mrs. Pearson stopped walking, and took him by the
shoulders. "Oliver, success is usually a feeling of mere

relief, where failure is pain. Happiness, you see, lies in neither, but in sticking to a daily ritual and becoming absorbed in something useful. When the war is over, even the greatest warriors do not exult. They go back to their garden or kitchen or library—or school—and resume life."

"Well, yes, but there's another problem," he gulped hard. "When I was, when I was bringing my father back and all, I tried to wait the full seven minutes, so that we would come back into the world at just the right moment. I got a little, well, panicky there, and I, well, I think I got us back thirty seconds too soon. I only realized it when I looked at the second hand on my watch. Nobody noticed, not even Charlie, but I think I just lost thirty seconds from world history and all. I hope no one notices."

Mrs. Pearson didn't seem a bit shocked. "Oh, they've noticed, but they don't *know* that they've noticed," she said. "A lost half minute? It's happened, several times before, when great heroes have launched themselves through the multiverse of time into the Way and forgotten to reset the clocks when they've come back. Orpheus, for instance, a real absentminded one. No one *knows* that people notice, but they do. What do you think everyone is always longing for?"

"How's that?"

"We don't know that we've lost a half minute from our lives but we feel it somehow, we feel its absence. *Something is missing*, we think. And so we long for the thing we've missed and can't name, and out of that wanting—well, everything else rises, good and bad. What do you think leads us to the windows in the first place? The light in your eyes shines because of the longing in your soul. And the longing in your soul rises because you are looking for the lost half minute."

They had come to the end of the avenue de Reine, the long broad street in Le Nôtre's wood. At its head was still another fountain, which was waterless for the winter, but whose golden figures of mermaids and river-gods shone bright even in the dull January light. Mrs. Pearson sat down on the edge of the fountain, just beneath the beard of one of the river-gods.

"You have driven back the mirrors, and the knights, and it was all extremely vivacious. The old king is dead, and— you know—you are the king, but you cannot be the king."

"Yes," said Oliver softly, "I was going to tell you that. My father and mother have decided we're moving back to New York. I just told the window wraiths that I can't be the King in the Window in New York, I don't believe. I don't think they have kings there, for one thing."

"Nor windows either, really. Not by Parisian standards, anyway. Just little portholes that open and shut, and with— what do they call those things? Oh, yes, with air condition-ers stuck right in their middles. Ugh. How unaesthetic you Americans really are!" Oliver noted that she was speaking of him as an American already. Nobody kept Mrs. Pearson's respect for long, not even the King in the Window.

"Well, the wraiths were impressed that I was abdicating. They said it showed that I really was the right choice after all."

Mrs. Pearson was silent.

"I mean, it's a bit ironic, considering. And a bit ironic that my whole relationship with the window wraiths should end in an irony, after all. I mean, don't ironies belong to the mirrors?" he said.

Mrs. Pearson, in her elegant Dior suit, began speaking more softly, even gently, than Oliver had ever heard her. "Oh, it's actually quite good to have an irony or two in your life to live with. Look at young Charlie! But it is better to have a metaphor to live for. Just as it is fine to live with a mirror to look into, but impossible to live without a window to look out of."

"Oh, that reminds me, Mrs. Pearson," Oliver said. "I think I figured out why everyone involved—you know, the Watchful, and the Witty, and the Wise—why they all begin with a 'W.'"

"Have you, then?"

"Yes. It's Double-U. Double you. It's what you see when you look into a mirror or a window. A double you: the you that's really there plus this other you that lies beyond. The double you in the windows is good, because it's sort of you plus something. The one in the mirror isn't, because it's just you staring at you staring at you . . . you know, on into the multiverse, nothing but you. But every you is a double you, and I think you have to choose which double you you want, if that makes any sense."

"Perfect sense. And quite wise, too," Mrs. Pearson said. "Did I say that?" She looked genuinely puzzled.

"By the way, Mrs. Pearson," Oliver said, after a

pause. "What happened to the Master of Mirrors?"

She yawned. "Oh, he's still in my spoon. Don't worry, he can't get out. Once upside down, always upside down. I left him permanently in the neck of a good bottle of the Billecart rosé, in my rooms on the rue Monsieur. The same kind of champagne that you and I shared during our first vivid dinner. It seemed a proper irony for him to contemplate. Who knows? Several millennia of absorbing all those bubbles may improve his character. I wouldn't count on it, but stranger things have happened. How odd to think that all he wanted was to go home, and he was prepared to cause so much suffering for so small a thing. In any case, thank God for Billecart, and thank God for these insulated bags that allow you to take it with you even on a winter picnic." She took another sip from her glass. "And thank God for Veuve Clicquot and all the other *grands marques*. Oh, by the way, that is the third thing that is both warm and cold: a chilled glass of good champagne. Now you know more than the Wise. And please do not forget that you still owe me a debt for that dinner, and I expect it to be repaid. Even from across the ocean."

She suddenly smiled and, to Oliver's great surprise, she took his hand and fell on one knee.

"Despite many obvious failures of judgment, Oliver, you showed charm and courage throughout your brief but eventful reign, and that is all that really counts. There could be no better king."

"Thank you, Mrs. Pearson." And then Oliver tried to

think of an image beautiful enough to express his debt to her. "You—you have helped to kick my pebble home," he said at last.

"Farewell, my king," she said, rising, and to Oliver's surprise, her eyes were briefly moist and then clear. "For you have been the spoon in my champagne. You have preserved my bubbles."

Oliver understood at once what she meant, and he was sure that they were the two best metaphors he had ever heard.

He found Neige, sitting by herself, in the upstairs balcony of the Petit Trianon. She looked at him scornfully as he came in.

"Neige, I'm sorry you're not a queen—" Oliver began.

"Oh, Oliver, had I become Queen of Crystals, I could have overseen every computer and television screen in the world. I could have saved them from being soul-traps, I could have . . . And by the way, what about my mother? Fine sentimental American moment you had with your father, but when you let the master break the seal, you drove my mother back into the mirrors, and now I shall have to go and find her." She frowned.

"But, your mother—I mean, she was all on the wrong side. And she didn't have, you know, much of a face."

"I know. But now that the master has fallen, the light in her eyes will come back on, and, however dim that light might be, still, she's my mother. And as for her face . . . well, better some face than none at all. But I still would have liked to be a queen."

"But then you would have been a subject of the Master of Mirrors."

She shrugged and made a little *moue*, which means a downward cast of the mouth. "Well, there's that. But I could have handled him, had we been married," she said. Then she looked at him, hard.

"Well, the truly amazing thing," Neige went on, "is that you actually came up with an intelligent, lucid plan at the end, which shows, I suppose, that even an American boy can learn to think, given the right teachers."

Oliver knew better than to be offended. "I would hope you would continue to be one of my teachers, Neige," he said.

"Perhaps, Your Majesty."

He had to tell her the news, too. "I'm not even a king anymore."

"I did not mean that you were. I meant only that you had . . . majesty." And she looked up at him, directly in his eyes.

Oliver blushed, absorbing the distinction she had made, and then she took his hand, and from within her sweater she drew out her crystal and held it high.

And for one last time, Oliver drew out the glass sword of the King in the Window and held it high.

The American boy's sword and the French girl's crystal touched and crossed in a gentle salute.

"Sword and crystal—the crystal sees, but the sword strikes," Neige said softly.

"Uh, I do have to give the glass sword back to the Louvre, Neige," Oliver said. "It should be safe there, I think."

"You do not have to hold the sword to own the sword," Neige said softly. "The king's true sword is always yours." And she leaned over and kissed him on the cheek, and then the forehead, and then the other cheek. "Anyway, we are even. I hold your beautiful soul in the mirror of my mind, and the light in my eyes shines for you alone, Oliver."

Oliver didn't know what to say to such a ferociously unpredictable and passionate French girl. He tried "Okay, thanks," but that seemed very inadequate. So then he thought hard, and took her hand, and tried to rise to one last burst of rhetoric, no matter how rhetorically worn-out he was.

"I would hope that those feelings will always be returned and reflected in the mirror—in the *true* mirror—of my mind, Neige."

He secretly thought that, though complicated, this was an even better metaphor than the ones he had exchanged with Mrs. Pearson, but he knew that he could never share this one with anyone but Neige.

That's all there is to the story, really, of how the King in the Window saved the entire cosmos, ended the war of the windows and mirrors, for a little while anyway, and got a passing grade on his paper on rhetoric and irony. Oliver went home to New York, where he found a new school where things were less rigorous and generally sloppier. Within a month, no one in Paris even remembered that the window wraiths had come out from their windows, or that the Eiffel Tower had bent itself down and become an arched bridge. If you mentioned it, they would turn their lips into "O"s and expel their breath as if to say *Please, don't expect me to be so naïve.* Between a pose of superior skepticism and the evidence of their own eyes, Parisians prefer the pose, and it is good that they do, or else, like Americans, they would always be looking past the present toward the future, and "improving" places, which, in Paris, would be no improvement.

Another family moved into Oliver's family's apartment on the rue du Pré-aux-Clercs, and then another one after that. They say, though, that if any family who lives there looks in the kitchen window on the evening of Epiphany, they will always see the family in the window—that is, themselves—but they will also see a grave and noble twelve-year-old boy at the table in the window with them, too, and he is always wearing a crown. Anyway, that's what they say.

A Note on Origins, and of Thanks

I WROTE this book in Paris, from Epiphany of 1997 to the summer of 2000, and then revised it on visits there, as well as in New York, in the following five years. I mention this because I would hate for my readers to think that I was still writing about Paris without being there; every book should have its *appellation controlé*, a declaration of the place it was made, as all wine does in France. This book's is Paris.

Many of the things in the book actually exist, in one dimension or another. A true, non-reversing mirror exists, and is made by John and Catherine Walter. (You can visit their Web site, www.truemirror.com.) Luc Gauric was a real person, and so were each of the window wraiths. I read many books about glass and mirrors before, or while I was writing about them, and learned a lot. Some good ones are *Mirror,*

Mirror, by Mark Pendergrast, and *The Mirror: A History*, by Sabine Melchior. A good beginning book on the multiverse and quantum computers (which don't quite exist yet, but may soon) is *How to Build a Time Machine*, by Paul Davies. The show at the hall of mirrors at the Musée Grévin has changed, and for the worse. Let's hope it is restored.

In the old days, before excessive acknowledgments in books became a plague, it was considered rude to thank an editor for helping to make a story, as it was rude to thank a chef for making a good meal; the excellence was taken for granted. In these degenerate times, however, an author can only thank exceptional efforts with spaniel-like gratitude and two editors contributed in so pressed and daily a way to these pages that I can't help but praise them here. They were David Groff, who applied his deep but gentle wisdom about story-telling to sharpen the point and soften the symbols of a long and often unwieldy narrative; without his help, Oliver and I might never have wandered into the Way. And then my sister, Alison Gopnik, expert on all things children-ish, longest of long-term readers, matchless analyst of mood (and the original Mrs. Pearson at that) without whose help I might never have found a path back out.

And thanks, too, to Isabella Giovannini, and Jacob Kogan, ten years old, but long in wisdom, who read so well and spoke so frankly.

Oh, yes. The Duc de Richelieu really did invent mayonnaise.

A.G.